Last Wish Wedding

Jeulia Hesse

Deep Creek Publishers

This novel is entirely a work of fiction. The names, characters, and incidents portrayed in it are the work of the author's imagination. Any resemblance to actual persons, living or dead, events or localities are entirely coincidental.

Deep Creek Publishers LLC

Whales Edits LLC

Cover Art: Jeulia Hesse

Also by Jeulia Hesse

The Stone House Inn Series
Deadly Inheritance
Killer Recipe
Soul Sentinel

The Deep Blue Sea Series
Secrets in The Deep Blue Sea
Sins in the Deep Blue Sea
Ghosts in the Deep Blue Sea
Curses in the Deep Blue Sea
Treasures in the Deep Blue Sea
Hearts in the Deep Blue Sea

Widow's Point Island Trilogy
Last Wish Wedding
Buried Secrets – Coming Soon
Widow's Walk – Coming Soon

For Jan, my sister-in-law and biggest fan

Contents

Prologue

The Vermont countryside unfurled in shades of delicate green, spring finally asserting itself after a brutal winter. Pink and white dogwood blossoms dotted the cemetery, their beauty an obscene contrast to the polished mahogany casket suspended above the raw earth.

Kelsey stood at the graveside under a mask of composure that belied the chaos roiling inside her. Her black dress strained slightly across her midsection. The barely visible curve of her pregnancy, five months along, was not obvious to casual observers but unmistakable to her with every movement, every breath.

She felt Amy's hand slip into hers, a lifeline of warmth in the cool spring air. Her sister stood close enough that their shoulders touched, as if physically bearing some of Kelsey's weight. Perhaps she was. The past five days had blurred together in a haze of arrangements and phone calls and decisions no twenty-seven-year-old should have to make.

"The Lord is my shepherd; I shall not want..." The minister's voice carried across the gathering, the familiar words washing over Kelsey without sinking in. All she could focus on was the casket. David was in there. David, with his crooked smile and terrible jokes. David, who had kissed her goodbye last Tuesday morning, promising to pick up Thai food on his way home from his meeting in Boston. David, who had never made it past the icy curve on Route 2 where his car skidded into the path of an oncoming truck.

Her knees buckled slightly. Amy's grip tightened, holding her upright as the minister continued, unaware of her momentary collapse.

"... though I walk through the valley of the shadow of death..."

Kelsey raised her eyes from the casket, letting her gaze drift across the gathering. Their friends from the hospital where she worked as a nurse stood in a tight cluster. Their faces were drawn with shock and grief. Dr. Matthews dabbed at her eyes with a handkerchief. Javier, from Radiology, had his arm around his wife, Irene, who had brought meals to their house every night since the accident.

And across the grave, standing separate from the hospital group, were the Prescotts. Margaret Prescott, David's mother, stood ramrod straight in an impeccable black suit, her silver hair swept into a chignon so tight it seemed to pull her features into permanent disapproval. She hadn't cried during the service. Not once. Kelsey wondered absurdly if the woman's tear ducts functioned properly.

Beside Margaret stood Jason, David's younger brother by five years and the golden child who had followed their father into the family business. His expression combined boredom and impatience, as if the burial of his only sibling was an inconvenient meeting he couldn't reschedule.

Every few minutes, he checked his watch. The gesture was so subtle most wouldn't notice, but Kelsey did. She noticed everything today, her senses painfully, unnaturally sharp.

Only Jennifer, Jason's wife, showed genuine emotion. She stood slightly apart from her husband and mother-in-law, and her delicate features were soft with sympathy whenever her gaze met Kelsey's. She had approached Kelsey before the service and embraced her with unexpected warmth, whispering, "I'm so sorry. If you need anything at all, please call me." The kindness had almost broken Kelsey's careful composure.

It made no sense to Kelsey how someone as gentle as Jennifer had ended up with Jason, who had, at their wedding, told David that marrying "the nurse" was "certainly a choice." They hadn't attended another Prescott family gathering since.

"... and I will dwell in the house of the Lord forever."

The minister closed his Bible, nodding to the funeral director. The mechanical whir of the lowering device jarred against the backdrop of birdsong and gentle spring breeze. Kelsey watched the casket begin its descent. Her body was rigid with the effort it took to not fling herself forward, to not scream at them to stop, to not demand one last look at David's face.

It was Amy who moved first, stepping forward to take a rose from the arrangement atop the casket before it sank too low. She handed it to Kelsey, then took one for herself.

"Goodbye, David," Amy whispered, tossing her rose into the grave.

Kelsey tightened her fingers around the thorny stem and welcomed the stab of pain. She tried to think of something to say, some final words that could possibly encompass what David had meant to her, what his loss had torn from her future. But there was nothing adequate, nothing big enough to hold the enormity of her grief.

Instead, she pressed the rose briefly to her lips, then to her belly, before letting it fall. It landed atop the casket with a soft thud that echoed in her bones.

The gathering began to disperse, people milling in small groups toward their cars, voices hushed out of respect. The Prescotts moved as a unit, Margaret leading, Jason and Jennifer following. They headed directly for their black town car without a backward glance at the grave. But Jennifer paused and said something to Jason that made him frown before giving a curt nod. She broke away and crossed the spring grass toward Kelsey.

"I meant what I said earlier," Jennifer said softly, her brown eyes warm with sincerity. "If you need anything, especially with the baby coming, please don't hesitate. I know things have been... strained... between David and the family, but I'd like to help if I can."

"Thank you," Kelsey managed. The words scraped her raw throat. "That's very kind."

She glanced over her shoulder where Jason stood by the car, checking his watch again. "I should go. Take care of yourself, Kelsey. And the little one."

As Jennifer walked away, Kelsey noticed how her shoulders seemed to stiffen with each step back toward her husband. Her posture gradually shifted from a natural grace to something more contained, more careful.

"Ready to go?" Amy asked gently. "Everyone's heading to the house for the reception."

The thought of returning to the small farmhouse she had shared with David, now filled with well-meaning people and casseroles, made Kelsey's stomach turn. But she nodded, knowing it was expected, knowing she had to go through the motions of this day like thousands of widows before her.

"Just... give me a minute," she requested.

Amy squeezed her hand. "Take all the time you need. I'll wait by the car."

Left alone at the graveside, Kelsey finally allowed herself to tremble. The careful mask she'd maintained cracked, her face contorting with grief too enormous to contain. Her knees gave way at last, and she sank onto the small metal chair that had been placed beside the grave. Her body folded in on itself as silent sobs wracked her frame.

"I can't do this," she whispered for David alone. "I can't do this without you."

A flutter of movement in her abdomen answered her. Not a kick, not yet, but the strange butterfly sensation that had started last week. The same day as the accident. As if the baby had somehow known, had chosen that moment to make its presence undeniably felt.

Kelsey pressed her hand to the small, sacred swell beneath the black fabric. Part of David, growing inside her. The only part she had left.

"But I have to do this, don't I?" she whispered to the grave, to the baby, to herself. "I have to keep going."

The flutter came again, stronger this time. Kelsey took a deep, shuddering breath to gather the broken pieces of herself back together. When she stood, her legs were steadier than she expected.

She looked down at the casket, now fully lowered into the earth. Cemetery workers stood at a respectful distance, waiting to complete their task once she left.

A cool breeze lifted the ends of her hair, carrying the scent of fresh earth and new growth. Kelsey took one final look at the grave, a final silent goodbye.

Then she turned and walked away. Each step was an act of sheer will, propelling her forward into a future she hadn't chosen but would somehow have to build, for the child who would need her to be both mother and father, both strength and tenderness.

For David's child. For Noah, the name they had chosen together just days before the accident while lying in bed with their hands intertwined over her growing belly.

Behind her, the cemetery workers moved in and their shovels bit into the pile of dirt beside the grave. She didn't look back, didn't allow herself to hear the first thud of soil hitting wood. Instead, she focused on Amy by the car, on the horizon beyond, on the life within her. One step, then another. It was all she could do.

It would have to be enough.

Chapter 1

The fog rolled in off the Atlantic like a living thing, swallowing I-95 in thick, gray tendrils. Preston MacCormack squinted through the windshield of his grandfather's Peterbilt eighteen-wheeler, his knuckles white on the steering wheel. The massive sailing yacht he was hauling behind him felt like a target in these conditions, and every car that zipped past sent a shudder through him. At least he was visible.

"Damn fools," he muttered, watching another set of taillights vanish into the fog ahead. At thirty-five, Mac had already seen enough of humanity's stupidity to last several lifetimes. It was partly why he'd bought the sailing yacht—a promise of solitude on the open water, away from everyone and everything.

The cab's heater fought against the early spring chill. He'd already slipped on the company jacket the usual driver had left in the cab and was eying the thick sweatshirt he'd brought lying on the passenger seat.

His grandfather would approve of Mac making this run himself, even if the old man might question Mac's plans for the boat. He was a man that loved being around people. "Learn it from the ground up, boy," he'd always said, his Irish brogue thick even after fifty years in the States. "That's how you respect what you've built."

Mac had learned, all right. Learned enough about people to know he was better off without them. The money he'd made on his own, plus his grandfather's pending inheritance, meant he never had to work another day in his life. But here he was, hauling his own boat because...

Brake lights blazed through the fog ahead.

Mac slammed his foot onto his brake, but physics had its own opinions about eighteen wheels and forty tons of momentum. He thanked his stars that he'd had the common sense to slow down. The truck's horn blared as he yanked it, but the sound was swallowed by the wall of gray. He could see it now—a pileup, cars crumpled like paper, and his rig sliding forward with inexorable certainty.

The world moved in slow motion. Mac's training kicked in—all those hours his grandfather insisted on drilling him on handling the rig in every condition imaginable. He fought the wheel, muscles straining as he tried to guide the massive vehicle toward the shoulder. Hitting the mass of cars would make things worse for everyone involved. The trailer with his yacht threatened swayed dangerously, threatening to jackknife.

Metal screamed against metal as the truck's cab clipped a silver sedan, pushing it sideways into the guardrail like a crumpled accordion. The impact jolted through the cabin, but the sedan was no match for the truck, and somehow he kept control until the rig finally shuddered to a stop.

Mac's hands trembled as he unclipped his seatbelt and grabbed his phone. The fog wrapped around him as he jumped down from the cab with the wet splash of his boots on asphalt. "Hey!" he shouted, running toward the sedan. "Anyone hurt?"

The driver's door groaned open. A woman emerged, moving with the kind of deliberate grace that suggested she was checking herself for injuries. She straightened, and Mac found himself frozen in place.

Her eyes were the color of Arctic ice, and they held about as much warmth. The look she fixed him with could have stripped paint off a wall. She was tall, maybe early thirties, with dark hair plastered to her face from the fog's moisture.

"Are you blind?" Her voice cut through the fog like a knife. "Couldn't you have missed my car?"

Mac felt his own temper flare. "Lady, if you could see past your own hood in this soup, you'd know I did everything I could to avoid—"

A chorus of horns blared behind them, followed by another sickening crunch of metal meeting metal at speed. The woman's eyes widened, and the anger in them was suddenly replaced by something else—fear, maybe, or recognition of just how bad this could have been.

Mac instinctively stepped between her and the ongoing chaos behind them, his earlier irritation forgotten. "We need to get off the road," he said, gesturing toward the guardrail. "More cars are coming, and they can't see a damn thing."

The fog made everything surreal, like a nightmare in slow motion. Mac wrapped his fingers around her arm to pull her toward the guardrail, but she twisted free with surprising strength.

Cries for help pierced through the fog's muffled silence. "I need my bag," she said, already rushing back to her crushed car. She reached through the passenger window and emerged with a large black duffel. "Call 911 and come with me."

Mac fumbled with his phone, punching in the numbers as he followed her. Her figure appeared and disappeared in the swirling mist like a ghost.

They found the cluster of people near a rolled SUV. A man lay on the ground, blood pooling beneath him. His wife knelt beside him with shaking hands as she tried to help. The metallic smell of blood mixed with gasoline and burning rubber.

The woman from the sedan transformed before Mac's eyes. Gone was the angry stranger who'd emerged from the wreck. In her place was someone else entirely—someone who moved with precise, professional certainty.

"My name is Kelsey. I'm going to help you." Her voice was steady and warm as she knelt beside the injured man. She swiftly found the source of bleeding in his thigh. "What's your name?"

"Tom," the man gasped. "Am I going to—"

"Tom, I need you to stay with me." Her hands were already crimson with his blood as she dug them into his leg. Mac's stomach turned as he realized what she was doing.

Without looking up, she addressed him. "Get into my bag. There's a tourniquet at the bottom."

Mac stood frozen, the 911 operator's voice tiny in his ear.

"My hands are occupied," she said, still remarkably calm. "Do it now."

The authority in her tone broke through his paralysis. He dropped to his knees and rummaged through the bag until he found what looked like a thick strap with a windlass.

"Good. Now, wrap it around his thigh, above my hands." Her blue eyes met his, steady and clear. "Pull it as tight as you can and secure it. Tom's life depends on this being done correctly. Do you understand?"

Mac nodded, then followed her instructions with trembling hands. The man's wife watched, clutching her husband's hand.

"Now," the woman commanded. "Pull it tight."

Mac twisted the windlass, watching her face for guidance. Blood covered her hands and splattered her blouse, but her voice never wavered as she talked to Tom, monitored his responses, and guided Mac's actions. In the distance, sirens began to wail.

"That's good," she said finally. "Hold it there." She looked at Mac with those crystalline eyes, and for a moment, he saw something like approval in them. "You did well. Now go tell those paramedics to come over here ASAP."

Mac had never felt more useless or more necessary in his life.

The paramedics materialized out of the fog like apparitions, their fluorescent vests glowing in the gray soup. They took over Tom's care with practiced efficiency, and the woman gave them a rapid-fire assessment of what she'd done and Tom's condition.

Before he could process it, she was moving again toward other people, her bloodied hands pulling fresh gloves from her seemingly bottomless bag. Mac trailed after her like a lost puppy and held her supplies as she worked her way through the wreckage.

She triaged each cluster of people with calm authority. A teenager with a nasty head wound. An elderly man complaining of chest pain. A young mother cradling a crying infant. At each stop, she knew exactly what to do, what to say, how to help until more first responders could arrive.

"Gauze," she'd say, or "The penlight," and Mac would dig through her bag until he became familiar with its organized chaos.

The fog was starting to lift, revealing the full scope of the pileup. Emergency vehicles now lined the highway, their lights painting everything in rotating red and blue. Mac noticed the woman had an easy rapport with the EMTs; she spoke their language, anticipated their needs.

"Are you some kind of doctor?" he finally asked as she stripped off another pair of bloody gloves. Things were starting to be more organized, and the injured were taken off on stretchers.

Those blue eyes flickered to his face, and for a moment he saw a hint of amusement there. "No," she admitted, reaching for her bag and wiping a bead of sweat from her brow with her unbloodied forearm.

"Did you say your name was Kelsey?" he asked.

"I don't typically make small talk with strange men I meet on the side of a highway. Especially men who've just plowed their trucks into my car."

Before Mac could respond, she was moving again, toward another call for help. He followed as though he had no other choice in the matter. "I'm Mac," he called after her. "Since we've now saved lives together, seems like I should know your name."

She glanced back over her shoulder, and this time he definitely caught the ghost of a smile. "You'll know it well enough, when our insurance settles this mess."

The EMTs had already reached the group calling for assistance, so Kelsey walked back to her crushed sedan. Mac's truck looked not-the-worse for wear. He guessed that if he could back it up from here, it would move on its own. Her car, however, was badly damaged, if not totaled.

A police officer approached them, handing Kelsey a business card with a number to call. A wrecker would tow her car to a garage in Portland along with the other damaged vehicles involved in the pileup. The officer took down her information and his, and moved along to get the highway cleared.

"Kelsey York," she said extending her hand as they looked over the damaged vehicles. "Looks like I'll need a ride to the ferry. Hopefully you're headed to Portland, or maybe you feel bad enough after wrecking my car to drop me off."

How could he say no to someone whose blouse was smeared with the drying blood of a dozen injured strangers?

"Of course. I am actually headed to the docks myself," he answered, gesturing to the still intact boat on the trailer.

Nodding, she gathered some items from her car and opened the passenger side of the cab. Mac hustled to move things around and make room for her on the seat. "Oh hey," she exclaimed, picking up the sweatshirt he'd tossed there earlier. "Do you mind if I borrow this?" She gestured to her bloodied shirt.

"Be my guest," he said. And stared opened-mouthed as she whipped off her blouse and donned the sweatshirt. The view of a black lace bra over a perfectly toned torso lasted only a second. But it was enough for his sex-deserted body to respond.

She smiled over at him. "Sorry, I'm sure that was nothing you haven't seen in your life. I just needed to get that off. Been awhile since I did trauma, and I still am not a fan."

Mac guided the truck carefully around the accident scene, following the police officer's directions until they were back on the highway. The fog had thinned considerably now, though his hands still felt tight on the wheel from the earlier tension.

"So," he ventured, glancing sideways at Kelsey. She was swimming in the over-sized sweatshirt but somehow managed to make it look good. "What you did back there... that was incredible."

She shrugged, looking out the window. "Just muscle memory, really. You never really forget the training, even if you choose a different path."

"You said you're not a fan of trauma anymore?" They weren't far from Portland now; the exit signs were coming up. He would have to take the exit to get down to the waterfront docks and the ferry, which would have the crane needed to lift the yacht into the water.

"No," she said, turning those striking blue eyes his way. "I'm a nurse practitioner now. I have a primary care practice at a rural clinic up the coast and function like a family doctor for the community. Much more my speed—helping people manage their aches and pains instead of packing a gushing artery on a highway."

Mac nodded, thinking about how even the EMTs had deferred to her expertise. "It seems like you're pretty good at it, though. That guy was lucky you were there."

"Yeah, well," she shifted in the seat, pulling her legs up under her. "Sometimes life gives you experience you didn't ask for. The clinic work suits me better. Regular hours, getting to know my patients, watching kids grow up healthy..." she trailed off, then changed the subject. "That's quite a boat you're hauling. Your customer must be very happy about their swanky new sailboat."

Mac recognized the deflection but didn't push. "Oh, he's definitely happy to be getting this one," he said, realizing she assumed he worked for the trucking company. It was a natural assumption, being that he *was* driving the truck, and wore the driver's jacket with the logo emblazoned across his chest.

Traffic began to pick up as they approached the docks. She was busy digging in her bag. "Let me give you my insurance information. Here is my name and number, just have your office or however it works for your employer give me a call about the details. Usually, we just let the insurance company work it out." She placed the note with the details on the seat between them. "I'll see if I can borrow a car in the meantime, but I'm not sure my policy covers a rental."

"I'll take care of it. I'm sure they'll give you whatever you need. Accidents happen," he tried to reassure her as, from the scowl on her face, the lack of a car distressed her. Of course she would need something to drive around. She had a job to get to, and for all he knew, she had a bunch of kids to chauffeur. A side glance at her hands revealed she didn't wear a wedding ring, but that didn't mean she didn't have any kids. People had all sorts of family arrangements these days, he reminded himself.

It bothered him slightly that he wanted to know what her living arrangements were, so he stopped himself from asking. It was very likely he would never see her again.

He'd chosen a life of solitude, and it had its price.

"I've got your companies information here, but what's your name?" she asked as they approached the docks.

"Mac... Actually, Preston MacCormack, with two *C*'s, one *K*."

She smiled at him as she wrote it down. He felt color rise in his face. He wasn't sure why he said his name like that, just a nervous habit from when he was a kid.

"Okay, this is me. You don't have to try to get this rig into the parking lot. I can walk from here." They had reached the docks for the car ferries that took residents and tourists to the islands outside of Casco Bay.

He pulled to the shoulder as best he could in the tight streets, and she opened her door to slip down to the sidewalk. "Well, thanks? I mean that. Thanks for your help back there."

"Sorry about your car..." he started.

A ferry blew its warning whistle. "I have to go. I guess we'll be in touch. Bye."

And with a slam to the cab door, she bolted to make the ferry.

Chapter 2

Kelsey pressed her forehead against the cold ferry window, letting the vibration of the engines rumble through her skull. The tears came silently, mixing with the salt spray on the glass. She'd held it together through the accident, through the aftermath, through the drive to the ferry with the stranger who hit her car. But now, alone in the corner of the passenger cabin, she was overcome.

Her hands were still shaking. Not from the accident itself. She'd handled that on autopilot. No, it was this morning's meeting in Boston that had her trembling. The cold conference room, Jason Prescott's perfectly tailored suit, the way he'd looked at her with that same condescending smile he'd always worn.

After the meeting, Jason had grabbed her wrist and hissed in her ear. "This is what's best for Noah," he'd said, as if he had any idea what was best for her son. As if the Prescotts hadn't completely ignored Noah's existence for the first three years of his life.

The Prescotts were old Boston money, their fortune built long before skyscrapers crowded the skyline. In the 1800s, they shipped cotton and rum across the Atlantic and ran half the city's textile mills. Today, their wealth is quietly diversified: real estate trusts that own blocks of Back Bay, a discreet private bank for the city's elite, and a family foundation whose name is etched into marble above every hospital wing and museum corridor in New England.

She wiped her eyes with the sleeve of the borrowed sweatshirt, the unfamiliar scent on it momentarily distracting her from her spiral of worry. Noah was everything she had left of David. He was her everything since that horrible day when the police had shown up at her door.

David had walked away from his family's money and expectations, and they'd never forgiven him for it. Now they wanted custody of her son, to raise him in their world of prep schools and summer homes on the Cape.

The ferry pitched slightly in the growing swells, and Kelsey's stomach lurched with it. She should be home already, picking up Noah from her sister Amy's house. Instead, she was stuck here, car-less, wearing a stranger's sweatshirt, and trying not to fall apart in public. At least the accident had given her something else to focus on for a while. Helping others had always been her way of coping, even after David's death, when she'd thrown herself into finishing her nurse practitioner program.

The familiar silhouette of Widow's Point Island emerged from the afternoon haze. The lighthouse first, then the scattered rooftops of the village, and finally the dark shape of the old mansion on the northern point. Its weathered shingles and empty windows seemed to watch over the island: half guardian, half ghost, holding stories in its bones. The mansion stood implacable and unmoved by human suffering, a monument to power and permanence while her own life felt suddenly built on shifting sand.

She'd chosen this place carefully—a fresh start, away from Boston, away from the Prescotts' influence. The small clinic, the tight-knit community, the way everyone looked out for each other—it had felt right. Safe.

But now? She pulled David's wedding ring out from under the sweatshirt where it hung on a chain around her neck and rolled it between her fingers. The meeting had made it clear; the Prescotts would not back down. Their lawyer had talked about "heritage" and "birthright" while her own attorney had whispered warnings to her about their influence over judges in both Boston and Portland. How could she fight them? A single mom barely making it at a small island clinic versus one of Boston's oldest and richest families?

She tried to be both mom and dad to Noah, but there were days when it felt as if she was failing at both.

The ferry's horn announced their approach to the dock. Kelsey stood, squaring her shoulders and wiping away the last traces of tears. She texted her sister to pick her up at the dock. Undoubtedly, she would worry why she was showing up without her car.

She couldn't fall apart. Not now. Noah needed her to be strong, just like all those people on the highway had needed her to be strong. One crisis at a time. First, she'd get home to her son. Then she'd figure out how to keep the life they'd built.

The ferry was just docking when Kelsey spotted Amy's ancient Subaru in the parking lot. Her sister was already out of the car, arms crossed, glasses perched on her head in her usual disheveled-yoga-instructor way. Noah's dark head was visible in the back seat, likely absorbed in whatever book he was reading now.

"So," Amy said as Kelsey approached, eyeing the oversized sweatshirt. "Interesting outfit for a meeting with your lawyer. What happened to your car?"

"Pileup on 95. It's not drivable, maybe totaled. I was rear-ended by a Mack truck. I'm fine," she added, knowing her sister would ask.

"Jesus Kel, you sure you're all right? Is that why you're wearing a man's shirt?"

"Long story." Kelsey gave her sister a grimace and tilted her head toward the car where Noah sat, already scrambling to greet her. "Mom!" Noah's face lit up as he allowed her to pull him close and breath in his familiar scent of soap and salt air. At seven, he was already showing signs of being as tall as his father, all legs and elbows. "You said you'd be home hours ago!"

"I know, sweet boy. The fog had other plans." They all climbed into the car.

"Well, you can tell me all about your 'interesting day' over tea later," Amy whispered after helping Kelsey with her bag.

They wound their way up the narrow island roads, past weather-worn cottages and early spring gardens. Amy kept glancing over at her, clearly bursting with questions she couldn't ask in front of Noah.

"The daffodils are starting to come up in the old gardens," Amy said as they turned onto the private drive that led to their cottages. "I found another patch yesterday, pushing through near the greenhouse ruins."

The massive bulk of the old, brooding mansion loomed above their cottages like a battered shipwreck run aground, its weathered gray shingles nearly black in the fading light—and nearly indistinguishable from the rocks on the nearby cliffs. Even after months here, Kelsey still caught her breath at the sight of it. Three stories of Victorian grandeur, with a widow's walk that looked out over the Atlantic. Dozens of windows glimmered in the shifting light, some winking with secrets, others blank-eyed and dark and seeming to watch their every move. The place held its breath, waiting for something, or someone, to return.

They continued down the winding drive, through what had once been formal gardens, but was now a tangle of old roses and unruly saplings. Kelsey and her sister lived in the cottages that had served as homes for the mansion's caretakers long before.

Amy's cheerful yellow cottage and neat herb garden came into view first. Kelsey could see the plots Amy had cleared in preparation for her summer vegetables, next to the old cook's kitchen garden she was slowly bringing back to life.

Kesley's own caretaker's cottage sat in a clearing, its simple Cape Cod style somehow both humble and dignified. The sound of waves drifted up from the hidden cove below, and Kelsey felt some of her tension ease.

"Can I go down to the beach?" Noah asked as they pulled up. "I want to see if any new shells washed up, and Mackie might be around."

"Not tonight, honey. It's getting dark, and we need to start dinner. I'm sure your little friend wouldn't be allowed out either." Kelsey caught Amy's eye. "But maybe Aunt Amy would like to come in for tea first?"

"You bet I would," Amy said, already turning off the engine. "I want to hear all about your 'foggy' day."

As they walked to the cottage, Kelsey noticed wisps of steam rising from the infinity pool at the house across the bluff, the one in which she assumed little Mackie lived. She'd never met the owners, though occasionally she saw lights on at night. The modern house somehow managed to look both impossibly expensive and perfectly at home among the island's traditional architecture.

Noah had befriended Mackie a few months ago, after she and Noah had moved here. It seemed they both shared interests in collecting the shells and trinkets that washed up on their shared cove.

Noah bounded ahead to unlock the door, and Kelsey settled herself for the conversation with her sister. How could she explain that the peaceful life they'd built here might be about to unravel?

Inside, Noah immediately headed to his room to unpack his backpack, calling over his shoulder, "Can I have macaroni and cheese for dinner?"

"We'll see," Kelsey answered and waited until she heard his door click shut before turning to her sister. Amy was already putting the kettle on, pulling two mugs from the cabinet with practiced familiarity.

"Okay, start with why you're hours late and wearing clothes that aren't yours," Amy said in a low voice, reaching for the chamomile tea.

Kelsey sank into one of the kitchen chairs, suddenly exhausted. Through the window, she could see the last of the daylight slipping through the trees. "I told you about the pileup on I-95. I had pulled over to the shoulder and a Mack truck came sliding out of the fog behind me..." She shuddered. "It was like slow motion. Thankfully, he wasn't going fast. My car got pinned against the guardrail and it crushed the back end."

"Oh my God, Kels!" Amy abandoned the tea preparation and looked her sister up and down. "Are you sure you're not hurt? Have you gotten checked out? You could have whiplash—you might not feel it yet, but tomorrow morning..."

"I'm okay, really. I was able to help with triage until the ambulances arrived. The truck driver gave me his sweatshirt because I was covered in blood... other people's," Kelsey clarified. She wrapped her arms around herself. "I'm preparing myself for the fact that my car is totaled. It's in pretty bad shape and my insurance doesn't cover rentals."

"The trucking company better be paying for everything," Amy said firmly. "Including a rental car. You need wheels out here—especially with your home care patients. They really count on you."

"I know. I'll call them tomorrow. For now..." Kelsey's voice cracked. "For now, that's actually the least of my problems. The meeting with Jason was... bad."

"That entitled—" Amy caught herself with a glance toward Noah's room. "What did your former brother-in-law want?"

"They want full custody. I would only get him for summer vacations, holidays, and school breaks. He would be living in Boston or on the Cape and go to one of the boarding schools Jason and David attended." Kelsey's hands trembled as she accepted the mug of tea Amy passed her. "He brought two lawyers, Amy. Two. They're talking about 'proper advantages' and 'family heritage' like the last seven years never happened. All the things of theirs David rejected."

"What's different now?"

Kelsey's voice turned bitter. "Besides that, he is fully potty trained and can fend for himself? Jason claims Matriarch Margaret is 'concerned' about him growing up on—and I quote—'some remote island without proper advantages.'"

"Remote island?" Amy snorted. "We have fiber internet and a year-round farmer's market. What we don't have is their toxic..."

A floorboard creaked, and both sisters fell silent as Noah appeared in the doorway. "Mom, can I work on my shell collection while you make dinner?"

"Of course, sweetie. Just keep it on the table by the window, okay?" Kelsey managed a smile as he retrieved his carefully organized boxes of beach treasures.

Amy waited until he was absorbed in his collection before whispering, "So what's the plan? You'll need a lawyer who can stand up to the Prescott empire. The one you have doesn't sound like she's got the balls you need."

"I don't know. I'm not sure I can fight them." Kelsey stared into her tea. "Between legal fees and now dealing with the car situation, I'm going to have to dip into Noah's college fund just to stay afloat."

"We'll figure it out." Amy squeezed her sister's shoulder. "I can drive you to your patients on Monday, or you can just take my car, if you haven't sorted out the rental. Maybe we can work out a schedule with some of the other clinic staff until this gets resolved."

"Mom?" Noah's voice made them both jump. "Are you okay?"

Kelsey lifted her head and forced brightness into her voice. "Just tired, honey. How about that mac and cheese?"

Chapter 3

Kelsey rubbed her temples while she stared at the patient schedule on her computer screen at the island clinic. The morning light shone through the windows, carrying the scent of salt air and early spring. Her phone buzzed again—another message from Pete's Garage on the mainland. The mechanic had promised to give her an quote for the repair this morning.

Frame damage is extensive... possible transmission involvem ent... will have to wait on the insurance adjuster... prepare that it may likely total loss given the age of the vehicle...

Her stomach clenched. Her car had been old but reliable. Perfect for island roads and Maine winters. More importantly, it had been paid off.

She pulled up the insurance policy on her phone, heart sinking as she confirmed what she already knew—no rental car coverage. And the local rental office had quoted her a weekly rate more than a new monthly car payment would be.

Maybe that was the solution, just going to the mainland and biting the bullet to get a new vehicle. It would take care of the problem for sure, but the thought of a car payment on top of looming legal bills made her head spin. She started to work through the logistics of getting off island and visiting a dealership around her work schedule and Noah's after-school activities. She'd figure it out, but it wasn't going to be any time soon.

The clinic's waiting room door creaked open, and Ruth, one of the home care nurses, poked her head in. "Just wanted to let you know about Mr. Costigan. The aide reported this morning that he fell in the bathroom the other day. No apparent injuries."

"Just a bruised ego I'm sure," Kelsey replied, shaking her head. Her favorite patient was one of her most stubborn. He insisted on staying home by himself even as his heart failed. "I'll check him out. How are his lungs?"

The nurse raised her eyebrows and said nothing, which spoke volumes. His condition was declining. Soon, they would need another plan for him. It would be a tough conversation, but a necessary one.

"I'm almost ready to head out. Amy let me borrow her car this morning."

"What did the garage have to say?"

"They think it might be totaled. They won't know more until the adjuster looks at it, but I think they're right. The truck basically crushed my car's back end into the guardrail." She ducked to grab her medical bag to hide her expression from Ruth.

"Thank goodness you're all right. Surely the truck driver has insurance that will cover it," Ruth replied and then headed out on her own visits for the day.

Ruth had a point, but Kelsey had given the driver her insurance information and hadn't yet heard a peep from his employer. So, Kelsey dialed the number to the trucking company and was re-directed several times as they determined who she needed to speak with. Eventually, she ended up leaving a voicemail for someone in their human resources department. Although the driver, Mac, had assured her it would be taken care of, it sure didn't start out promising.

The car she borrowed from Amy sat in the clinic's parking lot, its faded red paint a stark contrast to her usual navy car. It even smelled different: of peppermints and old leather, nothing like her car's familiar mix of coffee and Noah's soccer gear. Kelsey tossed her bag in the back and checked her watch. She planned to make several stops around the island today in case she didn't have a car later in the week.

The coastal road wound past weather-worn cottages and patches of stubborn snow hiding in the shaded parts. Kelsey downshifted carefully on the steep sections, still adjusting to the unfamiliar clutch.

Mr. Costigan's cottage appeared through the morning mist. Its weathered shingles and climbing roses made it exactly the sort of place you'd expect to find in rural Ireland, not on an island off the coast of Maine. Costigan had lived in the house and in Portland on and off with his wife of seventy years before finally moving here full time after they retired. His wife had died a few years ago, and Kelsey knew from Ruth his health had been declining since then. Smoke curled from the chimney, and the front windows gleamed with fresh washing.

Before stepping from the car, her phone rang. The trucking company returning her call from earlier.

"So ma'am, you're saying that one of our trucks hit you on I-95 on Saturday? And the driver was called Mac or Preston MacCormack?" A chill entered her gut at the tone of the woman on the other line, she sounded like she had her hackles raised. "I'm sorry to say, we don't have any employees with that name ma'am, and I just spoke to our dispatch, and we didn't have any drivers out on that route Saturday. Are you sure it was our company?"

"I'm sure," she answered. "I have a picture I took of the wreck. Truman Trucking..."

"I'm quite sure, too, ma'am. But if you want to send me the photo, I'd be happy to research it for you. But as of right now, I can't confirm the information you've provided."

Disbelief welled in her stomach. There had to be some mistake. Could she have gotten the trucking company name wrong? She hastily wrote the woman's email down and promised to send the photo right away. Ending the call, she pulled up the pictures she snapped at the last minute on Saturday. The trucking logo was clear in all of them. As she quickly sending the photos with a brief email, a realization dawned on her.

He'd lied.

The driver of the truck. He lied to her about how it would all be taken care of. Even his name was likely fake, "Mac" who drove a Mack truck. What if he had stolen the truck, and the sailboat it was hauling? The company didn't have a record of him driving because he wasn't supposed to be.

How could she be so stupid to fall for that!

Worse, now what was she going to do? If her insurance covered the damages, she still had a high deductible on her policy she would have to pay, which made the premiums more affordable. And they would likely raise her rates. And then there would be car loan payments. Her earlier bravado to go buy a new car evaporated.

Tears streamed down her face. This was a disaster.

Out of the corner of her eye, she caught Mr. Costigan standing at the open door to his cottage, peering out curiously at the strange car in his driveway.

"Ah, my favorite lady!" Mr. Costigan's voice, still rich with Cork County despite over seventy years in Maine, carried from the front door. He stood in the doorway, one hand pressed against the frame for balance, his shock of white hair wild as ever. "Where's your usual chariot, lass? Don't tell me you've traded it in for this wee red devil?"

"Had a bit of car trouble." Kelsey managed a smile before gathering her bag and following him inside to the book-lined sitting room that smelled of pipe smoke and earl grey tea.

"Trouble, is it?" Mr. Costigan settled into his armchair by the fire, wheezing slightly. "Who's working on it for you? I hope you avoided Jones over in the Northwest Harbor, doesn't know the right end of a screwdriver..."

She smiled at him despite her troubles, gathering her blood pressure cuff from her bag. "It's in Portland with a body shop. I was hit on Saturday by a truck. It's going to need a lot of work. Now, Ruth tells me you had a spill the other day. Are you all right? Did you hurt yourself?"

"I'm fine. Just a stupid thing," he said brushing her off as she inflated the blood pressure cuff. "Hey, I know the face of a girl whose been crying. Is it all that bad?"

Tears renewed, and it was hard to rebuild on her professional demeanor. She chastised herself for getting personal with a patient. "It's fine. It's just, the trucking company just told me that the driver who hit me doesn't work for them. Not sure what to do now."

"Well you make them pay, lass. What was the name of the company?" Mr. Costigan asked, as Kelsey tried to steer the conversation back to him.

"Truman Trucking & Transport. Now let me check your vitals."

Mr. Costigan flinched as she pumped up the blood pressure cuff. "Oh, I'm sorry. Did I pinch you?"

"No dear. I'm fine."

"This is reading much higher than normal, Mr. Costigan. Have you been taking your medication as we discussed? Any chest pain? Staying away from salt?"

"Aye. I've been a good boy," he replied pulling his arm away from her. "Did the driver give you his name?"

"Funny. He said his name was Mac," she winced. Kelsey recognized that the conversation was heading where she didn't want it to go. Her patients didn't need to know everything about her. It was tough keeping to yourself living in as close-knit a community as Widow's Point. She got used to the questions and scrutiny when she'd first arrived, as the islanders got to know and trust her, but Mr. Costigan didn't need to know the finite details of her life, and she needed to turn the conversation back to him. "Not sure if that was his real name or not. Now let me listen to those handsome lungs of yours."

The moon cast long shadows across Kelsey's small bedroom as she finally crawled into bed. Her body ached from the tension of the day and the stress of struggling with the stick shift in someone else's car all day. And she had to admit she was a little sore from Saturday's accident.

She'd meant to tackle some paperwork after Noah went to bed, but their evening's walk to their little cove had drained what was left of her energy.

The sailing yacht docked at the neighboring property had captured Noah's attention.

"Mom, it's huge! Like a floating house!" his face had been excited as he marveled at the boat.

The sleek vessel, easily worth millions, had seemed to mock her current situation. The crumpled insurance paperwork still sat in her bag, along with the useless note where she'd written "Mac" and the trucking company's phone number that now led nowhere.

A car payment. She turned the words over in her mind, adding figures she already knew wouldn't balance. The clinic paid well for the island, but between Noah's school activities, the rent on the cottage, and now Jason's custody threats... She pressed her face into the pillow, feeling the dampness spread.

"Preston MacCormack," she whispered into the darkness, the fake name bitter on her tongue. How could she have been so naïve? She should have taken more pictures, gotten his license plate, something. Instead, she'd let his kind eyes and borrowed sweatshirt lull her into thinking someone was actually going to help.

From her window, she could see the yacht's running lights reflecting off the quiet water of the cove. Someone's weekend toy probably cost more than she'd make in ten years. And here she was, with seven years of education all done on her own, working full time, raising her son, and she couldn't even figure out how to replace her car.

The tears came faster now, hot and angry. She could hear Noah's steady breathing from his room across the hall, reminding her why she'd chosen this life, this island, this escape from the Prescotts' suffocating world. But tonight, she staggered under the weight of every decision, every sacrifice, every moment of pretending to Noah that everything was fine.

He deserved so much more; more time, more patience, more than a mother who was always tired and always worrying about the next bill or the next shift. She was doing her best, but sometimes she wondered if her best was enough.

Would Noah resent her later on for not allowing him all the opportunities that his father's family offered, even though David had rejected them himself?

The foghorn sounded in the distance, low and mournful. Kelsey pulled her old quilt tighter around her shoulders, allowing herself this one night of self-pity before tomorrow's realities settled in.

"Mom, can I have more syrup?" Noah asked, his fork poised over the last bite of waffle.

"What you have is plenty." Kelsey sipped her coffee, scanning her phone for any messages from the insurance company. The morning sun streamed through their small kitchen window, catching the dust motes dancing above the worn table.

A sharp knock at the front door made them both jump. Noah's fork clattered against his plate.

"Are we expecting someone?" he asked, already sliding off his chair to investigate.

"Finish your breakfast," Kelsey said, tightening the belt of her robe. Through the door's warped glass panel, she could make out the silhouette of a man in what appeared to be a suit.

She opened the door cautiously, immediately noticing the crisp leather portfolio tucked under his arm. Great. Another lawyer.

"Ms. York? Kelsey York?" The man consulted a tablet.

"Yes?"

"I need your signature here." He extended a clipboard. "And here. Initial here."

"I'm sorry, what is this for?" Kelsey didn't take the pen he offered.

"Vehicle delivery, ma'am."

"There must be some mistake. I haven't—"

"Mom!" Noah's voice carried from the kitchen window. "There's a new car in our driveway!"

The man merely extended the clipboard again. "If you could sign, please. I have to make the ferry."

Kelsey's hand trembled as she took the pen and scanned the delivery receipt. Her name was there, along with the car details. A 2024 Subaru Forrester.

The man produced a set of keys and a sealed envelope from his portfolio. "Registration and insurance cards are in the glove box. Have a nice day."

"Wait!" Kelsey clutched the keys, hurrying after him as he turned toward a waiting taxi. "I didn't order a car. There has to be some mistake."

He paused and adjusted his tie. "No mistake, ma'am. Vehicle's paid in full and registered in your name. All legal and proper."

He gestured to the envelope in her hand. "Think that explains everything."

Noah burst out the front door, still in his pajamas. "Mom! Mom! It's a Subaru like Aunt Amy's but better! Can we look inside? Please?"

The delivery man smiled slightly, climbing into the taxi. "Enjoy your new vehicle, Ms. York."

Kelsey stood barefoot on the damp grass, watching the taxi disappear around the bend. Noah was already circling the gleaming, dark blue Forester, pressing his nose against each window.

"Look! It has a sunroof! And the seats are leather!" He tugged at her arm. "Can we try it out? Please?"

"In a minute, honey." With trembling fingers, she tore open the envelope. The note inside was typed on plain white paper:

To replace your car. Apologies for the delay in getting it to you. But it's all yours. Mac.

"Mom?" Noah's voice seemed far away. "Are you crying?"

Kelsey touched her cheek, surprised to find it wet. The morning sun caught the car's pristine paint, and for a moment, she couldn't breathe.

"Can we go for a ride?" Noah bounced on his toes, still in sock feet. "Please? Just to Aunt Amy's and back?"

"You need to finish breakfast. And put on shoes." Her voice sounded strange to her own ears. "And I need to... I need to figure out what to do and how to thank him..." So, this *Mac* was not a con artist, but perhaps something even more elusive.

"Who?"

She looked at her son's eager face, then back at the note. "How to thank the person who sent the car."

Chapter 4

M ac stood at the cottage window, watching the morning fog roll across the bay. Behind him, his grandfather's wheezing had grown more pronounced over breakfast, though the old man insisted on making them both proper Irish tea. The dense mist obscured the island's familiar contours, turning the harbor into a ghostly dreamscape where boats appeared as mere shadows, their moorings uncertain. It suited his mood perfectly.

"She's beautiful," Mac said, referring to his new boat, the *Nereid*. "Forty-two feet, state-of-the-art navigation. Perfect for solo sailing."

"Mmph." Truman Costigan settled into his worn leather chair, teacup rattling slightly in his hands. "And how long do you plan to run away for this time?"

"I'm not running, Grandad. It's an adventure. Six months exploring the Caribbean, maybe longer."

"Adventure?" The old man's brogue thickened with emotion. "It's hiding, boy. Same as selling your business, same as getting rid of the Boston house. You can't sail away from grief."

Mac turned from the window, jaw tightening. "I'm not having this conversation now."

"No? Then when?" Truman's voice softened. "You're thirty-five, Mac. She's been gone ten years. She wouldn't want..."

"Don't." Mac paced the small room, dodging piles of books. "You don't get to tell me what she would want."

"I'm dying, lad."

"You've been 'dying' for two years now."

"And this time I mean it." Truman set his tea aside and fixed Mac with a stern look. "My heart's giving out. I'd like to see you settled and happy again before I go."

Mac dropped into the chair opposite his grandfather, running a hand through his dark hair. "I am settled. I've got the boat. I'm fine."

"Alone on the sea for months? That's not living, that's existing." Patrick leaned forward. "Speaking of existing, did you take care of that nurse you crashed into?"

Mac stiffened. "How did you...?"

"Small island, boy. She's my nurse practitioner. Comes by once a week to make sure this old heart keeps beating." Truman's eyes twinkled. "And I still have a way with women. She also called the trucking office. Apparently, they told her no one by the name of Mac worked there. She believes you lied to her."

"I had Johnson handle it. New Subaru, delivered this morning."

"Bit extravagant, buying her a whole new car." The old man gave him a sidelong look.

Mac studied his hands. "It wasn't her fault. Just in the wrong place at the wrong time." Mac's voice softened. "I couldn't... after she helped those people. You should have seen her, Grandad. In the middle of chaos, she was just... calm. Competent. She likely saved the life of some guy who was bleeding out on the road. Didn't blink an eye doing what needed to be done and getting herself covered in blood in the process."

Truman's smile deepened, crow's feet crinkling around his eyes. "Sounds impressive."

"She was." Mac stood abruptly and stalked back to the window. "Anyway, it's handled now. Registration, insurance paid, everything transferred to her name."

"Mmm." Truman sipped his tea. "You know, she comes by on Mondays. Usually around ten."

"Grandad…"

"Just saying. If you wanted to check on your investment, make sure she likes the car."

Mac watched a pair of gulls wheeling over the bay, their cries carrying faintly through the glass. Around the bend out of view floated the *Nereid*, with promises of escape and solitude in her sleek lines.

"More tea?" Truman asked innocently.

"You're impossible." But Mac found himself checking his watch, noting it was only nine thirty.

"Got anything better to do today?"

He smiled at the old man. The only family he had left in the world. And Mac saw what he hadn't before—the dark circles beneath Truman's eyes, the hollows in his cheeks that hadn't been there a few months ago. He wondered if Truman was being truthful this time about his health.

And then he wondered if he could bear it.

Mac's footsteps crunched on the gravel path leading from his grandfather's cottage.

His grandfather's wheezing echoed with every step. How had he missed the changes? The tremor in those once-steady hands, the way he'd needed three tries to stand from his chair. Mac pulled out his phone, scrolling to his calendar. When was the last time he'd actually attended one of his grandfather's medical appointments?

Four years as his durable medical power of attorney, and he'd been letting his assistant handle all the medication changes and other issues. He'd been available for any emergencies of course, living mostly on the same island, same estate. But his software business kept him away for most of it. It was easier that way. Safer. Like everything else in his life since Marlene.

The memory hit without warning, Marlene's laugh as she'd told him about the baby, her hand pressed to her still-flat stomach. "A late September baby," she'd said. "Perfect timing for leaf-peeping." They had both been so young and in love, with the world and their lives in front of them.

They'd never made it to September.

Mac leaned against a weathered fence post, forcing air into his lungs. Ten years, and sometimes the grief still felt fresh as yesterday. His grandfather was right. The boat was an escape. Another way to run from people and empty houses with unending quiet days and nights. Exactly what he needed it to be.

He walked toward his Range Rover keys heavy in his hand. His grandfather's words echoing. *I'd like to see you settled, happy again, before I go.*

It was a tall request for someone like him. What he wanted from humanity was for it to leave him alone.

The morning sun caught the brass numbers on his grandfather's mailbox. It was the same address that had welcomed his grandparents when they were first married and full of dreams.

They could afford to live anywhere they wanted, and have staff waiting on them day and night, but it was here in their humble cottage where his grandmother had spent her final days, where his grandfather now insisted on staying until the end. It had been here where they raised their daughter, his mother, and built their business empire.

His grandmother had been a maid at the large mansion that graced the island, now sitting empty as the center stone for both their houses and a few other cottages. He didn't know the full story, but he knew his grandfather had purchased the whole estate for his grandmother. Since then, the mansion had stood empty. Maintained, and preserved. Just unused.

All Mac knew was this was how his grandmother had wanted it. And so it was.

Mac slid behind the wheel. *I'd like to see you settled, happy again, before I go.*

Mac stood at the water's edge, the gentle April waves licking at his boots. The sun had burned off the morning's fog, but a stubborn chill lingered in the air, an undercurrent of cold that the sunlight couldn't quite reach. Even as the sky promised summer, the Atlantic's restless surface told a story of waiting, of old wounds slow to heal. He drew his jacket tighter. The wind pressed salt and loneliness against his skin, as if the island itself echoed the hollow places inside him, the ones he kept hidden even from himself.

Out here, there was nothing to demand a smile, or an answer, or a promise he couldn't keep. He preferred it that way. At least, that's what he told himself.

He scanned the empty, silent cove. He'd spent hours doing general chores around his house and tending to his new boat, but his mind kept drifting back to breakfast with his grandfather. Mrs. Anderson, the head of the board of directors for the community clinic, had also called to talk again about her suggestions to honor his grandfather. She even wanted Mac to give a speech. Mac had put her off for months. But after the conversation today with Truman, maybe it was time to throw him a party, let him know how much he was appreciated.

The memory of his parents' swift decline surfaced. He'd been twenty-three, fresh out of business school, when cancer took them both. His mother first, then his father following barely three months later, as if unable to exist in a world without her. Before Marlene, before the baby, before everything fell apart.

But his grandfather had been there, steady as the lighthouse beam that now flashed its warning from the point. Truman Costigan hadn't just given him a job at Truman Transport—he'd insisted Mac learn every aspect of the business. "Can't lead men whose work you don't understand," he'd say, sending Mac out on routes with the drivers, having him load trucks, teaching him to read both balance sheets and people.

It was from that experience in learning the business that Mac later developed a specialized software—a groundbreaking tool for shipping and transport companies that allowed them to manage inventory in every warehouse they owned as well as those abroad. It helped companies increase their efficiency and shipping times, beating their competitors by miles in reliability and costs. He later sold the software, making him rich beyond his wildest dreams.

Wandering down to the little beach, Mac picked up a piece of driftwood, turning it over in his hands. His own company had been his life for so long. Work had kept him busy and occupied his mind. Some days he still questioned selling it, even though the offer had been too good to refuse. His grandfather had understood, even supported the decision. "Money's just paper, boy. It's what you do with your time that matters."

Time. The one thing his grandfather might be running out of.

More of his grandfather's words, this time from breakfast, echoed back. *You can't sail away from life.*

The old man had built an empire from nothing, and now wanted just one thing before he died: to see his grandson build a life worth living. Not just wealth and solitude, but a legacy of his own.

"Mackie!"

The familiar voice pulled him from his thoughts. The neighbor kid was picking his way down the beach, careful not to slip on the seaweed-covered rocks.

"Found any treasure today?" the boy called out.

Mac managed a smile. "Just started looking."

Mac watched as the little boy joined him in his search along the shoreline.

"Mom says I can play until supper's ready, then I've got to get my homework done," Noah stood and handed him a piece of sea glass. "Do you think this came from pirates?"

The little boy had started showing up on the beach a few months ago. Mac assumed he lived in one of the rentals from the old estate. He liked him even though he had many questions about whatever they found on the beach. He was entertaining, easy to be around and a distraction from his thoughts. "Your mom sounds pretty wise."

Chapter 5

Kelsey hummed as she climbed out of her new Subaru, catching whiffs of that new-car smell. The heated seats had been heaven on her back after a long day of house calls, part of the primary care she'd brought to the island. Visiting patients in their homes who found it hard to get out to the clinic. She'd never owned anything so nice. Her old car had been practical, but this... this was a luxury she'd never allowed herself.

She had already decided that the insurance check for her totaled car would go straight to her benefactor, once she tracked him down. It was the right thing to do, even if it wouldn't come close to covering what he'd spent. She didn't like being beholden to someone else. Retaining her independence was important to her.

She slipped her shoes off at the door of their rented cottage. Noah was so excited about going beach combing after school she had let him go down right away, ensuring he knew his homework would need to be done after dinner. It was a safe place for Noah to explore, with the cliffs just beyond their neighbor's house where he wasn't allowed to wander. And the weather was too nice to squander. Maybe they could eat dinner on the back deck, make the most of this perfect spring evening.

Through the kitchen window, she could see the beach path winding down through the scrub pines. The late afternoon sun painted everything golden, reminding her why she'd chosen this tiny rental despite its distance from town. Worth every penny of her strict budget just for views like this.

Kelsey grabbed a light sweater and headed down the path to surprise Noah. Maybe they'd find some sea glass together before dinner. The waves lapped gently at the shore, seabirds wheeling overhead, and then she heard it—Noah's laugh, floating up from the beach.

She rounded the last bend in the path, and her heart stopped.

Noah stood at the water's edge next to a tall man with dark hair. A stranger. Her son was holding something out to him, completely at ease, while this unknown man—this *man*—leaned down to look at whatever Noah was showing him.

Every maternal instinct screamed danger. Every awful story she'd ever heard about missing children flashed through her mind. Her feet were moving before she could think, almost stumbling on the rocky path in her haste to reach her son.

"Noah!" Her voice came out sharp with fear.

"Mom!" Noah's face lit up. He waved the piece of sea glass in his hand. "Come see what Mackie and I found!"

Kelsey's stride faltered as Noah grabbed her hand and pulled her toward the stranger. The man straightened, and she found herself looking into familiar eyes, the same ones that had met hers across bloody limbs and smashed metal just days ago.

"You're..." they both said simultaneously.

Noah bounced between them. "Mom, this is my friend Mackie. He knows all about the stuff that washes up here."

"We've met," Mac said quietly.

Kelsey's mind raced. "You live here?"

"Yes." He ran a hand through his wind-tousled hair after gesturing to the house on the bluff. "I... that was my grandfather's company's truck."

"Look what we found!" Noah thrust a handful of treasures between them. "Mackie says this one might be from an old medicine bottle."

"That's very cool honey," Kelsey stammered trying to find her voice. "I need to thank you. For the car. It's too much though. I'll have the insurance check in a few days—"

"No." Mac's response was firm but gentle.

"But—"

"Mom, can Mackie come for dinner?" Noah interrupted. "I want to show him my shell collection!"

"Oh, honey, I'm sure Mac's son is waiting for him at home..."

Mac's brow furrowed. "My son?"

"Don't you..." Kelsey gestured vaguely toward the big house up the beach. "I assumed you lived there with your family. Noah's been talking about playing with another boy..." Realization dawned on her. He was Mackie.

"Just me." Something flickered across his face. "Noah's been my beach-combing buddy these past few months."

Noah tugged at her sleeve. "Please, Mom? We're having chicken casserole, right? That's the best one!"

Kelsey looked between her son's hopeful face and Mac's carefully neutral expression. The same man who'd gifted her the car, who apparently owned the mansion on the point, had been spending his afternoons beach combing with her son while she thought he was another kid around the same age as Noah.

"Please?" Noah tried again. "He shows me cool stuff, Mom. Like today he told me about how sea glass gets all smooth and frosty-looking."

Against her better judgment, Kelsey heard herself say, "Well, there's plenty to go around."

Mac stiffened, as if he'd been expecting her to decline. "Perhaps another time." His voice was cold and rough as he nodded and turned on his heel.

Instantly, Kelsey thought herself foolish. Of course, he wouldn't want to join them for her budget chicken casserole; he likely had other plans for a fancy dinner cooked by a top model girlfriend. Nevertheless... "Well, the invitation is open, feel free to stop by any time, around this time. It's the least I can do to thank you."

"Mom, my shoe." Noah whined. "My hands are all sticky with sand."

Kelsey kneeled to tie Noah's shoe, glancing up just as Mac's gaze dropped to her hands. Their eyes met, and her breath caught. Had she noticed how blue they were before? Beyond them, the surf roared as the incoming tide announced its intentions. Kelsey stood, clearing her throat and brushing the sand from her knees, acutely aware of Mac's lingering gaze.

A scowl formed between his eyes. "You don't need to thank me, I was the one who totaled your car. You were the hero."

"Oh, come with us Mackie. I really want to show you my collection," Noah half whined.

She smiled at him. "Thank me, then, by making my son happy."

Mac's shoulders drooped, and she knew they had defeated him. He followed them up the path to their cottage, with Noah chatting excitedly the whole way.

Back in the cottage kitchen, Kelsey pulled the casserole from the oven on autopilot while keeping one ear tuned to the living room where Noah's excited voice carried.

"And this one's from last winter," Noah was saying. "See how it's kind of purple?"

"That's rare," Mac replied. "Probably from an old perfume bottle." Mac then called toward the kitchen. "Can I help with anything?"

"No, I've got it," Kelsey answered, watching through the doorway as Noah spread his collection across the coffee table. Mac sat cross-legged on the floor beside him and examined each piece with genuine interest. There was something both familiar and strange about seeing this clearly wealthy man so at ease on their worn carpet, listening intently to her son's stories about each find.

With the table set, Kelsey called them to dinner. Noah barely paused for breath between bites and questions.

"Your boat is huge! Is it really yours? Can I see it sometime?"

Mac glanced at Kelsey before answering. "That's up to your mom."

"Is that what you were towing the other day?" Kelsey asked, pieces falling into place.

Mac nodded. "Just picked her up."

"Do you go on lots of trips?" Noah asked around a mouthful of casserole.

"Planning to." Mac pushed a piece of broccoli around his plate. "Thought I'd head down to the Caribbean, maybe explore the islands for a while."

"By yourself?" Kelsey found herself asking.

"That was the plan." His voice grew quieter. "But my grandfather's not doing well, so... everything's up in the air right now."

"I'm sorry to hear that," Kelsey said softly.

Mac just nodded, and Noah filled the pause. "Jimmy brought his new Pokémon cards to school today. He got a holographic one!"

The conversation drifted to safer waters—school projects, Noah's friends, the unseasonably warm weather. When Noah finished eating, he looked expectantly at his mother.

"I suppose I need to go do my homework now?"

"That's right honey, if you want to finish before bedtime. Did you thank Mac for joining us?"

"Thanks Mackie!" Noah called over his shoulder, already heading for his room.

"He's a great kid, downright tolerable," Mac said.

Kelsey started gathering plates, but Mac was already standing. "Let me help with these at least."

She wanted to refuse, but he was already running water in the sink. They fell into an easy rhythm, her washing, him drying. With his sleeves rolled up, he looked like he fit right in. Less like a man who could casually buy luxury cars for strangers.

It was a nice domestic scene, something she and David never got the chance to do together. Kelsey found herself glancing at Mac's strong forearms and large hands. They were not the hands of a wealthy man who spent time behind a desk; they were rough and callused. And very unlike her privileged brother-in-law Jason, whose hands were softer than even her own. It made her wonder about Mac.

Kelsey reached for a glass in the soapy water and a large hand closed over her own. "Oops," Kelsey laughed, but Mac didn't remove his hand right away. She found herself again locked in on his face. The weathered lines around his eyes softened as he looked at her, his expression unreadable. His calloused fingers remained warm against hers beneath the water's surface, a point of connection that sent an unexpected current up her arm.

A heartbeat thudded and she stepped away, breaking the contact. The space between them suddenly felt charged like the static electricity before a summer storm. She busied herself with the dishtowel, avoiding his gaze until her pulse gradually steadied itself to normal.

"Would you like a coffee and some cookies?" Kelsey offered as she stepped away from the sink. "It's decaf."

She watched while he hesitated and twitched like he wanted to bolt out the door. But instead, he said, "Sounds great, just the coffee though. Trying to stay away from sweets."

She smiled, thinking he had no fat on his tall frame. He was muscle-bound and fit. Blushing a bit, she admonished herself for noticing. They took seats at the kitchen table and Mac sipped his coffee.

"If you don't mind my asking—from our earlier conversation when you asked if I was married—I was wondering, he's such a great kid... his father?"

"Yes. I was married. Noah's father died before he was born." Kelsey took a deep sip of her own coffee. The emotional baggage behind this statement was not new to her. But it startled her to see Mac's reaction. His face had paled and his expression turned stoney.

"You sure about the cookie? They're Noah's favorite, chocolate chip." She opened the canister, broke off a piece for herself, and popped it in her mouth with relish. "I don't think you've told me about you. Not married, and no children. But are you..."

"My fiancé was killed in a car accident," he whispered. "Ten years ago."

Kesley was speechless, caught mid bite of a second cookie. She swallowed hard, trying not to choke.

Mac rose to his feet awkwardly. "Thank you for dinner." He hung the dishtowel he still held in his hand neatly over the sink. "It's been a while since I had a home-cooked meal."

At the door, Kelsey found herself saying, "Noah's usually down at the beach after school. Which you know. If you're around and hungry, you're always welcome to follow him home for dinner."

Mac gave her a curt nod and turned to leave.

She watched him walk down the path.

Then on an impulse, she followed him, closing the door behind her. "Mac!" she called after him. She didn't want him to leave upset. He stopped before reaching the end of the garden path, and she caught up to him easily. She reached out to touch his arm, slipping her hand up his forearm to his shoulder.

"It doesn't get easier. I think you know that. Life just works its way around the pain. If I didn't have Noah, I'm not sure I would have survived it."

She moved without thinking and embraced him. It felt like the most natural thing in the world to stand in her dooryard hugging this man who had experienced a loss like her own. He held himself stiffly in her arms. When she stepped back from the embrace, Mac's hands were holding her forearms.

"You're the first person I think, who's told me that. Everyone else seems to think it's time to move on and get over it," he said.

She struggled with what to say next, worrying that she'd said something distressing instead of helpful. But she looked up into his face and was surprised to find a smile there. She let out a sigh of relief.

Their eyes met in the dim light, and something shifted in the air between them, it carried something deep, a recognition, an understanding between two people who had known loss.

Kelsey's heart thundered in her chest. A gust of cool evening air brought her back to herself. She stepped back.

"I should go," Mac whispered, though he made no move to step away.

"Yes," Kelsey agreed, equally motionless.

Finally, he took a step back and turned down the shore path.

She watched as his figure disappeared into the gathering dusk.

Chapter 6

Kelsey's hands shook as she set her phone down on the kitchen counter. The afternoon sun streamed through the window, catching dust motes in its beam, but she felt cold despite the warmth.

"Ms. York?" Her attorney's voice continued from the speaker. "Are you still there?"

"Yes." The word came out barely above a whisper. She cleared her throat. "Yes, I'm here."

"As I was saying, Maine law is very specific about grandparent rights. They would need to prove an existing relationship with Noah, which from what you've told me..."

"They see him every other month for a weekend." Kelsey pressed her palms flat against the counter to steady herself. "Noah tells me the last time he was there, he barely saw his grandmother."

"That works in our favor. And Jason Prescott, he's David's brother?"

"Yes." The memory of Jason at David's funeral surfaced—standing stiffly beside his mother, not even looking at her. "He does plan activities with Noah, but it's things like a business meeting over golf, and Noah's his caddy. Noah tells me he spends most of his time with Jason's wife Jennifer, or with the staff instead of with his uncle."

"His involvement in this suit is peripheral at best. It would be Margaret Prescott who'd need to prove standing."

Kelsey sank into a kitchen chair, the familiar scrape of wood on linoleum grounding her somehow. "David used to tell me stories about how his father would make problems... disappear. About judges who suddenly ruled in their favor despite all indications. Businesses that mysteriously failed after crossing them."

"Ms. York, Kelsey, those kinds of tactics don't work as well as they used to. Especially in family court. Everything's too public, too scrutinized."

Her eyes drifted to Noah's school picture on the fridge. His father's smile, his father's eyes. "They're going to say I can't provide for him. That I work too much, that I can't care for him adequately."

"You're a nurse practitioner with a stable income. Noah's in school, he's healthy, he's well-adjusted. There's nothing here that suggests unfitness."

"But they have money." Her voice cracked. "So much money."

"Money isn't everything in these cases. The courts look at the child's best interest, and uprooting a child from their only remaining parent to place them with virtual strangers even for partial custody is a stretch." Papers rustled over the line. "You've been cooperative with the visitations so far, so that's also in your favor. It would take extraordinary circumstances for them to be granted custody."

Kelsey wiped her eyes, forcing herself upright. There would be time to grieve, but not now. "David never wanted them involved. He said his mother only knew how to love things she could control. But for Noah's sake, I tried. I've documented every visit, every call, every excuse they made not to see him."

"Good," her lawyer said. "Keep it up. Save everything. And Kelsey—"

"I will," she cut in, her voice steadier. "If they want a fight, I'll give them one."

She pressed her phone to her ear, mentally composing a list of details and allies to contact. There was power in action. She would not sit in this kitchen and simply *wait* for her son to be taken from her.

"That's good, but don't let them provoke you. That's probably what they're hoping for."

"They have asked for him to spend spring break with them."

There was silence for a moment on the line. "Maybe that's all they are looking for, a chance to spend more time with him? And get to know him a bit more? If you let it happen, maybe they will stand down on the full custody."

"I don't know. I don't trust it."

"It may make this whole thing go away, if you allowed additional visits as an alternative to any custody rights. It might be something to consider. Think about it, and we can talk again." With that, her attorney ended the call.

Kelsey sat in the dimming light of late afternoon spring, mulling the advice from her attorney. Having Noah spend additional time on his own with the Prescotts didn't sit well. She didn't trust them, didn't know them at all. And with this attempt to obtain custody, it just made her more uncertain.

The sound of the waves below, and the breeze in the pines beside her cottage anchored her. Noah would be home soon, full of stories about his day, completely unaware that strangers were trying to claim him as their property.

She pressed her hands to her mouth, holding back a sob. The Prescotts' power scared her especially now, when she finally felt like they were building a real life here on the island. It hadn't been easy, but she'd done it, and done it all on her own. Noah was a great kid, and dammit she was a good mother.

In her time as a nurse, she'd seen unfit parents who loved their kids but just couldn't pull their lives together. She wasn't one of them. She'd be damned if someone tried to say she was.

The tears came then, hot and silent, falling onto the smooth surface of her kitchen table while the clock ticked steadily onward.

The jarring ring of her phone cut through the darkness. Kelsey's heart leaped as she fumbled for it, mind immediately going to Amy.

"Hello?" Her voice was thick with sleep.

"Kelsey?" Ruth's usually steady voice wavered. "I'm sorry to wake you, but I'm over at Mr. Costigan's. He's had an episode. His breathing's labored, and he's refusing transport to the hospital. I can't get him comfortable. He's asking for you specifically."

Kelsey sat up, already reaching for clothes. Ruth would never call her in the middle of the night if she could handle the situation on her own. "What are his vitals?"

"O2 sats are at 89, BP's elevated. He's on and off confused, agitated. I've never seen him like this." In the short time Kesley had worked with Ruth, she'd never heard such a tremor in Ruth's voice.

"I'm calling the family too, but—"

"I'm coming." Kelsey was already pulling on scrubs. "Give me fifteen minutes."

She hung up and reached for her phone again to call Amy, then remembered—her sister was at a conference in Boston. Reality crashed in. No babysitter. No choice.

"Noah." She gently shook her son's shoulder. "Honey, wake up. We need to go."

"Mm?" Noah blinked in confusion as she helped him into a sweatshirt. "Where're we going?"

"One of my patients needs help." She grabbed his blanket and pillow. "You can sleep in the car."

The drive up the coast was a blur of yellow lines and concern. Noah dozed in the back seat as Kelsey ran through possible scenarios in her head. Ruth wouldn't have called without good reason.

Headlights appeared in her rearview mirror, gaining quickly. Another car followed her turn onto the long drive to the Costigan cottage, gravel crunching under tires.

Ruth's silhouette appeared in the doorway as Kelsey parked. She was reaching for her medical bag when the other car's door slammed.

"Kelsey?" A familiar voice called out.

Kelsey froze, one hand on Noah's car door. "Mac?" They hadn't spoken since the dinner.

He was hurrying toward the house, looking nothing like the man she'd last seen. The pieces clicked into place as she struggled with Noah's seatbelt.

"Mr. Costigan is your father?"

"Grandfather. Here." Mac reached past her, gently gathering the sleeping Noah into his arms. "Let me take him. You go on in."

"But—"

"Trust me." His eyes met hers in the dim light. "I've got him. Go help my grandfather."

Noah stirred slightly, then settled against Mac's shoulder as if it was the most natural thing in the world. Kelsey hesitated for a split second, then grabbed her bag and rushed for the door.

Kelsey burst through the door, listening to Ruth's rapid-fire report as she assessed Mr. Costigan.

"Onset about an hour ago, nitro didn't touch it. Oxygen's helping some, but..."

"Mr. Costigan?" Kelsey knelt beside the recliner where the elderly man sat, his skin ashen, struggling for each breath. She pressed her stethoscope to his chest and was greeted by telltale crackles. "Can you tell me what you're feeling?"

"Like... an elephant..." He gasped between words. "Sitting right... here." His trembling hand pressed against his sternum.

"Ruth, has he had any morphine before?"

Ruth shook her head. "Just the nitro and his regular meds. We've never..."

"It's okay." Kelsey kept her voice calm, though her mind raced. Of course they hadn't. End-of-life care on the island was still catching up mainland practice. On her agenda to change. "Mr. Costigan, I'm going to give you something under your tongue to help with the pain and breathing, alright?"

He managed a nod, his knuckles white where they gripped the chair's arm.

Kelsey retrieved the comfort pack from the kitchen refrigerator. Although Mr. Costigan wasn't yet enrolled in a hospice program, Kelsey'd had an inkling he might be headed in that direction, so she'd gone ahead and prescribed the pack a few weeks ago. It was a small cardboard box that contained small doses of prescription medications for pain, nausea, and anxiety for use in emergencies instead of rushing to the ER.

"Ruth, watch closely, these drops go under the tongue. Start with two." She demonstrated the technique, then turned back to her patient. "This will help soon. Try to relax."

A floorboard creaked, and she glanced up to see Mac standing in the doorway, Noah still asleep against his shoulder. Their eyes met briefly before she returned her attention to Mr. Costigan.

"Your legs are pretty swollen," she noted, pressing gently against his ankle. The indent remained. "How's your urine output been?"

"Not... much..." His breathing was already becoming less labored as the morphine took effect.

"Ruth, let's add an extra dose of his diuretic. I have an injection I can give him now," Kelsey continued her assessment, noting with relief as Mr. Costigan's color gradually improved. "Better?"

He nodded, managing a weak smile. "Much. Knew... you'd know... what to do. I don't want to go the hospital. I'd die there. This is where I want to be."

"Your grandfather's in good hands," Ruth said softly to Mac, who hadn't moved from his position by the door, watching everything with wide eyes.

"The best," Mr. Costigan agreed with a stronger voice. "Though... surprised to see... my grandson... playing nursemaid."

Mac shifted Noah's weight carefully.

Mr. Costigan chuckled weakly, then sobered. "Sorry to... wake the boy."

"He could sleep through a hurricane," Kelsey assured him, checking his pulse again. The rhythm was steadier now. "How's the pain?"

"Fading." His eyes were heavy. "Thank you... for coming."

"I'll stay until you're sleeping," she promised, then adjusted his oxygen. She glanced at Ruth. "We should talk about updating the comfort protocols. There are other measures we can put in place. For now though, it's time to figure out his care for tonight."

Already Ruth's cell phone buzzed at her waist. "Busy night for on call."

Kelsey listened to the one-sided conversation as the triage service gave Ruth information on another patient. "I really need to head over to the other side of the island," Ruth whispered to her. "I hate to leave, but it must be a full moon. Everyone has issues tonight that can't wait until morning."

"I can stay with Mr. Costigan and show Mac how to administer the morphine if he needs it again. But we need a better plan for him if he is going to stay home. Time to not be on his own," Kelsey replied softly to Ruth.

The room fell quiet except for Mr. Costigan's now-steady breathing and Noah's soft snores. Mac stood sentinel-like, holding her sleeping son. The expression on his face was unreadable.

"Mac, why don't you lay Noah on the sofa over there by the window?" Kelsey guided him. "And come over here where we can talk with your grandfather."

He did as she instructed woodenly, eyes following Ruth as she excused herself and slipped out the front door. Kelsey sat on the love seat directly across from Mr. Costigan, who watched her with knowing eyes. "Sit down boy, she wants to be sure we both hear what she has to tell us."

Mac sat with wide eyes.

"You see my boy, it's true that I'm dying." Mr. Costigan's color was back, and there were tears in his eyes as he spoke to his grandson. "I know I've said it a thousand times, but this time Kelsey can back me up." He smiled in jest.

Kelsey gently reached over to touch Mac's knee and leaned forward in her seat toward Mr. Costigan. "Tonight is evidence that your condition is changing, and you'll need to have more care."

"No hospital. No nursing home. Here is where I want to be," Mr. Costigan pronounced stubbornly.

"I'm in agreement with your choice, however we have to make sure you're still well cared for. I don't want you to staying alone any longer. So we need to talk about what that can look like for you. Hospice agencies do come to the island and work with us to provide the supportive care you need to stay home. The nurses can increase their visits and send in aides for personal care. But the constant presence of someone here is needed. We'll train them in how to give you medication to make you comfortable, just as I did tonight, and a nurse can come to help relieve your symptoms with medications we'll anticipate that you'll need. But it's going to be up to you and Mac to decide how you want to structure things so you're not alone," Kesley explained. She was at ease with what needed to be done for Mr. Costigan. But delivering the information to the patient and family had to be done clearly and kindly.

"I can stay with him," Mac started. "But wouldn't the hospital be the best place for him? Can't they do something to make him better?"

"My heart's shot, son. All they want to do at the hospital is stick you with needles, make noise, and feed you army rations. And you're not exactly the nurse I had in mind," Mr. Costigan started. "Anyway, that shot you gave me is starting to work. I need to head to the bathroom."

He started to get up and both Mac and Kelsey stood to help him. "Take it slow, Mr. Costigan. I don't want you to get dizzy with the pain medication."

While Mr. Costigan was out of the room, Kelsey explained more of the hospice protocol to Mac. "If you or I, young and healthy, were experiencing heart failure, we'd call an ambulance. The emergency room would stabilize us and then fix whatever problem caused the heart failure in the first place. For your grandfather, though, there is no fixing the problem. It's only going to keep happening, and constant visits to the ER would be painful and traumatic. Instead, hospice's goal would be like what we did tonight. Make him comfortable and manage him at home. Not save his life but make what remains of it a peaceful experience."

Once they got him settled again, he began to doze off in his favorite chair. Kelsey tucked a hand knitted afghan around his shoulders.

"Okay Mac, let me show you how to give him morphine if he needs it again tonight. I should get Noah home." Kelsey demonstrated how much to drop under Costigan's tongue and wrote down the instructions. He'd said very little since they arrived at the house, but did seem to be absorbing everything. She felt for him. This was a lot to be taking in all at once. "Call me if you need anything tonight and I can walk you through it. I'll come over to check on him after I drop Noah off at school," she tried to reassure him.

Mac lifted the still-sleeping Noah from the couch and helped her get him in the car. Noah had never opened an eye in the entire process.

"Thanks for everything, Kelsey," Mac said, holding her car door open as she loaded her bag in the passenger side. "I don't know how I can thank you for all of this. I still have a lot of questions..."

Even in the porch light, she could see his eyes well with tears. "I'll be back in the morning. We can talk more then." She touched his arm, and he nodded and closed her door as she settled into the driver's seat.

No matter who you were, this part of life was hard. Kesley wiped at her own tears as she made her way home.

Mac sat in his grandfather's study, the glow of his laptop the only light besides the gradually brightening eastern sky. He'd spent the night alternating between watching Truman sleep and searching online for private hospice care agencies, his mind churning with everything that needed to be done. The reality he'd been avoiding for months was finally staring him in the face.

His grandfather was dying.

He rubbed his tired eyes, glancing at the collection of family photos on the desk. There he was at his high school and college graduations, Truman beaming beside him. Others of his grandparents laughing together, smiling at each other as though they were the only two people in the world. Older pictures including his parents at family gatherings filled in the rest of the display. It was humbling to consider that soon, he would be all that's left of his family.

The coffee maker in the kitchen beeped. Mac prepared two cups—black for himself, cream and sugar for his grandfather, just as he'd always taken it. When he returned to the living room, Truman was already awake, gazing out the window.

"Brought your coffee, Gramps."

"About time." Truman's voice was stronger than last night but still carried an unfamiliar fragility. "Help an old man up? I want to watch the sunrise from the deck. It's cold, but I want to be out there, just for a few minutes."

Mac covered his grandfather's shoulders with the afghan, then supported his elbow as they made their way outside. The sky was painting itself in shades of red and gold, the ocean reflecting the colors like scattered diamonds. It was truly beautiful.

"I've got some calls set up," Mac said, settling into a chair beside Truman. "For care agencies. We can find someone to stay with you all of the time. I'll get Johnson on it today."

"Mac." Truman's hand found his arm. "I'm not afraid."

"Well, I am." The words escaped before Mac could stop them.

"I've had over ninety years, boy. Saw you grow into a fine man. Built something meaningful." Truman took a sip of his coffee. "Only one thing left I want to see."

Mac knew what was coming. "Gramps—"

"You're lonely." Truman's voice was gentle but firm.

The sunrise painted the clouds crimson as Mac struggled to find words. "I'm fine on my own."

"Are you?" Truman's eyes held a knowing look.

"It's complicated."

"Life usually is." Truman smiled. "But that's the beauty of it."

The statement didn't need Mac's reply, nor did he have one, so they sat in comfortable silence and watched the red sun climb higher over the Atlantic. An old saying moved through Mac's thoughts, *Red sun at night, sailor's delight. Red sun at morning, sailors take warning.*

Chapter 7

"Mom, where's my red swimsuit?" Noah's voice carried from his bedroom.

"Already packed!" Kelsey called back, folding another t-shirt. The suitcase on Noah's bed was nearly full—shorts, swimsuits, sunscreen, and his favorite stuffed whale that he still slept with but wouldn't admit it to anyone else.

"What about my shell collecting bag?"

"Front pocket, with your goggles." She zipped the mesh compartment closed. "And don't forget, your grandmother said there's a pool at the house too."

Noah appeared in the doorway, clutching his tablet. "And the golf course! Grandmother said she'd teach me how to play."

Kelsey smiled, though something twisted in her chest. She'd been dreading this week but couldn't find reason to deny the visit. Margaret Prescott herself had reached out to her. There would be other cousins, her sister's grandchildren. It would mean a lot to her for Noah to know his extended family. "Remember to say please and thank you and listen to your grandmother."

"I know, Mom." Noah rolled his eyes. "Can I bring my new Pokémon cards to show Cousin Joseph?"

"Already in your backpack." She checked her watch. Jason would be here soon to pick him up. "Did you brush your teeth?"

"Going!" He dashed toward the bathroom.

Kelsey sat on the edge of the bed, running her hand over the packed clothes. A week. She hadn't been away from Noah for more than a weekend since... ever. But the Prescotts had been persistent. And this added time was meant to be a panacea. She hoped it worked and took their minds off custody.

At least she had projects to keep her busy. The closets desperately needed organizing, and maybe she'd finally paint the bathroom like she'd been planning.

The doorbell rang.

"That's probably Uncle Jason!" Noah called.

"I'll get it!" Kelsey headed for the door, mentally reviewing Noah's packing list one more time. She pulled it open, ready to greet her brother-in-law.

Instead, Mac stood on her doorstep. He held a bouquet of spring wildflowers and looked at her like he wished she wasn't at home. Her heart skipped at the surprise.

"Here," he said shoving the bouquet into her hands. "Thank you for all you've done with Grandad." He turned to leave but stopped in his tracks when footsteps thundered down the stairs.

"Mac!" Noah shouted, nearly tripping over his backpack as he careened through the open door and pulled Mac in the house by his sleeve. "Look how big my suitcase is! I'm going to Hilton Head!"

"Hilton Head?" Mac grinned at the enthusiastic boy. "Pretty fancy. I hear they have some great beaches there."

"And we're taking a private plane!" Noah bounced on his toes. "Have you ever been on one?"

A smile flickered across Mac's face. "Once or twice."

Kelsey stepped away to put the flowers in water as Noah rattled off his planned activities and Mac asked thoughtful questions about each one.

"Mom, I can't find my hat!" Noah suddenly remembered.

"Check the coat rack—" Kelsey called from the kitchen.

The crunch of tires on gravel interrupted her. Through the window, she watched a sleek black limousine pull up.

"Whoa!" Noah pressed his face to the glass. "Uncle Jason got a limo!"

The front door opened, and Jason Prescott strode in without knocking, his designer suit perfectly pressed despite leaving for vacation. His meek wife Jennifer trailed behind with a pinched, apologetic face. "Ready to go, sport?" His smile faltered when he saw Mac. "MacCormack."

"Prescott." Mac's already rough tone turned to ice, making Kelsey shudder.

She glanced between them as tension crackled in the air. "You two know each other?"

"Harvard Business School," Jason said shortly.

"Among other things," Mac added, his jaw tight.

Noah, oblivious to the undercurrents between the adults, grabbed his suitcase. "Mom, can you help me get this in the car?"

"I can help you Noah," Jennifer replied and took the bag from him. Kelsey and Noah followed her closely.

Outside, Kelsey hugged Noah fiercely. "Be good, okay? Call me when you land."

"Mom, you're squishing me!"

"Sorry, baby." She kissed his head, aware of Mac and Jason's stony silence behind her as the men continued to glare at one another.

"We'll take good care of him," Jason clipped, but his tone gave her the ironic impression that she wasn't supposed to care if Noah was taken good care of or not.

She watched as the limo disappeared down the lane, Noah's face pressed against the window, waving until they turned the corner.

Mac watched the limo disappear, his jaw still clenched from the encounter. "I had no idea you were connected to the Prescotts. Didn't know Jason had a brother..."

A soft sound made him turn. Kelsey stood frozen where she'd been waving to Noah's limo, tears streaming down her face. Her shoulders shook with silent sobs. Christ. He'd rather face a nor'easter naked than a crying woman.

He hesitated, wishing he could turn around and quietly leave her to break down in private, but her shoulders shook, small and fragile. He couldn't just abandon her like that, even if every bone in his body told him to run.

"Hey... hey." He stepped toward her uncertainly. "Let's get you inside."

She didn't resist as he guided her up the path, one hand at her elbow. In the kitchen, she collapsed into a chair while he searched for a glass, filling it with water.

He thunked it down on the table, rougher than he meant. "Here." He slid it toward her without meeting her eyes. When her hands fumbled, he steadied them, more out of reflex than comfort.

"I'm sorry," she gasped between sobs. "I'm so sorry. I don't usually... I can't..." Her words tumbled out, brittle. "You probably think I'm pathetic."

He let out a short, humorless laugh. "I think you're human."

She drew a shuddering breath. "They're trying to take him from me."

"What?"

"The Prescotts. They're... they're suing for custody." Her voice broke. "They say the island's too remote, that Noah needs more opportunities, better schools—"

"Jesus," he cut her off, voice sharper than he meant. "Let me guess. They never cared to help before, and now they want to play hero."

She gave a bitter laugh. "They've never lifted a finger. Now suddenly they want to sweep in and play grandmother and uncle of the year." Fresh tears spilled. "How am I supposed to compete? They have houses everywhere, private planes, the best of everything."

"That doesn't make them better parents."

"Doesn't it? In court?" Her fingers twisted the handkerchief. "They'll hire the best lawyers. Throw their influence around. They'll drag out every mistake I've ever made, my work hours, the little cottage, every penny I don't have. They'll make me look unfit." A sob caught in her throat. "And maybe I am."

He stared at her. "That's crap. Noah's a good kid because of you. Anybody can see that."

"But what if it's not enough? What if..." She pressed her hands to her face. "Maybe I am selfish, bringing him here. Maybe I'm not what he needs."

"You're his mother, just what he needs. Money isn't everything." The words came out sharper than he intended. "Trust me on that."

She looked away, wiping her eyes. "You don't understand. I keep telling myself I'm fighting for him, but maybe I'm just fighting for me. Maybe I'm the one who can't let go."

Mac felt helpless in the face of her pain, uncertain whether to reach for her or give her space.

"Are they are supposed to bring him back after school break?" He watched as Kelsey nodded silent tears streaming down her face. "Have you talked to a lawyer?"

"I have, and she suggested I offer additional visits to placate them. She also says the money arguments shouldn't hold up in a custody case. But I'm not sure she's right, and I know even with a decent lawyer I can't fight against their team. I'm trying not to let Noah know anything about this, I don't want to sour him on his family. But it's getting hard to deal with. At some point he'll find out."

Something hot and angry coiled in his chest. The Prescotts and their arrogance, their assumption that money could buy any-thing—even a child's love.

It made him wonder why Jason was so invested in the situation. Perhaps it wasn't the grandmother that was driving the case. Mac would bet money that this was all Jason's doing.

Chapter 8

Kelsey wiped her eyes with Mac's handkerchief, now thoroughly damp. "I must look a mess," she said, attempting a weak smile. "I'm not usually. This isn't..."

"Here." Mac slid a fresh cup of tea across the table. He'd been quietly making it while she pulled herself together. Likely something to keep his hands busy while she melted down. "My grandfather always said tea fixes everything."

"Even custody battles?" The words came out more bitter than she'd intended.

Mac's jaw tightened. "It appears Jason Prescott hasn't changed since Harvard. Still the same entitled—" He caught himself.

Kelsey wrapped her hands around the warm mug. "You seem to know more than I do about him. Tell me what you know."

Mac leaned back in his chair, his expression darkening. "Let's just say his reputation for getting what he wants, regardless of who it hurts, was well established even then."

"David said that about him as well. That's what scares me." She stared into her tea. "David had walked away from all of it, the money, the privilege, the family. Said it wasn't worth it. They never offered to help financially after he died."

Mac watched her carefully, a scowl between his eyes. "And only now, after years of visitations with his grandmother, Jason is more interested?"

"They both are. Jason is likely driving his mother, or helping her. I don't know them well enough to say."

"You barely know them, and yet you trust them with your child?" His tone was lightly accusatory, making her shift uncomfortably.

"They're his family. His father's family. He should know them, and they should have a chance to know him. I've tried very hard to keep Noah out of the drama so he isn't jaded unnecessarily. But it's been hard." Tears renewed as she fought to control her raw emotions. Kelsey set her cup down with shaking hands. "God, I'm sorry. You came over for something and here I am, falling apart and dumping all my problems on you."

"Yeah." He cleared his throat. "Actually, Grandad and I are going for a sunset cruise tonight. The weather's perfect, and he's feeling stronger today. But I was wondering if you... that is, I'd feel more comfortable if you were along, in case..." He jammed his hands deeper into the pockets of his jacket, scowling at the table for a second before looking back up at Kelsey. "If you want, I mean. Grandad likes company, and the weather's..." He shrugged, as if annoyed at himself for offering. "Not a private plane or anything, obviously. Just the same old sunset and sea breeze." He rubbed the back of his neck, gaze drifting to the door as if he half-expected her to say no, but Kelsey couldn't fit a word in between all his stammering. "If you're busy, don't worry about it."

"Oh, I couldn't—"

"It was Grandad's idea to have me invite you, he's demanding his nurse's company. Plus, it would be a nice distraction from your troubles."

Despite everything, Kelsey felt a smile tugging at her lips. "Using your grandfather's lure to convince me?"

"Is it working?"

"Maybe. What time?"

"An hour or so before sunset. We'll have dinner, watch the light change over the water. No pressure, no problems. Just good food and better company."

Kelsey met his eyes, finding something steady there, even through his exterior gruffness. "Okay."

"Okay?"

"Yes." She squeezed his hand. "Thank you. For everything."

Mac stood. "I'll pick you up at four." At the door, he turned back. "Be sure to dress for the weather. It will be warm, but it'll get cold quickly as soon as the sun goes down."

The Range Rover pulled up to her front steps at exactly four. Kelsey smoothed her skirt, second-guessing her choice of outfit, but the feminine floral print made her feel pretty, even if she'd layered it with practical tights against the evening chill. She'd taken extra care with her makeup, telling herself it was just to cover the evidence of crying.

"There she is!" Mr. Costigan's voice carried as Mac helped her into the back seat. "Looking lovely as a spring morning."

"You're looking well yourself," Kelsey said, noting with professional satisfaction his good color and clear eyes. "The new regimen seems to be agreeing with you."

"Aye, though this one fusses worse than any mother hen." He jerked a thumb toward Mac, who was settling behind the wheel. "Won't let me do a thing for myself."

"That's because you tried to carry firewood yesterday," Mac said, meeting Kelsey's eyes in the rearview mirror. "Outfit is a little light for later though. You're going to freeze."

Heat crept up her neck. "I brought warm things too." She patted her backpack. "Maine weather's too unpredictable not to."

"Smart girl." Mr. Costigan nodded approvingly. "Mac, she's got more sense than you."

"Here." Mac interrupted, passing back a small medical bag. "Ruth packed this. I assume you know what's in there?"

Kelsey peeked inside, checking through the medications Ruth had packed for outings. "Perfect. Though I'm hoping we won't need any of it."

"The only medicine I need is good company and maybe a wee drop of whiskey," Mr. Costigan declared as they pulled up to the dock.

"We'll see about that." Kelsey moved to help him from the car, but Mac was already there, supporting his grandfather with practiced care.

"Easy does it," Mac murmured, matching his pace to the old man's shuffling steps.

"I'm not made of glass," Mr. Costigan grumbled, but he leaned heavily on Mac's arm. "Though these legs aren't what they used to be."

The sailing yacht loomed before them, gleaming in the late afternoon sun. Mr. Costigan paused at the bottom of the gangway to catch his breath.

"The weatherman said we might see the aurora tonight," he said, gazing northward. "Wouldn't that be something? Haven't seen the lights dance since I was a boy in Ireland." His voice softened. "Would like to see them one more time."

"Grandad—"

"Oh hush, boy. We all know where this is heading." He patted Kelsey's hand where it rested on his other arm. "But tonight's for living, eh? And maybe if we're lucky, the lights will give us a show."

They helped him aboard, his jokes masking the effort it took. But his eyes sparkled with genuine joy as he settled into a cushioned seat on deck, the spring breeze ruffling his white hair.

"Now then," he announced, "who's going to fix an old man a drink while my grandson gets us underway?"

The auxiliary engine's gentle rumble vibrated through the deck as Mac guided them out of the harbor. Kelsey sat with Mr. Costigan, watching the island's familiar shoreline slip past from this new perspective.

"The old mansion looks different from here," she mused. She spotted her cottage above the cove. "Less intimidating."

"Everything looks different from the water, lass." Mr. Costigan sipped his whiskey, neat. "Makes you see things fresh. Like that sunset starting up there."

The sky was indeed beginning to paint itself in watercolors, streaks of pink and gold threading through the clouds. Mac stood confidently at the helm, occasionally adjusting their course, his profile strong against the darkening sky.

"He's a natural sailor," Mr. Costigan said softly. "Gets it from his grandmother. She could read the water like a book."

The wind picked up as they cleared the harbor, and Kelsey pulled her down jacket from her pack. "Do you need another layer, Mr. Costigan?" she asked, noting how he tugged his sweater closer.

"Not yet. The whiskey keeps me warm." He winked. "But I wouldn't say no to that blanket there. And for heaven's sake love, call me Truman."

She tucked it around his legs just as Mac cut the engine. The sudden quiet was broken only by waves against the hull and distant seabirds.

"Perfect spot," he called down from the helm. "We'll have a great view of the northern sky from here, Grandad."

The anchor chain rattled as it descended. Mac disappeared below deck, returning moments later with covered dishes that released wonderful aromas when he lifted their lids.

"Hope everyone's hungry," he said, setting out plates. "The chef at the club outdid himself."

"Is that lobster stew?" Truman leaned forward eagerly.

"And fresh rolls from the bakery." Mac served his grandfather first, then Kelsey. "Wine?"

The food was incredible, but Kelsey found herself watching the easy interaction between grandfather and grandson—the gentle teasing, the shared memories, the way Mac anticipated the old man's needs before he could voice them. It was nice to see this tender side of Mac.

"Remember that storm we got caught in off Mount Desert?" Mr. Costigan was saying. "Your grandmother read those clouds an hour before the radio warning came through. Had us safely anchored while other boats were still scrambling."

"She always knew." Mac's voice held a wealth of affection. "Though if I remember right, you were the one who forgot to secure the coffee pot."

"Ach, we were finding grounds in strange places for weeks." Mr. Costigan chuckled, then caught his breath slightly.

"Time for your evening dose," Kelsey said, reaching for the medical bag. The old man didn't protest as she administered his medication, and she saw Mac's shoulders relax.

The sun was barely kissing the horizon now, painting the water in shades of fire. Mac cleared the dishes and returned with coffee and what looked suspiciously like bread pudding.

"Look there," Mr. Costigan pointed north, where the first stars were appearing. "Sky's clear as crystal. If the lights are going to show, this would be the night."

Mac settled beside Kelsey on the cushioned bench, close enough that she could feel his warmth. Above them, the sky deepened to indigo, while somewhere in the darkness, a sea bird called its haunting cry.

"It's gotten chilly out here," Mac stated, rubbing his arms and watching Kelsey draw her knees up under the jacket. He reached for a soft wool blanket and draped it over both of them.

Mr. Costigan had dozed off in his chair. The bread pudding sat half-eaten between them, fragrant with vanilla and cinnamon.

"This is nice," Kelsey said softly to not wake the old man. "Being out here, away from everything."

"Look." Mac's voice was close to her ear as he pointed upward. "First one's out."

The evening star hung bright and clear in the darkening sky, soon joined by others as night crept in. The water lapped gently against the hull, creating a peaceful rhythm.

"Mac..." She turned to find his face inches from hers. "Thank you. For today. For being there when I fell apart."

"Humph." He shifted in his seat.

A flash of green-white light streaked across the northern sky, making them both start.

"Grandad," Mac called gently. "Wake up. The lights are starting."

Mr. Costigan stirred, his eyes brightening as another shimmer of aurora danced overhead. "Would you look at that," he breathed. "Just like when I was a boy."

The three of them sat in wonder as ribbons of light began to wave across the stars, like celestial curtains stirred by an otherworldly wind. Colors shifted from green to purple and back, reflecting off the dark water around them.

"Your grandmother would have loved this," Mr. Costigan said softly. "Thank you both for this. For getting an old man out to see it one more time."

Kelsey squeezed Mac's hand under the blanket, and he squeezed back. The lights continued their ethereal dance overhead, but she found her attention drawn to the profile of the man beside her, his face tilted skyward, new vulnerability written in every line.

After a while, Mr. Costigan's quiet snore made them both smile.

"Should we head back?" Kelsey whispered.

Mac shook his head. "Let him sleep a bit longer. He's comfortable, and his breathing's good." He paused. "Unless you need to go?"

"No," she said, letting herself lean slightly against his solid warmth. He didn't move away from the contact. "I'd like to stay."

Above them, the lights shimmered like dreams made visible, while below, the gentle rocking of the boat began to unknot something tight inside her chest. For the first time since Noah left in the Prescotts' limo, she felt herself truly breathe.

The aurora's dance gradually faded, leaving only stars scattered like diamonds across black velvet. Mr. Costigan's peaceful snoring mingled with the soft splash of waves against the hull. Mac hadn't moved. His shoulder was warm against hers, their fingers still intertwined beneath the blanket.

"Now we should probably head back," he whispered reluctantly. "The temperature's dropping."

As if to emphasize his point, a cool breeze swept across the deck. Kelsey shivered despite her layers. Mac pulled the blanket tighter around them. "Thank you for the distraction."

"Grandad's pretty good at that." Mac replied, looking down into her face. "Though, I think he's got ulterior motives."

"Oh?"

"He's been not-so-subtly trying to play matchmaker since the accident."

Kelsey lifted her head to look at him. In the starlight, his eyes were dark and serious. "Has he now?"

"Mhm." Her eyes fell to his lips, and she thought about how they would feel on hers.

But Mr. Costigan stirred, mumbling something, and they pulled away from each other.

"We should get him home," Mac said, standing.

Mac bustled around the deck, preparing for the return journey. Kelsey tucked another blanket around the sleeping grandfather.

The ride back to shore was silent except for Mr. Costigan's soft snores. Mac navigated carefully through the darkness, the *Nereid*'s running lights casting a gentle glow across the water. When they docked, it took both of them to help the sleepy old man to his feet.

"Come on, Grandad," Mac murmured. "Just a few steps to the car."

"I wasn't sleeping," Mr. Costigan protested drowsily. "Just resting my eyes."

Kelsey supported him from the other side as they made their way slowly up the dock. The night air had grown crisp, their breath visible in small clouds.

The drive to the Costigan house was short. Rita, the overnight aide, was waiting at the door when they arrived.

"Did you see the lights, Mr. C?" Rita asked, helping guide him inside.

"Beautiful as angels dancing," he mumbled.

Kelsey helped Rita get him settled in his bedroom after Mac turned down the bed. There was an ease to their teamwork.

"Goodnight, Grandad," Mac said softly, but Mr. Costigan was already asleep.

The drive to Kelsey's cottage was quiet. Mac pulled into her driveway and cut the engine. The cottage was covered in shadows from the surrounding pines. "It's really dark here. Let me walk you to your door."

Their footsteps crunched on the gravel path. At the door, Kelsey turned to thank him, but the words died in her throat at the scowl on his face. It was the same scowl he'd had when inviting her out on the sunset cruise. The same scowl he's worn when she'd thanked him. It wasn't an angry scowl—or maybe there was some anger, but it wasn't directed at Kesley. Instead, it seemed to be directed at himself. As if he thought whatever he was doing was a silly idea but he couldn't stop himself from doing it anyway.

His hand came up to cup her cheek, thumb brushing across her skin. She held still. A breath in the space between them, the warmth of his skin on hers, and her eyes fluttered closed. A heartbeat, then another, another—slow, steady, and strong pulsed against her ribs.

Suddenly, Mac stepped back, breaking contact. He turned the doorknob behind her, pushed her inside the cottage, and closed the door between them. Through the entry window, she watched him stride to his car without looking back, then pressed her fingers to her tingling cheek as his taillights disappeared into the darkness.

Chapter 9

The shrill ring of her phone jolted Kelsey awake. Her heart leaped into her throat as she fumbled for it on the nightstand, Noah's name flashing through her mind. The display showed Mac instead.

"Hello, Mac? Everything all right?" Her voice was still raspy with sleep.

"Still sleeping?" Mac's voice was also rough, but it didn't sound sleepy. "I guess I didn't realize how early it was."

Kelsey glanced at her bedside clock: 7:15 a.m. Through her window, morning sun sparkled on the water of the cove. "No, it's fine. I was just..." She trailed off, memories of last night flooding back—his hand on her cheek, the way he'd pushed her inside and walked away. Such memories made his next words all the more confusing.

"You probably have better things to do today"—he paused—"but weather's perfect for sailing and I need to practice sailing her on my own, I was going to run some errands in Portland. And I have a meeting with my attorney. I thought with Noah gone and all, you might like to come along?"

Her pulse quickened. "I don't know, Mac..."

"A day on the water would be a good distraction."

A gull cried outside her window. She could smell salt air drifting in through the screen, feel the ghost of his touch on her skin. "What time?"

"Could you come over in about an hour? Bring whatever you'd like to read or work on, as there won't be any entertainment. We can grab lunch in Portland."

She should say no. Should keep her distance after last night, should stay out of his hot and cold game. But... "Okay."

"Yeah?" Something in his voice lightened.

"Yes." She pressed her fingers to her temple.

After they hung up, Kelsey sat on the edge of her bed, staring at her phone trying to ignore the flutter in her stomach at the thought of spending a whole day with him on the boat.

"Helloooo!" Amy's voice rang through the cottage, followed by the bang of the screen door. "I brought those apple cinnamon muffins you love!"

Kelsey padded downstairs in her robe to find her sister already brewing coffee in the kitchen. Amy's long, dark hair was pulled into a messy bun, and she was in her usual massage therapy uniform: yoga pants and a flowing top.

"You're here early," Kelsey said, reaching for a muffin.

"Thought you might need company." Amy poured two cups of coffee. "Any word from Noah?"

"Not since yesterday." Kelsey wrapped her hands around the warm mug. "He sounds like he's having more fun than usual because there are some other cousins on this trip, Margaret's sister's kids."

Amy rolled her eyes. "I hope their spoiled bratness doesn't rub off on him. Speaking of which, I'm heading to Costigan's later. Ruth put in a referral for some massage therapy."

"Oh? That's actually a great idea. He had some additional activity last evening, so I bet he could use it. Mac and I had him out on the boat pretty late." Kelsey tried to keep her voice neutral while studying her muffin intently.

"Say what? You and Mac had him out late?"

"Yes. We saw the Northern Lights. Apparently something about a solar flare made them visible this far south."

Coffee sloshed as Amy set her mug down too quickly. "Mac? As in Mack truck, new car and rich as all get out? Mr. Tall-Dark-and-Brooding who barely speaks to anyone?"

"He speaks to people," Kelsey protested weakly.

"Mm-hmm, right..." She took a sip of her coffee. "So, Mr. Costigan. Thought I'd ask him about the old mansion while I'm there. Such a waste, sitting empty all these years. I'd love to make it into a retreat, a health retreat. I'd make a killing."

"Why ask Mr. Costigan about the mansion? What would he know about it?"

Amy looked at her as though she had two heads. "He owns it. He owns half the island or something. He's a real big deal around here. Very rich man. His grandson even more so. Rumor is that he sold some software he developed a year or so ago. Made a killing at it."

Amy tilted her head. "Why are you blushing?"

"I'm not." Kelsey stood abruptly. "I should get dressed. I'm going sailing."

"Sailing?" Amy's eyebrows shot up. "With whom?"

"Mac."

A slow grin spread across Amy's face. "Oh my God. Something happened between you two."

"Nothing happened."

"Liar. Your face is bright red." Amy leaned forward. "Spill. Now."

"I have to get ready. He's picking me up in," Kelsey glanced at the clock, "thirty minutes."

"Oh no you don't." Amy blocked her path to the stairs. "You're not going anywhere until you tell me everything. Since when do you and Mac MacCormack go sailing?"

"Since last night. He wanted to help me keep my mind off Noah," Kelsey admitted.

"I see. And?"

"And nothing. I think he just feels sorry for me with Noah gone."

"Huh," Amy nodded her tone skeptical. "Is that why you're wearing your special occasion perfume?"

Kelsey touched her neck where she'd already dabbed the scent. "I'm going to get dressed."

"This isn't over!" Amy called after her. "I want details when you get back!"

The morning sun warmed Kelsey's face as she followed the shore path, waves lapping gently at the beach to her right. Ahead, Mac's sailing yacht bobbed at the dock, its white hull gleaming. Mac moved efficiently around the deck, checking lines and equipment.

Her shoes clunked on the wooden gangway. "Permission to come aboard?"

He looked up, a half-smile playing at his lips. "Depends. Did you bring coffee?"

"In my thermos." She held up the bag over her shoulder.

Mac took it from her, his fingers brushing hers.

They cast off smoothly, the engine purring as Mac guided them out of the cove. Once they cleared the headland, he unfurled the sails, and they caught the wind with a satisfying snap.

Kelsey wandered the deck, trailing her hand along the polished railings. Everything about the *Nereid* spoke of careful maintenance—gleaming brass, fresh paint, clean lines. She made her way to where Mac stood at the helm, his stance relaxed but alert as he watched the sails.

"She's beautiful," Kelsey said. "What made you choose this one?"

"Good size for single-handed sailing. Sturdy enough for ocean crossings." His eyes remained on the horizon. "She'll do well anywhere I take her."

The casual implication made her curious. "How long will you be gone?"

He shrugged. "No set timeline. That's the point. Maybe a year. Maybe more."

"Sounds lonely," she said softly.

"Sounds perfect." His jaw tightened slightly. "No responsibilities. No expectations. No people. Just me and the sea."

Kelsey watched his profile, noting the tension around his eyes. She thought of Mr. Costigan, growing frailer each month, and how Mac checked on him multiple times a day. She didn't need to ask when he would be leaving. That timeline was pretty clear. After his grandfather didn't need him anymore.

"The Caribbean's beautiful in winter," she said instead of all the things she wanted to say. "All those little hidden coves and islands."

Mac glanced at her then, something softening in his expression. "Ever been?"

"Once, years ago. Family cruise." She smiled at the memory. "I got terribly seasick."

"You seem fine now."

"Don't jinx it." She bumped his shoulder with hers, and he chuckled.

The sound warmed her more than the sun.

Mac adjusted their heading slightly, his movements easy and practiced. "So, I know you aren't from around here. Where did you and your sister grow up?"

"We're from Vermont originally. Small town near Burlington." Kelsey settled onto the bench near the helm. "Amy moved here first, about three years ago. Said she fell in love with the island the minute she stepped off the ferry."

"And you followed her?"

"Amy kept telling me I needed a change. When the nurse practitioner position opened up at the clinic, it felt like a sign. It was an opportunity to be in private practice with a physician partner in a small town. I could see my patients in the office and on home visits as their primary care provider." She hadn't meant to mention that, but something about the gentle roll of the waves made it easier to talk.

Mac nodded, watching a pair of gulls wheel overhead. "Is it just the two of you?"

"Both our parents died when we were in college. Dad was a retired high school principal, Mom taught piano." She smiled. "They were great, a lot older than my friend's parents, but they tried very hard to fit in."

"And how do you like the island? Noah seems to have friends and activities he loves." He smiled at her. "We talk when we are looking for shells. He's a great kid."

"I love it here. The pace, the people." She paused. "Even the isolation. My sister worries I'll become a hermit."

"I can relate to that, it's a good place to not have to deal with too many people." He smiled at her then, his white teeth bright against his darker sunglasses. "Your sister doesn't seem the hermit type."

Kelsey laughed. "God, no. She knows everyone on the island. Always planning something—yoga classes, meditation groups, those full moon ceremonies on the beach."

"I've heard about those." The corner of his mouth twitched. "Grandad keeps threatening to join in."

"You should let him. I bet Amy would say he has 'good energy.'" Kelsey gathered her hair into a ponytail to tuck under her hat, as it was blowing wildly about her head. Mac watched her hands, the familiar scowl on his face, his eyes unreadable behind his dark lenses.

"She's actually seeing him today for a massage. I hope she doesn't talk his ear off about the mansion."

Mac's expression softened slightly. "She really wants to buy it from him. That I know. But he promised my grandmother to keep it as it was. She worked there you know, when they were first married. I don't know the whole story, but I think she had some sentimental reason."

"I'm surprised you know Amy." Kelsey watched his profile. "I mean. Amy says you've barely spoken."

He was quiet for a moment, adjusting a line. "I know most people on the island, I just don't find it necessary to socialize.

And I do try to know who my neighbors are, especially as their landlord."

"Oh, right." Of course he was. "But isn't that what we're doing? Socializing?"

His eyes met hers, his expression unreadable. "No. You're just... someone I respect."

A gust of wind blew her hat, and he caught it for her just in time, re-adjusting it on her head. A strand of hair had come loose, so Mac reached out to tuck it behind her ear. "And someone who isn't a pain to be around."

The way he said it made her breath catch. Before she could respond, the wind shifted, and Mac stepped away to adjust the sails. The moment slipped away like water through her fingers.

Chapter 10

Mac expertly maneuvered between the forest of masts and hulls at the Portland waterfront, responding with a nod of his head to occasional greetings to other boaters as they made their way to the dock. Once secured, he led Kelsey to a silver Range Rover parked in a private slip holder's lot.

"You keep a car here?" Kelsey asked as he unlocked the doors.

"Easier than dealing with cabs or rentals." He started the engine. "Portland's my supply stop for everything from boat parts to decent coffee beans."

Traffic was light as they wound through the cobblestone streets of the Old Port. The morning sun glinted off storefronts and coffee shops already bustling with tourists.

"I've got that meeting with my attorney at ten," Mac said, checking his watch. "Shouldn't take more than an hour. And then I have to meet with Johnson for some paperwork he's been nagging me about."

"Johnson?"

"My PA. Keeps my life from falling apart while I plan to sail away from it." He smiled wryly. "We're meeting at Arabica after."

"Oh, I love that place!" Kelsey brightened. "Look, why don't I wander a bit? I've been wanting to check out Sherman's Books, and there's that little shop on Exchange Street that carries those bath products Amy loves. I haven't had a proper Portland shopping morning in ages. Noah isn't exactly the best shopping companion." She adjusted her bag.

"I can relate to the kid. I'm not the best shopping companion either."

"What time should I meet you?"

"How's eleven thirty at Arabica?" Mac drummed his fingers on the steering wheel. "After, if you're up for it, I know this place up the coast. Best lobster rolls in Maine. We could grab lunch, maybe some takeout for dinner, then sail around the islands for a bit before heading back. I need to practice my navigation techniques anyway."

"Sounds perfect." She tried to ignore the flutter in her stomach at the thought of spending the afternoon with him, which could be exactly what he had in mind, too, because he really didn't seem to need any navigation practice.

He pulled into a spot near the waterfront. "You remember where Arabica is?"

"Down Middle Street, past the kitchen store with all the copper pots in the window."

"Right." He hesitated, then leaned over to pull a business card from the glove box. "You have my cell number, right?"

His sudden proximity had her holding her breath. Their fingers brushed as she took the card from him, and for a moment, neither moved. Then a car horn blared nearby, breaking the spell.

"Eleven thirty," she said, opening her door.

"Don't get lost in the bookstore," he called after her.

Kelsey waved without turning around, already planning her route through the familiar streets. Behind her, she heard his car door slam and tried not to think about how much she was looking forward to seeing him again in a few hours.

Kelsey hummed to herself as she pushed open the door to Arabica, her shopping bags rustling. The scent of coffee and pastries enveloped her as she spotted Mac at a corner table with a lean, thirty-something man in a crisp suit.

Mac stood as she approached. "Kelsey, this is Johnson."

"Nice to finally meet you," Johnson said, already gathering his things. "Mac's told me about your situation."

Her smile faltered. Her situation?

"Before I go—" Johnson reached into his briefcase. "Here's that research you asked me for on the Maritime Holdings merger and on Margaret Prescott's will. The PI was thorough." He handed Mac a thick manila folder. "Your assumption was correct."

The world tilted sideways as Mac held the folder out to her. Noah's grandmother's will? A private investigator?

"Thanks, Johnson," Mac said, seemingly oblivious to her shock.

Johnson nodded and left. The café chatter continued around them, but Kelsey couldn't hear it over the roaring in her ears.

"You ready?" Mac asked, gathering his coat. "That place I mentioned is about forty minutes up the coast, but the drive's gorgeous..."

Mac took Kelsey's shopping bags from her as they walked outside. They made their way to the parked car with Mac chatting behind her, Kelsey stonily unable to comprehend what he had done.

"What is this?" she said once they were both inside the vehicle. Her voice was barely a whisper as she stared at the folder in her hands.

"I had Johnson look into—"

"I heard what he said." The paper crinkled under her tightening grip. "You hired a private investigator? To look into the Prescotts?"

"I just wanted to confirm a suspicion. I thought it might help with your case."

"My case?" Her voice rose sharply enough that his eyebrows quirked and a look of concern entered his eyes. She lowered it to a harsh whisper. "What gives you the right to investigate my personal business?"

"Kelsey—"

"Take me to the ferry. I'll just make the noon crossing."

Mac just looked at her incredulously.

"The ferry," she repeated through gritted teeth.

Mac pulled the car out of the parking spot a little too fast. A few minutes later, tires squealed as he pulled into the marina parking.

"I was trying to help."

She whirled to face him. "By going behind my back? By digging into private matters that have nothing to do with you?"

"I have resources—"

"I don't need your resources!" She poked a finger into his chest. "I don't want you interfering in my life like this. God, Mac, I barely know you!"

"That's not—"

She was already out the door, the folder crumpled in her hand. Without looking behind her, she hurried to the ticket booth and just barely made the ferry before they raised the gangway.

She took a seat outside to gather herself. She just needed to breathe for a moment. The folder burned in her hands like a bomb about to detonate, and Kelsey stared out at the water, blinking back angry tears.

"I hate men," Kelsey announced, sprawled on her couch as Amy poured them each a second glass of wine.

"All of them, or just the ones who think they know what's best for us?" Amy settled into the armchair, tucking her feet under her.

"Yes." Kelsey stared at the folder on the coffee table. She'd thrown it there when she got home, but somehow it seemed to take up the whole room.

"So, what happened? One moment you're all perfumed up for your sailing date, the next you're home looking like someone killed your puppy."

Kelsey took a long drink of wine. "He hired a private investigator."

"Who did?"

"Mac. To look into Noah's grandmother's will."

"He what?" Amy sat up straight. "Without asking you?"

"Just had his assistant hand me the folder, like it was nothing. Like he hadn't completely overstepped."

"Dick move," Amy agreed, taking a sip of her wine. "Though... have you read it?"

Kelsey nodded.

"And?"

"And I'm still trying to process it."

"Kels." Amy leaned forward. "You can't drop a bomb like that and not tell me."

Kelsey pressed her fingers to her temples. "Margaret is leaving half of everything to David. And if David isn't alive when she dies, it will go to his children."

"Okay... How much are we talking about?"

"Over half a billion dollars."

Amy choked on her wine. "I'm sorry, what?"

"Apparently the Prescotts aren't just rich, they're rich rich."

"Holy shit." Amy set her glass down carefully. "So all this time, while you've been working your ass off to provide a decent life for you and your child..."

"They've been sitting on a fortune? Yeah." Kelsey laughed bitterly. "And now suddenly they want custody."

"Because Margaret's getting old," Amy's eyes widened. "That's why Jason is pushing for it now. He wants to control Noah's inheritance."

"Got it in one."

"Those absolute—"

A knock at the door cut her off. Through the screen, they could see Mac standing on the porch, holding Kelsey's shopping bags in one hand and what looked like takeout in the other.

"I should go," Amy said, reaching for her purse.

"Don't you dare." Kelsey grabbed her sister's arm. "I can't deal with him right now."

Another knock. "Kelsey?" Mac's voice was hesitant. "I brought your shopping bags. And I... I brought dinner. If you're hungry."

Amy raised an eyebrow at her sister. "Want me to tell him to fuck off?"

"I can hear you," Mac said from the door.

Both sisters looked at each other, and Amy started to laugh. Kelsey couldn't contain herself and joined in. After a moment, she smothered her smile and went to the door.

"Why are you here?" she demanded as Amy guffawed behind her.

Mac shifted uncomfortably on the porch, another of his scowls between his eyes. "I wanted to tell you that I'm sorry. I wasn't thinking clearly when I asked for the information. I thought it would be useful, but I was wrong to do it. And I want to apologize. I think too much of you to have you angry at me, and I'd like to make it up to you somehow."

Amy resolutely gathered her purse and jacket. "Well sis, I think maybe you should let him in. It's a rare thing when a guy admits to being wrong right off the bat like that." She opened the screen door and pushed past Mac, stumbling a bit on the steps. "Don't worry, I'm walking home... See you later."

The screen door closed again between them, and Kelsey stood looking down at Mac on her doorstep. "I don't appreciate having something like this done for me. Next time please ask before you take my private life into your own hands."

"Next time?" Mac whispers as Kelsey swings the door open to let him in.

"I haven't decided if I forgive you yet. I'm still mad. But I'm also very hungry, and whatever you have in that bag smells delicious."

Mac smiled at her and dropped the bags on the kitchen table. "I'm sorry we missed the lobster rolls. So, I stopped at the next best thing here on the island."

Kelsey dove into the still steaming bag of deliciousness, suddenly famished as she hadn't eaten since breakfast. And the wine had gone straight to her head. She picked up one of the lobster rolls and took an enormous bite. Mac watched her, open mouthed.

"Plates are up there," she said, pointing to the cupboard above the sink. Mac helped himself to a plate and gave Kelsey one as well. "Wine is here if you want some." Kelsey poured herself another glass, then handed Mac the bottle.

He grabbed a glass from the cupboard and poured the thimbleful of what was left of the bottle. "Looks like you and Amy did this justice."

Kelsey sat on the couch, quickly making her lobster roll disappear. Mac sat at the opposite end, and both faced the folder on the coffee table.

"Did you know?" Mac asked quietly, breaking the comfortable silence that had settled between them. "About the inheritance?"

Kelsey shook her head. She reached for her wine glass. "Not a clue. I mean, I knew they had money, but this," she gestured vaguely at the folder. "This is different."

"It's a lot."

"Yeah." She tucked her feet under her, feeling the wine's warmth spread through her limbs. "You know what's weird? I'm happy for Noah. He deserves every good thing. But I'm also..." She trailed off, searching for the right words.

"Worried?"

"Terrified." She took another sip of wine. "This changes everything, doesn't it?"

Mac set his plate down and turned to face her fully. "I know Jason. Our paths have crossed in business circles. He's... not a good person, Kelsey. The kind who sees dollar signs where he should see people. And if Margaret gets custody, Jason will have easy control of Noah's inheritance until he turns twenty-one." Mac's voice was gentle but firm. "This isn't about being a family. It's about money."

Kelsey felt tears prick at her eyes. "Noah's just a little boy. He doesn't deserve to be a pawn in their games."

"That's why I—" Mac stopped himself. "That's why I thought you should know. Even if I went about it the wrong way."

"You did." But the words had lost their earlier anger, softened by wine and understanding. She yawned, her head feeling fuzzy. "But thank you. For caring enough to try."

The words hung in the air between them as Kelsey's eyes grew heavy. She shifted, letting her head rest against the couch cushions. "I don't usually drink so much." Another yawn interrupted her, and she just thought she would close her eyes just for a minute.

The next thing she was aware of was the soft weight of the afghan being draped over her and then Mac gathering the plates and water running in the sink. Through half-closed eyes, she watched him move quietly through her kitchen, putting things away.

The last thing she heard was the gentle click of the door as he locked it behind him on his way out.

Chapter 11

M ac drove the winding coastal road to his grandfather's cottage, his mind churning over Jason Prescott's financial reports, which he'd spent half the night analyzing. The pattern was there: leveraged investments, mounting debt hidden behind shell companies, desperate moves by a desperate man. The kind of desperation that made people dangerous.

The image of Kelsey asleep on her couch last night, vulnerable and trusting despite her anger at him, made his chest tight. He'd watched her longer than he should have, wanting to protect her and Noah. But he'd already overstepped once. She was unaware that in addition to Margaret's will, he'd also looked into Jason Prescott's financial situation.

He shouldn't care so much, but he did. Somehow Kelsey York had gotten under his skin.

Though, admittedly, he'd requested the information before he learned about the custody case due to an imminent merger with another transport company Jason dealt in.

The weathered shingles of his grandfather's cottage caught the morning light. If anyone could help him understand the full scope of Jason's dealings, it would be Truman Costigan. The old man might be dying, but his mind was still razor-sharp when it came to business.

Mac found his grandfather lounging in the sun by the picture window, surrounded by the morning paper and a half-eaten breakfast. Truman looked up as he entered, eyes keen despite his frail appearance.

"You're here early." Truman folded his paper.

Mac pulled out the chair across from him. "What do you know about Jason Prescott?"

Truman's eyebrows rose. "Bit of a wastrel. Why?"

"He's on the board of Maritime Holdings."

"Ah." Truman nodded slowly. "Where we have considerable shares. Big merger coming up for them. We stand to make a bundle."

"He's been making some interesting moves lately. Taking out loans against future earnings, selling personal assets."

"Sounds like someone who needs money." Truman studied his grandson. "I thought you didn't like him. More so than the rest of the human race, that is."

Mac smiled at the dig and brushed it off. He leaned forward, choosing his words carefully. "I didn't know he had an older brother. But do you remember David Prescott's death a few years back?"

"Terrible business. Car accident, if I remember it right."

"Turns out his wife was pregnant at the time, and she had a son, Noah." Mac paused. "You know his mother, actually. It's Kelsey."

"My Kelsey?" Truman sat up straighter. "I had no idea..."

"She's been raising Noah alone, with no help from them." Mac's jaw tightened. "Meanwhile, Margaret Prescott, no doubt urged by Jason Prescott, has filed for custody of Noah. Her will leaves Noah over half a billion dollars, what was his father's inheritance."

"Margaret's a bit old to want to be raising a child. And what of Kelsey? Surely she's fighting them."

"You know how that will go. She doesn't have a chance. Once Margaret's gone, Jason will have control..."

"And by the sounds of it, he'll spend it all before Noah can inherit anything. Kelsey doesn't deserve that. Sweet girl. Excellent with old coots like me." Truman's eyes narrowed. "Those bastards."

"I think Jason's in trouble. Deep trouble. And he sees Noah's inheritance as his way out. This merger was likely going to hold him over financially until he could get his hands on the kid's money."

"Over my dead body." Truman pushed himself up from his chair with surprising vigor. "Get me my phone."

"Grandad—"

"That woman is an angel. You've seen her with the people here, how she cares for them. For that boy." Truman's voice shook with anger. "And they want to make her worry about losing him? Criminal. Absolutely criminal."

"What are you planning?"

A slow, dangerous smile spread across Truman's face. "Before I die, I'd like to see Jason Prescott's balls in a vise. And thanks to those Maritime Holdings shares, I think I know just how to do it."

Mac watched his grandfather shuffle toward his study, phone already in hand. He hadn't seen the old man this purposeful in months.

Mac drummed his fingers on the steering wheel, replaying the morning's conversation. The old man had spent three hours making calls, pulling up old files, sketching out strategies. They'd even ordered lunch brought in so they wouldn't lose momentum.

"Damn Prescotts," Truman had muttered more than once. "Always taking what isn't theirs."

The feud went back decades. Mac remembered the stories—how the Prescotts had tried to squeeze Truman out when he was just starting, using their old money connections to block his contracts. But where they ruled from mahogany boardrooms through layers of managers, Truman had built his kingdom from the ground up. He knew every captain who'd ever sailed his ships, every foreman who'd run his warehouses.

"People make the profit, boy," Truman always said. "They are the company."

The Costigan wealth had begun with a single truck and warehouse, and had grown into a multi-billion dollar international shipping industry across land and sea. If you bought something online to be delivered to your home in the US, there was a good chance one of the Costigan transport lines had a hand in making sure it arrived unscathed and on-time.

Mac turned onto the coastal road, mind churning. What his grandfather had in the making would put a hurting on Jason Prescott, if they were right about this deal tiding him over until he got his hands on Noah's inheritance. But it wouldn't do anything to stop the custody challenge.

Even with all their resources, even if Kelsey accepted their help—and that was a big if after his recent misstep—money alone wouldn't win this fight. The Prescotts had generations of influence behind them. Judges who owed them favors. Kelsey on her own, a nobody in the world of capital empires, was not going to win.

It burned him. And burned him again that he cared.

He found himself taking the turn toward Kelsey's house instead of his own, barely registering the decision until he was pulling into her driveway. This was how it went with all of his decisions lately, decisions to invite her to sunset cruises or a jaunt to Portland. He didn't think about them until the words were already tumbling out of his mouth faster than he could stop them.

The bass line of "Another One Bites the Dust" thundered through her open windows. Mac knocked, but the music drowned him out. After a moment's hesitation, he pushed the door open.

"Kelsey?" he called out. Nothing.

Then a shriek from upstairs. His heart jumped to his throat as he took the stairs two at a time, following the sound to the bathroom. He burst through the door to find Kelsey balanced precariously on a stepladder, paintbrush in hand, ineffectively trying to squish a large black spider.

She screamed again—this time in surprise—as she spun toward him. The paint can teetered, then tipped, sending a cascade of seafoam green down the front of her old t-shirt and onto the drop cloth below.

"Mac!" She grabbed the ladder to steady herself, eyes wide. "What the hell?"

Paint dripped down Kelsey's shirt as she stared at Mac standing in her bathroom doorway, his chest rising and falling quickly from his sprint up the stairs. His hair was rumpled, and he looked somehow even more appealing than usual in this frantic state.

"Mac! What are you doing here?" she asked, climbing down from the ladder. Her foot slipped slightly on the wet drop cloth, and Mac's hand shot out to steady her elbow. The touch sent warmth spreading up her arm.

"Are you okay? I heard screaming," he said, still not letting go of her arm.

"Oh God." She felt her face flush. "You must have thought I was being murdered up here."

"Something like that."

"It was a spider." She grabbed an old towel and started mopping up the spilled paint. "A really big spider. We had a disagreement about bathroom occupancy."

Mac's laugh was rich and deep. "So you're telling me I rushed up here to save you from an arachnid?"

"My hero," she said dryly, but couldn't help smiling. "Though next time, maybe knock louder?"

"I did knock. And yelled, but Queen was drowning me out."

She grimaced. "I guess I got carried away with my painting playlist."

Mac looked around at the half-finished walls. "Seafoam green?"

"It's soothing," she defended, watching as he rolled up his sleeves to expose muscular forearms. "What are you doing?"

"Helping. I can reach the high spots so you don't have to be on that rickety ladder. And I think painting responsibilities are the landlord's. Unless you'd rather do it alone?"

"No, I..." She swallowed hard. "Help would be nice."

They worked in comfortable silence for a while, the music now at a more reasonable volume. Mac painted with surprising efficiency, his brush strokes even and careful. They were making quick work of the small space.

"You're good at this," she observed. "David couldn't tell a Phillips-head from a flathead."

Mac dipped his brush in the paint. "My parents and grandfather saw to it I knew how to do things. I enjoy it really. Even helped design and build my house. Makes it more mine."

She watched him stretch to reach a high corner, his shirt pulling tight across his shoulders and baring part of his mid-drift. She tried not to stare. "I'm the same way. I like to do things for myself, relish in the satisfaction of a job well done. And it also helps keep my mind occupied and off of my troubles."

Mac's brush stilled, and Kelsey realized she'd made him uneasy. Maybe he was truly sorry for yesterday. The silence stretched between them.

"Mac?" she finally asked. "Why did you really stop by today? Did you come to apologize some more?"

He turned to face her, paint smudged on his cheek. He seemed unsure of himself. "I..."

"Maybe you wanted to ask me if I wanted to try that boat trip again. A do-over?"

His eyes met hers. "I *would* like to make up for yesterday properly. If you're willing."

She studied him. He'd clearly not had any idea why he'd stopped by, and she was pushing him into spending time with her.

"You've got paint on your face," she said finally, stepping closer. Without thinking, she reached up to wipe it away with her thumb. Mac caught her wrist gently, his thumb brushing over her pulse point.

"Is that a yes?"

"Yes," she whispered, suddenly very aware of how close they were standing. "It's a date."

Relief flooded his face. She stepped closer, feeling emboldened. There was no denying the attraction she felt for him. She pressed herself closer and watched his eyes darken. "I wanted to make that clear, Mac, about this being a date. The idea appeals to me."

Shock rippled through his body, but his arms curled around her back to pull her closer. "Kelsey... I can't give you... I'm leaving soon..."

"I know." She tilted her face upward.

He hesitated for a millisecond, then his thighs pressed against hers, and his hands moved lower on her waist.

That's all it took for her. She pulled back. "Okay, now let me finish up this bathroom. I think we're pretty much done. What time do you want me to come over?"

Mac stepped back, his mouth agape as he collected himself and stowed his brush with hers in the paint pan. "Tomorrow? How about one-ish?"

"Sounds great." Kelsey replied, trying to hide her smile, as she picked up the painting materials. "See you then."

Mac hesitated a moment before stepping from the confined space. "Okay then. See you tomorrow."

After Mac left, Kelsey leaned against the door jam, admiring the fresh paint job and not caring if she got more paint on her clothes. Her skin tingled from their embrace and her heart was racing. The look of shocked desire in his eyes had been worth every ounce of courage it had taken to invite herself on a date and step into his arms.

For the first time since David died, she felt truly alive—and terrified. Not of Mac, but of the intensity of her desire for him. There had been a few men since David had died, but she'd never felt close to the passion she felt near Mac.

He said he couldn't give her what she wanted, and she wouldn't force him. But whatever it was between them deserved to be explored. Life was fleeting. They both knew that.

Still, as she surveyed the finished bathroom, she couldn't stop smiling. Tomorrow couldn't come soon enough.

Chapter 12

Mac slammed his car door harder than necessary, striding toward his house with agitated steps. The feeling of Kelsey's body pressed against his lingered, making it impossible to think clearly. He yanked off his paint spattered shirt as he entered his living room.

"Damn it," he muttered, pacing the hardwood floors. What was he doing? He'd gone over there without a real plan, but definitely not to invite her out *again*.

He ran his hands through his hair. The boldness in her eyes. Heat coursed through him at the memory.

"A date," he said to the empty room. "She wants a date."

His upcoming sailing trip was supposed to be his escape. He'd been planning for years, organizing his life around the goal of getting away from everything. Leaving it all behind.

But now his grandfather needed him. And instead of doing the right thing—calling it off, maintaining distance—he was reaching for his phone to call his favorite caterer. He caught his reflection in the window as he detailed the menu, barely recognizing the spark of life in his own eyes.

This was dangerous. Kelsey wasn't some casual fling. She was his grandfather's nurse, Noah's mother. She deserved better than a man with one foot already out the door. A man who couldn't offer her anything beyond temporarily scratching an itch.

Mac sank onto his couch, head in his hands. She knew he was leaving. Knew about his late fiancé, about his broken pieces. And still, she wanted whatever this could be, even if it was temporary.

What made it worse was he wanted it as well. How was he supposed to keep his distance when she made him feel more alive than he had in years?

"Fine," he said aloud, making his decision. "If she wants a date, I'll give her a date she won't forget."

He pulled up his contact list again, determined to make every detail perfect. Maybe he couldn't give Kelsey forever, but he could give her this—one perfect evening on the water. One chance to explore this electricity between them before reality caught up.

Kelsey clutched her phone after ending the call, the echo of Noah's excited chatter about shells still ringing in her ears. His voice had been bright, happy—the way a seven-year-old's should be. No mention of custody battles or inheritance. No hint that his grandmother and Jason were probably watching his every move, documenting any perceived failing in Kelsey's parenting.

She wandered into his room, running her fingers over the collection of shells arranged meticulously on his bookshelf. Each one was labeled in his careful handwriting: *Found at Bass Point*, *From the cove behind Mackie's*, *Beach near the nursing home*. Their life together mapped out in calcium carbonate and mother-of-pearl.

The bed was still unmade from his hasty departure a few days ago, she hadn't had the heart to straighten it. His pajamas lay crumpled on the floor, one sock inside out. The familiar mess of a boy who knew he had a home to come back to.

"Please," she whispered to the empty room, sinking onto his bed. "Please don't take him from me."

The tears came then, hot and fierce. She pressed her face into his pillow, breathing in the lingering scent of his shampoo and that indefinable something that was just Noah. Her son. Her anchor. The reason she'd learned to smile again after David died.

What would she do if they won? If some judge decided that Margaret's mansion and Jason's connections were better for Noah than their cozy house and quiet life? Would Noah become the person that his father didn't want to be? Privileged and removed from the rest of the world? Had she really done enough for Noah? Could she give him everything he needed, or had her stubborn pride blinded her to what was best for him? Was she selfish for wanting to keep him close, even if it meant denying him opportunities she couldn't provide?

She glanced at her watch, two hours until she needed to meet Mac. Enough time to pull herself together. To pretend she wasn't terrified of losing everything that mattered. The idea that this was a real date was helping to distract her, but obviously not entirely.

Kelsey forced herself up from Noah's bed, wiping her eyes with the back of her hand. Her reflection in his mirror showed tear tracks, she'd need to fix that before seeing Mac. Before pretending everything was fine.

Her phone buzzed—a new picture from Noah. He'd arranged shells in the sand to spell *HI MOM*. Her heart squeezed.

Tell Mac I found a Junonia! Super rare!!!

She smiled through fresh tears, typing back: *Will do! Enjoy your time.*

Such a normal conversation. As if lawyers weren't already drawing up papers to try and take him away. But she was glad he was having a good time, and there were other kids along for this trip.

Kelsey checked the time again and headed to her bathroom. The fresh seafoam green walls reminded her of yesterday with Mac, of his kiss, of the way he'd looked at her. For a moment, she let herself imagine a future where she could have both—Noah and maybe something real with Mac. But Mac was leaving, and Noah...

She squared her shoulders, reaching for her makeup bag. She could handle Mac leaving. She could handle being alone. But losing Noah? That would break her completely.

The woman in the mirror straightened her spine, wiped away the last tears. She had two hours to become someone who deserved a perfect date. Someone who wasn't falling apart inside.

"You can do this," she told her reflection. "You can have one afternoon of normal. One afternoon of just being a woman on a date with a handsome man."

Wandering back to her room her eyes landed on Noah's latest school picture smiling at her from her nightstand, gap-toothed and gleaming, so much like David around the eyes. But the gentle spirit behind that smile? That was all Noah.

"I won't let them take you," she promised the photograph, her voice stronger now. "Whatever it takes, baby. Whatever it takes."

The late afternoon sun glinted off the water as Kelsey made her way down the dock. Mac was adjusting something on the sail, his movements precise and practiced. He looked up at her footsteps on the gangway, and his hands stilled.

"Wow," he said softly. "You look... beautiful."

Kelsey smoothed her sundress, suddenly glad she'd taken extra time with her hair. "Thanks. You clean up pretty nice yourself."

And he did. The careful shave highlighted his strong jaw, and his fitted polo and deck shoes managed to look both casual and expensive. She tried not to stare at how the fabric stretched across his shoulders as he reached for her bag.

"Brought clothes for later?" he asked, peeking inside.

"Ever the girl scout."

His fingers brushed hers as he took the bag, and that same electricity from yesterday sparked between them.

They stood there awkwardly until Kelsey blurted, "Oh! Noah texted. He wanted me to tell you he found a junonia shell."

Mac's face lit up. "Really? Those are pretty rare around here. Did he find it near the point?"

"I think so. He was excited to tell you about it."

"That kid has a good eye." Mac disappeared below deck to stow her bag and was back quickly. "You know, there's this little island about three miles out, uninhabited, great shelling. I'd love to show you and Noah sometime. It would give me practice anchoring and taking the skiff. We'll be going past it today. It's on the route I had planned."

"I'd love that." Kelsey settled onto one of the cushioned seats and watched Mac whirl around the deck with fluid efficiency. Every motion seemed purposeful, from the way he checked the lines to how he adjusted the wheel.

The auxiliary engine hummed to life, and they glided out of the cove. Mac kept up a running commentary about wind directions and tides, but Kelsey found herself focusing more on how the sun brought out golden highlights in his dark hair, the way his forearms flexed as he handled the wheel.

"See that island ahead?" He pointed. "It's got these hidden coves where the shells wash up after storms. Noah would love it."

"You seem to know every inch of these waters," she said, admiring how naturally he stood at the helm.

"Spent most of my life out here. It's home." He glanced over, catching her watching him. His smile turned softer, more intimate. "You're staring."

"Just admiring the view," she said boldly.

Color touched his cheeks, but his eyes held hers. "It is beautiful out here."

"I wasn't talking about the scenery."

Mac's hands tightened on the wheel. "Kelsey..."

"Sorry," she said, not feeling sorry at all. "Does it make you uncomfortable when I flirt with you?"

"No," he said after a moment, a ghost of a smile on his lips.

The wind caught her hair, and she saw his eyes follow the movement.

He adjusted their course slightly. "See that lighthouse? There's a story about it being haunted by a keeper that was lost in a storm. He still walks the tower at night, making sure the light stays on."

"You're changing the subject."

"Yes, I am." But his smile was warm, playful even. "Is it working?"

"Maybe." She stood, moving closer to where he stood at the helm. "Tell me about the ghost."

As Mac launched into the story, Kelsey watched the animation in his face, the way his hands waved as he talked. He was coming alive out here on the water, she realized. The familiar frown had vanished from his features.

The mansion appeared through the sea mist like something from a gothic novel. Its weathered gray exterior was stark against the clear blue sky. Kelsey moved closer to the helm, her shoulder brushing Mac's arm as she pointed.

"That's the mansion? It looks more imposing from this view."

"Yeah." Mac adjusted their course slightly, his body warm beside her. "Beautiful, isn't it?"

The boat rocked in the waves, Kelsey struggled to keep her footing, and Mac reached out to steady her. His hand lingered on her back.

"Why do they call the island Widow's Point?" She turned to look at him, close enough now to see the faint stubble he'd missed while shaving along his jaw.

"You want the romantic version or the practical one?" His eyes crinkled at the corners when he smiled.

"Both."

"Well, the house was built in the late 1800's by Captain Wilson for his new bride." Mac's voice took on a storyteller's cadence.

"Story goes that she'd walk the widow's walk, that railed platform on top, watching for his ship whenever he was due home."

"Did something happen to him?"

Mac nodded. "One winter, his ship never made it back to port."

"That's heartbreaking." Kelsey shivered despite the warm air. Mac's fingers spread over small of her back.

"The interesting part is what she did after," he continued. "Instead of retreating into mourning, she turned the house into a haven for other widows and unwed expectant mothers. Gave them a safe place to land while they figured out their next steps. I understand it was a pretty busy place."

"Your grandmother worked there, right? You mentioned that before."

"She did. By then it was owned by a foundation that kept up the work the widow had started. That's actually how she met my grandfather." His thumb traced small circles on her back, probably unconsciously, but it was doing delicious things to her senses. "He used to deliver supplies to the house. When the foundation that ran it decided to sell, he bought it. It's been empty since."

"I bet there's quite a story there."

Mac laughed. "Several. But that's the mansion, not the island. It's not why the island is called Widow's Point." He reached past her to tap the sonar display, his chest pressing briefly against her shoulder. "See those dark spots? Underwater rocks, just below the surface. They've claimed more than a few ships over the years. The lighthouse was built to warn sailors away, but before that..."

"The rocks made widows of sailor's wives," Kelsey finished.

"Exactly. Here, look." He adjusted something on the screen, and the underwater typography became clearer. "They're practically invisible, especially in storms."

Kelsey studied the underwater rocks on the display, acutely aware of the clean scent of Mac's aftershave. "Is that why we find so much sea glass in the cove?"

"It is." His breath stirred her hair. "Every piece you pick up probably has a story behind it. Cargo from shipwrecks, bottles thrown overboard—decades of maritime history tumbled smooth by the waves. The currents bring it to our cove."

"Noah would love hearing about this."

"I've told him about it, but you're right. We should bring him out here sometime. Show him the rocks, tell him the stories. He'd go nuts," Mac paused, seeming to realize what he'd said. "I mean if it's okay with you."

Kelsey turned to face him, his arm encircling her waist as she moved, and touched a hand to his chest to keep herself steady. "You'd do that?"

His eyes searched her face. "Yeah, I would. He's a great kid. I really enjoy talking with him. And he loves the history of this place."

The moment stretched between them. Mac's hand was still on her back, and Kelsey could feel his heartbeat where her palm rested against his chest.

"The widow," she said softly. "Does her ghost still walk up there, watching for her captain?"

"I've never seen her." Mac's voice was equally quiet. "But people say, on stormy nights, you can see a woman in white up on that platform."

"Do you believe in ghosts, Mac?"

Chapter 13

"No," Mac said firmly, his hand tightening slightly on her waist. "When you're gone, you're gone. That's it."

Kelsey's laugh was soft, almost sad. "You sound so certain."

"You're not?"

"I used to be. Before David." She glanced away, watching the waves break against the hull. "After he died, there were moments. I've never seen anything, exactly. Just... a presence. A certainty that he was there."

Mac's jaw tightened, but he didn't pull away.

"What was her name?" Kelsey asked gently.

"Marlene." His voice was rough. "Her name was Marlene."

"Don't you ever feel like she's watching over you? Or with you?"

"Kelsey..." Warning threaded through his tone.

"I'm serious, Mac. Wouldn't it be comforting to think that Marlene's still around, wanting you to be happy?"

"I doubt either of them would approve of... this." His fingers flexed against her hip.

"This isn't betraying them." Kelsey met his gaze steadily. "They're gone. We know that better than anyone. Moving on, living our lives, it doesn't diminish what we had with them. Or make our love for them any less."

Something shifted in Mac's expression, his eyes darkening as they dropped to her lips. His other hand came up to trace the curve of her waist, and Kelsey's breath caught at the heat in his touch.

"You feel very real," he murmured, voice dropping to a dangerous register that made her skin tingle. "Very alive."

His hands slid lower, pulling her closer until their bodies aligned. Kelsey's heart thundered against her ribs as Mac dipped his head, his breath warm against her lips.

A sharp electronic beeping cut through the moment. Mac's attention immediately snapped to the instrument panel.

"Damn it," Mac muttered, releasing her to adjust the controls. "Getting too close to those rocks I was just warning you about. Some sailor I am."

Kelsey stepped back and steadied herself against the rail. "I might have been distracting you."

"You think?" His smile was rueful. Mac busied himself with the boat for several moments while Kelsey continued to enjoy the view. It felt good to talk to him this way.

"Nobody's ever talked about Marlene like that before. People usually tiptoe around it, like mentioning her might break me," Mac said, turning back to her.

"Loss doesn't seem to work that way. They're always there, part of us, just under the surface."

Mac's hands moved over the screens and buttons on the console, displaying what Kelsey assumed were underwater objects, as well as the boat's speed and direction. "You were the first person to tell me the pain doesn't go away. Most people promise it gets better."

"Maybe I missed my calling as a grief counselor?" she laughed. "This is going to hurt forever."

"It's a true statement." He glanced at her. "The way you put it, about the pain becoming part of who you are."

Kelsey noted how his shoulders had tensed at the subject. She suspected he hadn't filled in the gaps Marlene's death left. Instead, he'd sold his company, retreated to the island, and was planning a solo sailing trip. All of it seemed less like moving forward and more like running away.

"Have there been others?" she asked quietly. "Since Marlene?"

"A few." His knuckles whitened on the wheel. "Nothing I would call a relationship. Nothing that lasted past them wanting more than I could give. You?"

"Oh, a lot of dating and fix ups. Two relationships that made it past a few months. Both ended when they realized Noah would always come first." She shrugged. "I'm used to being on my own. Between Noah's activities and work, I don't have much time anyway."

Mac gestured between them. "So where do you see this going? If we're being honest."

She moved closer, laying her hand over his on the wheel. "I'm not asking for anything. You're a decent guy, buying me a new car when you didn't have too, and how you care for your grandfather. And you actually enjoy spending time with Noah. I like being with you, even as ornery as you are and even when you put your nose in my business without asking first."

"I'm not ornery..."

She laughed. "We're here. We're alive. The sun is shining, and I'm wearing a very pretty dress." She squeezed his hand. "Can't that be enough for now?"

The tension in his shoulders eased slightly. "You make it sound simple."

"Stop overthinking it."

The sun painted the water in shades of gold and red as Mac dropped anchor in a sheltered cove. True to his word, Mac had guided them through a maze of rocky islands with seabird nests and scraggly pine trees.

When he finally disappeared below deck, she expected him to return with sandwiches. Instead, he emerged carrying a wicker basket that smelled like heaven and what looked suspiciously like wine glasses.

"You planned a picnic on the ocean," she said, delighted when he spread out an actual tablecloth on the small deck table.

"You said you wanted a date. So it's a date." He produced a bottle of white wine and a container of what turned out to be grilled salmon. "I might have had some help from that little café in town."

"And flowers?" She touched the small vase of wildflowers. "You're full of surprises."

"Don't get used to it." But his smile was pleased as he poured the wine.

The food was excellent, but the company was better. As the sky deepened to purple, and stars began to light the sky, Mac told stories about growing up on the island, his voice warm with memory and showing a side of himself Kelsey knew now not many people saw.

"Grandad used to let me take out this tiny sailboat," he said, gesturing with his wineglass. "I must have capsized it a hundred times, but he never worried. Just waited until I figured it out."

"That sounds wonderful. Noah has that kind of freedom here too. With so few people on the estate. He has the run of it." Kelsey pulled her knees up to her chest, getting comfortable. "Though I nearly had a heart attack when I saw him out on the beach with you that day."

"I wouldn't have let anything happen to him."

"I know that, *now*. Then, you were just some strange man with my son."

Mac leaned back, studying her. "He's a smart kid. Reminds me of myself at that age, always collecting things, wanting to know how the world works."

"He adores you, you know. All I hear about is Mackie this, Mackie that."

Something flickered across his face, and they looked at each other. She shivered, though it wasn't entirely from the cooling air.

"You're cold. Why don't you go below to change? I put your bag down there before we left, it's on the couch or the bed. You'll see it. I'll clean this up."

Grateful for the suggestion, Kelsey stood. "I'll just be a minute."

As she headed below deck, she could feel Mac's eyes on her. Her skin tingled at his attention.

Kelsey found her bag on the narrow bed in the cabin below. The space was cozy but efficient, every inch carefully planned to accommodate the needs of the passengers.

She imagined Mac here alone, sleeping in this small berth during his sailing trips. The thought made her oddly sad.

Chapter 14

Mac expertly guided the boat through the evening light and they arrived back at his dock. He was quiet again, withdrawing into himself. Kelsey wondered if pushing him into this date had crossed a line with him, and he was now regretting bringing her out.

She didn't regret their time out on the water, but a snag of guilt picked at her consciousness. It was clear Mac had other plans in his life, and dating her was not one of them. The heat was there between them, and they kept appearing in each other's orbits, but Mac... well she was beginning to doubt they would turn friends to lovers any time soon.

Once they closed up the yacht for the night, Mac took her bag. "Let me walk you home?"

She nodded silently and they walked side by side through the moonlight back to her cottage.

When they arrived at her door, he turned to her and ran a hand through his hair. "Listen, my grandfather's birthday is this Saturday. Mrs. Andersen from the board at the clinic has been forcing me to organize a big party for him here. They want to present him with an award for all he's done for the community. It's supposed to be a surprise. But I can't count on that after inviting half the town."

She smiled at the look of pure disgust on his face. "Forcing you?"

He snorted and kicked something on the step. "Can't think of anything else I would hate more, but it's for Grandad."

Kelsey nodded. "He's a wonderful man. I actually have him on my schedule this week. A regular check-up."

"Wednesday, right?" At her surprised look, he smiled. "He mentioned it."

She smiled back at him. "What time is the party?"

"Starts at six on Saturday. I've even planned fireworks out on the cove."

"He'll love that."

Mac stepped closer to her, his fingers brushing hers. Her breath caught.

"I know Noah's due back Sunday." His voice was soft. "He'll be sorry to miss the fireworks. I'll see you Wednesday?"

She nodded. "And Saturday."

He started to turn away, then looked back. "Maybe we could get coffee tomorrow? Just... coffee."

The hope in his voice made her chest tight. "Okay. Just coffee."

She watched him walk away before retreating into her dark and empty cottage.

The next morning, Kelsey hummed to herself as she went about her morning routine. Little memories flickering through her mind of their time together on the boat.

"Get it together," she muttered, but couldn't stop smiling as she pulled cleaning supplies from under the sink.

The bathroom closet had been on her to-do list for weeks. She sorted through old lotions and half-empty shampoo bottles, humming to herself. When she finished, the shelves gleamed, neatly organized with fresh towels.

Her phone buzzed just as she was admiring her work.

"Mom! You won't believe what we found!" Noah's excitement burst through the speaker.

"Hey, sweetie! What did you find?"

"We went to this amazing island where Blackbeard used to hide! Aunt Jennifer knows all about it. There were these cool markers that the Gullah people used to help guide escaped slaves to safety. Did you know they have their own language? It's called Geechee."

"That sounds fascinating, honey."

"Cousin Kyle says some of the Gullah traditions came from West Africa. We met this lady who makes these cool baskets from grass, just like her great-grandmother taught her."

Kelsey sat on the edge of the tub, smiling at his enthusiasm. "You're learning so much."

"Oh! And we found this old coin in the sand! Uncle Jason says it's probably not from a pirate ship, but it's still really old."

"Speaking of ships," Kelsey said, "I went out on Mac's boat yesterday."

"You did? Did you see any sharks?"

"No sharks, but he showed me where all those shipwrecks happened—you know, where the sea glass you've been collecting comes from."

"No way! Mom, can we go out there when I get back? Maybe Mac could teach me about sailing!"

Kelsey's heart squeezed. "I'm sure he'd love that, honey."

"This is gonna be so cool! Oh, okay. We're going to get ice cream. Love you, Mom!"

"Love you too, baby. Have fun."

The call ended, and Kelsey stared at her phone, guilt and happiness warring in her chest.

Kelsey sank into her favorite armchair. It would be so easy to get used to having Mac in her life. He fit so naturally into her world, into Noah's world. But there was something haunting about the way he lived, like he was just passing through his own life.

A knock startled her from her thoughts.

Amy stood on her porch, holding two cups from the coffee shop. "Thought you might need this after your... boat trip." Her smile was knowing.

Kelsey felt herself flush. "Come in. And wipe that smirk off your face."

"Can't help it." Amy handed her a cup. "So? How was it?"

"It was..." Kelsey searched for words that wouldn't reveal too much. "Nice."

"Nice? That's all I get?"

"What do you want me to say?"

"That you had an amazing time? That Mac MacCormack is actually human under all that brooding?" Amy settled onto the couch. "Speaking of humans, I had the most interesting conversation with his grandfather yesterday."

Kelsey curled deeper into her chair. "Oh?"

"After his massage and reiki session—which he pretends to hate but actually loves—we started talking about the mansion."

"Why am I not surprised?"

Amy smiled. "Right, not a surprise. But it was actually a little strange—he said his wife was really adamant about buying it *because* she didn't want anyone living there." Amy leaned forward. "Apparently, something about the place really upset her. The way the foundation that owned it had changed over the years, what they were using it for. She was determined to stop whatever evil was happening there."

"Did she ever tell him what they were doing?"

Amy sipped her coffee. "That's where it's really strange. He said she'd told him once that people had been murdered. But there was no proof when he and the sheriff dug into it. By then, he said, he wasn't sure if it was her dementia or the truth. But there wasn't any evidence."

Their subsequent gazes were an unspoken conversation of intrigue between sisters.

"Mac told me about a local legend of the widow of the sea captain that built the house. She can still be seen some stormy nights walking the widow's walk, searching for her husband," Kelsey said.

Amy paled. "That's creepy. On top of the murders, if it's true."

"I know, right?"

"But let's get back to you and Mac. Are you going to see him again?"

Kelsey thought about their coffee date tomorrow, about his grandfather's birthday party. "Maybe."

"Maybe? Girl, you're grinning from ear to ear."

"It's complicated, Amy. He's... he's not staying around. After his grandfather dies, he's leaving. He's made that very clear."

"And you're okay with that?"

Kelsey looked out the window toward the water. "For now? Yeah, I think I am."

"So..." Amy tucked her legs under her on the couch and changed the subject. "Have you heard anything about the custody situation?"

Kelsey's fingers tightened around her coffee cup. "I'm calling my attorney today."

"Good."

"I know." Kelsey set her cup down. "I keep thinking about that will, Amy."

Tears welled in her eyes as the idea of losing Noah surfaced. The tight control she had on her emotions boiled over. When Amy embraced her, she let her tears fall. "Everything will be all right, Kel. You've got this."

After Amy left, Kelsey dialed her attorney's number and paced the living room as it rang.

"Sandra Mitchell."

"Sandra, it's Kelsey Prescott."

"I was going to call you today, Kelsey."

Something in Sandra's tone made Kelsey's stomach drop. She sank onto the couch.

"What's wrong?"

"I received a courtesy call from Margaret Prescott's attorneys this morning. They're preparing to file additional evidence in the custody case—I don't know what yet, but they're making a move."

Kelsey's throat tightened. "But Noah's spending more time with them. He's with them this week on spring vacation. *You* thought that was going to appease them."

"Apparently they're not looking for any conciliation. I'm sorry."

"I should tell you, I was recently informed that Noah is to inherit what was my husband's inheritance when he turns twenty-one. It's a sum of roughly half a billion dollars." Kelsey's fingers were white as she clenched the phone, pressing it to her ear. "Sandra, I need you to be straight with me this time. Could I lose him?"

The silence stretched too long.

"Sandra?"

"It's highly unlikely. You're a good mother, you have a stable home, a good job. Noah is thriving."

"I hear a 'but'?"

Sandra sighed heavily, Kelsey could hear her shuffling papers on her desk. "Knowing now that they will not be satisfied with increased visitation, they will likely drag this out. Make it expensive, complicated." Sandra's voice softened. "I think we need to consider a worst case. If they want this badly enough Kelsey, you could lose."

Dead silence answered her, making Kelsey swallow deeply fighting the lump in her throat that threatened to choke her.

"Margaret is in her eighties and her health is diminishing, so Noah could be inheriting this money in a few years. Kelsey, who else in the family would take part in his care and manage his trust if they were granted custody?"

"I believe it would be David's brother, Jason. He's been involved with him during visits."

"Jason Prescott?" Kelsey was certain she heard Sandra swear beneath her breath.

Kelsey stared at the photo on her mantel—Noah at his last birthday, grinning with chocolate cake on his face. Tears began anew. "What do we do?"

"We fight. And Kelsey? It's my job to prepare you legally, but it is your job to be prepared emotionally. They'll use anything they can against you to make their case."

She sighed. "I understand."

"I'll call as soon as I know what they're filing, and we'll strategize from there. Try not to worry."

But after hanging up, Kelsey couldn't stop the tears. She pulled her knees to her chest and let herself cry.

Chapter 15

Mac stood at his kitchen counter, marking off names on the party list, something he'd never thought he would ever do in his lifetime. In spite of himself, he was unable to wipe the stupid grin off his face he'd been wearing since dropping Kelsey at her door.

"Get it together, MacCormack," he muttered, turning his attention back to the list.

The guest list had grown from a simple party of old friends to what looked like a town gathering. Even Pete from the marina had asked if he could bring his wife and kids. Old Joe Martin would need a ride; his daughter said he couldn't drive anymore but was too proud to admit it. And Eleanor Thompson—she'd been Gram's best friend—would need her oxygen concentrator.

Mac reached for his phone, thumbing through his contacts to arrange transportation for the older guests. His thumb hesitated over Kelsey's name.

"Don't do it," he told himself, but typed anyway: *Breakfast tomorrow at Annie's before work? 7:30?*

He set the phone down, determined not to watch for her response. Instead, he pulled out the plans for the fireworks setup. The weather report promised clear skies, perfect for the display he'd planned. Grandad always loved fireworks, said they reminded him of celebrating the end of the war. Mac had never gotten clarity on which war.

Ten minutes passed. No response.

Mac picked up his phone, checked his message had gone through. It had.

"She's probably busy," he said aloud to his empty kitchen. "She has a life. Unlike you, sitting here staring at your phone like a—"

He shoved the phone in his pocket and grabbed his keys; he needed to head into town on Mrs. Andersen's orders. The party supplies weren't going to order themselves.

In his car, his hand kept straying to his pocket. Still nothing.

What was she doing? Probably cleaning, like she'd mentioned. Or maybe she was having second thoughts. Maybe she was trying to figure out how to let him down easy. Maybe—

"Jesus Christ," he growled, pulling onto the only store on the island that would have what he was looking for in the way of party decorations. "You're not doing this. You're not getting attached."

But he couldn't stop thinking about her.

His phone buzzed. His heart jumped.

Sure, sounds great! See you then!

The relief that flooded through him was immediately followed by self-recrimination.

But he was already typing back: *Can't wait.*

Mac leaned his forehead against the steering wheel. "Who *are* you? You're in trouble, old boy."

He thought about their conversations. How she'd known exactly when to push and when to let him be quiet. It was easy to talk to her. He'd not encountered anyone quite like her before.

"Temporary," he reminded himself firmly. "She knows that. You know that. Keep it simple. Damn it." He sat up, shoving his phone deep in his pocket. "Focus on the party. Focus on Grandad."

But even as he walked into the store, part of him was already counting the hours until breakfast.

Annie's morning rush was in full swing when Kelsey pushed through the door at 7:25, the bell jingling overhead. Mac was already there, commandeering a corner booth by the window. He stood when he saw her, and her stomach did an annoying flip.

He'd clearly come straight from his morning run in wind pants and a fitted quarter-zip that showed off his shoulders in a way that should be illegal before coffee. His hair was still damp and curled slightly at his neck.

"Morning," he said, touching her arm as though hesitating whether to kiss her cheek or not. That smile again, the one that crinkled the corners of his eyes and made him look younger.

"Morning." She settled in and tried not to notice how good he smelled—some intoxicating combination of soap and sea air.

Annie herself bustled over, coffee pot in hand. "Well, well. Mac MacCormack dining in instead of grabbing coffee to go? Must be special company." She winked at Kelsey while filling their mugs. "What can I get you two?"

"What's good?" Kelsey asked, scanning the menu.

"Everything's good," Mac said. "But Annie's blueberry pancakes are legendary."

"Flattery will get you everywhere, Mac." Annie beamed. "Those pancakes kept this one alive through high school. He'd come in looking half-starved after morning practice."

Mac rolled his eyes. "I was a growing boy."

"You were a bottomless pit. Still are, I'd bet." Annie turned to Kelsey. "How about it, honey?"

"The pancakes sound perfect, actually."

"Make that two," Mac added.

As Annie walked away, Kelsey noticed at least three tables pretending not to stare at them. Mrs. Peterson, she recognized from the clinic, was practically falling out of her booth to eavesdrop.

"So," Mac said, leaning back in his seat. "Get everything done on your spring cleaning list?"

"Most." She smiled at him. "How's the party planning going?"

Before he could answer, a man Kelsey recognized from the hardware store approached, his nametag on his chamois shirt displaying "Joe." "Mac! Just the man I wanted to see. Heard what you're doing for that grandfather of yours. Sorry to hear he isn't doing well—did I ever tell you about the time he helped me save the store?"

"No." Mac said. It wasn't rude though, it was more like he couldn't decide if he wanted to hear the story at the risk of inviting Joe to stay.

"I'd love to hear it," Kelsey said for him, her tone warm. "Pull up a chair."

Joe launched into the story of how Truman had co-signed a loan during the recession of '08, saving the hardware store from foreclosure. Kelsey watched Mac listen, noticed how he kept his body angled toward her even as he gave Joe his attention.

Their pancakes arrived, and with it came more visitors. Sarah from the post office had a story about Truman helping her son get into college. Bill from the marina remembered when Truman had quietly paid for his wife's cancer treatments.

"Your grandfather's quite something," Kelsey said when they finally had a moment alone. "I didn't realize any of this about him."

Mac's expression softened. "Yeah, he is. Always had an interest making sure the island and the people stayed vibrant. This island helped him and my grandmother before he built his business, so he wanted to give back. He did what he could and never took any credit for it. He'd kill me if I told him I knew about half these stories."

His eyes met hers over the rim of his coffee cup, and that current of awareness crackled between them again. Kelsey focused on her pancakes, trying to ignore how her skin tingled where his knee brushed hers under the table.

"These really are amazing," she said, gesturing with her fork.

"Told you." He was watching her with that intense look again, the one that made her forget to breathe. "We'll have to make this a regular thing."

She reminded herself he was leaving soon before saying, "I'd like that."

Then, checking her watch, she sighed. "I should head in. Staff meeting at eight." She gathered her things, warmth spreading through her chest when Mac stood as she did. "Thanks for breakfast."

"Kelsey?" His voice stopped her at the door. When she turned, he was still standing by their table, hands in his pockets. "Do you have dinner plans?"

"No."

His answering smile stayed with her all the way to the office, along with the memory of how he'd looked in that damn quarter-zip. The whole town would be talking by lunch, but somehow, she couldn't bring herself to care.

The conference room smelled like coffee and sugar from the pile of donuts sitting untouched in the center of the table. Kelsey slid into her usual seat just as a vendor was setting up a presentation, her mind still half-stuck on breakfast and Mac's smile.

"Alright everyone," William, the clinic's physician announced as the vendor clicked to the first slide. "I know it's early, but this is important." He held up a small black device, about the size of a car key fob. "After what happened in Connecticut..."

One of the newer nurses shifted uncomfortably in her chair. They'd all heard about it—the home health nurse who never made it back to her car. Murdered by her patient.

"The board has requested we implement a new safety protocol." The sales vendor passed small key fobs around. "These connect directly to emergency dispatch. Three clicks," he demonstrated, "and help is on the way. They work off satellite, so even up on North Point where cell service is spotty at best, you'll have coverage."

Kelsey turned the device over in her hands. Marveling a little at the small size, no bigger than a key. She'd done hundreds of home visits in her time doing rural primary care and had few issues. Maybe an overzealous dog or two, but still—sometimes walking into a stranger's house alone... You just never knew what or who was going to be there.

"Questions?" William looked around the room.

"Do we have to wear them all the time?" The new nurse asked.

"During home visits, yes. Non-negotiable." William's usually easy-going expression was stern. "This isn't just about you. As your employer, we have a responsibility to do what we can to keep you safe. A couple of us have been testing them, and I just keep mine on my keychain all the time. Having to squeeze the alarm three times really eliminates any accidental activation."

The meeting wrapped up with scheduling updates and case reviews. Kelsey hung back as others filed out, fiddling with her new fob.

"William? Got a minute?"

He looked up from gathering his papers, smiling kindly at her. "For you, always. What's up?"

"It's about Truman Costigan's case." She perched on the edge of the conference table. "I wanted to talk about conflict of interest—I'm friendly with him and his family outside of work."

"You're worried about professional boundaries?" William smiled, pushing his reading glasses up. "Kelsey, this is Widow's Point. We've got what, the two of us for the whole island? It's taken a while for the community to get used to a nurse practitioner as their primary care provider, but they like and trust you. Some overlap between family and personal connections is inevitable. I wouldn't worry about dating his grandson."

"Not sure I would call it *dating*... And how did you..."

"Like I said, Kelsey, this is Widow's Point. News travels fast. My wife was having breakfast this morning at Annie's. Apparently it was obvious."

Obvious? Kelsey let out a breath of air.

"Has it affected your treatment of Truman?"

"No! Of course not."

"Has Truman or his family expressed any concerns?"

"No, nothing like that."

"Then I'd say we're good." William gathered his things. "I'll take a look at his chart today, but as with everyone else, Kelsey, your clinical assessments and decision-making have been spot-on. I'm grateful you're here. Just keep documenting everything clearly, and if you ever feel the relationship is impacting your treatment decisions, call me and we'll decide together. Deal?"

"Deal." She stood, relief loosening her shoulders. "Thanks, William."

"Don't thank me yet—you're on for the clinic office visits this morning and Mrs. Henderson at nine, and she's convinced her new hip is talking to her."

Kelsey groaned, but she was smiling as she headed to her office.

Mac balanced the takeout bags from Napolitano's as he knocked on Kelsey's door, taking in the small pot of lavender by the steps. The whole drive home, his phone had pinged with texts from well-meaning townspeople offering party planning advice. He'd never cared about tablecloth colors or flower arrangements be-fore, and he sure as hell didn't now. But he'd gritted his teeth. It was for Grandad. He pulled together what he considered to be a decent party, and so far, Mrs. Anderson had approved.

Kelsey opened the door, still in her work clothes but barefoot, her dark hair falling loose around her shoulders. The sight did something to his chest—that intimate combination of profession-alism and relaxation that made him want to pull her close. "My hero," she said, taking one of the bags. "I'm starving."

Inside, the cottage was warm and inviting, with soft lamp light and the faint scent of vanilla from the candles scattered through-out. They settled at her small kitchen table, its scratched surface covered with a bright yellow cloth.

Mac watched her twirl spaghetti around her fork and caught himself staring at the elegant line of her neck, the way her fingers curved around her wine glass.

"So," he said, dragging his attention back to conversation, "ap-parently we're getting married in September."

Kelsey choked on her wine. "What?"

"According to Mrs. Dawson. She's already planning the flower arrangements. Oh, and we're having twins next spring."

"Twins?" Kelsey laughed. The sound made his stomach flip. "The town works fast." She took another sip of wine, and the crystal caught the light. "How was party planning?"

"Brutal. I now know more about appetizer options than any man should." He ran a hand through his hair. "How was your day?"

"Clinic days are fast-paced; we see so many people. It's why I like home visits better. You can spend more time with your patient, get to know them better." She took a bite. "We got a new gadget to call for help in the field and I had a conversation with Dr. David about my conflict of interest in caring for Truman."

"Truman would raise hell if they tried to replace you. You're the only one who stands up to him."

143

"But at the same time, I needed to acknowledge it professionally. He said it's inevitable in a town this size. As long as it doesn't affect my decision making, we're fine."

Mac stilled. This was something he hadn't considered. "What then, though? I wouldn't want anyone else for him."

"I would just reach out to David, have him go over my plans. It shouldn't be an issue at all. You should be aware in case you question something I'm doing."

Mac gathered the empty wine glasses while Kelsey wrapped the leftover pasta in foil. She hummed something graceful under her breath. The domesticity of it all should have made him uncomfortable but instead, he felt settled. Right.

The thought stopped him mid-reach for a container lid.

Trust.

It had crept up on him so gradually he hadn't noticed. But there it was, solid and undeniable as granite. He trusted her. Not just with Truman's care, though watching her handle his grandfather's stubbornness with that perfect blend of firmness and compassion had been something to see. Competent. Kind. Strong.

No, he trusted her with... himself. With everything.

"Mac?" Kelsey's voice pulled him back. She was looking at him curiously, head tilted. "You okay? You went somewhere else just now."

"Yeah." He surprised himself with how steady his voice was, considering his world had just shifted on its axis. "Yeah, I'm good."

Better than good, really. For the first time in years, he felt like he could breathe properly. Like some weight he'd been carrying had finally eased. Relieved, Mac helped her clear the dishes.

After the kitchen was tidied, they migrated to the couch, a plush navy thing with too many throw pillows. The TV cast flickering shadows across Kelsey's face as she curled against the pillows with her feet tucked under her. He was close enough that he could breathe in the scent of her shampoo, something citrusy and fresh, like summer.

"Can I ask you something?" she said softly after a stretch.

"Anything."

"Did you ever want kids? Before?"

The question hit him like a wave, unexpected and strong. He took a long breath, watching the wind stir the branches outside her window. "Marlene was four months pregnant when she died."

Kelsey's hand found his and squeezed gently. Her skin was soft, but he could feel the strength in her fingers. "I'm so sorry, Mac. I can't imagine losing even the thought of a child. Losing Noah would..."

He heard the catch in her voice, her eyes now more gray than blue in the dim light. "Has there been more activity in your custody issue?"

"I talked to my lawyer yesterday. Prescott's attorneys gave her a courtesy heads up that they are pulling together a filing. They didn't give details. But I did share with her what you found out about Noah's inheritance."

"What was her reaction?"

"Not good. Says it gives them incentive to put a lot of resources behind winning." She started to worry her bottom lip between her teeth.

He'd seen enough of Noah and Kelsey together to know separating them would destroy them both.

Over his dead body would he let that happen.

The strength of such a response frightened him. Who was he becoming?

Chapter 16

Surprising her the next morning, Mac stood on her porch with takeout coffee from a local shop. "Heading out so soon?" he asked, handing her a cup.

"Some of us have to work. I've got two visits before Truman's."

"About that. I need your help with something."

"Ahh coffee with a catch? The birthday party?" She started loading her car with her home visit bag and other supplies.

"Yeah. I'm telling him the board of directors from your community clinic wants to do a dedication ceremony for his donation. Think you could back me up?"

"Lying to my patient? How unethical." But she was smiling. "What time?"

"I'll be there around eleven."

Her phone buzzed again—Noah's daily morning call. "That's Noah. I need to take this."

"Hey baby," she answered, stepping away.

"Mom! Guess what? We're going to see another pirate house today!"

"That's amazing! Tell me everything when you get back—"

There was a scuffle, and suddenly Jason's voice came through, cold and hard. "Listen here, Kelsey. I know you've been digging

147

around in my business. My accounts. You really think that's going to help your case?"

Her blood ran cold. "I haven't been—"

"Don't lie to me. Back off, or things will get very unpleasant. You have no idea what I'm capable of."

"Is Noah there? Can he hear you threatening me?"

A pause. "Noah, say goodbye to your mother."

"Mom?" Noah's voice was small. "Is Uncle Jason mad at you?"

"No, honey, everything's fine." She kept her voice steady through sheer will. "Adults just disagree sometimes. You go have fun. You can tell me more about it tomorrow?"

"Okay. Love you."

"Love you too, baby. So much."

The call ended and Kelsey gripped the porch railing, fury burning through her veins. How dare he? Using Noah like that, trying to frighten him, to turn him...

Wait.

She hadn't been investigating Jason's finances. But obviously someone had. Someone with resources, with connections to be able to accomplish something like that.

"Mac?" she called out across the driveway where he waited for her to end the call, her voice carefully neutral. His easy smile faded when he saw her face, returning to his typical frown.

"Everything okay?"

"You tell me." Kelsey set her coffee mug down with deliberate care. "Why is Jason Prescott accusing me of investigating his finances?"

Mac went still, as though he was choosing his words carefully. It was answer enough.

"What did you do?"

148

"Kels—"

"Don't 'Kels' me. What did you do?" Her voice cracked slightly. "He just threatened me with Noah on the line. He's trying to use this to turn my son against me."

Mac's expression darkened. "He what?"

"Answer the question, Mac."

He crossed the driveway, not quite meeting her eyes. "I had our team look into his business dealings. There were... irregularities."

"Irregularities?" The word tasted bitter. "So you, what? After Margaret's will, you decided to play private investigator again? Knowing how I felt about it? Without considering how it might affect my custody case?"

"I was trying to help!" Now he did look at her, jaw set. "This guy is trying to take your kid, Kelsey. I couldn't just sit back and—"

"It's not your decision to make!" The fear she'd felt hearing Jason's voice transformed into anger, hot and sharp. "This is my son, my fight. You had no right—"

"No right to what? To care? To want to protect you both?"

"To go behind my back! To potentially make things worse!" She ran her hands through her damp hair. "God, Mac, do you have any idea what you might have done? If he can prove I was investigating him, I've already lost Noah."

"He can't. The people I used are discrete."

"That's not the point!" Her voice rose. "The point is you didn't tell me. Didn't ask me. Just decided you knew better than I did how to handle my own business."

Mac took a step toward her, reaching out. She stepped back.

"I have to get to work." She grabbed her bag, her keys. The new safety fob clattered against them. "I'll see you at Truman's."

"Kelsey, wait—"

But she was already slamming the door, heart hammering. In her car, she gripped the steering wheel until her knuckles went white. Deep breaths. She had patients to see. Had to be professional, focused.

Her phone buzzed with a text from Mac: *I'm sorry. We should talk about this.*

She turned her phone face-down on the passenger seat and started the car. Right now, she needed to think. About Jason's threat. About Mac's interference. About what it meant that even as angry as she was, part of her was touched that he'd tried to help.

Most of all, she needed to figure out what to do next. Because one thing was crystal clear—Jason wasn't going to back down. And now he would be playing dirty.

But first, she had patients to care for. The rest would have to wait. The morning fog hung thick over the island as she drove to her first appointment.

After her first two visits, Kelsey pulled up to Truman's cottage, fatigue weighing on her shoulders. Her earlier anger had cooled to a dull simmer, but seeing Mac's Range Rover already parked in the driveway made her stomach knot. She sat for a moment, gathering her professional composure. Her patients deserved her focus, regardless of her personal turmoil.

The cottage door was ajar when she arrived, voices drifting from inside. She knocked lightly before entering, medical bag in hand.

"... should've told her from the beginning," Truman was saying, his voice carrying from the living room.

"I know that now," Mac's response was quieter, tinged with frustration.

Kelsey stepped into the doorway, clearing her throat. Both men looked up and their conversation halted abruptly. Mac stood by the window, arms crossed, while Truman occupied his usual armchair beside a stack of financial reports scattered on the side table.

"Good morning," she said with a professional formality. "How are we feeling today?"

Truman waved a weathered hand. "Come in, come in."

Kelsey managed a small smile and deliberately avoided Mac's gaze as she set her bag down. "Let's check your vitals, shall we?"

Mac shifted uncomfortably. "Kelsey, about this morning—"

"Not now," she said quietly, wrapping the blood pressure cuff around Truman's arm. "I'm working."

"Actually," Truman said, "I think now is exactly the right time. My grandson tells me he's made a proper mess of things."

"Grandad—"

"Hush, boy. Let me speak." Truman patted Kelsey's hand as she checked his pulse. "My dear, we owe you an explanation, and more importantly, an apology."

Kelsey kept her focus on her watch, counting beats. "Your pulse is strong today."

"And my head is clear enough to know when my family has overstepped." Truman fixed her with a direct gaze. "The situation with Jason Prescott isn't just about your boy, though God knows that's reason enough to be concerned."

Despite herself, Kelsey looked up. "What do you mean?"

Mac stepped forward. "Maritime Holdings is undergoing a major merger. They do about forty percent of the shipping business in and out of the New England ports. My grandfather and I own a significant position in the company."

"Twenty-two percent," Truman supplied.

"Jason sits on the board," Mac continued. "We started looking into his finances because of some unusual trading patterns before the merger announcement. This was before I knew about your custody situation."

Kelsey finished recording Truman's vitals, the numbers perfectly within normal range. "So, you were investigating him for the merger, and then decided to dig deeper when you learned about Noah?"

"Yes," Mac admitted. "I should have told you. Both times."

"Both times? So you admit there's a pattern here?" She pulled her stethoscope from her bag, the metal cold against her fingers.

"I do," Mac said and ran a hand through his hair. "And I'm sorry, Kelsey. I was trying to help, but I went about it all wrong."

"The boy's got the tactical sensitivity of a charging bull," Truman sighed. "Always has. Gets that from me, I'm afraid."

Kelsey positioned the stethoscope on Truman's chest. "Deep breath, please."

Truman complied, then said, "Jason Prescott is in serious financial trouble, lass. He's over-leveraged, and this merger is his Hail Mary pass. Which explains his sudden interest in Noah's inheritance."

She moved the stethoscope to listen to his lungs.

Truman continued. "The man's desperate, and desperate men are dangerous."

"This was important for us to know in this business deal, I thought having it would help you," Mac's voice was low, earnest. "I was wrong not to tell you before."

"Yes, you were." She stood, wrapping the stethoscope around her neck. "That's twice now you've decided what's best for me without asking. First the investigation into Margaret's will, now this."

"I know," Mac stepped closer. "But Kelsey, Jason threatened you this morning. Which just confirms our suspicions of him."

"That's not the point!" Her professional mask slipped. "The point is trust, Mac. How can I trust you when you keep making these unilateral decisions that affect my life? My son's life? How can I trust you when you apologize and say you won't do it again, but then you do?"

Truman cleared his throat. "If I may, Kelsey. My grandson has many virtues, but sometimes his desire to protect the people he cares about overrides his common sense."

"Is that supposed to make me feel better?" Kelsey turned back to her medical bag, organizing instruments to steady her hands.

"No," Truman said softly. "But perhaps it helps explain. He's not had many people to care about these past years."

"Grandad..." Mac shook his head at his grandfather, a warning tone in his voice. "I'm sorry, Kelsey. Truly."

Kelsey met his gaze, wanting to believe him but hesitant. "Twice is already a pattern, Mac."

"Then let me break it," he said quietly. "Let me earn back your trust."

Truman shifted in his chair, wincing slightly. "My blood pressure medicine is making my ankles swell again."

The professional in Kelsey couldn't ignore this. She knelt to examine his ankles, finding significant edema. "We should adjust your dosage. I'll call it in today."

"Before you go making medical decisions," Truman said with a twinkle in his eye, "perhaps you should consult with me first? Seeing as it's my body and all."

Kelsey sighed, a reluctant smile tugging at her lips despite herself. "That's different."

"Is it?" Truman raised a bushy eyebrow. "People who care sometimes overstep, lass. The trick is finding someone who learns from their mistakes."

She glanced at Mac, who was watching her with those intense dark eyes, genuine remorse evident in his expression.

"I appreciate the apology," she said finally. "Both of you. But I need time to think about this. And in the meantime," she turned fully to Mac, "no more investigations, no more surprise solutions. Nothing that concerns me or Noah without talking to me first."

"You have my word," Mac said solemnly.

"And what about Jason?" she asked. "What happens now?"

"That," said Truman, picking up one of the financial reports beside him, "depends entirely on what you want to happen next, because there's something else you should know about our position with Maritime Holdings."

"What's that?"

"With one phone call," Truman said, his Irish brogue thickening as it often did when he was passionate about something, "I can orchestrate a complete takeover during this merger."

Kelsey's pen stilled mid-sentence. "A takeover?"

"Aye." Truman's eyes gleamed with a shrewdness that belied his frail appearance. "The board doesn't know that Mac and I have been quietly acquiring shares through various subsidiaries. So, rather than twenty-two percent, we own more like seventy-four. Thus, rather than a merger, it will become a covert acquisition; we can absorb the Prescott stake in Maritime Holdings through a hostile takeover."

Mac moved closer to his grandfather. "If we execute this strategy, Jason Prescott will lose the bulk of his investments. He'll be financially ruined."

"Ruined?" Kelsey repeated, the word tasting sharp in her mouth.

Truman nodded. "He's heavily leveraged, borrowed against everything he owns. He's betting his entire financial future on this merger going through on terms favorable to him."

"And you can just..." Kelsey snapped her fingers, unable to articulate the enormity of what they were suggesting.

"That's about the size of it," Truman confirmed. "One call to our attorneys, and Jason Prescott would be finished in Boston financial circles."

Kelsey sank onto the ottoman, her mind racing. The casual way they discussed destroying someone's livelihood—even someone as despicable as Jason—made her head spin. This was a world she'd never navigated, where fortunes rose and fell on single decisions, where people wielded power she could barely comprehend.

"There is nothing," Truman continued, his voice hardening, "that would give me greater satisfaction than to see Jason Prescott brought low. Not just for what he's putting you through, lass, but for decades of underhanded dealings. The Prescotts have never played fair."

Kelsey looked between them, these two powerful men who had somehow become her allies. "Just like that? You could just ruin him?"

Mac nodded, his expression grim. "Just like that."

"But," Truman added, reaching for her hand, "I won't make that call without your consent. This affects you and Noah most directly. You should have a say."

Her laugh came out strangled.

"What's so funny?" Mac asked.

"Nothing's funny," she said, shaking her head. "It's just... I was just upset about you making decisions about my life without my input, and now you're offering me the devastating power to destroy someone else's."

She stood, pacing the small living room. Outside, birds called to each other. How surreal that such peaceful surroundings could contain such momentous decisions.

"I don't know how to think about this," she admitted. "I'm a healthcare provider. I help people. The idea of deliberately ruining someone, even Jason..."

"He wouldn't hesitate to do the same to you," Mac pointed out quietly. "He's trying to get custody of your son,"

"I know that." Kelsey stopped by the window, staring out at the water. "But if we destroy him financially, wouldn't that make him even more desperate to get control of Noah? For the inheritance?"

Truman nodded gravely. "It's possible. Desperate men are unpredictable."

"Then I can't." She closed her eyes briefly. "I can't endorse that. Not when Noah might end up bearing the consequences."

"Then what do you propose?" Mac asked.

Kelsey turned back to face them. "I don't know enough about high finance to propose anything. This is your world, not mine. I take care of people for a living—I help them heal, help them find comfort. I don't... I don't ruin people." She took a deep breath. "You need to do what's best for your business interests. I won't ask you to make decisions based on my situation."

Truman studied her, something like admiration in his eyes. "You're a remarkable woman, Kelsey York. Most people, given the chance to strike at their enemies, would take it."

"Maybe I'm just a coward," she said. "Maybe I'm afraid of the blowback."

"No," Truman shook his head. "It takes more courage to show restraint than to attack. I've lived long enough to know that."

Kelsey ran her fingers through her hair, overwhelmed. "This is so far beyond anything I'm equipped to handle. One minute I'm worried about Noah's science project, the next I'm discussing corporate takeovers and my enemy's downfall." She gathered her medical bag. "I need space to process this. All of it."

"Of course," Truman said gently. "Take whatever time you need."

As she headed for the door, Mac followed. "Kelsey, I know you're still angry with me, but—"

"I'm not angry anymore," she interrupted, surprising herself with the truth of it. "I'm... overwhelmed. There are forces at play here I never imagined, and my son is somehow caught in the middle of all of it. I need to figure out what's best for Noah."

"I'd like to help," Mac said softly.

She studied his face—the sincerity in his eyes, the tension in his jaw. Part of her wanted to lean on him, to accept his help navigating this unfamiliar terrain. But another part needed to stand on her own.

"I need to think," she repeated. "About everything. About what kind of person I want to be in all this."

Mac nodded, respecting her space. "Call me when you're ready to talk?"

"I will," she promised. As she walked to her car, the significance of what had just been offered settled on her shoulders. The power to crush an opponent with a single phone call—it was like something from a movie, not real life. Not her life.

Yet here she was, somehow entangled with people who could reshape financial landscape at will. People who were willing to use that power on her behalf. It was terrifying and humbling all at once.

As she drove away, Kelsey wondered what David would think of all this. Would he have wanted her to use the Costigans' power against his brother? Or would he have counseled restraint, as she had?

Either way, one thing was certain: her simple island life had become anything but simple.

Chapter 17

The evening air carried the scent of freshly turned soil and salt from the nearby cove. Kelsey perched on an overturned whiskey barrel that Amy had repurposed as a garden seat, watching her sister attack a particularly stubborn root with a pickaxe. The determined swing of the tool sent soil flying. Her little terrier was happily running around, getting his snowy white feet plastered with dirt.

"I still can't believe they just offered to destroy him," Kelsey said, twisting the stem of her wineglass between her fingers. "Like they were deciding what to have for dinner."

Amy paused to wipe sweat from her brow with the back of her gardening glove, leaving a streak of dirt across her forehead. "The ultra-wealthy live in a different universe than the rest of us." She leaned on the pickaxe handle. "Pass me that wine, would you?"

Kelsey reached for the bottle nestled among Amy's garden tools and topped off her sister's glass. The late-evening sun flickered across the garden beds Amy had been rehabilitating for months. Behind them, the vacant old mansion's windows caught the fading light, making them glow like watchful eyes.

"What exactly did the old man say again?" Amy asked, then took a generous sip.

"Something about controlling shares they've been secretly acquiring." Kelsey shook her head. "I don't understand the mechanics of it, but the outcome would be Jason's financial ruin."

Amy whistled low. "And they were just going to do this for you? No strings attached?"

"That's what they said." Kelsey stared toward the mansion. "It's like they have this biblical power to smite people. And they're just sitting on it, waiting for the right moment."

"Or the right person," Amy pointed out, returning to her digging. The pickaxe hit something solid, and she grunted with effort. "The stump of whatever was planted here goes down to China, I swear."

Kelsey set her wine aside and stood. "Want me to take a turn?"

"Nah, I've almost got it. Just needed to vent." Amy paused, leaning on the handle again. "So what are you going to do? Let them unleash financial Armageddon on Jason Prescott?"

"I told them no," Kelsey admitted. "It just felt wrong somehow. Like it would be stooping to their level."

"Their level being wealth and power?" Amy's tone was teasing, but her eyes were thoughtful.

"You know what I mean. Crushing people, even terrible people like Jason."

Amy attacked the stump again, loosening more earth around it. "Have you considered that if they did this, it wouldn't really be you doing it?"

"What do you mean?"

"I mean," Amy paused, "that Mac and Truman would be the ones making the call. They'd be the ones initiating the takeover. For their own business."

"They'd be doing it because of me," Kelsey countered.

"Maybe partly." Amy set the pickaxe down and crouched to tug at the stump. "But they clearly have their own history with the Prescotts. Their own scores to settle."

Kelsey helped her sister pull, feeling the wood begin to give way. "That doesn't make it right."

"No, but it also means it's not entirely on your conscience." With a final heave, they freed the gnarled stump, falling backward from the effort. Amy laughed, raising her dirt-covered hands in triumph. "Victory!"

Kelsey smiled despite herself and retrieved their wine glasses from where they'd set them. She handed Amy hers, and they clinked them together in celebration. "To conquering stubborn obstacles."

Amy settled onto a nearby garden bench. "If Mac and Truman did ruin Jason..."

"Yes?"

"What happens when Mac sails away? When Truman..." Amy gestured in the direction of the old man's cottage on the other side of the estate. "When he's gone?"

Kelsey's stomach tightened. "What do you mean?"

"I mean," Amy said carefully, "that their protection is temporary. Mac's made it clear to you he's leaving once his grandfather passes. If they destroy Jason now, who's going to protect you when they're gone? The Prescotts have been in Boston society for generations. Even if Jason's broke, he still has connections, influence. You'd be facing a vengeful man with even more reason to go after Noah's inheritance—but alone, this time."

The realization hit Kelsey like a punch. "I hadn't thought of it that way. But you're right. It would just postpone the problem, maybe even make it worse."

"Not to mention," Amy added, "if Mac is truly going to sail away and leave all this behind, what's to stop him from using this takeover power for himself? They both care about you, sure, but business is business."

"I don't think they'd do that," Kelsey said, though a seed of doubt had been planted.

Amy shrugged. "Maybe not. But my point is, any solution that depends on their continued protection is temporary at best."

They sat in silence for a moment, the crickets beginning their evening chorus around them. Amy brushed dirt from her jeans and stood to retrieve her tools.

"You know what you need?" she said suddenly. "A permanent solution. Something that doesn't depend on Mac or Truman to stick around."

"And what would that be?" Kelsey asked, helping her gather the garden implements scattered over the ground.

"I have no idea." Amy grinned. "But that's what sisters and wine are for. To figure these things out together."

As they walked back toward Amy's cottage, Kelsey glanced over her shoulder at the massive silhouette of the mansion against the darkening sky. Its empty windows watched them, keeping century-old secrets in its silent halls.

The island suddenly felt smaller. Its boundaries confined more than protected, the surrounding ocean less a buffer against the outside world than a keeper of the island's own dark history and the mournful ghosts that still kept watch.

"I still think it's weird how much Truman's wife wanted this place," Amy said, following her gaze. "What could have happened here that made her so determined to keep it empty?"

"I don't know. But maybe her dementia had a part in it after all?"

Amy gestured toward the overgrown gardens she'd been working to restore. "This place has such potential for use. It's just a shame to leave it. I wonder what will happen to it after he dies?"

Kelsey rolled her eyes, she'd heard her sister's ideas on this place so many times that it was old news, but she still couldn't suppress a shiver as they passed a particularly tangled section of garden that hadn't yet been cleared. Something about the dense undergrowth seemed almost deliberately concealing.

"Come on," Amy said, looping her arm through Kelsey's. "Let's finish this wine inside where it's warmer. And we can strategize about how to keep Noah without relying on billionaire ex-boyfriends."

"He's not my ex," Kelsey protested automatically. "He's not even my boyfriend."

Amy's laugh echoed across the garden. "Keep telling yourself that, sis. Keep telling yourself that."

As they walked away, Kelsey caught a glimpse of Amy's little dog with a bone in its mouth. Clearly, she'd been digging in the dirt near a corner of the garden, revealing the edge of something pale and curved beneath the earth.

More roots for Amy to tend to for certain.

Kelsey smoothed the front of her emerald silk dress, checking her reflection one last time. The elegant boat neck flattered her collarbone, and the skirt floated just at her knees   formal enough for a supposed board-of-directors event, but comfortable enough for the real celebration to follow.

Her phone buzzed with a text from Mac: *On my way. Grandad's ready and excited.*

She smiled despite herself. They'd been texting constantly since Wednesday, finalizing party details while carefully avoiding deeper subjects. Their messages remained cordial and focused—who was bringing what, when guests should arrive, how to ensure Truman wouldn't suspect anything. A fragile peace treaty conducted through emojis and short sentences.

The crunch of tires on gravel announced Mac's arrival. Through the window, she watched him emerge from his Range Rover looking devastatingly handsome in a charcoal suit that fit his broad shoulders perfectly. He'd even added a tie, navy blue with silver flecks that caught the early evening light.

When she opened the door, his gaze traveled the length of her dress and lingered appreciatively. "You look beautiful," he said simply.

"Thank you," she replied, grabbing her wrap and small purse.

The drive to Truman's cottage was a short one, filled with last-minute details.

"Johnson's handling the caterers," Mac said, then turned onto the narrow lane leading to his grandfather's place. "Eleanor insisted on bringing her famous coconut cake, though, so I made room for it on the dessert table."

"Smart move. I've tasted that cake—it's worth rearranging a party for."

Mac's smile was quick but genuine. "Fireworks are set for nine thirty. The company assured me everything's ready to go."

Truman was waiting on his front porch when they arrived, leaning on his cane but dressed impeccably in a tailored navy suit that hung on his diminished frame but still held an undeniable elegance. A white pocket square and polished shoes completed the look.

"Look at you two," he called as they approached. "Giving an old man hope for the next generation."

"You're looking rather dashing yourself," Kelsey said, accepting his kiss on her cheek.

"This old thing?" Truman brushed nonexistent lint from his lapel. "Had it since '92. Still fits, though the tailor had to take it in a bit. Apparently dying makes you skinny."

"Grandad," Mac's tone was warning but affectionate.

"Just stating facts, boy." Truman allowed himself to be helped into the front seat of the Range Rover. "Now, what's this about a dedication ceremony? Seems like a lot of fuss."

"The board wants to recognize your contributions to the island," Mac explained smoothly while sliding behind the wheel. "You've done a lot for the community over the years."

"Hmph. Just good business sense. Take care of the people, they take care of you."

Kelsey turned slightly in her seat. "Everyone's excited to honor you. It means a lot to the island."

Truman harrumphed again, but she caught the pleased glimmer in his eyes.

As they neared Mac's house, he suddenly patted his pockets. His performance was convincing enough that Kelsey almost believed his dismay.

"Everything okay?" she asked on cue.

"My wallet," Mac said, turning onto his driveway. "I must have left it at home when I changed. Would you mind if we stop for a minute? I need it for the donation they're asking for tonight."

"Always asking for money, these things," Truman grumbled good-naturedly. "Fine, but make it quick. I'd like to get there before I croak."

Mac parked in front of his house, which sat in apparent darkness. "Won't take long. Why don't you both come in? No sense sitting in the car."

Kelsey helped Truman by supporting his elbow as they walked toward the front door. Mac went ahead, unlocking it and stepping inside first.

When Truman crossed the threshold, the lights blazed on and a chorus of voices shouted, "SURPRISE!"

Truman stumbled backward slightly, clutching Kelsey's arm. For a terrifying moment, she feared they'd given him a heart attack. Then his face split into a smile of pure delight.

"You crafty devils," he laughed. Tears sprang to his eyes as he looked around at the crowd filling Mac's spacious living room. "You got me, you really got me!"

The room was transformed. Twinkle lights draped from every surface, flowers adorned every table, and a banner reading *Happy 95th Birthday Truman!* stretched across the far wall. Dozens of familiar faces beamed at them—shopkeepers, fishermen, nurses from the clinic, and many of the older residents who had known Truman for decades. To Kelsey it looked as though most of the population of Widow's Point was there.

Eleanor Thompson stepped forward first, her oxygen concentrator slung over her shoulder. "Happy birthday, you old scoundrel," she said, patting his cheek affectionately.

A line quickly formed. Each guest wanted to personally greet the guest of honor. Mac slipped beside Kelsey as they watched Truman soak in the attention, laughing and clasping hands with each well-wisher.

"You did good," she said softly. "Look how happy he is."

"We did good," Mac corrected, his hand briefly touching the small of her back. "Couldn't have pulled it off without you."

The evening flowed beautifully. The caterers kept glasses filled and platters circulating. Musicians played in the corner—a local trio whose gentle jazz created the perfect backdrop for conversation. Truman held court from a comfortable chair near the fireplace, receiving guests and telling stories that grew more colorful with each glass of whiskey.

Kelsey found herself drawn into conversations with islanders she rarely saw outside the clinic, discovering new facets of the community she'd come to love. Throughout the evening, she was aware of Mac circulating among the guests, the perfect host, but his eyes frequently found hers across the room.

Around nine, Mac appeared at her elbow as she chatted with Ruth. "Almost time for fireworks," he murmured. "Would you mind helping me get everyone outside?"

Together, they guided the partygoers onto Mac's expansive deck and the lawn beyond, where blankets had been spread and chairs arranged facing the cove. Truman was given a place of honor in the center, a plush chair with a clear view of the water.

Mac stood behind his grandfather, one hand resting on the old man's shoulder. "If I could have everyone's attention," he called, voice carrying across the gathered crowd.

The conversations quieted as all eyes turned to him.

"First, thank you all for coming tonight. It means the world to my grandfather—and to me—to see how many lives he's touched." Mac's voice carried emotion Kelsey rarely heard from him. "For those who don't know, my grandfather started with nothing but determination and a beat-up fishing boat. He built a shipping empire, yes, but more importantly, he built relationships. He taught me that success isn't measured by what you have, but by what you give."

Truman reached up to pat Mac's hand, visibly moved.

"Grandad, you've given me everything—a home, a purpose, a moral compass that sometimes I've ignored but never forgotten." Light laughter rippled through the crowd. "Tonight is our small way of saying thank you for ninety-five remarkable years. We love you."

Applause broke out, along with a few whistles. Truman waved them off, but his eyes glistened.

"Now," Mac continued, checking his watch, "if you'll direct your attention to the cove, we have one more surprise."

The first firework shot into the sky, exploding in a shower of gold that reflected off the dark water. More followed—red, blue, green—painting the night with ephemeral fire. The crowd oohed and aahed as the display grew more elaborate.

Kelsey found herself drifting to the edge of the deck, slightly removed from the crush of people. The cool evening air carried the scent of salt and gunpowder, an oddly compelling mixture.

She felt rather than saw Mac approach until his presence was warm beside her. "Beautiful, isn't it?" she murmured, eyes on the sky.

"Yes," he answered, but when she glanced over, he was fixated on her, not the fireworks.

The next explosion illuminated his face—strong jawline, those intense blue eyes. The moment stretched between them, charged with everything they hadn't said over the past days.

"Kelsey," he began. His voice was barely audible over the whistling rockets. "I—"

His hand found hers in the darkness between them, fingers intertwining. Another burst of light painted them in momentary gold, then blue, then red.

The fireworks reached their crescendo, multiple shells exploding simultaneously in a kaleidoscope of color. In that brilliant moment, Mac turned to her fully, and his free hand came up to cup her cheek.

"May I?" he whispered.

Her answer was to rise onto her toes to meet him halfway. It was the ghost of a kiss, only the few nearest atoms of their lips brushing in the air between them that tasted like whiskey and promise. Before their kiss could deepen, a particularly spectacular burst illuminated them fully, followed by a chorus of cheers and whistles that Kelsey initially attributed to the fireworks. Mac's arm wrapped around her waist and he pulled her closer.

Then she registered Truman's distinctive voice rising above the others: "That's my boy!"

They broke apart to find many of the party guests applauding their way, with good-natured enthusiasm. Truman was beaming from his chair and raised his whiskey glass in salute.

Kelsey felt heat flood her cheeks, but Mac merely laughed and kept his arm firmly around her waist as he raised his free hand in acknowledgment of the crowd's approval.

"Well," she murmured, "small towns..."

Mac smiled down at her, visible even in the dim light between fireworks. "Any regrets?"

The final barrage of rockets soared skyward, filling the night with cascading light and thunderous applause. Kelsey leaned into Mac's solid warmth and watched the spectacle with a curious sense of rightness.

"Not one," she said, and meant it.

The last of the guests departed just after midnight, leaving a wake of empty glasses and the lingering scent of perfume mixed with whiskey. Kelsey helped Amy gather Truman's gifts while Mac tipped the departing caterers.

"Best party I've had since VE Day," Truman declared, his voice raspy from hours of storytelling and laughter. Despite his insistence that he wasn't tired, his eyelids drooped heavily.

"Let's get you home, old man," Mac said fondly, then helped his grandfather to his feet by his elbow.

"I can still outlast you youngsters," Truman protested. He immediately yawned widely. "Just... perhaps not tonight."

The four of them made their way to Mac's Range Rover, Amy and Kelsey flanking Truman while Mac carried the gifts. The drive back would be a short loop—Kelsey's cottage first, then Amy's, and finally Truman's.

"Did you see Eleanor's face when Joe started dancing?" Amy asked from the back seat, where she sat beside Truman. "I thought she was going to faint from shock."

"Joe Martin always could cut a rug," Truman replied. "Even with that new hip of his."

Kelsey smiled, watching the moonlight play across the coastal road as Mac drove. His hand rested on the console between them, and she found herself wanting to reach for it, to maintain the connection they'd forged during the fireworks. Instead, she kept her hands folded in her lap, quiet in the intimate confines of the car.

"I think everyone had a wonderful time," she said. "You're well-loved, Truman."

"Bah," the old man waved dismissively, but his pleased expression belied his gruff response. "They just came for the free food."

Mac turned onto the lane leading to Kelsey's cottage. As they rounded the final bend, the official markings of a sheriff's department cruiser in their headlights cut through the night. A uniformed deputy stood on her front porch, holding a large manila envelope.

"What on earth?" Amy murmured from the backseat.

Kelsey's heart lurched sickeningly. "Noah," she whispered, fumbling with her seatbelt before Mac had fully stopped the car. "Something's happened to Noah."

She was out of the vehicle before it came to a complete stop, stumbling slightly on the gravel as she ran toward the deputy.

"Ms. York?" the deputy asked. His expression was carefully neutral.

"Yes," she gasped. "Is it Noah? Has there been an accident?"

The deputy shook his head. "No ma'am, nothing like that. I'm here to serve you with these papers." He held out the manila envelope. "I'm required to deliver these personally and confirm receipt."

Relief washed through her, quickly followed by confusion. "Papers? What papers?"

"Court order, ma'am. That's all I know."

With trembling fingers, Kelsey tore open the envelope, vaguely aware of Mac approaching behind her. In the harsh porch light, the legal letterhead swam before her eyes until she forced herself to focus.

EMERGENCY ORDER OF TEMPORARY CUSTODY, the heading read. As she scanned the document, certain phrases leapt out: *granted to Margaret Prescott... immediate effect... pending further hearing... concerns regarding maternal fitness*.

"No," she whispered, her voice breaking on the word. "No, this can't be right."

She fumbled through the remaining papers and found a stack of photographs paper-clipped together.

Photographs that made her stomach lurch. There she was with Mac on her front porch, on the boat, and walking along the shore. Others of her and Noah coming home after dark, a pizza box in her hand, another speaking to Noah with a cross expression on her face while Noah stood before her with his head bowed.

The images blurred as tears flooded her eyes. "They've been watching us? Taking pictures of us?"

Mac's hand touched her shoulder. "Kelsey, what is it? What's happening?"

She thrust the papers at him, unable to speak as the full horror of the situation crashed over her. They had Noah. They had taken custody of her son while she was celebrating, drinking champagne, almost kissing Mac under the fireworks. Her knees buckled.

"They took him," she choked out, sinking to the porch steps. "They took my son."

The world tilted crazily, and all sounds became distant and distorted. She heard Mac's voice, sharp with fury, demanding answers from the deputy. Amy's gasp of horror. Truman's Irish curse cutting through the night air.

"On what grounds?" Mac was clutching the papers in his white-knuckled grip. "This is outrageous!"

The deputy shifted uncomfortably. "Sir, I'm just delivering the papers. You'll need to take this up with the court."

A strange keening sound filled the air—it took Kelsey a moment to realize it was coming from her own throat. The photographs slipped from her fingers and scattered across the porch like fallen leaves.

"Noah," she moaned, curling forward as physical pain lanced through her chest. "My baby... they took my baby..."

Mac was on his knees beside her, his arm around her shoulders, saying something she couldn't process. Amy's face appeared before her, pale and frightened in the porch light.

The world contracted to a single point of agony—Noah was gone. Those bastards.

She needed to get him back.

Without thinking, she broke away from her sister and Mac and ran to her car. She slammed the driver's door and stomped on the gas, revving the engine as it turned on. She would not stop driving until she got to Boston. Until she stormed onto the front steps of the Prescott mansion and took her son back even if she went to prison for trying.

Beside her, the passenger door opened and Mac slid in beside her. He leaned over to place his hands on hers as she slammed the gear into reverse.

"Whoa there, Kelsey. Let's think this through. Plus, you're about to crash into my car and Truman is in there..."

Then the driver's side door opened, and Amy leaned in. Mac pushed the ignition button to shut the engine off. Amy wrapped her arms around her, and then the tears came.

The next thing Kelsey knew, she was on Truman's couch, a blanket draped over her legs, Mac's arm solid around her shoulders. The transition was jarring—she had no memory of leaving her car, of being driven here. The cottage was warm, lamps casting a gentle glow that did nothing to dispel the cold horror in her chest.

"... called Sandra," Amy was saying from somewhere nearby. "She'll be on the first ferry in the morning."

"Did you get through to the Prescott house?" Mac's voice rumbled against Kelsey's side.

"Straight to voicemail," Amy replied, her voice tight with anger. "I left a message that would make a sailor blush."

Truman sat in his armchair, looking every minute of his ninety-five years but with fire in his eyes. "This is dirty, even for the Prescotts," he said.

"It looks like I abandoned my son to have an affair." Kelsey's voice was a hollow whisper. She became fully present again, the fog of shock receding enough for raw pain to flood in. "That's exactly what they wanted it to look like. That's why they were photographing us. And then they struck when Noah was already physically with them." A fresh wave of anguish washed over her. "He must be so scared. Does he think I know? That I let this happen?"

"No," Amy said firmly, kneeling before her sister. "Noah knows you would never abandon him. Never."

"He's just a little boy," Kelsey whispered. Tears streamed down her face. "He thinks he's coming home tomorrow."

Mac's arm tightened around her. "We're going to fix this," he said, his voice low and fierce. "I promise you, Kelsey. Whatever it takes."

Kelsey looked up at him, seeing the determination in his eyes, the same expression Truman wore. For the first time since the envelope was placed in her hands, a small flicker of hope kindled in her chest. She had powerful allies at her disposal.

"How?" she asked, her voice steadier than she felt.

"By any means necessary," Truman said gravely from his chair. "Any means necessary."

Chapter 18

The night aide, Mrs. Henley, had arrived shortly after they'd settled at Truman's, and her familiar presence was a small comfort in the chaos. With practiced efficiency, she'd prepared Truman's evening medication and gently but firmly steered him toward his bedroom despite his protests.

"I'm perfectly capable of staying up during a crisis," Truman grumbled, though the exhaustion etched in the lines of his face belied his words.

"You'll be more help tomorrow if you rest tonight," Mrs. Henley replied, a statement that brooked no argument. She'd been managing Truman's care long enough to know which battles to fight.

Mac stood in the doorway of his grandfather's room, watching as the old man settled reluctantly beneath the covers. "We'll be back first thing," he promised. "Johnson's contacting our attorneys now."

Truman's eyes, rheumy but sharp, fixed on him. "Don't let her be alone tonight, boy. I'd hate to see her try to take them on alone."

"I won't," Mac replied quietly.

Now, as he guided his Range Rover along the darkened coastal road, Mac glanced at the two women beside him. Amy sat in the back, her face drawn with worry as she stared out the window. Beside him, Kelsey was frighteningly still, her earlier collapse having given way to a hollow-eyed stoicism that concerned him even more.

They reached Amy's cottage first. Mac put the car in park but left the engine running.

"I'll come by in the morning. Let me know if you hear anything," Amy said, leaning forward to squeeze her sister's shoulder. When Kelsey didn't respond, Amy met Mac's eyes with a silently pleading expression.

"I've got her," he assured her quietly. "Try to get some sleep."

Amy nodded, though they all knew sleep would be elusive tonight. She slipped out of the car and hurried up the path to her door, turning to wave once before disappearing inside.

The drive to Kelsey's cottage took less than five minutes, but the silence stretched it into an eternity. Mac parked and came around to open Kelsey's door, offering his hand. She took it mechanically and allowed him to help her from the vehicle.

On the porch, she fumbled with her keys, dropping them twice before Mac gently took them from her trembling fingers. He unlocked the door and guided her inside, flipping on lights as they went.

The cottage felt wrong—too quiet, too empty without Noah's presence. Mac felt it immediately, and he saw from Kelsey's flinch that she did too.

"I'll make some tea," he said, just to break the silence.

Kelsey finally spoke, then, her voice paper-thin. "Will you stay? Please?"

"Of course," he answered without hesitation. "As long as you need me."

She nodded, then disappeared into the bathroom. Mac heard water running and moved to the kitchen to fill the kettle and search the cupboards for tea. He found a box of chamomile and set two mugs on the counter.

While the water heated, he sent Johnson a text update and requested that his assistant bring a change of clothes when they meet tomorrow. The reply came almost instantly—Johnson had already arranged it, along with a nine-a.m. meeting with their top attorneys.

When Kelsey emerged wearing flannel pajamas, her face scrubbed clean of makeup, she looked impossibly young and vulnerable. The kettle whistled, and Mac poured the steaming water over the tea bags.

"I have a sleeping pill," she said, her voice hollow. "I think I need it tonight."

Mac nodded. "I'll be here," he promised. "Go ahead and take it."

She disappeared into the bathroom again and returned with the pill in her palm. She took it with a sip of tea, then carried her mug toward the bedroom. At the doorway, she paused, looking back at him with an unspoken question.

"I'll be on the couch," he said.

She shook her head. "No, I... I don't want to be alone. Would you...?" She gestured toward the bed.

"Of course." He followed her into the bedroom.

They settled into an awkward dance—Kelsey sliding beneath the covers while Mac removed his shoes and jacket, debating whether to keep his dress shirt and slacks on before deciding it would be ridiculous to sleep fully clothed. He stripped down to his undershirt and boxers, then carefully slipped under the covers beside her, leaving a distance between them that Kelsey could fill if she wanted.

Kelsey closed that distance immediately. She turned to press herself against his side, her head finding the hollow of his shoulder as if it belonged there. Her body trembled with suppressed sobs.

Mac pulled her closer. "We're going to get him back," he said, the only thing he could think to say. "I swear to you, Kelsey. Whatever it takes."

She nodded against his chest, tears dampening his shirt. "I can feel the pill starting to work," she murmured. "Don't leave, okay?"

"I won't," he vowed, stroking her hair gently. "I'm right here."

Her breathing gradually slowed and deepened as the medication took effect. Even in sleep, her body remained tense, and small tremors ran through her occasionally. Mac held her, one hand continuing its soothing rhythm through her hair, and stared at the ceiling.

How had he come to this moment? Six months ago, he'd been in Singapore, selling his company worth billions. Minimal attachments, maximum freedom, his focus entirely on relinquishing any connections. Exactly as he wanted it.

After Marlene died, Mac had sworn never to make himself that vulnerable again. Never to let someone become so essential to his happiness that they could destroy him with their absence.

Yet here he was, lying in Kelsey's bed, his heart racing with fury at what had been done to her and her son, his mind already calculating exactly how much of his considerable fortune and influence he would spend to make it right.

The answer, he realized with a mixture of wonder and terror, was all of it. Every penny, every favor, every resource at his disposal.

When had it happened? When had this woman and her son become more important than his carefully constructed independence?

Perhaps it had started that first day, when she'd turned those ice-blue eyes on him at the pile-up. Or maybe during her visits to his grandfather's cottage, her gentle competence as she tended to Truman. Or was it seeing her with Noah, their bond so genuine it made his chest ache with something like envy?

Whenever it had begun, he knew with absolute certainty there was no going back. The thought should have terrified him, it did terrify him, but lying here with her nestled against him, the fear seemed distant and academic.

Tomorrow, he would mobilize every resource at his command. The Prescotts had money and social standing, yes, but they had no idea what they'd provoked. His grandfather hadn't built an empire by playing nice, and Mac hadn't expanded it by being squeamish.

Let the Prescotts see what happened when they threatened what belonged to him.

His train of thought jarred him. Kelsey didn't belong to him. Noah wasn't his son.

Yet the fierce possessiveness he felt was undeniable. Somehow, without his permission, these two had become his to protect, his to defend. His family.

The realization should have sent him running for the door. Instead, he tightened his arms around Kelsey's sleeping form and made silent promises to her and her son. Promises that scared him with their intensity, their lack of conditions or limits.

Outside the window, the first hint of dawn lightened the sky. Mac watched it grow while he worked through their approach and contingencies.

By the time Kelsey stirred in his arms, he had the beginnings of a plan.

She would need to agree to them, of course.

Truman's cottage felt crowded with bodies and tension. Mac leaned against the mantelpiece while Kelsey sat rigid on the edge of the sofa, her fingers twisting together in her lap. Amy perched beside her, one hand on her sister's shoulder. Johnson stood in the corner like a sentinel, his tablet at the ready, while Sandra Mitchell and Mac's attorney, Harrison Wells, occupied the armchairs opposite Truman.

The old man looked worse than Mac had seen him in weeks. His skin had a grayish cast, and his breathing came in shallow rasps despite the oxygen cannula. Yet his eyes remained sharp, following every word exchanged with hawkish intensity.

"So let me understand this correctly," Sandra was saying, her reading glasses perched on the end of her nose as she examined the court order. "They're claiming that Kelsey is an unfit mother because she's allegedly engaged in a series of... indiscretions?"

"That's the gist of it," Harrison confirmed. "The photographs were presented as evidence of moral turpitude and neglectful parenting."

"It's ridiculous," Amy burst out. "Kelsey's the most devoted mother I've ever seen."

"Unfortunately," Harrison continued, his tone measured, "the Prescotts have painted it as Kelsey prioritizing a new relationship over her child's welfare. To not return Noah as planned at the end of vacation was justified as 'preventing further emotional harm and instability.'"

Mac watched Kelsey flinch at the words, her knuckles whitening as her hands clenched.

"It's a temporary order," Sandra reminded them. "We can fight this at the full hearing."

"When?" Kelsey asked, her voice barely above a whisper.

Sandra hesitated. "The judge set it for three weeks from now."

"Three weeks!" Kelsey's composure cracked. "Noah will be terrified for three weeks?"

"We can try to move it up," Harrison offered, "but given Judge Harmon's relationship with the Prescott family—"

"He'll drag his feet," Mac finished flatly.

"What are our options?" Amy demanded. "There has to be something we can do."

Harrison and Sandra exchanged a look that made Mac's stomach sink. "We can file a counter-motion," Harrison began carefully. "Present evidence of Kelsey's fitness as a parent. Character witnesses, testimony from Noah's teachers, medical records showing regular checkups..."

"But?" Mac prompted, recognizing the hesitation in the attorney's voice.

"But the Prescotts have already demonstrated their willingness to use their considerable resources and influence," Harrison admitted. "They'll hire expert witnesses, potentially even pay for psychological evaluations that favor their case."

"I hate to say it," Sandra added bluntly, "but they can outspend us in legal costs by a factor of ten. Kelsey and I have discussed this. They can drag this out, file motion after motion, request continuances."

"Until what?" Kelsey asked. "Until I'm bankrupt? Until Noah thinks I've abandoned him?"

"Until you give up," Mac said quietly. "That's their game. They know you can't match their war chest."

"This is just about money," Amy said bitterly. "They're using a child as a pawn in their sick game."

"It's about power," Truman rasped from his chair, speaking for the first time. All eyes turned to him. "Jason Prescott wants to prove that no one can stand against him."

A painful coughing fit seized the old man. Mac crossed quickly to his side, supporting his grandfather as his thin frame shook. Mrs. Henley appeared from the kitchen with a glass of water, her face creased with concern.

"You need to rest, Mr. Costigan," she murmured.

"I'll rest when I'm dead," Truman wheezed, waving her away. "And that'll be soon enough."

The blunt statement hung in the air, heavy and undeniable. Mac felt Kelsey's eyes on him, knew she was thinking of her promise to stay until the end. That end seemed closer today than it had last night.

"What do we do, then?" Kelsey asked, directing the question to the room at large. "How do I fight this?"

Harrison shifted uncomfortably. "Ms. York, the odds are not in your favor."

"There has to be a way," she insisted, looking from Harrison to Sandra. "I can't just give up."

"There is a way," Truman said. His voice was quiet but steadier now. "But it requires a sacrifice."

Mac looked sharply at his grandfather, recognizing the gleam in the old man's eye—the same calculating look he'd worn during high-stakes business negotiations.

"What sacrifice?" Kelsey asked.

Truman's gaze shifted to Mac, then back to Kelsey. "Marriage."

The word landed like a stone in still water, ripples of shock expanding outward through the room.

"Excuse me?" Amy was the first to recover.

"Marriage," Truman repeated. "To my grandson."

Mac felt all eyes turn to him, but he kept his own fixed on his grandfather. The old fox had been thinking along the same lines Mac had—the radical solution that had occurred to him last night.

"I don't understand," Kelsey said, though the slight tremor in her voice suggested perhaps she did.

"It's quite simple," Truman continued, gaining strength as he warmed to his subject. "As Kelsey York, you're a nurse with modest means fighting Boston aristocracy. As Kelsey MacCormack, you become part of a family with deeper pockets and a longer reach than the Prescotts."

"That's..." Sandra began, then paused, looking thoughtful. "Actually, that would significantly change the equation."

Harrison nodded slowly. "Marriage to Mac would give you immediate financial stability and negate the recent allegations—rather than neglecting Noah for an irresponsible tryst, you were pursuing a rounded family. The court would have to consider the changed circumstances."

"And Mac could petition to adopt Noah," Truman added. "Creating a legal relationship that would supersede Jason's connection."

"This is insane," Amy protested. "You can't just get married as a legal strategy!"

"People do it all the time," Harrison countered. "Green cards, tax benefits, inheritance rights."

"We're talking about my sister's life," Amy snapped. "Not some transaction."

Mac finally spoke, his voice quieter than he intended. "We also have another weapon."

Everyone turned to him.

"Do you mean...?" Kelsey asked.

Mac pushed away from the mantelpiece to stand before Truman's chair. "Grandad and I have the means to put Jason Prescott in a very uncomfortable financial position. To essentially destroy him, if we chose to."

"The takeover," Johnson murmured.

"Yes," Mac confirmed. "But as things stand, there would be nothing stopping him from coming after Noah again once he recovered. Nothing stopping him from using other tactics to gain control."

"But if you and I were married," Kelsey continued, "if you adopted Noah..."

"Then Jason would have to go through the both of us," Mac finished. "And more importantly, through the full might of our wealth while he had nothing left in his pockets."

"We'd put his balls in a vice," Truman said with grim satisfaction. "Cut off his financial oxygen until he begged for mercy."

"Jesus, Truman," Amy muttered, but there was a note of admiration in her voice.

"It's more than that," Truman continued, his voice growing weaker again. "If you two were married, it would make an old man very happy. My final wish, you might say."

Mac recognized the manipulation for what it was but couldn't begrudge his grandfather the attempt. Truman had been pushing them together since the beginning, convinced they were meant for each other despite Mac's insistence that he wasn't staying.

"This is..." Kelsey stood abruptly and paced to the window. "This is a lot to consider."

"It would be a business arrangement," Mac said, trying to give her an out to make it less overwhelming. "We could draw up terms, set conditions."

"A prenuptial agreement would be advisable," Harrison added.

"Nothing says romance like a prenup," Amy muttered.

"It's not about romance," Mac said, though something in him protested the statement. "It's about protecting Noah. And yes, about giving my grandfather peace of mind in his final days."

Truman coughed again, the sound wet and concerning. Mrs. Henley appeared with his medication, insisting he take it this time. The interruption gave Kelsey a moment to think with her back still to the room as she stared out at the ocean.

"The court would scrutinize your relationship carefully," Sandra warned. "If they suspect the marriage is solely for custody purposes, it would do more harm than good."

"Then we make them believe it's real," Mac said firmly. "We move in together. We present ourselves as a family."

"You'd have to sleep in the same room, display affection, care for Noah together," Harrison noted. "The Prescotts would almost certainly have you watched for any evidence the marriage is a sham."

"They've already proven they're not above spying," Amy agreed, gesturing to the file containing the damning photographs.

Kelsey returned to her seat with deliberate movements. "If we do this," she said, her voice steady now, "how quickly could we get Noah back?"

"We could file for an emergency review of the custody order based on changed circumstances," Sandra said. "With Mac as your husband and petitioning to adopt Noah, we'd have a strong case for immediate return while the full hearing proceeds."

"Days, not weeks?" Kelsey pressed.

"Potentially," Harrison nodded, clearing his throat, "Especially if we can get it before a different judge. One with an alliance to Mac."

"And the takeover?" Amy asked. "How does that factor in?"

"We hold it as leverage," Kelsey whispered with bright eyes, as if a lightbulb had gone off. "We let Jason know it's on the table if he doesn't back off. If he chooses to fight anyway, we execute."

"Scorched earth," Truman added with satisfaction.

Kelsey closed her eyes briefly. Then she looked at Mac, really looked at him, as if searching for something in his expression.

"I'll do it," Kelsey heard her own voice saying. "I'll marry you."

She stood up and faced Mac as Truman looked on. Both men were stunned into silence.

"I'll marry you. If you can help me to get my son back. I'll do anything, sign any agreement you want. I believe it'll work, I'm in."

The room was silent. Outside, the sound of the waves washing on the shore beneath them was the only sound.

Mac's expression changed a hundred times as he absorbed what Kelsey was saying. She stepped toward him.

Then Truman rasped from his chair.

Kelsey rushed to his side. "Are you all right? Do you need more medication?"

He squeezed her hand tightly and reached his other hand to Mac, who took it, his face stony. "I know I don't have much time left on this earth. So forgive me for putting this on you two. But nothing would make me happier than seeing you married. You may not realize it now, but you were meant for each other. Now make an old man's day, and let's do this now. I can die happy and you can get your boy back."

Truman leaned back on the cushions, his face gray. Kelsey turned on his oxygen and settled him so his head was elevated. Color returned to his face.

Comfortable, he pointed to Sandra. "How can we get this done today? I'd like for them to be married here if we can."

Everyone in the room exchanged glances. Mac's eyes never left Kelsey's face.

"There is no waiting period in Maine. As soon as they have the license, they can be married. If I remember correctly, Kelsey you'll need David's death certificate," Sandra answered.

"Perfect, I'll call Judge Thorton to come over and perform the ceremony. The town offices open at nine, why don't you kids get what you need to process the paperwork before then. Kelsey, I'm sure you want your sister here for it. The sooner we get this taken care of the sooner we can get the ball rolling."

Her feet felt like they were encased in cement. But Mac took her hand, and she felt her body follow him out the door. He guided her to his car, helped her into the passenger seat. They drove the distance to her cottage in silence.

Once inside, Mac spoke. "Go ahead and pack a bag for a few days, Kel. We'll head to Boston as soon as we're done. Get what you need for Noah too. I'm going to stop by my place and I'll do the same. I'll be back in half an hour?"

Kelsey went upstairs and gathered the needed paperwork for their marriage license. Everything felt surreal, and doubts streamed in her mind. *Get it together,* she told herself. Mac and Truman were giving her the tools she needed to fight the Prescotts and finally put Jason in his place.

Catching a glimpse of herself in the mirror, Kelsey decided to jump in the shower, hoping one of her special-occasion dresses would fit, Sandra's warning to make the marriage appear real resonating in her mind. She dressed quickly and put her hair up into a quick bun so loose tendrils fell curling around her face. She took precious moments to apply makeup and was pleasantly satisfied with the results.

The last twelve hours had ripped out her soul. Now, having the power to get him back gave her hope.

A door closed downstairs. "You ready?"

"Yes, coming." Kelsey replied and banged the two suitcases down the stairs. Mac came up to help her but stopped in his tracks at her appearance.

"Wow, Kelsey. You look beautiful."

She noticed that he had also showered and shaved. He wore an expensively cut suit without a tie and looked like a million bucks.

Mac loaded the suitcases in the back, and they left for the town offices.

They drove past the mansion on the winding driveway from Amy and Kelsey's cottages. Its window eyes tracked her movement, questioned her presence on this island of wealth and older secrets. The Georgian columns stood like sentinels, their rigid symmetry a silent rebuke to the messiness her life had become. It was if the mansion measured her and found her wanting. She shivered as they drove past.

"Mac, I was serious about signing anything you need me to. Like a prenup."

He nodded, his eyes locked on the road. "I know," was all he answered.

"Well, I think you should have something. I don't want to take advantage of you any more than I already am."

"I'm not worried about it."

"But—"

"You won't Kelsey." Mac turned to her, his fingers touching her knee. "If it bothers you, we'll come up with something. But I'm not worried about it today. I'm sure Harrison will have a heart attack, but I'm not concerned."

Soon, they were pulling into the three-space parking lot to the town offices. Kelsey hesitated as Mac opened the door for her. "Are you sure this is what you want?" she asked him, sliding off the seat to stand close to him.

He chucked her chin. "It solves a multitude of problems. And it gives Grandad his dying wish."

"What about you?"

"My plans haven't changed, if that's what you're asking. For me, putting Jason Prescott into a world of hurt? That's something I am going to enjoy immensely."

He took her elbow and guided her into the office.

The fluorescent lights hummed overhead, making everything feel even more surreal. The clerk looked up, recognition crossing her face. Everyone knew everyone on the island. By sunset, the whole town would know about their marriage, if not by noon. It would help sell their story, Kelsey realized. Small towns loved romance.

"Ms. York?" The clerk's voice pulled her back. "I need your signature here."

As she signed, she caught Mac watching her with an unreadable expression. He'd been so quick to agree to this plan, to offer himself as a solution. But what was he really thinking? His plans to leave, his trip, weren't changing. He'd made that clear.

An image of David's face entered her mind, their wedding, how happy they'd been. She wondered what he would think of her now, marrying a man she didn't love and didn't really know only to have the ammunition she needed to fight his family? It was for Noah, all for Noah, truly she believed David would understand. But he would also want her to be happy.

The clerk stamped their license with a heavy thunk that made Kelsey jump. "Congratulations," she said, sliding the paper across the counter.

Mac took the license, and his hand found the small of Kelsey's back as they walked out. The familiar gesture felt different now, felt weighted with their impending vows.

In the car, Mac cleared his throat. "We can still—"

"Don't," Kelsey interrupted softly. "Don't give me an out. I want Noah home."

"Yeah." His knuckles whitened on the steering wheel. "Grandad would never forgive me."

They drove in silence, the license lying between them like a promise or a threat—Kelsey wasn't sure which. But as they turned onto the coastal road leading to Truman's, she felt a strange sense of peace settle over her. Whatever came next, at least she wasn't facing it alone.

Chapter 19

Kelsey gripped Mac's hand as they approached Truman's cottage for the second time that day. The afternoon sun cast a golden glow over the weathered shingles, the ocean beyond sparkling as if nothing momentous were about to happen. As if her entire life weren't about to change with a few simple words and a signature.

"You're sure about this?" Mac asked quietly, pausing at the bottom of the porch steps.

She looked up at him. His casual elegance somehow made him even more handsome.

"I'm sure about getting Noah back," she answered honestly. "The rest... we'll figure out as we go."

He nodded, and his thumb brushed across her knuckles. "One step at a time."

Inside, the cottage had transformed. The morning's atmosphere of crisis and strategy had given way to something unexpectedly festive. Flowers adorned the mantle and side tables—arrangements of white roses and blue hydrangeas that Amy must have sourced from the island's only florist. Soft music played from the speaker system, and sunlight streamed through the windows that Mrs. Henley had clearly just cleaned.

"There they are!" Amy called, emerging from the kitchen with a champagne flute in hand. She'd changed into a pale blue dress that complemented her dark hair and had applied makeup—something she rarely bothered with. "The bride and groom!"

The words sent a jolt through Kelsey's chest. Bride. Groom. This was really happening.

"Where's Grandad?" Mac asked, scanning the room.

"Mrs. Henley's helping him get ready," Amy replied. "He insisted on wearing his good suit. Oh! I almost forgot—" She thrust her glass into Mac's hand and disappeared into the kitchen, returning moments later with a small bouquet of white roses tied with a blue ribbon. "For you, sis."

Kelsey took the flowers, emotion welling unexpectedly. "Amy, you didn't have to..."

"Yes, I did," her sister replied firmly. "If you're getting married—even for practical reasons—you're doing it properly. And I'm including this in the photo album I'll be making for Noah to help him understand."

The thought of Noah, confused and frightened at the Prescotts', made Kelsey's throat tighten. "Thank you," she managed.

A door opened down the hallway, and Mrs. Henley appeared, guiding Truman. The old man looked remarkably improved from that morning—still frail, still attached to his portable oxygen, but his color was better, his eyes bright with anticipation. He'd dressed in a gray suit that hung loosely on his diminished frame, a blue pocket square adding a touch of color.

"There she is," Truman said, his voice stronger than it had been all day. "My granddaughter-to-be."

The words, spoken with such warmth and certainty, made Kelsey's eyes sting. She crossed to him and bent to kiss his papery cheek. "You look very handsome, Truman."

"Had to make an effort for my grandson's wedding day," he replied with a wink. "Never thought I'd live to see it."

Mac joined them, resting a hand on his grandfather's shoulder. "Don't start getting emotional on me, old man. You'll ruin your reputation."

Truman harrumphed, but his eyes glistened suspiciously. "I have something for you two," he said, reaching into his jacket pocket with trembling fingers. "Been holding onto these, hoping for the right moment."

He withdrew a small velvet pouch and tipped its contents into his palm. Two gold bands gleamed against his wrinkled skin—one larger, one delicate and feminine, a diamond and emerald glinting in the light.

"These were mine and Eleanor's," he explained, his voice roughening. "Had them polished and refurbished. We can get them sized if they don't fit."

Mac stared at the rings. "Grandad... I don't know what to say."

"Say you'll take them," Truman replied simply. "Nothing would make me happier than seeing them worn again, by two people I love."

The sentiment hung in the air and threatened to crack Kelsey's carefully maintained composure. This was supposed to be a business arrangement, a strategic alliance—not this intimate family moment that made her heart ache with its bittersweetness.

"We'd be honored," Mac said finally, his voice unusually husky as he took the rings.

A knock at the door interrupted the moment. Mrs. Henley opened it to admit Judge Thorton, a tall man with silver hair and kind eyes whom Kelsey recognized from town events. He carried a leather portfolio and wore a formal suit that suggested he took this impromptu ceremony seriously.

"Mac, Kelsey," he greeted them with a nod. "Truman explained the situation. I must say, this is the most romantic shotgun wedding I've ever been asked to perform."

Mac huffed a laugh. "Thanks for coming on such short notice, Judge."

"For Truman Costigan? I'd have swum across the bay if necessary." The judge glanced out the window at the perfect blue sky beyond. "Seems a shame to waste such a beautiful afternoon. Shall we do this outside?"

"Excellent idea," Truman agreed. "The deck has the best view on the whole island."

With gentle efficiency, Mrs. Henley helped guide Truman outside while Amy fluttered around Kelsey, straightening her dress—a simple ivory sheath she'd found in the back of her closet—and tucking a stray curl behind her ear.

"You look beautiful," Amy whispered, giving Kelsey's hand a squeeze. "Are you okay?"

"I'm fine," Kelsey replied automatically, then amended, "I'm getting through it."

Amy studied her face. "You know, I think you could actually be happy with him. He looks at you like—"

"Please don't," Kelsey cut her off gently. "Let's just get through today."

Her sister nodded. "One step at a time."

The deck had been transformed as well, with more flowers in ceramic pots and a white runner leading to the railing that overlooked the ocean. Mrs. Henley had positioned Truman's chair at an angle that allowed him to observe the ceremony while taking in the spectacular view. The afternoon sun cast everything in that special golden light photographers called "magic hour," turning the ordinary into something enchanted.

Judge Thorton took his position at the railing, opening his portfolio on a small table someone had thoughtfully placed there. "Shall we begin?"

Mac extended his hand to Kelsey with a question in his eyes. She took it, surprising herself with how steady her own fingers felt. They walked together down the makeshift aisle and stopped before the judge with the vast expanse of ocean at their backs.

"We are gathered here today," Judge Thorton began, his voice carrying on the salt-tinged breeze, "to join Preston MacCormack and Kelsey York in matrimony."

The traditional words washed over Kelsey, familiar from her own wedding with David, yet utterly surreal in this context. She studied Mac's profile as the judge spoke of commitment and partnership, of facing life's challenges together. His jaw was set in that determined line she'd come to recognize, his eyes focused on the judge with the same intensity he brought to everything.

"Mac and Kelsey have chosen to exchange traditional vows," the judge continued. "Mac... Preston, if you would repeat after me..."

Mac turned to face her fully, taking both her hands in his. His eyes, that impossible shade of blue, locked onto hers with an expression she couldn't quite decipher.

"I, Preston MacCormack, take you, Kelsey York, to be my wife," he repeated, his voice clear and steady. "To have and to hold from this day forward, for better, for worse, for richer, for poorer, in sickness and in health, to love and to cherish, until death do us part."

The sincerity in his tone caught her off guard. He wasn't simply reciting words; he was making a promise. A promise she knew, intellectually, was part of their arrangement. Yet, in this moment, with the sun warming her skin and the ocean stretching endlessly behind him, it felt like something more.

"Kelsey," Judge Thorton prompted gently. "Please repeat after me."

She took a steadying breath. "I, Kelsey, take you, Preston Mac-Cormack, to be my husband." The words felt simultaneously familiar and foreign on her tongue, yet not as wrong as she'd feared. "To have and to hold from this day forward, for better, for worse, for richer, for poorer, in sickness and in health, to love and to cherish, until death do us part."

Mac's hands tightened slightly around hers. His eyes never left her face.

"The rings, please," Judge Thorton requested.

Amy stepped forward with Truman's rings on a small blue pillow she must have found in the cottage. Mac took the smaller band first and poised it at the tip of Kelsey's finger.

"With this ring, I thee wed," he said, the traditional phrase carrying on the breeze as he slid the gold band onto her finger. It fit perfectly, as if it had been made for her.

Kelsey took the larger ring. "With this ring, I thee wed," she echoed, sliding the band onto Mac's finger. The inherent intimacy of the act superseded her detachment to the wedding and her hands trembled slightly.

"By the power vested in me by the State of Maine," Judge Thorton declared, "I now pronounce you husband and wife." He smiled warmly. "Mac, you may kiss your bride."

Mac hesitated, the briefest pause that only Kelsey noticed. Then he leaned forward, one hand coming up to cradle her cheek as his lips met hers in a first kiss that was gentle but not perfunctory, lingering but not passionate. A perfect middle ground for their complicated situation.

Applause erupted from their small audience—Amy's enthusiastic clapping, Mrs. Henley's more subdued appreciation, and Truman's delighted "That's my boy!" cutting through it all.

When they parted, Kelsey was surprised to find herself slightly breathless. Mac's expression had softened, a smile playing at the corners of his mouth as he looked down at her.

"Hello, Mrs. MacCormack," he murmured, just for her ears.

The name sent a shiver through her that she attributed to the ocean breeze.

"Champagne!" Amy declared and hurried inside to retrieve the bottle she'd apparently been chilling. She returned with five glasses and the bottle, already working the cork loose. "We need to toast the newlyweds before you dash off to Boston!"

The cork popped with a festive sound, and Amy poured the golden liquid into their glasses. Mrs. Henley helped Truman with his, ensuring he received just a small amount in deference to his medication.

"To Mac and Kelsey," Judge Thorton said, raising his glass. "May your union bring you every happiness."

"And may it restore your family quickly," Amy added, raising her own glass toward her sister.

"To family," Truman said. His frail voice carried surprising weight. He looked at Mac and Kelsey with undisguised affection. "The one we choose and the one that chooses us."

They clinked glasses. The crystal produced a clear, bright sound that seemed to hang in the perfect afternoon air. Kelsey sipped the champagne, and the bubbles tickled her nose as she tried to process the fact that she was now, legally, Kelsey McCormack.

"I almost forgot!" Amy exclaimed, setting down her glass and hurrying inside again. She returned moments later with a small white bakery box. "It's not a wedding without cake!"

She opened the box to reveal a miniature wedding cake, elegantly decorated with white buttercream and tiny blue flowers that matched her bouquet. "Eleanor Thompson's coconut cake," she explained with a conspirator's smile. "I called in a special favor this morning."

"Amy," Kelsey said, touched by her sister's thoughtfulness despite the bizarre circumstances. "You didn't have to go to all this trouble."

"Of course I did," Amy replied firmly. "This may not be the wedding you dreamed of, but someday you'll tell Noah about it, and I want it to be a story worth telling."

Mac's hand found the small of Kelsey's back, a gesture that was becoming familiar. "She's right. Besides, I've never met a situation that wasn't improved by Eleanor's coconut cake."

Mrs. Henley produced plates and forks, and Amy ceremoniously cut two small slices for the bride and groom. There was laughter as Mac and Kelsey awkwardly managed to feed each other bites without making a mess—a wedding tradition Amy insisted upon.

"Pictures!" she declared next, producing her phone. "Stand together by the railing, with the ocean behind you."

Mac and Kelsey obliged, posing first formally side by side, then with his arm around her shoulders. Amy directed them through several poses, including one with Truman seated before them, his gnarled hands holding theirs and face alight with genuine joy.

"Time check," Mac said finally, glancing at his watch. "We should get on the road if we want to reach Boston before dark."

The reminder of their mission—of Noah waiting, confused and likely frightened—sobered the mood instantly. Kelsey's single-minded determination returned full force.

"Yes," she agreed, setting down her champagne glass. "We should go."

Truman reached for Mac's hand, pulling him down to whisper something in his ear that made Mac's expression soften. Then he turned to Kelsey and took her hand in his papery grip.

"Bring my great-grandson home," he said simply. "And then bring him to meet me."

"I will," Kelsey promised, bending to kiss his weathered cheek. "As soon as we get back."

"Take care of each other," Truman added. "That's what marriage is, when you strip away all the nonsense. Taking care of each other."

The sentiment, spoken with his ninety-five years of experience, lodged somewhere deep in Kelsey's chest. She nodded, not trusting herself to speak.

Amy hugged her fiercely. "Call me the minute you have him," she instructed. "I don't care what time it is."

"I will," Kelsey promised.

Final goodbyes were exchanged, and then she and Mac were walking down the cottage steps toward his Range Rover, husband and wife on their way to claim their child. The reality of what they'd done—the irrevocable step they'd taken—began to sink in as Mac held the passenger door open for her.

"Ready for this?" he asked quietly.

Kelsey looked down at the gold band on her finger, gleaming in the late afternoon sun. "For Noah? I'm ready for anything."

Mac nodded. "Then let's go get our son."

He closed her door and rounded the vehicle to the driver's side. As they pulled away from Truman's cottage, Kelsey caught a glimpse of Amy and Mrs. Henley helping Truman wave from the porch, the three of them silhouetted against the ocean backdrop like a scene from another life—one where this hasty marriage might have been the joyful celebration it appeared to be, rather than the tactical maneuver it actually was.

She touched the ring on her finger, turning it slightly, feeling a weight that hadn't been familiar for over seven years. Mrs. Mac-Cormack. The name that would open doors, command respect, and most importantly, bring Noah home. Whatever it cost her, whatever complications lay ahead, that was all that mattered now.

The Range Rover sliced through the afternoon stop-and-go traffic heading into Boston with minimal fuss. Mac adjusted his grip on the steering wheel, glancing at the navigation screen that estimated their arrival time at just under two hours. Traffic thinned slightly as they passed an accident on the shoulder, emergency lights flashing in his rearview mirror.

Beside him, Kelsey sat perfectly still, her gaze fixed on the road ahead, the bouquet Amy had given her resting in her lap. Her left hand lay on her thigh, the gold band catching the sunlight that streamed through the windshield. She hadn't said much since they'd left the island, the enormity of their situation seeming to settle more heavily with each passing mile.

Mac cleared his throat. "Traffic's not as bad as it could be. Mostly outbound at this time of day."

"That's good," Kelsey replied, her voice distant. She twisted the ring on her finger, as if testing its weight and presence.

"You okay?" Mac asked, though it was a ridiculous question. Of course she wasn't okay. Her son had been taken from her, and she'd just married a man she'd known for mere weeks and who's leaving soon for the middle of the ocean as a legal strategy.

She gave him a thin smile. "I'm focused on Noah. Everything else is just... background noise right now."

Mac nodded, understanding completely. "I need to make a call. Do you mind?"

"Go ahead."

He pressed a button on the steering wheel. "Call Judge Michaels."

The car's Bluetooth system dialed, and ringing filled the cabin. After three rings, a deep voice answered. "Mac? Twice in one month—to what do I owe the pleasure?"

"James," Mac said, his tone deliberately casual. "I need to cash in a favor."

A chuckle came through the speakers. "You never call just to chat anymore Mac. What's going on?"

Mac glanced at Kelsey, who was listening intently. "I got married today."

A startled pause. "You're joking."

"Not at all. Eloped this afternoon with the most incredible woman." Mac's eyes remained on the road, but he felt Kelsey's gaze shift to his profile.

"Well, I'll be damned," Judge Michaels said, genuine surprise in his voice. "Congratulations, I guess? This seems rather sudden. But I know Marlene would be happy for you."

"When you know, you know," Mac replied after a brief pause in which he had to brush off the last part of that statement. "But we've hit a complication. My wife's son was taken from her last night on an emergency custody order. Judge Harmon signed it."

"Ah," the understanding in the judge's voice was immediate. "Harmon's involved. Now I begin to see why you're calling me."

"We're petitioning to get the order reversed. We need to expedite the process and get an emergency hearing to review the custody situation. I'm also petitioning to adopt the boy."

"I see," Judge Michaels asked carefully, "were there any actual grounds for the emergency order? Abuse? Neglect?"

"None," Mac said firmly. "It's a power play by the mother's ex-brother-in-law. He wants control of the boy's inheritance. You remember Jason Prescott?"

"Jesus Mac," Judge Michaels swore under his breath. "And the boy's father?"

"Deceased," Mac answered. "Before the boy was born. David Prescott."

"I see." There was a pause, the sound of papers shuffling. "I can't promise anything, Mac but I'll see what I can do to expedite the process. Have your attorney send me the details and I'll make some calls."

"Thank you, James. I appreciate it."

"Don't thank me yet," the judge cautioned. "And Mac? I expect to meet this woman who convinced you to give up bachelorhood. Must be quite something."

Mac's eyes shifted to Kelsey. "She is. More than you know."

Kelsey looked at him and blushed before returning to staring out the windshield. "That seemed helpful."

After they disconnected, the GPS interrupted with mechanical precision: "In one mile, merge onto I-93 South."

"James owes me," Mac explained, merging smoothly into the left lane. "His son got into some trouble last year. I helped make it go away."

She gave him a sharp look. "Is that legal?"

A smile tugged at Mac's mouth. "Perfectly. I just funded the endowment for the community center the kid had vandalized and convinced them dropping charges would be better for everyone."

"Oh." Kelsey seemed to absorb this, then asked, "Do you have these kinds of connections throughout Boston?"

"Not throughout, but in the right places." He navigated around a slow-moving truck. "The Costigan and MacCormack names still carries weight in this city."

"The MacCormack name." She fingered the ring again. "I should probably start getting used to that."

The traffic slowed to a crawl as they approached a construction zone. Mac reached out to touch her hand. "Having second thoughts?"

"No," she answered quickly. "Not if it gets Noah back. It's just... a lot to process."

Mac nodded, understanding the sentiment all too well. This morning, he'd been a single and brooding widower with a broken heart. Now he was a married man, soon to be a stepfather if everything went according to plan. The speed of the transformation was dizzying, even for someone accustomed to making multi-million-dollar decisions on the fly.

Kelsey pulled her phone from her purse, swiping through it with a frown. "Still nothing from Noah."

"Try calling?" Mac suggested. "They might be screening texts."

She nodded, pressing the phone to her ear. After a moment, her face fell. "Voicemail again." She waited for the beep, then spoke, her voice softening. "Hi sweet pea, it's Mom. I just wanted to check in and see how you're doing. I miss you so much. I'll see you really soon, okay? I love you more than all the stars in the sky."

She ended the call, her eyes suspiciously bright. Mac reached across the console, squeezing her hand briefly before returning his to the wheel.

"Makes me wonder what sort of nonsense they are filling him with," she said.

"Traffic detected ahead," the GPS announced suddenly. "Alternate route suggested."

"Accept," Mac responded, and the screen adjusted, showing a new path through the city. "Kids are resilient," Mac offered, though he had little experience to base this on and thought better of saying it immediately after.

"They shouldn't have to be," she replied, a flash of anger breaking through her worry. "Not like this."

They fell silent as Mac navigated a complex interchange, following the GPS's instructions through an unfamiliar neighborhood of Boston. When they emerged back onto a main thoroughfare, Kelsey spoke again.

"We should talk about how to handle this with Noah."

"The marriage, you mean?"

She nodded. "He knows you as his friend and neighbor. Now suddenly you'll be his stepfather? It's a lot for a seven-year-old."

"We can take it slow," Mac suggested, braking as traffic came to another standstill. "For now, maybe we explain that we care about each other and decided to get married. The details can come later, when he's settled."

"And living arrangements?" Kelsey asked. "He'll have questions about where we're staying."

Mac considered this. "We could stay at the cottage together, at first. Let him get used to the idea. Then, after some time, maybe he could come see my house, *our* house, and pick out which room he'd like, decorate it how he wants. Ideally you would be all set up before I set sail."

A small, genuine smile touched Kelsey's lips. "He'd love that. He's been through a dinosaur phase, a space phase, and now he's obsessed with the ocean. Sharks, specifically."

"A boy after my own heart," Mac said, surprised by the warm feeling that spread through his chest at the thought. "We could do an ocean theme. I know some artists who could paint a mural if he'd like."

"In one-quarter mile, turn right onto Commonwealth Avenue," the GPS interrupted.

Kelsey adjusted her seatbelt, shifting to face Mac more directly. "We'll also have to talk with him about the adoption. How he feels about that."

The comment caught Mac off guard. He'd been thinking about the adoption purely in legal terms—a strategy to secure Noah's position. The emotional reality of it hadn't fully registered until now.

"I haven't spent much time around kids," he admitted. "How do you think he'll respond to that?"

Kelsey considered, her expression thoughtful. "I think we should give him choices where we can. Maybe about his name—whether he wants to take yours, keep Prescott, or hyphenate."

The thought of Noah carrying his name sent an unexpected surge of pride through Mac. Noah MacCormack. It sounded right in a way he hadn't anticipated, fulfilling a desire he hadn't known he harbored.

"You think he might want that?" Mac asked, his voice rougher than he intended. "My name?"

Kelsey studied him, seeming to notice something in his expression. "I think he might. Noah never knew David. He knows about him from pictures and stories, but he's never had a father figure in his daily life. He might welcome it, but he might need time."

"Turn right at the next intersection," the GPS instructed.

Mac made the turn. The idea that Noah thought about him, asked after him, warmed something deep in his chest. "I'd like that," he said finally. "If he wanted my name. But no pressure, of course. It's his choice."

Traffic opened up suddenly as they left the congested area behind, the Range Rover accelerating smoothly. Mac's phone rang through the car's speakers, interrupting their conversation. Harrison Wells's name flashed on the dashboard display.

"Harrison," Mac answered, exchanging a quick glance with Kelsey. "What have you got for us?"

"Good news," Harrison's voice filled the cabin. "Judge Michaels works fast. We've got an emergency hearing scheduled for nine a.m. tomorrow with Judge Rivera. She's already reviewing the case and, between us, she's not impressed with how this was handled."

Kelsey leaned forward, hope lighting her features. "Does that mean we can get Noah back this week?"

"Better than that," Harrison replied. "Judge Rivera has issued a stay on the current custody order, effective immediately. We'll have the sheriff accompany us tomorrow morning to enforce it if necessary."

Mac's jaw tightened. "What time tomorrow?"

"We'll meet the sheriff at the Prescott estate at eight thirty. I've already informed Jason Prescott's attorneys of the judge's decision."

"And their response?" Mac asked.

"Professional obfuscation," Harrison said dryly. "But they know they've been outmaneuvered, at least for now. They'll try again with a different strategy, but this round goes to us."

Kelsey pressed a hand to her mouth, tears welling in her eyes. "So we'll have Noah back tomorrow morning?"

"Yes, Mrs. MacCormack," Harrison confirmed, using her new name with deliberate emphasis. "Your son will be returned to your custody tomorrow morning."

The GPS interrupted: "Continue straight for two miles."

"Thank you, Harrison," Mac said, his voice steady despite the relief flooding through him. "We'll see you in the morning."

After disconnecting, Mac glanced at Kelsey, who was wiping tears from her cheeks with trembling fingers.

"One more night," she whispered. "Just one more night and he'll be home."

"We did it," Mac said, reaching for her hand. "Or rather, you did it. Agreeing to this crazy plan."

She interlaced her fingers with his, the gold bands on their hands touching. "We did it together. I couldn't have done this without you, Mac."

The GPS announced their impending arrival at the Prescott estate, but Mac was already changing their destination. "Take us to the Four Seasons, please," he instructed the system.

"Recalculating," the mechanical voice responded.

"The Four Seasons?" Kelsey questioned.

"We need a place to stay tonight," Mac explained. "And we might as well start our marriage in style."

A surprised laugh escaped her. "Our very unusual marriage."

"Unusual, yes," Mac agreed, his thumb brushing across her knuckles. "But effective. And besides, my grandfather hasn't looked that happy in years."

"Truman," Kelsey said with affection. "He's probably still gloating."

"Undoubtedly," Mac replied, a smile tugging at his lips. "He always did like to win."

"In five hundred feet, merge left," the GPS instructed.

Mac followed the direction, navigating through the thinning evening traffic with one hand, the other still holding Kelsey's. Tomorrow they would face the Prescotts, retrieve Noah, and begin the complicated process of becoming a family. But tonight, they would rest, regroup, and prepare for the battle ahead.

Noah MacCormack. The name echoed in his mind again, stirring something primal and protective he'd never experienced before.

Chapter 20

Kelsey stepped into the suite at the Four Seasons, her small overnight bag suddenly seeming shabby against the backdrop of cream-colored luxury. Floor-to-ceiling windows showcased the Boston skyline, city lights twinkling against the darkening sky. She set her bag down and wandered to the window, pressing her fingertips against the cool glass.

"Quite a view," she murmured, more to fill the silence than anything else.

Mac moved around the suite with comfortable familiarity, setting down his own leather duffel, checking the minibar, adjusting the thermostat. "I've stayed here a few times."

"Of course you have," Kelsey said with a small smile. She turned to face the room properly. She took in the king-sized bed dominating one side, the elegant sitting area with a sofa and armchairs, the discreet door that presumably led to a bathroom she was already certain would be obscenely luxurious.

"Are you hungry?" Mac asked, already slipping from his jacket and unbuttoning his shirt. "We could order room service."

Kelsey realized she hadn't eaten since the wedding cake, and even that had been just a few bites. "Starving, actually."

"Here," Mac handed her a leather-bound menu from the desk. Their fingers brushed, and she felt the unfamiliar coolness of his ring against her skin.

She sat on the edge of the sofa, studying the offerings while Mac hung his jacket carefully in the closet.

They had shared a bed last night, but this was different.

Now, they were husband and wife, at least on paper, and the formality of that commitment hung in the air between them.

"See anything you like?" Mac asked, and Kelsey startled slightly, realizing she'd been staring at the menu without reading it.

"The salmon sounds good," she managed. "And maybe a glass of wine."

"Let's make it a bottle," Mac suggested, loosening his cuffs. "I think we've earned it."

He placed their order over the phone—salmon for her, steak for him, a bottle of Pinot Noir, and a chocolate soufflé to share. His voice was steady, confident, the voice of a man accustomed to giving instructions and having them followed.

When he hung up, he turned to her with his familiar scowl back in place. "Thirty minutes. I'm going to change. You?"

Kelsey nodded. She retrieved her bag and retreated to the bathroom, which was indeed as luxurious as she'd expected—all marble and gleaming fixtures, with plush towels and high-end toiletries.

She splashed water on her face, then studied her reflection in the mirror. The woman who looked back at her seemed changed somehow, though she couldn't pinpoint exactly how. Same honey-brown hair, now slightly mussed from the day's events. Same blue eyes, perhaps a bit more shadowed than usual. Same mouth, set in a line of determination.

But now, for the first time in seven years, she wore a wedding ring—Eleanor Costigan's ring—and called herself Kelsey Mac-Cormack. Now she was a wife again, after years of being simply "Noah's mom."

"Get it together," she whispered to her reflection. "This is for Noah. Everything else is secondary."

She changed into the more comfortable clothes she'd packed—dark jeans and a soft blue sweater—and tried to tame her hair into something presentable. When she emerged from the bathroom, Mac had also changed into jeans and a gray henley that clung to his shoulders in a way that made her stomach flutter despite everything.

He looked up from his phone and smiled, a small genuine smile that reached his eyes, definitely more relaxed than he'd been moments ago. "Feel better?"

"Much," she admitted, setting her bag aside. "Washing your face can do wonders after a day like today."

"A day like today," Mac echoed with a soft laugh. "Not many of those in my experience."

"Mine neither," Kelsey said, settling onto the sofa.

"Just the one other, I assume?" Mac asked lightly, though something in his tone suggested genuine curiosity.

Kelsey nodded. "David and I had a big wedding. Two hundred guests, cathedral ceremony, the works. His family insisted. Even though they didn't approve, it was a social event."

"And what would you have wanted? If it had been entirely up to you?"

The question caught her off guard. "Something more intimate. Just family and close friends. Like ours." She smiled at the memory. "Though I did love my dress."

JEULIA HESSE

A knock at the door interrupted them. Mac answered it, admitting a server with a rolling cart. He set up their dinner on the small table near the windows, uncorked the wine with practiced efficiency, and slipped out after Mac signed the check.

"Shall we?" Mac gestured to the table, now set with covered plates and gleaming silverware.

Kelsey took her seat, the view of Boston spread out before her. The rich burgundy of the wine Mac poured caught the light.

"To new beginnings," he said, raising his glass.

"And to Noah coming home," she added, and touched her glass to his.

They ate in companionable silence for a few minutes. The food was surprisingly good despite Kelsey's distracted state. The wine warmed her from within, loosening some of the tension that had held her rigid all day.

"Tell me about Noah," Mac said suddenly. "I know him pretty well from our talks on the beach. He's curious and smart. What's he like when he's just being himself?"

Kelsey felt a smile spread across her face. "You're right, he's curious about everything. Always asking questions, wanting to know how things work. And he's sensitive—picks up on moods instantly, wants everyone to be happy."

"He gets that from his mother," Mac observed.

"Maybe," she acknowledged. "He's also stubborn. Once he gets an idea in his head, good luck changing his mind."

"That also sounds familiar," Mac said with a teasing note.

"Are you calling me stubborn, Mr. MacCormack?"

"Determined," he corrected smoothly. "Which is a quality I admire greatly."

Their eyes met across the table, and something flickered between them—the same chemistry that had drawn them together, now complicated by the gold bands on their fingers.

Mac cleared his throat. "More wine?"

"Please." She held out her glass, watching as he refilled it.

The conversation flowed more easily as they finished their meal, sharing stories about Noah, about Mac's travels, about the island they both loved. By the time they dug into the chocolate soufflé, Kelsey felt almost relaxed, the strange circumstances of their marriage temporarily receding in the face of good food, good wine, and good company.

Mac set down his dessert spoon and regarded her thoughtfully. "I've been thinking about what you said earlier, about your wedding to David."

"Oh?" Kelsey took a sip of wine.

"If we're going to do this—actually be married, I mean—perhaps we should have a proper wedding at some point. For Noah's sake, and for appearances."

The suggestion startled her. "You mean beyond what we did today?"

"Something more planned," Mac clarified. "Something Noah can be part of. On the island, over the summer. We could invite friends, make it a real celebration."

The image was unexpectedly appealing—standing with Mac and Noah on the beach, surrounded by people they cared about, making promises they intended to keep. But it also felt dangerous, like a step beyond their current arrangement into something more meaningful.

"That's... thoughtful," she said carefully. "But don't you think it might confuse Noah? And complicate things when..." She trailed off, unwilling to finish the sentence.

When you leave. When this ends. When we go back to being whatever we were before.

Mac's expression shuttered slightly. "Just a thought." He stood and gathered their empty plates. "No need to decide anything now."

Kelsey felt a pang of regret at having dampened his enthusiasm. "It's not that I'm opposed to the idea," she tried to explain. "It's just—"

"Complicated," he finished for her. "I know. This whole situation is complicated."

He moved to the entertainment system, tapping at a screen until soft music filled the room. The melodic strains of an old standard—Ella Fitzgerald—created a cocoon of warmth around them.

Mac extended his hand to her. "Dance with me?"

"What?" Kelsey blinked in surprise.

"Dance with me," he repeated. "We didn't have a first dance at our wedding."

The gesture was so unexpected, so disarmingly sweet, that Kelsey found herself rising from her chair and stepping into his arms without further thought. Mac's hand settled at the small of her back, the other clasping hers, holding it against his chest. She could feel his heartbeat beneath her palm, steady and strong.

They swayed together. The city lights twinkled beyond the windows as Ella sang about stars falling on Alabama. Kelsey allowed herself to relax into Mac's embrace, her head finding a natural resting place against his shoulder.

"This is nice," she murmured, and breathed in the scent of him—expensive cologne layered over something distinctly Mac.

"Mmm," he agreed, his chest rumbling beneath her cheek.

The song shifted to something slower, more intimate. Mac drew her closer, his hand splaying across her back. They weren't so much dancing now as holding each other and swaying gently to the music.

"Kelsey," Mac said, his voice low near her ear. "I know this isn't how either of us planned things, but I want you to know—I'm not sorry we did this."

She lifted her head to find his gaze intent on hers. "Neither am I," she admitted. "Not if it brings Noah home."

"Not just for Noah," Mac said, eyes darkening. His hand moved to cup her cheek, and his thumb brushed across her lower lip. "For this too."

He leaned down, closing the distance between them with deliberate slowness. It gave her every opportunity to pull away. But Kelsey found herself rising to meet him, her lips parting as they connected with his.

The kiss was different from their previous ones, at the fireworks and then at their wedding. Mac's hand cradled her face as if she were something precious. His touch was gentle but confident. Kelsey sighed against his mouth, her arms winding around his neck, drawing him closer.

When they separated, both slightly breathless, Mac rested his forehead against hers. "I've been wanting to do that since the day we met." His voice was rough. "That day at the wreck when you changed your blouse in the truck. I've thought about that every day since."

"Why didn't you?" Kelsey asked, her voice barely above a whisper.

"I wasn't sure if you wanted me to." His thumb traced the curve of her cheek. "If this was just business for you."

Kelsey shook her head slightly. "It's not just business. It's complicated. I mean Mac, we just started dating, if that's even what you want to call it... but it's not just business."

That seemed to be all the confirmation Mac needed. He kissed her again, deeper this time, one hand tangling in her hair as the other drew her flush against him. Kelsey responded in kind, her fingers finding the hem of his shirt, slipping beneath to touch warm skin.

They moved together toward the bed and discarded clothes along the way. There was a tenderness between them as Mac's hands mapped her body with reverent care, his eyes holding hers in the dim light of the suite.

"You're beautiful," he murmured while he pressed kisses along her collarbone. "So beautiful."

Kelsey felt herself blush under his attention, her own hands exploring the planes and angles of his body, his strong shoulders, firm chest, the dip of his spine. The gold band on his finger caught the light as his hand traced down her side, a visual reminder of the commitment they'd made, however pragmatic its origins.

Their lovemaking was slow, deliberate, charged with emotions neither of them seemed ready to name. Mac watched her face intently, learning her responses, adjusting to please her. Kelsey felt herself unraveling under his touch, all the stress and fear of the day transforming into something warm and bright that spread through her limbs.

When they finally came together, skin to skin with nothing between them, Kelsey felt tears prick behind her eyelids, not from sadness but from the overwhelming intensity of the connection. Mac kissed them away with movements gentle but insistent, bringing her to the edge and then following her over.

Afterward, he held her close, her head pillowed on his chest, his fingers tracing idle patterns on her bare shoulder. The city continued to glow beyond the windows, but Kelsey's world had narrowed to this bed, this man, this peace in the midst of chaos.

Mac's breath was warm against her hair. Eventually, his breathing deepened and his body relaxed into sleep. But Kelsey remained awake a little longer, listening to the steady beat of his heart beneath her ear, watching the city lights play across the ceiling.

Her last conscious thought before sleep claimed her was how strange life could be—how the worst day of her recent life had somehow led to this moment of unexpected comfort.

Chapter 21

The predawn light cast a glow over Boston's skyline, the same soft-edged dawn that had crept over the island every morning since Kelsey moved there. But here, the light rebounded off steel and glass, making the city glitter like a jewel box. Kelsey held her coffee mug in both hands and let the warmth seep into her palms as she stood by the floor-to-ceiling windows.

Noah would be waking soon. Did he have his favorite cereal for breakfast at the Prescotts'? Had he remembered to brush his teeth without being reminded? Was he scared, confused? Her chest tightened at the thought of her son thinking, even for a moment, that she had abandoned him. The whole situation was surreal, that they had come to this point was unthinkable just last year at this time.

The gold band on her finger caught the light as she raised the mug to her lips. Twenty-four hours ago, she'd been a single mother, widow, desperate and alone. Now she was married to a man whose quiet breathing she could still hear from the bedroom. The speed of the transformation made her head spin.

Behind her, the sheets rustled. Mac appeared in the doorway moments later, hair tousled from sleep, wearing only his pajama bottoms. She tried to not stare at his fit chest she'd used as a pillow last night.

His eyes found hers immediately, as if he'd been searching for her.

"You're up early." His voice was still rough with sleep.

"Couldn't stop thinking." She gestured toward the city with her mug. "Beautiful morning, though."

Mac crossed to her, his footsteps silent on the plush carpet. He stood beside her, close but not touching, both of them gazing out at the awakening city.

"What's on your mind?" he asked after a moment.

"Noah," she admitted, but it was of no surprise to either of them. "I'm worried about what they've told him. If he thinks..." Her voice caught. "If he thinks I gave him up."

Mac ran a hand through his hair. "You wouldn't ever. He knows you better than that."

"He's seven, Mac. Seven-year-olds don't have the most sophisticated understanding of court orders and custody arrangements." She set her mug down on a side table with perhaps more force than necessary. "What if they're telling him I don't want him? What if he believes them?"

"Hey." Mac's hand found her shoulder, and he turned her gently to face him. "Noah loves you. He knows who his mother is, who's always been there for him. That foundation doesn't crumble in a couple of days."

Kelsey wanted to believe that, needed to believe it. But the knot of fear in her stomach wouldn't ease. "What if he's scared? What if he was crying for me and they wouldn't let him call?"

"Then we deal with that today," Mac said firmly. "We get him back, we reassure him, we make things right."

Kelsey looked up at him, seeing the flash of conviction in his eyes. This man who had been a near-stranger a few weeks ago was now her husband, now fully invested in helping her retrieve her son. Their son.

She swallowed deeply.

"We should talk about how we're going to tell him. I don't want him to get involved in the adult drama surrounding this whole mess. But he needs to understand what is happening."

Mac nodded, moving to the coffee maker to pour himself a cup. He took it black. A detail she hadn't noticed about him, but it was now one of countless things she would need to learn about her new husband.

"What do you think is best?" he asked, returning to stand beside her.

"Honesty," Kelsey said without hesitation. "Noah does best with frankness. He doesn't need all the adult details or the legal jargon, but he needs the truth at a level he can understand."

"What would that look like?"

Kelsey considered, trying to frame the complexity of their situation in terms a seven-year-old could grasp. "We tell him that sometimes grown-ups get married quickly when they care about each other, like we do. That we were already friends who liked spending time together, and now we're a family. Also that being a family helped us to be allowed to see him again. For us to stay together."

Mac looked up at her, surprise turning into a smile at her words. He turned his face from hers for a moment to take a sip of his coffee.

"And what about his uncle and grandmother?"

"We will likely have to improvise a bit there; I'm not sure what they've told him. But we can start with the fact that they made a mistake, thought I wasn't taking good care of him, but the judge fixed it." She sighed. "We keep it simple, but true. And we give him plenty of space to ask questions, to express his feelings."

Mac appeared to absorb this, sipping his coffee thoughtfully. "I'll follow your lead on that. We're already friends, Noah and I. I'd like to build on that foundation."

"He likes you," Kelsey agreed. She felt a small easing of the tension in her shoulders. "He talks about you all the time, your beach walks, the things you teach him."

A small smile touched Mac's lips. "He's a great kid."

"He is." Kelsey was warmed by Mac's genuine affection for her son.

"What about the adoption?" Mac asked after a moment. "You mentioned he might want it, but how do we approach that subject?"

Kelsey settled onto the small sofa in the corner. Mac followed, sitting at the opposite end, giving her space while remaining connected. Another thing she was learning about him: how he seemed to intuit what she needed. A contrast to the gruff persona he shared with the outside world.

"Same approach," she said. "Slowly, with frankness. That if he wants, I'd like you to adopt him, which means legally becoming his dad. And remember, the most important thing is that we don't push."

"I wouldn't," Mac assured her. "This has to be his choice."

The words settled an uncertainty in Kelsey's chest. Mac understood that Noah's feelings mattered, that they couldn't simply reconfigure the boy's life without his consent, even if it was in his best interest.

"Thank you," she said quietly.

Mac tilted his head. "For what?"

"For caring about how Noah feels in all this. For recognizing that he's not just a legal pawn to be moved around."

Mac's expression softened. "Kelsey, I may not have much experience with kids, but I know what it's like to have decisions made for you. To feel powerless. My father made some decisions for me when I was young I could do nothing about—sending me away to a boarding school. Away from my family and friends, from the island." He paused, something vulnerable flickering across his features. "I wouldn't put Noah through that."

The sincerity in his voice touched her. It gave her hope that maybe, just maybe, they could make this complicated arrangement work.

"We should get ready," she said finally, glancing at the clock. "Harrison will be meeting us downstairs."

The hotel restaurant buzzed with early morning business meetings, the clink of silverware against china providing a soothing backdrop as Kelsey stirred her second cup of coffee. Across the table, Harrison arranged documents with methodical precision, his tailored suit and precisely knotted tie projecting exactly the image of legal authority they needed today.

"The sheriff will meet us at the estate at eight thirty," Harrison reminded, sliding a document across the polished table. "Judge Rivera was quite clear in her order. The Prescotts are to turn over Noah immediately, with all his personal belongings."

Kelsey scanned the court order, her eyes catching on phrases like *immediate return to maternal custody* and *pending full hearing*. The legal jargon blurred together, but the bottom line remained crystal clear: Noah was coming home today.

"They've been notified?" Mac asked, his voice steady beside her. He'd dressed in a charcoal suit that made him look every inch the powerful businessman. Kelsey had chosen a navy dress in an effort to appear more confident than she was. A subtle armor against whatever the Prescotts might throw at them.

Harrison nodded. "Their attorneys were informed last night. They'll have prepared the Prescotts for our arrival."

"What kind of resistance should we expect?" Mac's hand found hers under the table, a grounding touch.

"More obfuscation, delay tactics, possibly emotional manipulation." Harrison's expression remained neutral, but his eyes hardened. "They may try to upset Noah to make the transition more difficult."

"And if Jason gets confrontational?" Mac pressed.

Harrison closed his portfolio with a snap. "That's why we have the sheriff. This isn't a negotiation; it's a court order. They comply or face criminal consequences."

Kelsey took a deep breath, eager to feel her son in her arms again.

"Keep your focus on Noah. The legal team and sheriff will handle the Prescotts."

Mac's thumb traced circles on her palm, a silent reassurance. "We won't let them manipulate this further," he said. "Noah's coming home with us today. That's all that matters."

The drive to the Prescott estate passed in tense silence. Beside her, Mac spoke briefly on the phone with Johnson, confirming details for their return journey. Outside the car windows, Boston's elegant neighborhoods gave way to the even more exclusive enclaves of the wealthy, houses set far back from the road behind imposing gates and manicured hedges.

When they turned into a long, tree-lined drive, Kelsey's heart began to race. The Prescott mansion loomed ahead, a colonial revival masterpiece with white columns and perfect symmetry. A place of cold privilege that David had fled and where her son had been all but imprisoned.

"Ready?" Mac asked quietly as Harrison's car pulled up alongside theirs, followed by the sheriff's official vehicle.

Speechless, Kelsey nodded. There was little likelihood that she would have been able to pull this together on her own. This was all Mac's influence. In minutes, she would hold Noah again because of him.

They walked up the stone path together, the sheriff—a no-nonsense woman with a salt-and-pepper hair—leading the way. Harrison flanked Kelsey's other side, his portfolio clutched in steady hands.

The massive front door opened before they reached it. A stern-faced housekeeper assessed them with a flat expression.

"Mrs. Prescott is expecting you," she said, stepping back to admit them to a grand foyer with a sweeping staircase.

Margaret Prescott stood at the base of the stairs, her silver hair perfectly coiffed and her tailored pantsuit impeccable despite the early hour. She looked more frail than Kelsey remembered from their last encounter. The lines around her mouth were deeper, and her hands were slightly tremulous where they clutched a cane.

"Sheriff Daniels," Margaret acknowledged with a curt nod.

"Mrs. Prescott," the sheriff replied, "we're here to execute Judge Rivera's order in returning Noah Prescott to his mother's custody."

Margaret's eyes slid to Kelsey, then narrowed at the sight of Mac standing protectively beside her. "I've been informed of the situation."

Mac stiffened but chose to say nothing to the old woman. Noah was all that mattered now.

"Margaret, I'd just like to take Noah home," Kelsey said, keeping her voice even. "This must be very confusing for him."

"Jennifer is gathering his things," Margaret replied, making no move to usher them further into the house. "Jason's attorney advised us to comply, though we will be challenging this hasty decision."

The sheriff stepped forward. "Mrs. Prescott, I'll need to see the child immediately."

Margaret's lips thinned, but she turned toward the staircase. "Jennifer!" she called. "Bring Noah down, please."

A flurry of movement upstairs, and then Jennifer appeared at the top of the stairs, her delicate features pinched with worry. Behind her, small sneakers visible at shin level, was Noah.

"Mom?" His voice, uncertain and small, broke something inside Kelsey.

"I'm here, sweet pea," she called, stepping instinctively toward the stairs.

Noah darted around Jennifer and flew down the stairs with reckless abandon. Kelsey caught him at the bottom, his small body crashing into hers with the force of his need. She wrapped her arms around him and breathed in the familiar scent of his hair, his skin. His heart race against hers.

"I knew you'd come," he whispered against her neck, his voice wobbling. "I knew you wouldn't leave me."

"Never," Kelsey promised fiercely. Tears threatened despite her determination to stay composed. "I will never leave you."

Noah pulled back slightly, his eyes shining. He seemed both smaller and older somehow, the stress of the past days evident in the shadows beneath his eyes.

"Mac!" he exclaimed suddenly, noticing the man standing a respectful distance behind Kelsey. "You came too!"

"Of course I did, buddy," Mac said. His voice was gentler than Kelsey had ever heard it.

Jennifer descended the stairs, carrying Noah's backpack and his small suitcase. "I've packed all his things," she said quietly, her eyes not quite meeting Kelsey's.

"Thank you." Kelsey was genuinely grateful for Jennifer's consideration. The woman had always seemed out of place among the Prescotts, too kind for their cold world.

"Noah," Margaret said in her imperious tone, "come say good-bye to your grandmother properly."

Noah tensed in Kelsey's arms but dutifully extracted himself to approach Margaret. The older woman bent stiffly to embrace him, her movements formal rather than affectionate.

"Remember what we discussed," she murmured, just loud enough for Kelsey to hear. "About your future and responsibilities."

Kelsey's jaw tightened, but Harrison's warning echoed in her mind. Stay calm. Focus on Noah.

"Time to go, Noah," she said gently, extending her hand.

Noah had just reached for it when the sound of a door slamming echoed through the foyer. Heavy footsteps approached from a side hallway, and then Jason Prescott appeared, his face flushed with barely contained anger.

"What is this circus?" he demanded, glaring at the assembled group before his eyes landed on Mac. His expression shifted from anger to surprise. "MacCormack. What are you doing here?"

"Jason," Margaret warned, but her son ignored her.

"You think you've won?" Jason stepped closer to Kelsey and dropped his voice into a menacing growl. "This isn't over. Not by a long shot."

Mac slid smoothly between Jason and Kelsey. His posture was relaxed but imposing all the same. "Careful, Jason. There's a child present."

Noah pressed against Kelsey's side, his small body tense. She hugged him protectively to her.

"My nephew," Jason spat, "who you're manipulating for your own ends."

"That's enough, Mr. Prescott," the sheriff interjected, stepping forward. "We're here to execute a court order, not engage in family disputes."

Jason's eyes narrowed as he took in Kelsey's hand on Noah's shoulder and the gold band glinting on her finger. "So that's your play?" He laughed, a harsh sound devoid of humor. "A convenient marriage to the richest man on that godforsaken island?"

Kelsey felt Noah looking up at her, confusion evident in his expression. Before she could respond, Mac spoke, his voice dangerously soft.

"I'd choose your words very carefully, Jason."

Something in Mac's tone must have penetrated Jason's anger. He stepped back, straightening his tie with a jerky motion.

"This isn't over," he repeated, but the threat sounded hollow now. "We're just getting started."

"No, Jason," Mac said. "It is over. Noah is going home with his mother and me. If you value what's left of your assets, you'll accept that reality."

Comprehension slowly flickered across Jason's face, followed by a flash of fear.

He knew, Kelsey realized. He knew now that it was Mac looking into his finances, and not her. And with Mac's wealth, that was a much scarier prospect. The tables had just turned on him.

The knowledge that this man who had caused her and her son pain and stress for no reason except for his own personal gain was now afraid of what they may do to him in retaliation made her feel powerful. She held the cards now.

"We're leaving now," Kelsey said, giving Noah's shoulder a gentle squeeze. "Noah, do you have everything you need, honey?"

Noah nodded, pressing closer to her side. "Can we go home?"

"Yes, sweet pea. We're going home."

Jennifer stepped forward, offering the suitcase to Mac, who took it with a polite nod. "Take care, Noah," she said softly, tears in her eyes as she waved her hand to the child.

"Bye, Aunt Jennifer," Noah replied. He hesitated, then added, "Bye, Grandmother."

Margaret remained rigid by the staircase, her expression unreadable. She inclined her head slightly but said nothing as the sheriff ushered their group toward the door.

Outside, the morning air felt cleansing after the stifling atmosphere of the Prescott mansion. Noah walked between Kelsey and Mac, one hand clutching Kelsey's, the other Mac's. His gaze moving between them as if reassuring himself they were both real.

"I'll follow up with the court to confirm completion of the order," Harrison said as they reached the cars. "You should head home, get settled."

Kelsey nodded, gratitude welling within her. "Thank you, Harrison. For everything."

Mac helped Noah into the back seat of the Range Rover, buckling him in with careful attention while Kelsey settled beside her son. She couldn't bear to be separated from him by even the width of a car seat.

As Mac pulled away from the Prescott estate, Noah's small fingers found Kelsey's, intertwining with desperate need. "Mom," he whispered, "I was really scared."

"I know, baby," she murmured, pressing a kiss to his temple. "I was scared too. But I never stopped trying to get you back. Not for one minute."

Noah leaned against her, some of the tension visibly draining from his small frame. "They said you were too busy with Mac to take care of me anymore."

Anger flashed through Kelsey, white-hot and consuming, but she tamped it down. "That's not true, sweet pea. You are the most important person in my life. Always."

In the driver's seat, Mac was quiet. But his eyes met Kelsey's in the rearview mirror, steady and supportive.

"Mom?" Noah's voice was still small but also curious now. "Why did Uncle Jason say that about you and Mac? About you getting married?"

Kelsey took a deep breath, remembering their conversation from that morning. Honesty at a level he could understand.

"That's something we wanted to talk to you about, honey," she said gently. "Mac and I did get married yesterday. We care about each other very much, and we both care about you."

Noah's brow furrowed as he processed this information. "Like, married married? With rings and everything?"

"Yes," Kelsey confirmed, showing him her hand with the gold band. "With rings and everything."

Noah looked toward the front seat, where Mac's left hand was visible on the steering wheel and his own wedding band caught the light. "So... is Mac my dad now?"

Mac glanced in the rearview mirror again, his expression carefully neutral, waiting for Kelsey's lead.

"Mac is my husband," Kelsey explained, choosing her words carefully. "And if you're okay with it, he'd like to be a part of our family. We can talk more about what that means when we get home."

Noah's seven-year-old mind visibly worked through the implications. "Does this mean we're moving to Mac's big house? The one with the pool?"

A surprised laugh escaped Kelsey, and the tension broke slightly. "We haven't figured out all those details yet, sweetie. But yes, if you want to."

"Okay." Noah seemed satisfied with this answer for now. He leaned more heavily against Kelsey, fatigue evident in the droop of his shoulders. "I'm really tired, Mom."

"Then rest, baby." She stroked his hair and felt him relax against her. "We've got a long drive ahead. When you wake up, we'll be closer to home."

Noah's eyes fluttered closed, the emotional toll of the past days finally catching up to him. As his breathing deepened into sleep,

Kelsey continued to stroke his hair. She reassured herself with each rise and fall of his chest that he was here, he was safe, he was coming home.

Mac's eyes found hers again in the mirror, a silent question in their depths. She nodded, offering a small, genuine smile. They'd done it. The first, most crucial step was complete.

One step at a time, she reminded herself, watching the city give way to highway. They were a family now. Unconventional, unexpected, and formed in the crucible of crisis. But a family nonetheless.

And for today, that was enough.

Chapter 22

Mac steered the Range Rover down the familiar coastal road leading to Kelsey's cottage, hyper-aware of the two passengers who had dozed off in the back seat. Noah's head rested against his mother's shoulder, their matching honey-brown hair mingling where they leaned together. The boy had finally crashed from the adrenaline and fear of the past days about an hour into the drive.

The late afternoon sun glared through the windshield as Mac parked on the gravel drive. He turned off the engine, and the resulting sudden silence was too loud. For a moment, he simply sat and watched in the rearview mirror as Kelsey gently roused Noah.

"We're home, sweet pea," she murmured. Her voice contained a tenderness he'd never experienced from anyone.

Noah's eyes fluttered open, momentarily confused before recognition flooded his features. "Home," he said.

Mac stepped out and opened the rear door, reaching for Noah's bags. "I'll get the bags, buddy."

Noah nodded, rubbing sleep from his eyes as he clambered out. "Thanks, Mac." The simple phrase, so casually offered, caught Mac off guard. As if the boy had always expected Mac to be there to handle, handling such mundane tasks.

Inside, the cottage felt simultaneously welcoming and strange, familiar from his previous visits yet different now that he entered as Kelsey's husband rather than her... whatever he'd been before. Friend? Neighbor?

"I'm starving," Noah announced and dropped his backpack by the stairs. "Can we eat soon?"

Kelsey glanced at the empty refrigerator, a flash of guilt crossing her features. "I don't have much in the house."

Mac sensed an opportunity. "I could grab some pizzas. Let you two settle in."

"Pizza!" Noah's face lit up, the first genuine excitement Mac had seen since retrieving him from the Prescotts. "Can I have pineapple and ham on mine?"

Mac raised an eyebrow at Kelsey, who nodded. "Afraid so," she confirmed with a small smile. "He's one of those."

"Hey, pineapple on pizza is awesome." Noah dropped onto the sofa with the easy physical abandon of childhood. "Uncle Jason said it was an abom... abomi..."

"Abomination?" Mac supplied.

"Yeah. He wouldn't let me order it." Noah's expression clouded.

Kelsey's jaw tightened minutely, and Mac made a mental note to add extra pineapple to the order.

"I should get a change of clothes anyway," Mac added, feeling suddenly like an intruder in the domestic scene. "While I'm out."

Understanding flashed in Kelsey's eyes. She knew he was giving them space, mother and son time to reconnect without his awkward presence.

"Thanks," she said softly. "That would be great."

"So how was the beach trip?" Mac asked Noah, trying to normalize the conversation while he pulled up the pizza place's online menu.

Noah perked up. "We went to this really cool museum with all these pirate things! And Aunt Jennifer took me to look for shark teeth on the beach." He tilted his head. "Did you and Mom really get married while I was gone?"

The directness of the question, delivered with a child's unfiltered curiosity, made Mac hesitate. The gold band felt tight on his finger.

"We did," he confirmed, looking to Kelsey for guidance.

She settled beside Noah on the sofa. "We'll tell you all about it after you got settled, honey."

"Was there cake?" Noah asked pragmatically.

Mac laughed, and the tension eased from his shoulders. "There was. Your Aunt Amy made sure of it."

"Did you save me some?"

"I think there might be a piece in the fridge at your great-grandfather's house," Mac said.

"I have a great-grandfather?" Noah asked as Kelsey slipped onto the couch beside him.

Mac took the opportunity. "I'll call in that pizza." He pulled out his phone and stepped toward the door. "See you in a bit."

Outside in his car, Mac leaned his head against the steering wheel, exhaling slowly. The past few days had been a whirlwind of legal maneuvering, emotional declarations, and now... domesticity.

He was a husband. A stepfather. Words that hadn't existed in his vocabulary forty-eight hours ago.

After calling in an order for two pizzas, including a small ham and pineapple monstrosity for Noah, Mac drove toward his own house. The property sat quiet and imposing, the modern architecture a stark contrast to Kelsey's cozy cottage.

Inside, the space echoed with emptiness. He'd never bothered with a security system, as there was no need, nothing to steal.

He waded through the sleek, minimalist rooms to gather clothes and toiletries and mentally catalog what else he'd need for an extended stay at the cottage. They'd need to live together, the attorneys had emphasized. The Prescotts would be salivating over any evidence their marriage was a sham. The sheriff's intervention had gotten Noah back, but the custody battle was far from over.

The prospect of sharing Kelsey's bed every night sent heat coursing through him. That part would be no hardship. But the rest of the day-to-day reality of family life was uncharted territory.

Upstairs, Mac paused in the doorway of an unused bedroom. It could be Noah's, he realized. The room had good light, a view of the cove. He would like that, being able to watch for marine life from his window.

Mac tried to envision dinosaur wallpaper or space-themed decorations, things he vaguely remembered wanting as a child. But Noah preferred the ocean. Sharks. A marine biologist in the making, perhaps.

He wandered through the upper floor and saw the house through new eyes. No photographs on the walls, no mementos displayed on shelves. Kelsey would probably want to soften the modernity with her personal touches, as she had in the tiny cottage. Throw pillows. Family photos. The kind of homey clutter that made a house feel lived in.

A home.

He'd existed in this pristine space for years, leaving no mark, as if prepared to disappear at any moment. Which was exactly the plan.

In his closet, Mac pulled out a duffel bag and began filling it mechanically. Jeans. T-shirts. He could come back and get a change of clothes when he wanted, so, just enough for a few days.

He caught sight of himself in the mirror, the gold band glinting on his left hand as he reached for a sweater.

Married. To a woman with a child. Living in domestic harmony in a cottage by the sea.

It wasn't real, he reminded himself. Or rather, it was legally real but emotionally temporary. He was still leaving. The *Nereid* was ready, the maps prepared, the adventure planned. Once Truman passed and Noah's custody was secure, Mac would be gone. The endless horizon and solitude of the open ocean was his future, not family dinners and homework supervision.

Wasn't it?

Mac zipped the duffel with more force than necessary. He was helping Kelsey and Noah and fulfilling his grandfather's dying wish. That was all.

He locked up the house and tossed the duffel in his car.

As Mac drove back toward the cottage, the pizza boxes warm on the passenger seat, he realized he was nervous about all this. After all he'd done in his life, a seven-year-old boy made him anxious. He went over potential answers to questions he thought Noah would ask and vowed to stay casual, calm. Letting Kelsey take the lead when he didn't know what to say.

He was out of his depth, navigating unfamiliar waters without a chart. But for now, he had pizza with extra pineapple. And maybe that was a good place to start.

The savory aroma of pizza filled the cottage's small kitchen as Mac set the boxes on the table. Noah was already there, plate in hand, practically vibrating with anticipation.

"Did you get the pineapple?" he asked, bouncing on his toes to peer into the box Mac opened.

"Extra pineapple," Mac confirmed, revealing the pizza laden with golden chunks. "Just to make up for lost time."

Noah's face lit up. "Awesome!" He reached for a slice before Kelsey could even get plates distributed.

"Noah David," Kelsey admonished gently, "hands, please. And we sit before we eat."

"Sorry," Noah mumbled, darting to the sink to wash his hands. He then slid into his usual chair at the kitchen table.

Mac took the seat opposite while Kelsey glided with practiced efficiency, getting napkins, pouring drinks, and finally settling in her own chair.

"This is so good," Noah declared around a mouthful of pizza.

"Don't talk with your mouth full, honey," Kelsey reminded him, though her expression was indulgent.

Noah swallowed dramatically. "Sorry, Mom." Then, turning to Mac with solemn formality: "This pizza is excellent, thank you very much."

Mac couldn't help but laugh. "You're very welcome."

The tension in Mac's shoulders eased as the meal progressed. They were still the same people they'd been before, Kelsey with her quiet strength, Noah with his boundless energy and curiosity. The wedding rings and marriage license hadn't fundamentally altered who they were.

As Noah's initial hunger abated, his questions began. "So, are we going to live in Mac's house now that you guys are married?"

Kelsey glanced at Mac, a silent conversation passing between them.

"We could," Mac said carefully. "If that's something you both want. It would need some changes first, though. New furniture, maybe different colors. To make it feel like home. You would need to pick out your own room."

Noah's eyes widened. "I get to pick out my own room?"

"Absolutely. Any room you want, except mine. Ours," he corrected, glancing at Kelsey. "And we could decorate it however you like."

Noah seized the opportunity. "Could I have a TV in my room?"

Kelsey raised an eyebrow. "Noah..."

"Worth a shot," the boy shrugged, unrepentant. "What about sleepovers? My friend Tyler has a game room where they have sleepovers. Do you have a game room, Mac?"

"Not yet," Mac found himself saying. "But we could make one, I suppose."

Noah seemed to consider this seriously. "And the pool, can we use it whenever we want? Even at night?"

"The pool is heated," Mac added. "So it's usable most of the year."

"With supervision," Kelsey interjected.

"Cool!" Noah's excitement was palpable. "And what about the boat? Can we take it out any time we want? Remember you promised we'd go?"

Mac smiled, warmed by the boy's enthusiasm. "I did promise that, didn't I? We'll definitely do that soon."

"When can we move?" Noah pressed, reaching for another slice of pizza. "Tomorrow?"

Mac laughed. "Not quite that soon, buddy."

"But when it's ready, we'll live there?" Noah persisted.

Mac looked to Kelsey, who nodded slightly. "Yes," Mac confirmed. "When it's ready and you both want to, we'll live there."

Noah seemed satisfied with this answer, turning his attention back to his pizza. Mac caught Kelsey's eye across the table. Her grateful smile sent warmth spreading through his chest.

After dinner, as Kelsey gathered the plates, she glanced at her watch. "Noah, honey, it's getting late. Why don't you and Mac go for a quick walk before your bath? It's a school night, and we need to get you back into your routine."

Mac and Noah put on their coats and made their way down the path to their beach. The familiar location had Mac feeling at ease, and he and Noah slipped into their comfortable routine of looking for treasures washed up in the sand.

As they walked along, Noah's expression grew serious. "Mac, Mom says Mr. Costigan really sick. That he's going to die soon."

Mac was startled by the directness of the statement. "You know about things like that?"

"Yeah, Mom tells me. Everyone dies. You know that right, Mac?"

Of course Noah would have a different relationship with death than most children, growing up with a mother who worked in healthcare and discussed these matters openly.

"Yes," Mac said finally, his voice rougher than he intended. "He is very sick."

"That's sad," Noah said simply. "But Mom says it's okay to be sad when people die. She says it means we loved them a lot."

Mac's throat tightened unexpectedly. "Your mom is very wise."

"I'd like to see him. Do you think he'd want to meet me? Before he dies?" Noah asked, his innocent question landing like a punch to Mac's solar plexus.

"I know he would," Mac managed. He recalled Noah had been sound asleep the night Kelsey had brought him to Truman's emergency. "He's asked about you."

Noah nodded, satisfied with this answer. A piece of sea glass got his attention for a moment. Then, after a brief pause: "So, *are* you my dad now?"

Mac felt something lurch in his chest. "Technically, I'm your stepdad."

"Mom said you might adopt me," Noah continued, his gaze direct and unflinching. "What does that mean, exactly?"

Mac took a deep breath. "It means I would legally become your father. Your name could be Noah MacCormack, if you wanted. And no one could ever separate you from your mom or me."

"Would it make you my real dad, then?" Noah's small face was serious.

Mac leaned forward, choosing his words carefully. "I would be your real dad in all the ways that matter. I would be there for you and take care of you. What is mine becomes yours. But I would never try to replace David, your father. He'll always be part of who you are."

Noah considered this solemnly. "But you'd be my dad who's here?"

"Yes," Mac said. Emotion made his voice unsteady. "I would be your dad who's here."

"Would I call you Dad?" Noah's forehead creased in concentration.

"Only if you wanted to," Mac assured him. "You could keep calling me Mackie. Whatever feels right to you."

Noah was quiet for a long moment, his young face pensive. Then, with decisiveness he said, "I think I'd like to call you Dad."

Something shifted inside Mac's chest, a strange, terrifying, wonderful sensation. "I'd like that very much," he managed to say. "But only if you're completely sure."

"I'm sure," Noah said. With the natural physicality of children, he tucked his small hand into Mac's larger one.

Mac stared down at their joined hands, overwhelmed by the simple gesture. His thumb brushed against Noah's knuckles, and he marveled at how small they were, and how perfectly they fit within his palm.

Chapter 23

The morning sun filtered through the kitchen curtains as Kelsey juggled a travel mug of coffee and Noah's nearly forgotten lunch box. Mac stood at the counter, spreading peanut butter on bread with practiced movements.

"Noah! Five minutes!" Kelsey called up the stairs while reaching to take over the lunch making from Mac.

"I've got it," Mac said, slipping the sandwich into a bag. "You finish your coffee before it gets cold."

Kelsey paused, coffee halfway to her lips. "Thanks. I'm still not used to having help in the morning."

Mac glanced up with a half-smile. "I'm not sure making PB&J qualifies as real help."

The thunder of small feet on the stairs announced Noah's arrival. He skidded into the kitchen, backpack hanging off one shoulder, hair still damp from his shower.

"Mom! I can't find my permission slip for the aquarium field trip!" Noah's voice carried the urgent desperation of a panicked seven-year-old in the morning rush.

"Check your homework folder," Kelsey said, taking a quick sip of coffee. "The blue one."

"I did! It's not there!"

Mac zipped the lunch bag closed after adding some fruit and a granola bar. "Try the side pocket of your backpack. That's where it was yesterday when you showed it to me."

Noah's face brightened. He dropped his backpack to the floor and unzipped the side pocket. "Found it!"

"Shoes," Kelsey reminded him and checked her watch. "Quickly, please. We're running late."

"I'm ready, I'm ready," Noah insisted, though he was clearly not. He shoved his feet into untied sneakers while simultaneously trying to stuff the permission slip into his folder.

Mac knelt down. "Here, buddy. Let me tie those while you fix your papers."

Noah automatically extended his foot, and the unconscious trust in the gesture made something catch in Mac's chest. Two weeks of marriage, and already these small intimacies had become routine.

"What time's your first appointment?" Mac asked, double-knotting Noah's laces.

"Ten thirty. I have a staff meeting at the clinic before hitting the road." Kelsey gathered her nursing bag. "I'll be at Truman's around one. Should we still plan to meet for lunch?"

"Perfect. I'm heading over there now, but I'll stick around. And I can pick up lunch for all of us from the café with those turkey sandwiches he likes."

"Guys," Noah interrupted, "we're gonna be late!"

"Right you are, Captain," Mac said, rising to his feet. "Your chariot awaits."

Outside, they split up at the driveway. Mac leaned in to give Kelsey a quick kiss goodbye, a reflex that surprised them both and left a moment of startled silence between them.

"I'll see you at lunch," he recovered with an awkward half-wave.

"Bye, Mac!" Noah called, already climbing into Kelsey's car.

"Bye, buddy. Learn something amazing today, okay?"

Mac watched them pull away before climbing into his own truck. As he started the engine, he caught sight of his reflection in the rearview mirror. The man looking back at him seemed different somehow—less fed up with the human race, if that was possible. The realization was unsettling.

The island elementary school nestled against a grove of wind-bent pines, its playground equipment gleaming in the morning sun. Kelsey pulled into the drop-off lane, joining the small procession of cars.

"Do you have everything?" she asked as Noah gathered his things. "Lunch, homework, permission slip?"

"Yes, Mom," Noah sighed with the particular exasperation reserved for mothers who asked the same questions every morning.

"Alright, smart guy. Have a good day and have fun on the field trip. Mind your manners and listen to your teacher. Love you."

"Love you too." Noah leaned over for a quick kiss on her cheek before bounding out of the car, joining the stream of children flowing toward the entrance.

Kelsey watched until he disappeared inside then began to pull away. As she checked her mirrors, something caught her eye: a man standing across the street, partially obscured by a parked van.

He held what appeared to be a camera with a long lens, pointed in her direction.

She slowed, frowning. The man lowered the camera and turned away quickly.

Kelsey pulled the car over and rolled down her window. "Excuse me!" she called out. But the man was gone.

Kelsey sat there for a moment, hand tight on the steering wheel. A coincidence, surely. Just a tourist taking photos of the charming island school. Yet the prickle of unease remained as she pulled back into traffic and headed toward the clinic.

The morning passed in a blur of patient visits. Truman was her last stop before lunch, and she found herself looking forward to seeing both him and Mac for a midday break. The thought brought a small smile to her face as she gathered her supplies from the clinic storage room.

"Someone looks happy today," observed Rina, the receptionist. "Marriage suits you."

Kelsey felt her cheeks warm. "It's been an adjustment."

"Mac MacCormack," Rina sighed dramatically. "Half the island women have been trying to land him for years. You swoop in and snap him up in a month. It's not fair."

"Hardly swooped," Kelsey laughed. "More like stumbled."

"Well, the two of you make sense together," Rina said, handing her a stack of files. "And Noah seems to adore him, from what I hear. That's what matters."

"It is," Kelsey agreed. It surprised her how true the words felt.

She shouldered her bag and headed for the parking lot, mind already shifting to her next patient. This late in the morning, only a few staff cars remained in the back parking lot, as most of the team was out making home visits.

As Kelsey approached her vehicle, movement at the tree line caught her attention. A figure stepped between two parked cars, then quickly retreated when she turned.

The same man from the school.

This time, she was certain. Without hesitation, Kelsey changed direction, walking purposefully toward him.

"Hey!" she called out. "I need to speak with you!"

The man quickly fled between the trees. By the time Kelsey reached them, he was gone, leaving only the sound of breaking twigs and rustling leaves to mark his hasty retreat.

Kelsey stood at the edge of the woods, heart hammering. She pulled out her phone and hovered her thumb over the emergency call button. After a moment's hesitation, she dialed Mac instead.

"Hey," his voice came through after two rings. "I was just about to call you, I'm at Grandad's. He had a rough night apparently."

Kelsey swallowed, suddenly reluctant to voice her concerns. It sounded paranoid, even to her own ears. "Do you need me to come right now?"

"No, no. He's sleeping now. We should let him rest and then you can have a look at him when he wakes later. Are you all right? You sound tense."

"I'm fine," she said automatically, then remembered that Mac was in this too, now. "Actually... I think someone is following me and taking pictures. At Noah's school, and just now at the clinic."

The silence on the other end lasted just a beat too long.

"What did he look like?" Mac asked finally, his tone carefully neutral.

"Tall, thin. Dark jacket. Baseball cap pulled low. I couldn't see his face clearly." She hesitated. "You think it's the Prescotts?"

Another pause. "We'll talk when you get here."

"Mac..."

"Let's just be careful, okay?" he said, too quickly. "Text me when you get to your next patient and when you leave, just so I know where you are."

Kelsey stood in the parking lot long after the call ended.

She glanced back at the tree line once more before getting into her car and locking the doors immediately. As she pulled out of the lot, she caught herself checking the rearview mirror every few seconds for a dark figure that wasn't there.

Yet.

Kelsey's hands gripped the steering wheel tightly as she left Mrs. Hendricks's cottage, her second home visit of the morning. The elderly woman's blood pressure had been stable, her medication working well, but Kelsey was distracted throughout the visit, eyes darting to windows and doorways.

"Get a grip," she muttered to herself, checking her rearview mirror for the third time since pulling away. Nothing but empty road stretched behind her.

She parked outside the Marshall residence, her last stop before Truman's. Before getting out, she sent a quick text to Mac:

Arriving at my last stop. Will head to Truman's after.

His reply came almost immediately: *Text when you leave there. Call if anything seems off.*

The care she took in checking her surroundings while walking to the front door made her feel foolish, yet she still carried the sensation of being watched. The visit passed without incident. Her patient's wounds were healing well, and her husband was learning to take over their care from the visiting nurses.

Back in her car, she texted Mac again:

On my way now. ETA 15 minutes.

As she drove the winding coastal road to Truman's house, Kelsey kept scanning the roadside and checking her mirrors. The rational part of her brain knew she was being hypervigilant, but Mac's wary voice during their earlier call had triggered her instincts.

Truman's cottage came into view. Mac's SUV sat in the circular driveway alongside a small sedan that belonged to Truman's day nurse. The familiarity of the scene brought a small measure of relief.

Kelsey gathered her nursing bag and hurried up the walkway. Before she could knock, the door swung open, and Mac stood there, shoulders tense, eyes quickly scanning the road behind her.

"Everything okay?" he asked, voice low.

"Fine. No sign of anyone following me."

Mac nodded and stepped back to let her in. The tightness around his eyes didn't ease. "Good. That's good."

"What's going on?" she asked. His tension seemed to stem from more than just the Prescotts taking photos of her again.

He glanced toward the living room. "Grandad had a rough night."

His tone shifted her focus immediately. Kelsey followed Mac into the main room.

Truman sat in his usual armchair by the window, but the commanding presence that had filled the space just two weeks ago had diminished. His skin had a grayish undertone that Kelsey recognized immediately with cardiac failure, and the effort each breath required was evident in the slight rise and fall of his shoulders.

"There she is," Truman said, his voice thinner than before but still carrying the warmth she'd come to expect. "My granddaughter."

Kelsey crossed to him and bent to kiss his papery cheek. "Good morning, Truman. I hear you had an eventful night."

"Overreaction," he waved a hand dismissively. "A bit of indigestion."

Mac made a sound of disagreement. "Angina, Grandad. Bad enough that the nurse had to give you nitroglycerin. And morphine."

"Details," Truman muttered.

Kelsey set her professional face in place, though her heart ached at the visible decline. "Mind if I check a few things?"

"If it will make my grandson stop hovering like a mother hen, by all means."

As Kelsey took his vitals, the three fell into conversation about Noah's field trip today to the Portland aquarium while carefully avoiding the elephant in the room. Truman's blood pressure was lower than before, and his oxygen saturation was concerning.

"Your color's a bit off today," she said gently, removing the blood pressure cuff. "How's your breathing?"

Truman sighed. "To be honest? Not great. Feels like I'm climbing a mountain just going to the damned bathroom."

"I noticed," Kelsey said. She glanced at Mac, who stood by the window, arms crossed tightly over his chest. "I think a wheelchair might help conserve your energy for moving around the house. And oxygen support throughout the day, not just at night."

"A wheelchair," Truman repeated, staring down at his hands. The momentary silence felt heavy with unspoken meaning.

Mac cleared his throat. "It's just to help with the longer trips, Grandad. From the bedroom to—"

"I know what it means, son." Truman's voice was quiet but firm. He looked up, first at Mac, then at Kelsey. The clarity in his faded blue eyes was startling against his ashen complexion. "This is it, isn't it?"

The directness of the question hung in the air. Kelsey felt Mac's eyes on her, silently pleading for reassurance she couldn't honestly give.

"Yes," she said softly.

Truman nodded. "How long?"

Kelsey moved to sit on the ottoman beside his chair and took one of his hands in hers. "It's difficult to say exactly. You may start to have more episodes like last night, which tells us your heart is giving out."

"How long, Lass?"

"Grandad," Mac's voice broke.

"Weeks, not months," Kelsey said.

"It's alright, boy," Truman said, extending his hand toward his grandson. "Come here."

Mac crossed the room slowly, as if each step required immense effort. He took his grandfather's offered hand then sank to one knee beside the chair. The set of his shoulders had collapsed, revealing a vulnerability Kelsey had never seen in him before.

"I thought we had more time," Mac said, his voice rough.

"I've had a good run, haven't I? Haven't we?" Truman squeezed Mac's hand. "Ninety-five years. Can't complain about that."

"Still not enough," Mac whispered.

Kelsey felt tears burning behind her eyes at the naked grief on Mac's face. His usual stoic expression had crumbled and left behind something raw and unguarded.

"The wheelchair is a good idea," Truman said after a moment, turning back to Kelsey. "And the oxygen. Whatever makes this easier." He paused, his breathing labored despite his attempt at nonchalance. "For all of us."

Kelsey nodded. Her professional mask was the only thing helping her maintain composure. "I'll arrange for both to be delivered today. And we should adjust your medication schedule again. The nitro helped last night?"

"Like magic," Truman confirmed. "Awful after-taste, though."

"We'll keep it close at hand," she said, making notes in his chart.

Mac still knelt beside the chair, one hand gripping his grandfather's, the other pressed against his own mouth, as if physically holding back words or emotions. Truman looked down at him with infinite tenderness.

"Don't go getting maudlin on me, lad," he said gently. "This isn't a surprise. We've known this was coming."

"Knowing and accepting are different things," Mac replied. His voice was steadier now, though his eyes remained bright with unshed tears.

"Well, I've accepted it," Truman said. "Now I need you to." He looked between Mac and Kelsey. "Both of you. No tiptoeing around. Just truth and as much laughter as we can manage in the time we have left. Bring that boy around more, I do enjoy talking to the lad." They had brought Noah to see Truman after school the week prior, and the two had hit it off.

Kelsey felt something shift in her chest, a deepening respect for this man, mixed with grief for what Mac was about to lose. What they were all about to lose. "Okay," she said.

"I'll try," Mac added, finally releasing his grandfather's hand and rising to his feet. "But I'm not making any guarantees about the laughter part."

Truman smiled, and the expression brought a momentary glow back to his face. "Fair enough. Now, wasn't there talk of lunch? Dying doesn't mean I've lost my appetite."

Mac let out a sound somewhere between a laugh and a sob. "Turkey sandwiches. I'll go get them."

"I'd like a few minutes with my new granddaughter, if you don't mind."

After he left the room, Truman watched Kelsey with knowing eyes. "He hasn't told you yet, has he? About the photographer."

Kelsey's breath caught. "You know about that?"

"My grandson thinks he can protect everyone by keeping secrets." Truman shook his head slowly. "Some lessons take longer to learn than others."

"What is it, Truman? The Prescotts again?"

The old man sighed, each word measured as if conserving energy. "It's not my story to tell. But make him talk to you. Tonight." He reached for her hand again. "Life's too short for secrets between people who love each other."

Kelsey felt the words like a physical touch against her heart. "We don't... it's not like that."

"Not yet, maybe," Truman said with a smile that held both wisdom and mischief. "But I've seen the way he looks at you when you're not watching. And how you look at him."

Before Kelsey could respond, Truman's expression shifted, a shadow of pain crossing his features. His hand tightened on hers.

"Truman? What's wrong?"

"Just a twinge," he said, though his breathing had quickened. "Would you mind... the oxygen?"

Kelsey quickly retrieved the portable oxygen concentrator and placed the nasal cannula. As she adjusted the flow rate, she watched Truman's face carefully. The relief was almost immediate, but the episode had drained what little color remained in his cheeks.

"Better?" she asked softly.

Truman nodded, eyes closed. "He'll need you," Truman said suddenly, voice barely above a whisper. "When I'm gone. He'll try to push you away. It's what he does."

"I'm stronger than I look," Kelsey replied.

Truman's eyes opened, finding hers with surprising clarity. "Good. Because so is the cell where his heart is imprisoned."

The afternoon sun was warm on Truman's driveway as Mac walked Kelsey to her car. Behind them, through the bay window, they could see Truman dozing in his armchair, oxygen tubing looped beneath his nose, a nurse quietly arranging his medications nearby.

Kelsey paused by her driver's side door. "He's resting comfortably now, but I adjusted his medication schedule. The morphine needs to be more regular."

Mac nodded, his gaze fixed on the window. "I've never seen him look so... small."

"Mac," Kelsey said softly, drawing his attention back. "Truman said you know something I don't about the photographer the Prescott's have following me."

Mac ran a hand through his hair, jaw tight. His eyes scanned the quiet street before meeting hers. "Not just a photographer, it's a private investigator."

"You're sure?"

"That same guy was at the courthouse the day we filed our marriage license," Mac said, his voice low. "I didn't mention it because... hell, I didn't want to worry you. But I've seen that car before, parked outside various places around town. Black sedan, tinted windows."

Kelsey leaned against her car. "So they're watching us for evidence that our marriage is a sham. This is exactly what we expected. What do you suggest we do?"

Mac's eyes hardened. "Remember that takeover we mentioned. We can execute it. I'll contact my lawyer today. By tomorrow, Jason Prescott will be on his knees."

Kelsey frowned. "Mac, that's the nuclear option."

"They started this," Mac said, an edge to his voice. "They're trying to take your son. Our son. Again."

"I know, but..." Kelsey hesitated. "It just feels wrong. There has to be another way."

Mac's frustration was visible in the tense line of his shoulders. "While you're contemplating the moral high ground, they're building a case against you."

"I'm not saying we don't act," Kelsey clarified. "I'm saying let's be thoughtful. Not reactionary."

Something in her steady gaze seemed to reach him. Mac exhaled slowly, and some of the rigidity left his posture with it.

"Okay," he conceded. "We'll talk about options tonight. But Kelsey, we're running out of time to play nice. The hearing is in two weeks and the window to pull off this takeover is closing."

She nodded. "We talk tonight. After Noah's in bed." She unlocked her car, and Mac reached out to touch her arm.

"Can I ask you something completely different?"

Kelsey nodded.

"The time Grandad has left... what's going to happen to him?"

She swallowed. "I meant what I said in there. He's close. Truly it could be any time, but more likely he will gradually get weaker, become bedbound and eventually slip into a deep sleep where he won't wake. He may have pain, or shortness of breath, which we'll manage with medication. And he may get confused, try to do things he shouldn't or talk to people that aren't there. But we won't be afraid; we'll do our best to manage his symptoms so he's comfortable as possible."

Mac nodded, words seemingly beyond him for a moment. His fingers tightened around hers before reluctantly letting go.

"I should get back to him," he said finally. "You have more patients?"

"No, I'm heading back to the clinic and then to pick up Noah from school. He'll be late, due to the field trip. We'll be home for dinner."

"I'll be there by six at the latest. Grandad'll throw me out by then."

Kelsey opened her car door. "Mac, about the Prescotts, I'm not saying we don't fight."

"I know," he said. "Tonight."

As she slid into the driver's seat, Mac rested his hand on the car door. "Kelsey?"

"Yes?"

"Thank you. For being honest about Grandad. Most people try to soften things, but..." He paused. "The truth is harder, but better."

"Always," she agreed.

As she drove away, Kelsey watched Mac in her rearview mirror. He stood in the driveway, watching her until she turned out of view.

Chapter 24

The school parking lot buzzed with anxious energy as Kelsey pulled into one of the few remaining spaces. Parents stood in small clusters between cars, checking watches and phones, faces pinched with concern. The ferry had docked and departed twenty minutes ago—without the field trip students from Portland.

Kelsey's stomach tightened as she scanned the lot. The private investigator from earlier flashed in her mind, followed by Mac's confirmation. She gripped her steering wheel, trying to calm the sudden spike in her pulse.

"Just late," she murmured to herself. "Field trips always run late."

Still, she couldn't fight the creeping dread as she stepped out of her car and joined the throng of waiting parents. She spotted Amanda Porter, Tyler's mother, standing near the school entrance and made her way over.

"Any word?" Kelsey asked. She tried keep her voice level.

Amanda turned, relief crossing her face at seeing her. "Oh, Kelsey! They just called the school office. The ferry is about fifteen minutes out."

"What happened? They missed the four o'clock?"

Amanda nodded, tucking a strand of hair behind her ear. "Apparently there was some kind of incident with one of the kids at the aquarium. They got delayed and missed the scheduled crossing."

"Incident?" The word landed like a stone in Kelsey's chest. "Did they say what kind?"

"Just that everyone's okay." Amanda offered a reassuring smile that did nothing for Kelsey's growing unease. "You know how kids are on field trips. Probably someone wandered off in the gift shop."

Wandered off. The words echoed in Kelsey's mind as she remembered the man with the camera. The Prescotts watching her. Watching Noah.

"Probably," Kelsey agreed, her mouth dry.

Parents continued to gather, their conversation a mix of minor irritation and good-natured jokes about teacher herding skills. Kelsey joined in automatically, laughing at appropriate moments, but her attention remained fixed on the road leading to the school.

When the yellow bus finally rounded the corner, a collective sigh of relief rippled through the waiting crowd. Kelsey moved closer to the designated drop-off area, stomach knotting as the bus doors opened and children began spilling out.

One by one, students descended the steps and ran to waiting parents, backpacks bouncing and voices excitedly talking about fish and sharks and the ferry ride. Kelsey scanned each face. The knot in her stomach tightened with every child who wasn't Noah.

Then the flow of children stopped.

Kelsey stepped forward. Mrs. Smith, Noah's teacher, appeared at the bus door, one hand on the shoulder of a subdued-looking Noah.

"There he is," Kelsey breathed, relief flowing through her until she registered her son's expression—head slightly down, with none of the other children's post-field-trip animation.

Mrs. Smith spotted Kelsey and guided Noah down the steps. As they approached, the teacher's professional smile did little to mask the concern in her eyes.

"Ms. York," Mrs. Smith said, then quickly corrected herself. "I'm sorry—Mrs. MacCormack." She kept one hand lightly on Noah's shoulder. "We had a bit of a situation today I wanted to discuss with you."

Kelsey knelt to Noah's level first. "Hey, buddy. You okay?"

Noah nodded, not quite meeting her eyes. "I'm fine, Mom."

"What happened?" Kelsey looked up at Mrs. Smith while keeping a hand on Noah's arm.

The teacher's expression was carefully neutral. "Noah disappeared for about fifteen minutes at the aquarium. As you can imagine, it gave us quite a scare."

"Disappeared?" Kelsey's voice sharpened.

"I'm sorry," Noah mumbled.

Mrs. Smith continued, "When we found him, he was with a woman he identified as his Aunt Jennifer. He said she was his uncle's wife."

The name hit Kelsey like a gut punch.

"I should have been notified immediately," Kelsey said, fighting to keep her tone even.

"There was no need. Noah was found quickly, and everything seemed to be in order." Mrs. Smith's brow furrowed slightly. "In the future, though, I'd appreciate if you'd let us know when family members might be meeting up with students on field trips. It's school policy that we need written permission for anyone else to have contact with students while they're in our care. She was quite... upset with me about it."

Kelsey stood slowly, one hand still on Noah's shoulder. "I didn't know she would be there."

Something in Kelsey's tone must have registered with the teacher because Mrs. Smith's expression shifted subtly. "I see. Well, no harm done this time, but perhaps a family conversation is in order."

"Absolutely," Kelsey agreed, her voice tight. "Thank you for bringing this to my attention."

"Noah was very cooperative once we found him," Mrs. Smith added, softening her tone as she addressed the boy. "And he did excellent work on his marine life observation sheet. One of the best in the class."

Noah looked up, a ghost of a smile crossing his face. "The octopus was really cool, Mom."

Kelsey forced a smile. "That sounds amazing, buddy. We should get home and you can tell me all about it." She looked back at Mrs. Smith. "Thank you for taking care of him."

"Of course. Have a good evening, both of you."

Kelsey guided Noah toward the car, keeping her movements deliberate and calm despite the fury building inside her. The Prescotts had made their move, and had put their hands on her son. The violation of it burned through her veins.

Once they were in the car, Kelsey took a deep breath before turning to face Noah. "So, tell me about seeing Aunt Jennifer. That must have been a surprise."

Noah buckled his seatbelt, his eyes downcast. "She said she came to the aquarium because she knew our class would be there."

Kelsey's hands tightened on the steering wheel. "What did she want, honey?"

"She said..." Noah's voice faltered. "She said she could take me to see Grandmother Prescott. That they had a room all ready for me at their house, with her and Uncle Jason." He looked up suddenly, with wide eyes. "She wanted me to go with her in her car, Mom. She said we could call you later."

"What did you tell her?"

"I said I needed to get back to my class." Noah's voice dropped to nearly a whisper. "She grabbed my arm kind of hard and said it would only take a minute to get her car." His bottom lip trembled slightly. "It scared me. That's when Mrs. Smith found us."

White-hot rage flooded Kelsey's system. Jennifer Prescott had tried to take her son.

Not just talk to him. Take him.

"Noah, you did exactly the right thing," Kelsey said, working to keep her voice steady despite the fury coursing through her. "I am so proud of you for knowing that wasn't right."

"Aunt Jennifer seemed different," Noah frowned. "She wasn't as nice. She kept saying bad things about you and Mackie."

"What kind of things, sweetheart?"

Noah shifted uncomfortably. "That you were keeping me away from my real family. That you got married to Mackie for his money." He paused, then added in a small voice, "She said you probably don't have time for me anymore."

Each word was like a dagger. The calculated cruelty of trying to plant those doubts in her seven-year-old's mind triggered a protective instinct so powerful Kelsey could barely contain it.

"Noah, look at me," she said, turning fully toward him at a stoplight. "What Aunt Jennifer said is completely untrue. You are the most important person in my life, always have been, always will be."

Noah nodded. "I didn't believe her, Mom. That's why it felt scary. She was all weird."

"It's okay buddy." Kelsey reached over to squeeze his hand. "Sometimes adults do things that are wrong. But you were very brave and very smart today."

"Is she going to get in trouble?"

Kelsey considered her answer carefully. "What she did was wrong, and yes, there will be consequences. But that's for me and Mac to handle. You don't need to worry about it."

As they pulled into their driveway, Kelsey's determination hardened into something sharp-edged and immovable. The Prescotts had attempted to abduct her child.

"Hey, Mom?" Noah's voice pulled her from her thoughts as she turned off the engine. "Mac said he'd show me how to build a model boat when he got home today. Do you think he still will?"

"I'm sure he will, buddy," Kelsey said, finding a genuine smile despite the storm brewing inside her. "Why don't you go get changed and set up your homework? Mac should be home soon."

Noah brightened, some of his usual energy returning. "Okay!" He unbuckled and was out of the car in a flash.

Kelsey sat motionless in the driver's seat after Noah disappeared inside. She pulled out her phone and stared at it for a long moment before typing a message to Mac:

Jennifer Prescott tried to take Noah from his field trip today. Literally tried to make him leave with her. Let's go nuclear on their asses.

She hit send, then leaned her head against the steering wheel, breathing deeply to calm the protective rage coursing through her system. The Prescotts had made their intentions clear. Now she would make hers equally transparent.

No one threatened her family. No one.

Mac sat beside his grandfather's bed, watching the older man's labored breathing. The afternoon sun slanted through half-drawn blinds, casting the room in amber light. Truman had been sleeping fitfully since lunch. After his bad night, Mac assumed he needed the rest. Kelsey's changes to his medications seemed to be working, keeping the pain at bay.

Mac's phone vibrated in his pocket. He pulled it out, expecting a message from the nurse. Instead, Kelsey's name appeared on the screen. As he read her message, his blood went cold.

"Jesus Christ," Mac muttered, rereading the words in disbelief.

"That bad, huh?" Truman's raspy voice startled him. The old man's eyes were open, clearer than they'd been all day.

Mac looked up, jaw tight. "They tried to abduct Noah. Jennifer Prescott showed up at his field trip and tried to walk off with him."

Truman's weathered face hardened. "Bastards."

"I'm going to destroy them," Mac said, his voice deadly quiet. "All of them."

Truman shifted in the bed, wincing as he reached for the water glass on his nightstand. Mac handed it to him, waiting as his grandfather took a careful sip.

"The takeover play?" Truman asked, handing back the glass.

Mac nodded. "Jason Prescott is going to have a bad day."

"Why were we waiting, exactly?"

Mac ran a hand through his hair. "Kelsey had reservations."

Truman made a sound somewhere between a laugh and a cough. "And now?"

"Now she's ready to burn it all down." Mac stood, pacing to the window. "Earlier today, she wasn't sure that was the right call. But..." He shook his head. "They tried to take Noah, Grandad."

"So what are you doing still standing here?" Truman's voice was weak but firm. "Go home to your family." Truman waved a dismissive hand. "I'm fine son, they'll give me something to eat and I'll fall asleep to the news."

"You sure?"

"I survived three years in Korea and sixty years married to your grandmother. I think I can manage an hour in this bed." Truman's eyes, though sunken, held a familiar spark. "Give 'em hell, boy. Nobody comes after a MacCormack and walks away unscathed."

Mac leaned down and squeezed his grandfather's shoulder. "I'll be back if you need me any time, even in the middle of the night."

"Don't bother. Be with your wife and boy." Truman fixed him with a stern look. "You protect what's yours, Mac. Nothing else matters."

"Yes, sir." Mac straightened, a cold resolve settling in his chest. "I'll send the nurse in now anyway."

Twenty minutes later, Mac pulled into the driveway of their cottage, his truck tires crunching on the gravel. The windows glowed with warm light against the gathering dusk. In any other circumstance, the scene would have filled him with peace. Tonight, it only intensified his determination to eliminate the threat to the people inside.

Mac entered through the kitchen door, the scent of garlic and tomatoes enveloping him. Noah sat at the table, math workbook open in front of him, while Kelsey stood at the stove stirring a pot of sauce. For a moment, Mac paused in the doorway, struck by how right the scene felt and how close they'd come to having it shattered.

Kelsey looked up and met his eyes. Without a word passing between them, he could see that her emotions matched his own.

"Mackie!" Noah spotted him and jumped up from his chair. "You're home early!"

"Hey, buddy," Mac said, forcing a smile as he ruffled Noah's hair.

He strode to Kelsey and placed a hand on the small of her back, pressed a kiss to her temple. "Hey," he murmured. He hoped the single word carried the weight of everything unsaid.

"Hey yourself," she replied softly, leaning into him briefly before turning back to the stove. "Dinner's almost ready."

Mac hung his jacket on the hook by the door. "So, Noah, how was the field trip today? See any sharks?"

Noah's face lit up. "Yeah! They had a huge tank with sand tiger sharks and these really weird flat rays that looked like they were smiling." His excitement faltered slightly. "But then some other stuff happened."

"Oh?" Mac kept his tone casual as he pulled plates from the cabinet.

Noah glanced at his mother, then back to Mac. "My Aunt Jennifer was there. She tried to make me go with her." His voice dropped. "She grabbed my arm really hard, Mac. It was scary."

Mac set the plates down carefully, fighting to keep his expression neutral despite the rage boiling inside him. He crouched to Noah's level. "Mom told me about it."

Noah nodded solemnly. "She said she and Uncle Jason have a room all ready for me at their house."

Mac's jaw tightened. He glanced up at Kelsey, who had turned from the stove, wooden spoon still in hand.

"Noah," Mac said carefully, "your mom is never too busy for you. Ever."

"I know," Noah said. "That's why it was weird." He frowned.

"You were very brave," Mac said, placing a hand on Noah's shoulder.

Noah seemed to consider this, then abruptly changed course. "Remember you said you would show me how to build that model boat tonight. Can we start after dinner?"

"Absolutely." Mac stood. "I brought home all the supplies last week. It's a clipper ship—fastest vessel of its time."

"Cool!" Noah's enthusiasm returned full force. "I told Tyler I was building a boat with you, and he didn't believe me because his dad doesn't know how to build stuff."

"Well, we'll have to take pictures to prove it," Mac said, helping Kelsey set the table. "Maybe we can even sail it when it's done."

Dinner passed with Noah chattering about octopuses and jelly-fish, the incident with his aunt temporarily forgotten.

Two hours later, Noah was tucked into bed, and the partially assembled boat model was drying on his desk. Mac found Kelsey in the living room, standing by the small fire in the hearth that warmed the still chill evening, her arms wrapped around herself.

"He's asleep," Mac said quietly, then closed the distance between them. "Wanted me to tell him more about clipper ships tomorrow."

Kelsey nodded while staring into the flames. "He adores you, you know."

"The feeling's mutual."

"They tried to take him from us, Mac." Her voice was steady but laced with a fury he'd never heard from her before. "Jennifer was going to put him in her car and drive away with my son."

"I know." Mac's hands clenched at his sides. "If I ever see her..."

"It's not just her," Kelsey interrupted. "It's all of them. The Prescotts think they can take whatever they want." She turned to face him, her eyes bright with unshed tears of anger. "This morning, I was worried about taking the high road. About what destroying Jason would teach Noah about how we handle conflict."

"And now?"

"Now I'm thinking about what would happen to Noah if we don't stop them." Kelsey's voice hardened. "I don't care what it takes. I don't care what bridges we burn. They tried to take my child."

Mac reached for her hands and held them between his own. "I called my attorney on the way home. He's drawing up the paperwork tonight. We're filing for an emergency restraining order against Jennifer Prescott and all members of the Prescott family," Mac explained. "Simultaneously, we are moving on the takeover. In the morning, Jason Prescott will be broke."

"And that will stop them?"

"It will destroy Jason's reputation and finances. He's already in debt up to his ears, debt he won't be able to pay," Mac said grimly. "He'll have burned through his trust. And the bank of Mama was closed long ago. His mother cut him off, refusing to give him another cent while she lives. What's left is Noah's. And the custody of Noah and his trust is becoming out of reach for him," Mac's expression was unyielding.

Kelsey nodded slowly. "Do it. All of it."

"You're sure?" Mac searched her face. "This morning you were concerned about morality."

"This morning they hadn't tried to abduct my son," Kelsey cut in. "Everything changed the moment Jennifer put her hands on Noah."

Mac nodded, pulling out his phone. "I'll check in with Harrison now." He dialed and put the phone on speaker after his attorney answered on the second ring.

"Mac, I was just finalizing the documents," Harrison's clipped voice came through. "You want me to proceed with everything we discussed?"

"Yes. First thing in the morning," Mac confirmed. "And Harrison? Make sure the restraining order includes all Prescott family members, employees, and representatives. I want a minimum thousand-foot perimeter around both Noah's school and our home."

"Already included. I've also drafted motions regarding attempted child abduction, which should get law enforcement involved. We'll need a formal statement from Noah's teacher and any witnesses."

"I'll contact the school tomorrow," Kelsey said.

"Mrs. MacCormack, good evening," Harrison acknowledged. "I should inform you both that once we file these actions, the Prescotts will likely contest vigorously. This won't be a clean or quiet process."

"I don't care," Kelsey said firmly. "They tried to take my son."

"Understood." Harrison's tone was grim. "In that case, I'll have the full package ready by eight a.m. The restraining order should be in place by noon. The takeover is already underway."

"Good," Mac said. "And Harrison? No mercy."

"None whatsoever," the attorney confirmed. "I'll call when it's done."

After they hung up, Kelsey let out a long, shaky breath. "It feels strange to be hoping for someone's downfall."

"It's not about vengeance," Mac said quietly. "It's about protection. There's a difference."

Kelsey nodded, then surprised him by stepping forward and wrapping her arms around his waist, letting her head rest against his chest. Mac hesitated only a moment before enfolding her in his embrace and cradling the back of her head with one hand.

"Thank you," she whispered against his shirt.

"For what?"

She looked up at him. "For being an ally."

Something shifted between them in that moment, an acknowledgment that what had begun as a marriage of convenience was evolving into something much more real. Mac leaned down and brushed his lips against Kelsey's gently. Her eyes fluttered and she gazed at him with those blue eyes that had startled him at their first meeting. Now their icy edges were almost purple in the firelight.

Reaching up on tiptoe, Kelsey kissed him back. The tenderness grew into something more, and heat sparked in his chest and spread through his body. Not the desperate passion they'd shared before, but something deeper and foreign.

Mac's hands framed her face, thumbs brushing her cheekbones as his mouth claimed hers more insistently. When she sighed against his lips and parted them to deepen the kiss, he felt it resonate somewhere beneath his ribs in a place left untouched since Marlene.

He hadn't planned this, hadn't expected this moment to transform into this smoldering need. But as Kelsey's hands slid beneath his shirt, fingers tracing the muscles of his back, all rational thought receded.

His hands found the hem of her sweater and lifted it slowly, giving her time to stop him if this wasn't what she wanted. Instead, she raised her arms, allowing him to draw the garment over her head.

The firelight played across her skin, turning it to gold. Mac's breath caught at the sight of her.

She sank slowly to her knees on the rug, drawing him down with her. The firelight caught in her hair, turning the dark strands to liquid ink as she reached for his belt.

Mac captured her hands and brought them to his lips. "Slow," he murmured against her fingers.

His shirt followed her sweater to the floor. Her bra. His jeans. Each article of clothing removed with careful attention revealed skin that demanded to be touched, explored. Mac traced the curve of her breast with his palm, watching her eyelids flutter as his thumb brushed across its peak. The soft sound she made ignited something primal in him.

He lowered her to the rug, his mouth following the path his hands had taken—the hollow of her throat, the sensitive skin beneath her collarbone, the gentle swell of her breast. Kelsey arched beneath him as his tongue circled her nipple, and she threaded her fingers through his hair to hold him against her.

"Mac," she breathed, the single syllable containing multitudes.

He continued his descent, hands spanning her waist, mouth trailing kisses across her ribs, her stomach, the jut of her hipbone. When he reached the waistband of her underwear, he looked up for permission. The naked want in her expression was answer enough.

The last barriers between them fell away. Mac settled between her thighs, taking his time, learning her body's responses. The way her breath hitched when he touched her just so. How her fingers tightened in his hair when his tongue found that perfect rhythm. The broken sound of his name when she shattered beneath his mouth.

Before she'd fully recovered, Mac moved up her body, claiming her lips again, letting her taste herself on his tongue. Her hands roamed his back, his shoulders, pulling him closer with an urgency that matched his own mounting need.

"Now," she commanded softly against his mouth. "I need you now."

Mac positioned himself at her entrance, the heat of her almost unbearable against his rigid length. He paused there, suspended in the moment, acutely aware that this crossing felt different, significant in ways he couldn't articulate.

Their eyes met as he pushed forward slowly, watching her lips part on a silent gasp as he filled her completely. For a moment, neither moved, locked together in a perfect stillness that seemed to extend beyond their bodies.

Then Kelsey rolled her hips beneath him, and thought became impossible. Mac began his long, measured strokes that had her clutching at his shoulders, legs wrapping around his waist to draw him deeper. The firelight danced across their joined bodies to create shapes on the walls that merged and separated with each thrust.

Mac braced himself on his forearms, keeping most of his weight off her smaller frame while maintaining the intimate press of skin against skin. He watched her face, the flutter of her eyelashes, the parting of her lips, the flush spreading across her cheeks, committing each detail to memory.

Kelsey's inner muscles tightened around him as her breathing fractured into soft moans that drove him toward the edge of his control. Her release came suddenly, her body arching beneath him, inner walls pulsing around him as she cried out his name.

The sight of her abandoned to pleasure, combined with the exquisite pressure of her body, toppled Mac over the edge after her. He buried his face against her neck as his hips jerked, emptying himself inside her with a groan that seemed torn from somewhere deep in his chest.

For long moments after, they remained entangled, sweat cooling on their skin, breath gradually slowing. Mac rolled to his side, bringing Kelsey with him to face the fire, her back pressed to his front, his arm around her waist. He pulled the throw blanket from the couch to cover them both against the evening chill.

Neither spoke. What words could possibly encompass the shift that had occurred between them? Mac pressed his lips to her shoulder, a wordless acknowledgment of... something.

This was temporary, he reminded himself, even as the thought caused a sharp pain in his chest. In a few months, after the custody battle was won and his grandfather was gone, he'd be on his boat, alone on the ocean.

This wasn't forever. Couldn't be.

Mac tightened his arm around her sleeping form, inhaling the scent of her hair, allowing himself this moment of pretense. He listened to her quiet breathing, the crackle of the fire in the hearth, until sleep finally found him.

Chapter 25

The spring sunshine filtered through the wide bay windows, casting its rays across Truman's bed. They'd moved it yesterday, positioning it to face the ocean view he loved so dearly.

Kelsey adjusted the oxygen flow, her movements automatic after so many days of tending to him. The medical part was easy, administering medications, ensuring comfort. It was watching him fade that broke her heart.

"How are you doing this morning?" Mac's voice was deliberately light as he entered with a tray carrying tea and toast. The circles under his eyes had deepened over the past several days, evidence of the nights he'd spent sleeping in the armchair beside his grandfather's bed.

"Tired of being fussed over," Truman rasped, though his smile belied the complaint. His skin had taken on the grayish pallor Kelsey recognized too well from her years in healthcare. The subtle transparency that meant the body was retreating, preparing for its final journey.

"The oxygen's helping," Kelsey said, noting the slight improvement in his saturation levels. "And he actually ate some oatmeal earlier."

"Barely a spoonful," Truman grumbled. "But it was good. Your grandmother's recipe?"

Mac nodded and set the tray down carefully. "Mrs. Henley found it in your recipe box. Thought it might tempt your appetite."

Truman's eyes drifted toward the windows, where whitecaps dotted the steel-blue water of the bay. "Beautiful day. Tide's coming in."

Kelsey followed his gaze, struck by how the timeless rhythm of the ocean continued regardless of human dramas. The tides didn't care about custody hearings or corporate takeovers or even death. They simply came and went, as they had for millennia.

"Any word from the Prescotts?" Truman asked suddenly, his mind still sharp despite his body's decline.

Mac exchanged a glance with Kelsey. "Nothing. Just the *see you in court* text to Kelsey."

"Radio silence," Kelsey confirmed. "I almost wish he'd do something so we'd know what we're facing."

"The hearing's in a week," Mac added, the tension evident in his jaw.

Truman made a dismissive noise. "Jason Prescott is drowning. The takeover cut off his credit lines, and those shell companies he was using to hide his debt are collapsing. You've beaten him, whether he knows it yet or not."

"But is it enough?" Kelsey asked, voicing the fear that had kept her awake at night. "The custody hearing isn't about finances. It's about Noah."

"It was always about the money." Truman's voice was momentarily strengthened. "Without it, Jason has no resources to pursue custody. No judges to buy out. He doesn't care about the boy, he cares about controlling his inheritance."

"Right, but these people, they're vindictive. They may do something out of spite," Kelsey said.

"The restraining order is in place," Mac replied, though the words provided little comfort. He had paced to the window, hands shoved deep in his pockets. "They'd be fools to attempt anything like what Jennifer tried at the aquarium again."

"They're desperate fools," Kesley countered. "Aren't those the most dangerous kind?"

Truman shifted in the bed, wincing slightly with the effort. "Listen to an old man who's seen more than his share of battles. When you cut off a snake's head, it might thrash for a while, but it's still dead. You've shown him your power, he'd be a fool to make any other move against you." Truman gazed out at the ocean again, a wistful expression crossing his face. "I'd like to go outside," he said suddenly.

Kelsey hesitated, glancing at Mac. "Are you sure you're up for that?"

"I'm dying, not dead," Truman replied with a flash of his old spirit. "And I'd like to feel the sun on my face while I still can."

"Let's do it," Mac decided, already moving toward the wheelchair they'd brought in earlier that week. "It's a perfect day."

Together, Mac and Kelsey helped Truman from the bed to the wheelchair, a process that left the old man breathless despite their careful movements. Kelsey adjusted the portable oxygen tank and made sure the tubing didn't tangle as Mac tucked a thick wool blanket around his grandfather's legs.

"Ready for your grand voyage?" Mac asked. His attempt at lightness didn't quite mask his concern.

"Aye, aye," Truman replied, his hands gripping the armrests as Mac wheeled him toward the French doors.

Outside, the spring air carried the scent of salt and pine, the temperature mild enough to be pleasant without being too cool for Truman's weakened system. Mac positioned the wheelchair in a sunny spot sheltered from the breeze, while Kelsey adjusted the blanket higher around Truman's shoulders.

Truman closed his eyes as the sunlight bathed his face, breathing as deeply as his failing lungs would allow. "Now that," he said after a moment, "is better than any medicine."

"I should have brought you out sooner," Mac said, pulling up a chair beside him.

"Don't start with the regrets, boy," Truman opened his eyes, fixing his grandson with a stern look. "Life's too short for what ifs and should haves. God knows I've had my share."

Kelsey settled into another chair, the three of them forming a small circle. Below the deck, waves crashed rhythmically against the shore, their sound both soothing and eternal.

"Your grandmother is waiting for me," Truman said after a comfortable silence, his voice contemplative rather than sad. "Been waiting quite a while, I imagine. She never was patient."

Mac's hand tightened on the armrest of his chair, but he didn't contradict his grandfather's calm acknowledgment of what was coming.

"I'm looking forward to seeing her," Truman continued, a smile touching his lips. "Almost sixty years together, and still not enough. But I'm ready to go to her now."

"Grandad..." Mac's voice caught.

"I'm at peace, son," Truman said firmly. "Truly. I've had a good life. Built something from nothing. Loved a good woman. Raised a fine daughter. And you..." he reached out to pat Mac's knee, "you've grown into a man I'm proud of."

Kelsey felt tears burning behind her eyes at the naked emotion on Mac's face. She started to rise to give them privacy, but Truman stopped her.

"Stay, Kelsey. You're family now." His gaze included her, warm and accepting.

"I've been thinking about the arrangements," Truman continued, shifting slightly in the wheelchair to ease his discomfort. "Nothing fancy, mind you. No black crepe and somber faces. A celebration—good whiskey, good music, good stories."

"Irish wake," Mac nodded, his voice rough. "Grandma would approve."

"She always did love a party." Truman's eyes were distant with memory. "Have it at the house, not that awful funeral home in town. And scatter my ashes in the bay, where I scattered hers."

"We will," Mac promised, reaching for his grandfather's hand. "Exactly as you want it."

Truman nodded, satisfied. "Now, about the will."

"Grandad, we don't need to discuss this now."

"When better?" Truman countered. "I've made some changes recently. Harrison has all the paperwork, but I wanted to tell you myself."

Mac's expression tightened, but he nodded for his grandfather to continue.

"Most of it's as you'd expect," Truman said. His breathing grew slightly more labored as he spoke. "The business, the investments, the real estate, all yours, as we've always planned."

Kelsey watched Mac's face, seeing the tension there. He didn't care about the inheritance; he cared only about losing the man sitting before them.

"But I've made provisions for Noah," Truman continued. "A separate trust for his education. College, graduate school, whatever he wants to pursue. And Kelsey you too."

Kelsey felt her throat constrict. "Truman, you didn't have to—"

"I wanted to," he cut her off gently but firmly. "You're family now, both of you." He paused, and a mischievous glint appeared in his tired eyes. "And I've left the mansion to Amy."

"What?" both Mac and Kelsey exclaimed simultaneously.

Truman chuckled, the sound dissolving into a brief cough. "Just for the hell of it. To see what she does with it."

"But Grandad, you always said..."

"Your grandmother's been gone a long time now. Whatever happened there, whatever she wanted to protect by keeping it empty, it's time for new life to fill those walls." Truman's expression grew more serious. "There's a condition, though. Amy has to maintain the historical status. She can turn it into that health retreat she's always talking about, but the structure, the façade, those stay. They're part of the island. There's a fund to help with the restoration."

Kelsey shook her head in wonder. "She'll be ecstatic. She's been dreaming about this for years."

"I know," Truman said with satisfaction. "I hear her plans every time she works on my shoulders. That girl can talk." His face softened. "But she loves this island the way my wife did. She'll do right by the old place."

A comfortable silence fell between them, broken only by the sound of waves and distant gulls. Truman's eyes drifted closed and his face turned toward the sun like a flower seeking light. For a moment, he looked peaceful, almost young again.

"I'm content," he said finally, opening his eyes to look between Mac and Kelsey. "My affairs are in order. My conscience is clear. And I know what matters most is taken care of."

"What's that?" Mac asked, his voice barely audible over the wind.

"You," Truman replied simply. "Finding your way back to life, to family. For a while there, I thought you'd turned away from everything that matters. But now," he glanced at Kelsey, "now I can go knowing you're happy again."

Mac's jaw tightened with the effort of holding back tears. Kelsey reached across the space between them and rested her hand on his knee, offering silent support.

"I don't know if I can do this without you," Mac admitted. The words seemed torn from him.

"You can," Truman said with absolute certainty. "And you will. You have responsibilities now, people who need you."

Kelsey felt a tear slip down her cheek at the unguarded emotion on Mac's face. This taciturn, private man who'd been determined to sail away from human connections was now fighting to hold on to the most important one he had.

"I think I've had enough sun for now," Truman said after another quiet moment, his voice noticeably weaker. "But this was good. Very good."

As they helped him back inside, Kelsey knew with the certainty of her medical training that Truman's time was measured now in days, perhaps even hours. But she also knew that he had given Mac an immeasurable gift today. Permission to grieve, yes, but also permission to live fully once he was gone.

Outside, the tide continued its eternal rhythm, waves breaking against the shore in a cadence older than humanity itself.

The courtroom's oak paneling seemed to absorb light rather than reflect it. She smoothed her navy skirt for the third time, forcing her hands to remain still on her lap afterward. Beside her, Mac sat rigid in his charcoal suit, the dark circles under his eyes more pronounced than ever. He hadn't slept properly in days.

"You okay?" she whispered, touching his arm lightly.

Mac's eyes focused on her as if from a great distance. "Fine," he said, and covered her hand with his. "Just ready for this to be over."

Harrison leaned forward from his position at the edge of their table. "Judge Abernathy is thorough but fair. She doesn't suffer fools or waste time with theatrics."

Kelsey nodded, grateful for the reassurance, though her stomach remained knotted. The door at the back of the courtroom opened, and she stiffened instinctively.

Jason Prescott entered, looking nothing like the self-assured man who had threatened her in the Prescott mansion. His expensive suit hung slightly loose, as if he'd lost weight rapidly, and a sickly pallor had replaced his usual tan. Jennifer followed with a slightly bowed head and hands clasped so tightly her knuckles shone white. A third person, a sharp featured woman in a severe black suit, trailed them, carrying a leather portfolio.

"Where's Margaret?" Kelsey whispered to Harrison.

"Apparently too ill to attend," Harrison replied, watching the trio with calculating eyes. "That's her personal attorney, Regina Walsh. I've known her for years, tough but usually reasonable."

Mac's jaw tightened as Jason and Jennifer took their seats at the opposite table. "He looks like hell."

"Good," Kelsey couldn't help the vindictive surge of satisfaction. After what they'd tried to do to Noah, after the sleepless nights filled with worry, after the private investigator and the attempted abduction, Jason deserved whatever ruin Mac had engineered.

"All rise," the bailiff called, and the courtroom rustled to its feet as Judge Abernathy entered. Her gray hair was cut close to her scalp, and her movements were efficient as she took her seat.

"Be seated." Her voice carried clear authority. She adjusted her reading glasses, reviewing the file before her with swift precision. "We're here regarding petition FCVS-2025-1187, Prescott versus York-MacCormack, a custody matter concerning minor child Noah York-Prescott, age seven."

She looked up at the two tables. "I've reviewed the extensive filings from both parties. Before we proceed, I want to acknowledge the restraining order currently in place against the Prescott family with regard to Mrs. MacCormack and her son."

The judge's eyes narrowed on Jason. "Mr. Prescott, I find it highly unusual to be hearing a custody petition from individuals who have been legally barred from coming within one thousand feet of the child in question due to an attempted removal from a school function. Would you care to explain this situation?"

Jason shifted uncomfortably, then leaned toward his attorney, who whispered something before standing.

"Your Honor, my clients wish to express their deep regret for the misunderstanding that led to the restraining order. Mrs. Jennifer

Prescott simply ran into him at the museum and wanted to spend time with her nephew while he was in Portland. There was no intent to remove him permanently from his mother's care."

Judge Abernathy's expression made it clear she wasn't buying the explanation. "A 'misunderstanding' that required a teacher's intervention and resulted in a restraining order? That's quite a stretch, Counselor."

The attorney pressed on. "Nevertheless, we maintain that Margaret Prescott, as Noah's paternal grandmother, has legitimate grounds for seeking a custody arrangement that honors the Prescott family's role in the child's life."

"And yet Mrs. Prescott isn't present today," the judge observed. "May I ask why?"

"My client is experiencing health issues that prevented her attendance, Your Honor. Mr. Prescott is authorized to represent her interests as Noah's uncle."

Judge Abernathy turned her attention to Harrison. "Counselor Harrison, what is your clients' position on these custody claims?"

Harrison rose smoothly. "Your Honor, my clients, Kelsey and Preston MacCormack, assert that this petition is without merit and represents a pattern of harassment against a stable, loving family. Mrs. MacCormack has been Noah's sole caregiver since his birth following his father's tragic death. Mr. MacCormack has recently married Mrs. MacCormack and is in the process of legally adopting Noah, with the child's enthusiastic consent."

The judge nodded and made a note. "And the Prescotts' involvement in Noah's life prior to this custody petition?"

"Minimal at best, Your Honor," Harrison replied. "They showed little interest in Noah for the first three years of his life. More recently, Margaret Prescott has maintained a visitation schedule consisting of one weekend every other month, which Mrs. Mac-Cormack has always facilitated despite no legal obligation to do so."

Kelsey watched Jason's face as Harrison outlined their case. The man seemed almost gray now, his eyes darting occasionally to the courtroom door as if planning an escape. Jennifer stared fixedly at the table before her, and her fingers worried at a tissue.

Judge Abernathy reviewed several documents, the courtroom silent except for the rustle of papers. Finally, she removed her glasses and looked directly at the Prescott table.

"I've reviewed the financial disclosures required for this case," she said, her tone measured but pointed. "Mr. Prescott, your recent financial difficulties are extensive. I can't help but notice they coincide precisely with your sudden interest in custody of a child who stands to inherit a significant trust."

Jason's attorney began to object, but the judge held up her hand. "I'm not finished, Counselor." She turned her attention to Kelsey and Mac. "Mrs. MacCormack, Mr. MacCormack, your home study indicates a stable, nurturing environment. Noah's teacher reports he's well-adjusted, academically engaged, and has shown remarkable resilience through these proceedings."

Kelsey felt a surge of hope, her hand finding Mac's under the table. His fingers tightened around hers, though his expression remained guarded.

Judge Abernathy replaced her glasses and consulted her notes once more. "After careful consideration of all evidence presented, I find the Prescott family has no standing for custody of Noah Prescott. Furthermore, I am extending the restraining order for a period of one year, at which time it will be reviewed."

She gazed unflinchingly directly at Jason. "Mr. Prescott, let me be very clear: This court takes a very dim view of custody petitions motivated by financial interests rather than the child's wellbeing. Nor does it tolerate the kind of behavior exhibited toward this child at his school field trip. I suggest you direct your energies toward resolving your own matters rather than pursuing custody of a child who is clearly well cared for in his current home." With a sharp crack of her gavel, she concluded, "Petition denied. Court is adjourned."

The sound reverberated through Kelsey's body like a physical release. Tension drained from her shoulders so suddenly she felt lightheaded.

They'd won. Noah was safe.

"Congratulations," Harrison said, shaking both their hands. "Abernathy couldn't have been clearer. The Prescotts have no grounds to appeal."

Some of the tension eased from Mac's face. "Good. Let's get out of here."

Across the courtroom, Jason was already striding toward the exit, not even glancing in their direction. Jennifer lingered briefly, and her eyes met Kelsey's with an unreadable expression before following her husband.

Outside in the corridor, Kelsey's knees felt suddenly weak. She leaned against the wall, closing her eyes briefly as relief filled her.

"We did it," she whispered, then looked up at Mac. "It's over."

"It's over." His hands found hers in that now-familiar gesture. Yet something in his expression remained distant, preoccupied.

Harrison excused himself to speak with the court clerk, leaving them alone in the busy hallway.

"Mac? What is it?" Kelsey searched his face. "Aren't you happy?"

"Of course," he said, but his smile didn't reach his eyes. "Just thinking about Grandad. I should get back to him."

"Of course," Kelsey nodded, pushing aside the unexpected hurt at his detachment. Today was a victory, they should be celebrating. Instead, Mac seemed a million miles away.

The drive back to the island passed mostly in silence, the coastal road winding beneath a perfect blue sky that seemed at odds with the strange new heaviness between them. Mac drove with mechanical precision, his gaze fixed on the road ahead, occasionally checking his phone at stoplights, presumably for messages from Mrs. Henley about Truman.

Kelsey watched the scenery pass. The Prescotts had been thoroughly defeated. So why did it feel like something else had just ended too?

"The restraining order extension was a nice touch," she said finally, unable to bear the silence any longer. "A whole year of not having to worry about them showing up unannounced."

Mac nodded. "Harrison thought she might do that. Abernathy has a reputation for being thorough."

Another stretch of silence followed, broken only by the rhythmic swish of windshield wipers as they drove through a brief shower.

"You seem..." Kelsey hesitated, searching for the right word. "Distant. Any updates?"

Mac's hands tightened on the steering wheel. "No."

"That's good," Kelsey said softly. She waited, hoping he would say more, but he simply nodded.

The thought that had been circling in her mind all morning finally broke free. "Mac, do you think..." She stopped, finding it hard to put her fears into words. "Do you think we rushed into this? The marriage, I mean?"

His head turned sharply toward her before returning to the road. "What?"

"The judge barely mentioned our marriage," Kelsey continued, the words spilling out now. "She focused on my parenting, on Noah's stability. I just wonder if we..." She swallowed hard. "If we needed to get married at all."

Mac pulled the car onto a scenic overlook, putting it in park before turning to face her fully for the first time since they'd left the courtroom.

Kelsey's heart hammered against her ribs as she watched the emotions play across Mac's face. Surprise, confusion, and something deeper she couldn't identify. But instead of speaking, he simply turned away and stared out at the view beyond the guardrail.

The silence stretched between them.

They'd faced down the Prescotts together, became a legal family, shared a bed and a home, and yet in this moment, Mac seemed as unreachable as the sky. She wanted him to reassure her, tell her the marriage was necessary, or even if it wasn't, that he didn't regret it.

Had she misread the past few weeks of the growing connection between them? All those tender moments, the way he'd stepped effortlessly into their lives, the genuine bond he'd formed with Noah?

She studied his profile, the strong line of his jaw now tense. The dark circles beneath his eyes spoke of sleepless nights at Truman's bedside, but there was something else there too, a withdrawal that had nothing to do with exhaustion.

Had it been naïve to think their marriage of convenience could ever be more?

Once the custody battle was won and Truman was gone, what reason would Mac have to stay? The *Nereid* was ready, waiting to carry him away from the complications of human connection, just as he'd planned.

The thought settled like ice in her chest. She'd let herself fall for him, let Noah get attached, knowing all along what was going to happen. He would leave, and they would be alone again. Different but the same.

Maybe that was for the best. Hadn't she managed perfectly well on her own before?

Yet the idea of returning to that solitary existence after experiencing the warmth of their improvised family felt unbearable. She'd grown accustomed to Mac's presence. She'd come to rely on his perspective, his unwavering support.

More than that, she'd begun to love him.

She loved him, not just for what he'd done for them, but for who he was. The man who built model boats with Noah. Who knew exactly how she took her coffee. Who traced patterns on her skin in the quiet darkness after making love. Who fought with every resource at his command to protect them.

But was she truly his? Had she ever been? Or was she simply a responsibility he'd taken on out of loyalty to his grandfather and a sense of justice?

Mac's phone rang, shattering the silence. He answered without checking the screen, his body tensing as he listened to the caller. When he hung up, he turned to her, his expression grim.

"It's Grandad," he said simply. "We need to go."

He put the car in drive without another word, pulling back onto the coastal road with careful precision. Whatever Kelsey had hoped to hear from him remained eclipsed by the more immediate concern of Truman's decline.

As the car accelerated toward the ferry stop, Kelsey stared out at the passing landscape, feeling strangely untethered. They had won the custody battle today, secured Noah's future, but now the victory felt hollow.

Chapter 26

The scent hit Kelsey first as they entered Truman's cottage—antiseptic mingled with something else, something medicinal and final that she recognized from years of nursing.

Death.

The curtains were drawn against the afternoon light, creating a hushed, timeless atmosphere that existed outside the ordinary world.

Ruth met them in the hallway, her normally cheerful face etched with professional concern. "He's been in and out," she whispered, guiding them toward the bedroom. "More out than in, this afternoon."

Mac pushed past Kelsey with silent urgency, his shoulders rigid with tension. She followed, her medical training warring with the personal grief already building behind her ribs. In the doorway, she paused, taking in the scene.

Truman lay centered in the bed that now dominated the main room, the one they'd moved to face the ocean view. Even from here, she could see the change in him—the deeper hollows beneath his cheekbones, the pronounced blue tinge around his lips despite the oxygen flowing through the nasal cannula. His breathing had the distinctive pattern she'd seen too many times before—shallow, with occasional deeper gasps.

A woman Kelsey didn't recognize stood by the window, making notes on a tablet. She looked up as they entered and offered a gentle smile.

"You must be Mac and Kelsey," she said, extending her hand. "I'm Lauren, the hospice social worker. I came over on the ferry when Ruth called."

Mac shook her hand mechanically, but his gaze never left his grandfather. "How is he?"

Lauren exchanged a look with Ruth. "Comfortable. We've adjusted his medication to ensure he's not in any pain."

Mac glided to the bedside, and his hand hovered uncertainly before settling on Truman's arm. The old man didn't stir.

"Can we talk in the kitchen?" Ruth murmured, gesturing for Kelsey to follow. She touched Mac's shoulder briefly before stepping away. Her nursing persona slipped into place like a familiar shield.

In the kitchen, the normalcy felt jarring—sunlight streaming through the windows, a half-empty teacup on the counter, yesterday's newspaper folded beside it. Ruth leaned against the counter, fatigue evident in the slump of her shoulders.

"He had an episode this morning," she said without preamble. "Chest pain. Bad enough that I thought..." She trailed off, shaking her head. "The extra nitro helped, but it took longer to work than usual."

"Cardiac insufficiency," Kelsey said quietly. "His heart's giving out."

Ruth nodded. "The oxygen levels have been dropping gradually all day. I've increased the flow rate twice."

"Has he been responsive?"

"In and out. More confused when he is awake, though he asked for Mac several times." Ruth passed her the medication chart. "I've had to increase the morphine substantially."

Kelsey scanned the updated dosages and nodded her approval at the adjustments. Ruth had followed the orders Kelsey had laid out. Lauren, the social worker, joined them, her voice pitched low.

"I've gone over the DNR paperwork again. Everything's in order. No heroic measures, no hospital transfers—exactly as Mr. Costigan requested. We have the number of the funeral home to call, and we are able to pronounce him at home."

"Thank you, I'll be here and I can take care of that." Kelsey said, grateful for her calm efficiency. These practicalities were necessary, though they felt almost obscene against the significance of what was happening in the next room.

Mac appeared pale-faced in the doorway. "He's stirring. I think he's trying to wake up."

Ruth and Lauren exchanged glances. "I should go," Ruth said, gathering her things. "My shift technically ended an hour ago, and it seems like..."

"Like family should be with him now," Lauren finished gently. "I'll stay a bit longer, but I won't intrude."

Kelsey squeezed Ruth's hand as she passed. "I'll take over. Go home to your kids."

"Call if you need anything," she said. "Anything at all."

After Ruth left, Kelsey returned to the medication chart, forcing herself to focus on the professional details. Proper dosing. Timing. Comfort measures. It was easier than facing the raw emotion in Mac's eyes.

"Kelsey." Mac's voice was rough with strain. "Is this... is he..."

She set the chart down and met his gaze directly. "His body is shutting down, Mac. His heart is failing."

"But how long?" The question contained a universe of pain.

"It's hard to say exactly," she answered honestly. "It could be hours. It could be a day or two. The timing isn't..." Kelsey swallowed, her medical detachment slipping. "It isn't predictable."

Mac nodded. His hand found hers, a desperate grip that betrayed his outward composure. "He's asking for us."

In the dim light, Truman's eyes were open though unfocused. His gaze drifted until it found Mac's face, and recognition filtered through the medication haze.

"There you are," he said, his voice barely a whisper. "How was court?"

Mac sat carefully on the edge of the bed and took his grandfather's hand between both of his. "We won, Grandad. The judge dismissed their case completely."

A ghost of Truman's old smile touched his lips. "Told you. Nobody messes with a MacCormack."

"You were right," Mac said. He traced his thumb back and forth across Truman's papery skin. "The judge saw right through Jason. She even extended the restraining order for a full year."

"Good." Truman's eyelids fluttered. "Noah's safe then."

"Yes," Mac's voice caught. "Noah's safe."

"And you?" Truman's gaze shifted briefly to Kelsey before returning to Mac. "You'll take care of them?"

Something passed over Mac's face—an emotion so raw Kelsey had to look away. "I will."

Truman seemed satisfied with this, his eyes drifting closed again. His breathing slowed, and for a terrifying moment, she thought it might have stopped altogether. But then his chest rose again, and the cycle continued its inevitable rhythm.

Mac remained motionless, still holding his grandfather's hand, his shoulders curved inward as if physically bending under the sorrow of approaching loss.

Kelsey moved to the other side of the bed to check Truman's oxygen and adjust the blanket that had slipped from his shoulders. She moved with professional ease while her heart ached for Mac, for Truman, for the inevitable parting coming closer with each labored breath.

"Eleanor," Truman murmured suddenly, his eyes still closed. "Patience, love."

Mac's head jerked up, his gaze meeting Kelsey's across the bed. She'd seen this before—the dying often spoke to those who had gone before, caught somewhere between worlds.

"It's normal. It's a known phenomenon in hospice patients," she whispered, though the knowledge did little to soften the moment's impact.

Truman's eyes opened again, clearer now, and focused directly on Mac. "Mac," he said, his voice suddenly stronger. "I love you, boy. Never doubt that."

Mac's composure finally cracked. A single tear tracked down his cheek as he leaned closer. "I love you too, Grandad."

"You'll be alright," Truman insisted, each word taking visible effort. "You've got..." His gaze drifted to Kelsey again. "You've got family now."

His eyes closed once more, and his breath settled into the shallow pattern of deep sleep. Mac remained frozen, still clutching his grandfather's hand as if it were an anchor in a storm.

After a long moment, he looked up at Kelsey. "Is this it?" he asked, his voice barely audible.

She moved around the bed to stand beside him, professional assessment warring with personal compassion. "It's... hard to say with certainty. His vital signs are declining, but sometimes this process takes time."

"Will he wake up again?"

Kelsey hesitated to take away hope, but she was unwilling to lie. "He might. Briefly. But he's slipping away, Mac."

Mac nodded again. Then, with visible effort, he straightened his shoulders. "I'm staying with him. I won't leave."

"Of course."

"Will you..." He looked up at her, vulnerability naked in his expression. "Will you stay too? I can't do this alone, Kelsey."

"Yes," she said without hesitation. "I'll just need to arrange for Noah."

"Noah," Mac repeated, as if just remembering.

"Let me call Amy," Kelsey suggested gently. "She can bring him for a short visit, then take him for the night."

Mac nodded gratefully, his attention returning to Truman's sleeping form.

She stepped into the kitchen to make the call. Amy answered on the second ring.

"How did it go?" she asked immediately. "The hearing?"

"We won," Kelsey said, the victory feeling strangely distant now. "The judge dismissed their case completely."

"That's amazing! I told you—"

"Amy," she interrupted softly. "Truman is passing. Mac and I are going to stay with him tonight. Could you pick up Noah from school and keep him?"

The line went quiet for a moment. "Of course," Amy said finally. "Should I bring him by first? To say goodbye?"

Kelsey glanced toward the bedroom and weighed the options. "Maybe for just a few minutes. He should see Truman, but I don't want to frighten him."

"I'll prep him on the drive over," Amy promised. "And Kels? I'm so sorry. I know how fond you've become of him."

"Thank you," she managed, her throat tight. "For everything."

"That's what sisters are for. We'll be there in about an hour."

When Kelsey returned to the bedroom, Mac hadn't moved. Lauren, the social worker, was preparing to leave, gathering her tablet and notes.

"I've left extra resources on the counter," she told Kelsey quietly. "Information about grief support for both adults and children. And my card, if you need anything at all."

She thanked her and walked her to the door. When she returned, she found Mac still sitting beside Truman, one hand holding his grandfather's, the other pressed against his mouth as if physically holding back his sobs.

"Amy's bringing Noah," Kelsey said softly, then settled into the chair on the opposite side of the bed. "Just for a short visit, then she'll take him for the night."

Mac nodded without looking up. "Thank you."

The room fell silent except for the whisper of the oxygen and Truman's labored breathing. Outside, the afternoon sun cast lengthening shadows across the porch, marking time's passage with silent precision.

"I called the funeral home," Mac said suddenly. "Last week. Made all the arrangements."

"That was wise," she said gently.

"He was very specific about what he wanted. No church service. A wake here at the house. Bagpipes, though where we'll find a bagpiper on the island..." His voice cracked.

Kelsey reached across Truman to touch Mac's arm. "We'll figure it out. One step at a time."

Mac lifted his gaze to hers, his eyes suspiciously bright. "That's what you said when we got married."

"It was good advice then too," she said. A small smile tugged at her lips despite everything.

Mac's hand turned, capturing hers across his grandfather's sleeping form. His thumb traced the gold band on her finger, the gesture achingly intimate in the room's stillness.

"It wasn't a mistake." His voice was so low she almost missed it.

"What?" she asked, unsure she'd heard correctly.

His eyes held hers, steady and certain despite the grief hanging over them. "Our marriage. It wasn't a mistake."

Before she could respond, Truman stirred slightly, drawing their attention back to him. His breathing had become more labored, and each inhale was a visible effort.

Kelsey checked his pulse automatically. She found it thready and irregular beneath her fingertips. They both fell silent, the moment suspended as they waited, watched, and held space for the inevitable transition.

Outside, the tide was turning, waves retreating from the shore in their ancient rhythm of departure and return. Inside, they sat vigil, hands joined across Truman's bed. They bore witness to life's most profound journey—one that, despite all Kelsey's medical training, remained the greatest mystery of all.

The crunch of tires on gravel cut through the room's stillness, pulling Kelsey from her vigilant observation of Truman's breathing. She touched Mac's shoulder lightly, reluctant to disturb the fragile peace that had settled over them.

"That'll be Amy and Noah," she said softly as she moved to meet them at the door.

Mac nodded without taking his eyes from his grandfather's face. The past hour had brought only subtle change. Truman's labored breathing had evened somewhat, settling into a deeper, more peaceful rhythm. It was the deceptive calm that sometimes came near the end, Kelsey knew.

Outside, the late afternoon sun warmed the porch as Kelsey stepped out to meet Amy's car. Noah was the first to emerge, his face solemn but composed. Amy had clearly prepared him, explained things in terms he could understand without frightening him.

"Hi, sweetheart," Kelsey said, kneeling to his level and pulling him into a hug. His small body felt solid and warm against hers, a vital counterweight to the atmosphere of quiet fading inside the cottage.

"Amy says Truman is going to heaven," Noah said when she released him.

"That's right," Kelsey confirmed, brushing his hair back from his forchead. "His body is very tired, and it's almost time for him to go."

"Is he scared?"

The simple question caught at Kelsey's heart. "No, honey. He's not scared. He's ready to see his wife again, Mac's grandmother, who died a long time ago. And his daughter, Mac's mother."

Noah considered this. His face was serious beyond his years. "Can I say goodbye to him?"

"Of course. Would you like to see him now? He's sleeping, but he might wake up for a little while."

Noah nodded and slipped his hand into hers with complete trust. Amy stepped forward, offering Kelsey a quick, fierce hug.

"How are you holding up?" she asked quietly.

"Managing." The single word encompassed all the complex emotions beneath her outward composure. "Thank you for bringing him."

"What are sisters for?" Amy squeezed her hand. "Is Mac okay?"

Kelsey glanced toward the house. "As well as can be expected."

Together, they entered the cottage. The transition from bright sunlight to the dimmed interior created a momentary disorientation, as if they'd stepped into another world entirely. Kelsey guided Noah toward the bed, keeping her hand steady on his small shoulder.

"Remember," she murmured, "he looks different than the last time you saw him. He's very weak now."

Noah nodded solemnly. They paused to allow him to take in the scene of Truman lying still beneath the blankets. Mac sat vigil beside him, the quiet hiss of the oxygen the only sound breaking the silence.

Mac looked up at their entrance, and his face softened as he spotted Noah. He motioned them in with a gentle wave.

"Come in to see Grandad," he said. His voice was rough from emotion and exhaustion.

Noah approached the bed cautiously and studied Truman's sleeping face. Kelsey remained close behind him, ready to intervene if the scene became too overwhelming, but Noah showed no signs of fear, only a solemn attention that seemed to draw from some deep well of intuitive understanding.

As if sensing their presence, Truman's eyelids fluttered open. For a moment, his gaze seemed unfocused, drifting around the room before settling on the small group gathered at his bedside. Recognition dawned slowly, and with it, a smile that transformed his drawn features.

"There's my family," he whispered. The words were slightly slurred but unmistakable.

Mac's hand tightened on his grandfather's, his throat working visibly.

"Noah's come to see you," Kelsey said, and gently encouraged Noah forward. "And Amy too."

Truman's eyes found Noah, and his smile deepened. "Come here, young man," he said, lifting one trembling hand in invitation. "Let me look at you."

Noah stepped closer, somber but unafraid. "Hello, Truman."

"Hello yourself," Truman replied, summoning strength from some hidden reserve. "You being good for your mama and Mac?"

Noah nodded. "I got an A on my boat project. Mac helped."

"Course you did," Truman said with satisfaction. His gaze shifted to Amy, who stood slightly apart to give the family their space. "Amy. Come closer, girl."

Amy stepped gingerly to the bedside. "Hey, Truman." She took his free hand in hers. "Not working your yoga routine, I see."

Truman's chuckle dissolved into a weak cough, but his eyes crinkled with genuine amusement. "Giving me sass till the end."

"Wouldn't want you to forget me," Amy replied.

"No chance of that." Truman's gaze moved between them all, something like contentment settling over his features. "Noah. Amy. Come give an old man a goodbye kiss."

Kelsey felt the lump rise in her throat as Noah leaned carefully over the bed and placed a gentle kiss on Truman's papery cheek. Amy followed. Her usually animated face was still with emotion as she pressed her lips to his forehead.

"I love you all," Truman said, each word deliberate and clear despite his weakening voice. "My family." His eyes found Noah's again. "You be good, young man. Take care of your mama."

"I will," Noah promised solemnly. "Me and Mackie will."

Something passed between Mac and his grandfather at these words. Truman nodded, satisfied, before his eyes drifted closed again.

"I think that's our cue," Amy said softly, placing a hand on Noah's shoulder. "We should let Truman rest."

Noah looked up at Kelsey, uncertainty crossing his face for the first time. "Will I see him again?"

The directness of the question demanded honesty. "I don't think so, sweetheart."

Noah accepted this with the same quiet gravity he'd shown throughout. He leaned against Mac briefly. "Bye, Mackie. I'll see you tomorrow?"

Mac gathered the boy in a quick, fierce hug. "You bet, kiddo. Take care of Aunt Amy, okay? Make sure she doesn't eat all the ice cream."

The small attempt at normalcy seemed to reassure Noah. He nodded seriously before taking Amy's hand.

Kelsey walked them to the door, kneeling once more to hug Noah. "I love you so much," she whispered against his hair. "Be good for Amy."

"I will," he promised. "Don't be sad, Mom. I love you."

His simple words made Kelsey's eyes sting.

After they left, the cottage felt simultaneously emptier and more intensely focused, as if all the world had narrowed to this small space where life was preparing to slip away. Kelsey returned to the living room to resume her place beside Truman's bed. Mac's vigil remained unbroken.

"Noah did well," she said softly, settling into her chair. "He understands, in his way."

Mac nodded, but his eyes never left his grandfather's face. "He's a remarkable kid."

They fell into silence again, the room growing dimmer as the sun dipped toward the horizon and painted the sky in crimson, a spectacular display neither of them moved to observe. The beauty seemed both poignant and irrelevant in the face of what was happening within these walls.

Sometime later, time had lost its usual meaning in the suspended reality of their vigil, Truman's eyes opened again. This time, they were startlingly clear, focused in a way they hadn't been for days.

"Outside," he said. The single word carried surprising strength. "Want to go outside."

Mac leaned closer. "Grandad?"

"The deck," Truman insisted. "Want to see the stars once more."

Mac looked at Kelsey, a silent question in his eyes. She assessed Truman quickly, his color, his breathing, the steadiness of his pulse beneath her fingertips. Despite everything, there was something in his clarity that gave her pause.

"It might be possible," she said carefully. "The patio doors are wide enough that we could move the bed."

"Is it safe to move him?" Mac asked.

Kelsey considered the question. "Safe isn't the right question at this point," she said gently. "It's what he wants. And we can switch him to portable oxygen."

Decision made, Mac rose with purpose. "Let's do it, then."

The logistics proved challenging but not impossible. Mac disconnected the bed from the wall, while Kelsey secured the oxygen tank to the mobile stand. Together, they carefully maneuvered the bed toward the French doors that opened onto the deck, inch by painstaking inch.

"Tight fit," Mac muttered as they angled the bed through the doorway and the frame scraped slightly against the wood.

"Almost there," Kelsey encouraged, guiding the oxygen tubing to ensure it didn't tangle in the wheels.

With a final push, they managed to position the bed on the broad wooden deck. The night had turned unseasonably warm for late spring, and the air carried just enough chill to feel fresh without being uncomfortable. Above them, a full moon hung suspended in a cloudless sky, casting silver light across the water below.

Truman's face seemed to transform as he looked up at the vast expanse of stars. His breathing deepened slightly, as if the sea air itself was infusing him with momentary strength.

"Beautiful," he murmured. He looked from the moon to the dark silhouettes of pine trees at the property's edge, to the silver-tipped waves breaking against the rocks below.

Mac pulled up a chair beside the bed. Kelsey checked the oxygen flow once more before joining him, and the three of them existed together in a moment of peace.

"Eleanor and I," Truman said suddenly, "watched a meteor shower from this very spot. 1958. The year before we married."

Mac leaned forward to capture this unexpected gift of memory. "You never told me that story."

"Didn't I?" Truman's eyes remained fixed on the night sky. "She wore a blue dress. Had a thermos of coffee laced with whiskey." A smile touched his lips. "Proposed to her that night. Couldn't help myself. She outshone the stars."

Kelsey's throat tightened at the simple poetry of his words, at the love still evident in his voice after so many decades.

They sat in companionable silence for a while longer, the rhythm of the waves below creating a soothing counterpoint to the night's stillness. The moon climbed higher, and its light turned the bay into a mirror of quicksilver.

"Look." Truman's gaze was fixed on the vast sky above. "Up there."

Mac and Kelsey lifted their eyes to the star-studded darkness. Just as they did, a bright streak of light cut across the night—a falling star, brilliant and ephemeral, trailing silver across the black canvas before disappearing.

"A shooting star," Mac said, wonder momentarily displacing grief in his voice. "Did you see it, Grandad?"

Kelsey turned back to the bed. A sense of foreknowledge had already settled in her chest. In that brief moment, while their eyes had been lifted to the heavens, watching the falling star trace its arc across the sky, Truman had slipped away.

He lay peacefully, eyes closed as if in sleep. But the labored rise and fall of his chest had ceased.

Mac made a small, broken sound as he moved swiftly to the bedside. His hand found his grandfather's, still warm but utterly still beneath his touch.

Kelsey was slower. She checked for a pulse out of professional habit, though she expected none. The stillness beneath her fingertips was final, unequivocal.

"He's at peace, Mac," she said softly, resting her hand on Mac's shoulder. "It was a good death. Gentle. On his own terms."

Mac nodded, unable to speak. His shoulders shook slightly beneath her touch as he bent over his grandfather's hand and pressed it to his forehead in a gesture of profound grief and love.

Around them, the night continued its ancient rhythms, the waves breaking on the rocks below, the moon tracing its arc across the star-filled sky, the world breathing in and out as it had done since time began.

Inside this small circle of moonlight, a life had ended. But something of Truman remained in the love that had gathered his family around him, in the peace that now settled over his features.

Kelsey stood beside Mac, her hand steady on his shoulder as he grieved.

Beyond the railing, the bay stretched away toward the distant horizon, carrying the whispered promise of life flowing onward.

Chapter 27

M ac stood in the foyer of his house, their house now, watching as Noah darted from room to room, whooping with each new discovery. The boy's energy contrasted sharply with the leaden grief that had settled in his own chest since Truman's death.

Ten days, and the fog hadn't shown any signs of lifting. If anything, it seemed to thicken with each passing day, memories of his grandfather ambushing him at unexpected moments. The scent of pipe tobacco that lingered in Truman's cottage, which Mac couldn't bring himself to empty. The half-finished book on the coffee table, the pages marked, that Truman would never read.

"Mackie! Mackie!" Noah's excited voice penetrated the gray haze of his thoughts. "My room has a window seat! With cushions and everything!"

Mac forced his lips into what he hoped was a convincing smile. "Your mom picked those out. Special order."

"It's perfect for reading!" Noah exclaimed, bouncing on his toes. "And I can see the whole bay from up there!"

"That's the idea." Mac ruffled the boy's hair.

Noah beamed up at him before racing off again, and his footsteps thundered up the stairs. The sound brought life to spaces that had been silent for too long. Mac had never noticed how quiet the place was until Noah filled it with his boundless enthusiasm.

He turned as Kelsey entered through the front door, carrying another box labeled *KITCHEN* in her neat handwriting. She set it down with a small grunt of effort then pushed a strand of hair from her face.

"That's the last of the kitchen stuff," she said, straightening up. "Amy's got Noah's books and toys in her car. She's stopping to get pizza before coming over."

Mac nodded and moved to help her with the box. "I'll take this to the kitchen."

"Thanks." Her eyes studied his face with the careful attention he'd grown accustomed to since Truman's death. "You okay? You seem..."

"Fine," he said automatically, knowing even as he said it that she wouldn't believe him. Kelsey had an uncanny ability to see through his defenses. "Just thinking."

She squeezed his arm lightly, a gesture of understanding that required no response, before moving toward the living room to continue unpacking. Mac was struck by how naturally she fit into this space that had felt like nothing more than an investment property until now.

She'd chosen new curtains, rearranged furniture, added touches of color that transformed sterile rooms into something warm and inviting. His empty rooms were becoming a home, not just a house.

In the kitchen, Mac set the box on the counter and began unpacking its contents, dishes, glasses, the mismatched collection of mugs that Kelsey inexplicably refused to part with. He mechanically organized items in cabinets while his mind drifted elsewhere.

Truman had always wanted him to stop running. But now that Truman was gone, the urge to run had only intensified. The *Nereid* would take him far from the complications of human connection, and away from the grief that seemed to follow him like a shadow.

And yet.

Noah's laughter echoed from upstairs, followed by Kelsey's answering call. The sound wormed its way into Mac's chest, creating a strange, tight feeling that wasn't entirely unpleasant.

This wasn't how it was supposed to be. He hadn't planned on the way Noah would look at him with absolute trust, or how Kelsey's hand would find his in quiet moments.

He hadn't planned on becoming a family.

"Earth to Mac." Kelsey's voice startled him from his thoughts. She stood in the kitchen doorway, an expression of mild concern on her face. "You've been staring at that coffee mug for three minutes."

Mac set the mug down, embarrassed to be caught woolgathering. "Sorry. Just distracted."

"You don't have to apologize." She moved into the kitchen, taking a glass from the box and placing it in the cabinet. Her expression was carefully neutral, revealing nothing of what she might be thinking.

"I wanted to show you something," he said, changing the subject. "Before I forget."

He led her to the study, the one room in the house that remained largely unchanged. The heavy oak desk still dominated the space, rows of legal binders lining the bookshelves behind it. Mac opened the desk drawer and withdrew a leather portfolio.

"These are the account details." He laid out various documents on the desktop. "Joint checking, savings, investment accounts. I've added your name to everything."

Kelsey's brow furrowed slightly as she looked at the papers. "Mac, I..."

"There's also this," he continued, pulling out a small box containing credit cards and an ATM card, all bearing her name. "Johnson handles the bills. He'll make sure everything gets paid on time. I've instructed the bank to send duplicate statements to you."

Harrison had almost had a heart attack when Mac had refused to put together any kind of post-martial agreement. His exact words were that he was a "damn fool." But he idea that his resources, his house, his money, his name, would continue to protect Kelsey and Noah after he'd sailed away was strangely comforting. Maybe that was what Truman had meant about finding happiness before he died. Not the romantic notion of falling in love again, but knowing his legacy would continue.

"Slow down," Kelsey said, placing her hand over his as he reached for another folder. "What is all this?"

Mac took a breath, forced himself to meet her eyes. "Our finances, and what you need to know to access our accounts. I'm making sure you and Noah have what you need."

"We're doing fine with what we have," she said quietly.

"This is different," Mac explained, opening the folder to reveal a thick document with Post-it notes marking specific pages. "This outlines the investment strategy. Gordon Winters manages it; he's conservative but gets solid returns. He is also managing Noah's trust from Truman, and this one is your account he set up for you. You don't have to touch it if you don't want to. All of the day-to-day expenses should be paid through our joint accounts. You can reach him at this number if you have questions."

Kelsey scanned the numbers, and her face blanched as she absorbed the information. "There's a lot of zeros here," she whispered, then stared at him. Her expression shifted from confusion to something more troubled. "Mac, why are you doing this now?"

He shrugged, attempting nonchalance. "Just being practical. You shouldn't have to worry about money."

"That's not what I asked."

Mac shuffled papers to avoid her searching gaze. "I also want you to know that you don't have to keep working if you don't want to. There's more than enough—"

"I like my job," she interrupted.

"I know. I'm just saying you have options. I know it can get hectic for you, with Noah. You could cut back if you wanted, or quit altogether." He closed the folder and tapped it with his fingertips. "If you're concerned about health care on the island, you could take a position on the clinic board. Use some of our resources to improve services for the islanders. Your expertise would be valuable."

Kelsey remained silent, studying him with an intensity that made him uncomfortable. When she finally spoke, her voice was carefully measured.

"You're leaving?"

Mac had rehearsed this conversation in his mind, prepared reasonable explanations, but now that the moment had arrived, the words felt inadequate.

"I've always planned to," he said finally. "Once Grandad was..." He couldn't finish the sentence.

"I know that," Kelsey said. "But this doesn't feel like you're planning a six-month sailing trip. This feels like you're handing over your entire life to us. Like you're leaving forever."

Mac walked to the window, looking out at the bay where the *Nereid* sat moored, white hull gleaming in the afternoon sun. "It was always the plan. Before any of this happened."

"Before us, you mean."

The simple statement cut through his careful evasions. He turned to face her and found an unreadable expression that somehow made this harder.

"Yes," he admitted. "Before us."

Kelsey leaned against the desk, arms crossed loosely over her chest. "And now?"

He looked at her then, really looked at her, searching for some hint of what she was feeling beneath the composed exterior, surprised that he wanted to see what she was keeping closely guarded.

Mac's hand clenched involuntarily at his side. "Now, everything's complicated. You. Noah. I didn't plan for any of it."

"Neither did I," Kelsey said quietly. "But here we are."

He faced her again and struggled to articulate the conflict raging within him. "I need to go, Kelsey. I can't stay."

Something flickered briefly across her face, disappointment, perhaps, or resignation, before her expression settled back into careful neutrality. "I see."

"Do you?" he asked, suddenly desperate to break through the wall of composure she'd erected.

"You want to leave," she said simply. "That's clear enough."

"That's not—" Mac broke off, frustrated. How could he explain the pull of the open ocean, the need for solitude to sort through the tangled mess of grief his life was? How could he make her understand when he barely understood it himself?

"It's okay, Mac," Kelsey said. Her voice was gentle but distant. "You don't owe us anything. The marriage was a legal arrangement that served its purpose. You deserve to go on with your life."

The clinical assessment of what had grown between them landed like a slap. "Is that all it is to you? A legal arrangement?"

"You tell me. You're the one making exit plans," she said, crossing her arms over her chest. For the first time, her composure wavered slightly.

Mac ran a hand through his hair. "I'm trying to make sure you're taken care of."

"We don't need taking care of," Kelsey replied, a hint of steel entering her voice. "We'll manage just fine after you go."

The quiet certainty in her tone—*after* you go, not *if* you go—stung more than he'd expected. "So that's it? You've already decided I'm leaving?"

"Haven't *you*? Mac, stop waffling. Choose to stay or choose to go," she countered, meeting his gaze directly.

The moment hung between them. Before Mac could respond, Noah's thundering footsteps on the stairs heralded his arrival.

"Mom! Mackie! Can we get a dog? There's a perfect spot in the backyard for a doghouse, and I promise I'll walk it every day."

"Whoa, slow down," Kelsey laughed, her demeanor transforming completely as she turned to her son. "We've barely moved in. Let's get settled first before we add a dog to the mix."

Noah's face fell momentarily before brightening again. "But you didn't say no!"

"I didn't say yes either," Kelsey pointed out. "Go wash up for dinner and set the table. Amy will be here with pizza soon."

As Noah raced off, Mac found himself caught by this kind of ordinary exchange he'd watched other families have from a distance, but had never imagined he'd be part of one.

"He's going to wear you down on the dog," he said, a small smile tugging at his lips despite everything.

"Probably," Kelsey agreed, though her smile didn't reach her eyes. "I'll go help him set the table."

As she moved to leave, Mac caught her hand. "Kelsey."

When she turned back, her expression was carefully neutral again.

"I..." He broke off, struggling to find the right words. "This isn't simple."

"Do whatever you want, Mac. Noah and I will be fine either way."

She left him standing alone in the study.

Chapter 28

The late afternoon sun filtered through the windows of Mac's house, reflecting off the hardwood floors. Kelsey adjusted a vase of fresh-cut hydrangeas, their blue heads nodding slightly under her touch. Around her, the house hummed with voices, laughter occasionally rising above the general murmur. This was exactly the kind of wake Truman had requested. Not a funeral but a celebration.

"He would have loved this," Ruth said, appearing at Kelsey's elbow with two glasses of whiskey. She handed one to Kelsey. "Especially the whiskey. He always said cheap stuff was for funerals, good stuff for wakes."

Kelsey accepted the glass, the amber liquid catching the light. "Mac made sure it was his favorite."

"Of course he did." Ruth's eyes tracked across the room to where Mac stood, deep in conversation with the harbor master. "How is he holding up?"

"As well as can be expected." The response was automatic and noncommittal—the kind of thing Kelsey had found herself saying repeatedly over the past few days when asked about Mac.

The truth was more complicated. Since their conversation in his study, a new distance had grown between them. It was as though the unspoken words between them had solidified into an impenetrable barrier.

"And you?" Ruth pressed, her shrewd eyes missing nothing.

Kelsey took a sip of whiskey and welcomed the burn. "I'm fine. Just focusing on getting Noah settled in."

Ruth's expression suggested she wasn't entirely convinced, but before she could pursue the matter, they were interrupted by Mrs. Henderson, the librarian.

"There you are, dear," she said, patting Kelsey's arm. "What a lovely service. So dignified, yet casual, very Truman."

"Thank you. Mac arranged most of it."

"You two make such a wonderful team," Mrs. Henderson continued, a gleam in her eye that Kelsey had come to recognize as the island's insatiable curiosity about their relationship. "Though I must say, we were all surprised by how quickly you married. When did you first meet?"

Kelsey had rehearsed this answer so many times it came automatically. "Mac rear-ended my car."

"And it was love at first sight?" The older woman leaned in, hungry for details.

"Something like that," Kelsey replied, but her smile didn't quite reach her eyes. She glanced across the room and found Mac's face in the crowd. He seemed distant, unreachable, though he was only a room away.

Mrs. Henderson followed her gaze. "Well, it's clear you're devoted to each other. And your little boy has certainly blossomed with a father figure in his life. I saw him at the library last week with Mac. They were picking out marine life books together. Thick as thieves, those two."

The observation lodged a splinter beneath Kelsey's ribs. Noah had indeed flourished under Mac's attention. What would happen when that attention was gone? She worried for her little boy, caught in an adult mess.

"If you'll excuse me," she said, "I should check on the food."

In the kitchen, Kelsey leaned against the counter, taking a moment to compose herself. Through the window, she could see guests spilling onto the deck, glasses in hand, the bay stretching beyond them in a glittering expanse. Exactly the view Truman had loved so much.

"Hiding out?" Amy's voice broke into her thoughts.

Kelsey turned to find her sister arranging canapés on a serving plate. "Just taking a breather. One more question about our whirl-wind romance and I might snap."

Amy snorted. "Island gossip. Better get used to it since we're both going to be permanent fixtures now."

"Still processing the inheritance?"

"Understatement of the century." Amy's hands stilled on the plate. "A historic mansion and twenty acres. What am I supposed to do with that?"

"Guess there is something to that saying, 'Be careful what you wish for.' From the way people have been bending your ear all evening, there's no shortage of suggestions."

"Tell me about it. Bed and breakfast. Art retreat. Summer camp. Wedding venue." Amy shook her head, bemused. "Old Mrs. Farnsworth actually suggested a cat sanctuary."

Despite herself, Kelsey laughed. "That's... specific."

"Apparently, she has seventeen cats and is 'concerned about their future.'" Amy grimaced. "But seriously, Kels. What if he made a mistake? I barely knew him."

"He knew you," Kelsey said softly. "He knew how much better you made him feel. How you could do that for others, too. He was a good judge of character, Amy."

Amy's eyes grew suspiciously bright. "I just wish I could thank him."

"You are. By being here. By celebrating him exactly as he wanted." Kelsey squeezed her sister's hand. "Also, don't think I haven't noticed you taking mental measurements of every room in the mansion."

"It has potential," Amy admitted, a smile breaking through her melancholy. "The acoustics in the main hall are incredible. And that staircase? Pure drama."

"See? You're already planning."

"Maybe." Amy picked up the platter. "Speaking of planning... have you and Mac talked?"

Kelsey busied herself with rearranging napkins. "About what?"

"Don't play dumb. About him leaving."

"There's nothing to talk about. He's always been clear about his plans."

Amy studied her sister's face. "And you're okay with that? Your husband sailing off into the sunset?"

"It's a temporary arrangement, Amy. You know that."

"Is it? Because from where I'm standing, it looks a lot like a real marriage. The way he looks at you."

"Don't," Kelsey interrupted, more sharply than she intended. "Please. Not today."

Amy sighed. "Fine. But you're going to have to face it eventually."

"Face what?"

"That you're in love with your husband."

Kelsey's denial died on her lips as Mac appeared in the kitchen doorway. Had he heard? His expression revealed nothing.

"There you are," he said. "The fireworks crew just arrived. They're setting up on the beach."

"Perfect timing," Amy said brightly, lifting her platter. "I'll announce it to the guests."

As she brushed past Mac, Kelsey was left alone with him for the first time that evening. The kitchen suddenly felt too small, too intimate.

"Everything okay?" His voice was carefully neutral.

"Fine," she replied automatically. "Just taking a moment."

Mac moved further into the kitchen, close enough that she could smell the faint woody scent of his cologne. "It's a good turnout. Grandad would have been pleased."

"Half the island, just like his birthday." Kelsey smiled despite herself. "He made an impact."

"He did." Mac's gaze softened with memory.

The moment stretched between them, taut with possibilities. Then Mac glanced at his watch. "We should get outside. Fireworks start in fifteen."

As they moved toward the deck, Kelsey found herself waylaid by more well-wishers, more curious questions about their relationship. She answered on autopilot, her awareness fixed on Mac as he moved through the crowd, accepting condolences with grace, raising a glass in his grandfather's memory, playing the role of grieving grandson with perfect composure. Only she seemed to notice the tension in his shoulders, the way his smile never quite reached his eyes.

Outside, guests gathered on the expansive lawn, necks craned toward the darkening sky. Noah darted up to Kelsey, his friend Tyler in tow.

"Mom! The fireworks are going to be epic! Mac says they ordered special ones that explode in blue because that was Truman's favorite color!"

Kelsey smoothed his wild hair. "That sounds perfect."

"Can I sleep over at Tyler's tonight? Please? His dad said it's okay, and they're making pancakes for breakfast!"

She glanced at Tyler's father, who nodded confirmation. "Alright. But don't stay up too late, and be good."

"Yes!" Noah pumped his fist in victory before turning serious. "Is it okay to be excited? Since it's a funeral and all?"

"It's a celebration of life," Kelsey corrected gently. "And yes, it's absolutely okay to be excited. Truman would have wanted you to enjoy every moment."

Satisfied, Noah raced off with Tyler, their young voices carrying back through the gathering dusk. The simple joy of his excitement stood in stark contrast to her complicated emotions.

The first firework shot into the sky with a distant whistle, exploding in a shower of blue sparks. A collective "ahh" rose from the assembled guests. More followed, illuminating upturned faces with flashes of blue, silver, gold.

Kelsey found herself standing beside Mac, close but not touching. Above them, the sky bloomed repeatedly with light, the explosions reflecting off the dark water of the bay. From the corner of her eye, she could see Mac's profile, strong and defined, but his expression was softened by the ethereal light from above.

"It's exactly what he would have wanted," she said softly.

Mac's hand found hers in the darkness, fingers intertwining with a familiarity that made her heart clench. "He told me he wanted his send-off to be memorable. 'Nothing too somber,' he said, 'or I'll come back and haunt you.'"

A particularly large burst of blue and silver lit up the night, casting momentary daylight across the lawn. In that frozen instant, Kelsey saw the glitter of tears in Mac's eyes. Then darkness fell again, and his expression was once more hidden.

They stood that way through the remainder of the display, hands linked, neither speaking. When the final volley exploded overhead in a cascade of blue stars, the crowd erupted in appreciative applause. Mac's hand tightened briefly around hers before releasing it. She wondered if he too was thinking about their first kiss, under the fireworks at Truman's first party.

The evening wound down gradually after that. Noah departed with Tyler's family, his goodbye hug fierce and quick. Guests drifted away in twos and threes, leaving behind empty glasses and plates of half-eaten food. Amy was among the last to leave, pulling Kelsey into a tight hug.

"Call me tomorrow," she whispered. "And remember what I said."

Finally, only Kelsey and Mac remained, moving through the quiet house collecting glasses, straightening furniture, postponing the moment when they would be truly alone with nothing to distract them from the conversation they'd been avoiding.

"Leave the rest," Mac said eventually, taking a stack of plates from her hands. "The cleaning service will handle it tomorrow."

When Kelsey relinquished the dishes, she was suddenly aware of how tired she was.

"I think I'll head up," she said, gesturing vaguely toward the stairs.

Mac nodded but made no move toward the staircase. Instead, he crossed to the cabinet and withdrew the bottle of Truman's favorite whiskey. "One more toast? For Grandad?"

Something in his voice made refusal impossible. "Of course."

He poured two fingers into each of two crystal tumblers and handed one to her. They stood in the center of the living room, glasses raised to the memory of the man who had, in his own way, brought them together.

"To Truman," Mac said simply.

"To Truman," she echoed, and the whiskey burned a warm path down her throat.

Silence settled between them, not entirely uncomfortable but weighted with unspoken words. Mac wandered to the large windows overlooking the bay, where the last of the firework smoke drifted across the night sky over the dark, endless bay.

"I'm leaving the day after tomorrow," Mac said, his voice low.

Kelsey gripped the back of the sofa, knuckles white. Even with the knowledge lurking in every quiet moment these past weeks, hearing it aloud felt like a wave breaking over her.

"For how long?" she managed.

"I don't know." The words were heavier than the gathering dusk. "Maybe months. Maybe longer."

Silence expanded to fill the room. Outside, the fog gathered in the hollows of the lawn, and the house felt colder, emptier.

Longer than months meant seasons. Years, even. The reality of what had always been an abstract concept suddenly crystallized.

"And when were you going to tell Noah?" Kelsey said, voice tight. "Or were you hoping I'd do the explaining when he wakes up and you're gone?"

Mac's shoulders stiffened. "I thought it would be easier for him."

"Easier for you, you mean." The accusation slipped out, sharp and unplanned, and she instantly regretted it. But she didn't take it back.

When Mac turned, the weariness in his eyes was almost worse than anger. "I'm not good at this, Kelsey. Goodbyes. Staying. Any of it."

"You're better at it than you think." She swallowed, fighting for composure. "But if you're going, then *go*. Don't make Noah—or me—wait for the other shoe to drop."

The wind rattled the windows. Somewhere in the distance, the lighthouse beam swept across the bay—steady, persistent, a promise of safe passage or of warning, depending on your direction.

Kelsey set her glass down with deliberate care. "He deserves a proper goodbye, Mac. Not just waking up to find you gone."

"You're right." Mac ran a hand through his hair, a gesture of frustration she'd come to recognize. "I'll talk to him tomorrow, when he gets back from Tyler's."

"And what am I supposed to tell him when he asks when you're coming back?" Kelsey asked, unable to keep the edge from her voice.

Mac was silent for a long moment. "Tell him the truth. That I don't know."

"*Are* you coming back?"

He moved closer then, his face shaded in the dim light of the room. "I don't know. That's the honest answer. I don't know what

I'm looking for out there, or if I'll find it. I don't know if what I'm running from will follow me."

She had no answer for that. Instead, she stepped closer and brushed her lips against his in a whisper of a kiss.

Looking down at her, his eyes darkened and flared, his mouth finding hers with a hunger that matched the need that had been building inside her for days. Her body arched into his, hands sliding into his hair to hold him closer.

The kiss deepened, desperation threading through desire. They had been here before, using physical connection when words failed, but this felt more urgent, as if they were both aware of the closing window of time.

Mac broke away first, his breathing uneven. His hands framed her face, eyes searching hers in the dim light. "I'm sorry. For a lot of things."

"Don't," she whispered, not wanting apologies, not now. "Not tonight."

She kissed him again, pouring into it all the words she couldn't say. Mac responded with equal fervor, his arms wrapping around her, pulling her flush against him as if trying to eliminate any space between them.

They stumbled toward the stairs, unwilling to break contact even as they navigated the steps. In the hallway, Mac pressed her against the wall, his mouth hot on her neck, hands sliding beneath her dress with possessive urgency. Kelsey gasped, her own fingers working at the buttons of his shirt, needing to feel his skin against hers.

In their bedroom, though it had never felt truly shared until this moment, Mac laid her on the massive king bed with a reverence that contrasted with the urgency of his earlier touch.

"Are you sure?" he asked, hovering above her, his body a shadow in the darkness.

In answer, Kelsey pulled him down to her. She needed the weight of him, the reality of his body against hers. They moved together with increasing desperation to imprint the memory of each other on their skin.

"Look at me," Mac whispered as they reached the edge together.

Kelsey opened her eyes to find his fixed on hers, dark with passion but also something that looked jarringly like he was trying to commit this moment to memory. The realization sent her over the edge, a sob catching in her throat as pleasure washed through her. Mac followed moments later, his body tensing as he buried his face against her neck.

In the aftermath, they lay tangled together, the sound of their gradually slowing breaths the only noise in the darkened room. Mac's hand traced idle patterns on her bare shoulder, his touch gentle now, almost reverent.

"I'm sorry, I—" he began, then stopped.

Kelsey waited, heart pounding, hope rising treacherously despite her best efforts to suppress it.

But Mac didn't continue. Instead, he pressed a kiss to her temple, then rolled away onto his back.

Kelsey turned onto her side, studying his profile in the faint moonlight filtering through the curtains. "Sorry for what?"

His jaw tightened, the struggle visible even in the dim light. "I'm sorry I'm not the man you and Noah need."

"You already are," Kelsey whispered. The admission cost her more than she wanted to show. Mac's hand found hers in the darkness, fingers intertwining. He brought her hand to his lips and pressed a kiss to her knuckles.

They made love again, slower this time, each touch deliberate, as if storing up the memory of each other's bodies for the long absence to come.

Later, as Mac's breathing evened into sleep, Kelsey remained awake, watching the play of moonlight across the ceiling. Beside her, Mac's arm lay heavy across her waist.

Tomorrow, she would need to be strong. Tomorrow, she would help Noah understand, would maintain the pragmatic approach that had gotten her through every other challenge in life to this point.

But tonight, in the darkness, she allowed herself to acknowledge the truth she'd been avoiding. Against knowing better, she had fallen in love with her husband.

In less than forty-eight hours, he would be gone.

Chapter 29

Kelsey opened her eyes to pre-dawn darkness and the sound of careful movement. The bedroom door closed with a barely audible click. Footsteps descended the stairs, deliberate and measured, avoiding the spots that creaked. The distant thud of the back door.

Gone. Just like that.

She rolled onto her side, facing the space where Mac had slept. The sheets were cool already. Had he been watching her sleep? Had he considered waking her for a final goodbye?

Realistically, Kelsey knew she had wanted to let him slip away with minimal fuss, minimal pain. Ensure that he couldn't see how his leaving was truly affecting her.

Outside, the distant rumble of an engine drifted up from the water. Kelsey knew the sequence by heart now. He would use the auxiliary motor to navigate the channel, then there would be silence as the sails caught the wind.

She remained motionless, listening to the sounds of departure. The sensible thing would be to get up, to go to the window, to mark this moment properly. To bear witness to his leaving. But she resisted the ritual, as if refusing to acknowledge his departure might somehow kccp a part of him here.

The space beside her felt impossibly vast. The king-sized bed that had seemed too intimate in those first awkward days of moving into his house now stretched before her like a miniature desert, empty and unforgiving. She traced her fingers over the pillow where his head had rested, catching the faint scent of his shampoo. How long before that, too, would fade?

The engine sound grew more distant as he headed out. Soon, he would be a silhouette against the dawn sky, and then not even that.

Kelsey closed her eyes, remembering yesterday morning when they'd told Noah. The boy had taken the news with surprising stoicism on the surface, though she'd noticed the slight tremble in his lower lip, the way his fingers had worried the edge of his shirt. Noah's small tells that betrayed his confusion, his hurt.

Mac had been gentle but firm, explaining he needed to sail away for a while. But at least he'd taken her concerns about Noah to heart; he had set up the email account on Noah's tablet and showed him how the video calls could work when Mac was near enough to land for a signal. For that, Kelsey was grateful.

What Mac hadn't done was set up any such system for Kelsey herself. The omission felt deliberate, a clear delineation of priorities, of relationships worth maintaining. Noah was the responsibility Mac had undertaken. Kelsey was... what? The means to that end?

The engine sound faded entirely. Kelsey finally rolled from the bed, drawing back the curtain just enough to see the bay. Mac's sailboat was a white speck against the darkened water, diminishing with each moment.

She watched until the *Nereid* disappeared beyond the channel markers, until there was nothing to see but the first pink streaks of dawn illuminating an empty horizon. Then she let the curtain fall back into place.

The house felt different already. Hollowed out.

Kelsey moved through her morning routine with deliberate care. Shower. Clothes. Coffee. The familiar motions were a bulwark against the tide of despair threatening to pull her under. She would need to wake Noah soon for school, as if they hadn't just lost a vital component of their newly constructed family.

The adoption would go through, Mac had assured her of that. Johnson had his instructions and the attorneys knew what to do. The paperwork would proceed without Mac's physical presence, grinding methodically toward making Noah officially a MacCormack. A strange comfort, knowing that despite everything, this part of Mac's promise remained intact.

The threat the Prescotts held was at bay, Jason effectively hoppled. The house was theirs to live in, and every material need was met.

Everything except the one thing she hadn't realized she wanted until it was already slipping away. Him.

Foolish, really. She'd gone into the arrangement with eyes wide open. A marriage of convenience. A solution to a specific problem.

Yet here she was, standing in the kitchen of a dream house, feeling as if someone had hollowed out her chest and replaced her heart with lead.

She'd been here before, she reminded herself. When she learned of David's death, pregnant and suddenly alone. Grief had seemed like an ocean too vast to cross. She had survived that. She had built a life for herself and Noah from nothing. She could do it again.

But this was different. David hadn't chosen to leave. He hadn't packed his things and sailed away. David's leaving had been absolute, irreversible. There was clarity in that, a definitive ending that allowed for eventual healing.

Mac's departure was all loose ends. Not knowing if he would return, or when. Not knowing if, somewhere out on the open ocean, he would find whatever he was looking for and decide that life was simpler without the complications of a family waiting at home.

Kelsey glanced at the clock. Time to wake Noah. She prepped herself for the questions that would inevitably come from the little boy, knowing she would need to strike the right balance between honesty and reassurance. Noah had never known his father, had never experienced the pain of someone walking away from him. Until now.

Climbing the stairs to Noah's room, she paused at the top, suddenly overwhelmed by a wave of déjà vu. How many times had she done this in the first months after Noah was born? Gathered herself, plastered on a brave face, determined not to let her infant son somehow absorb her grief even though he was too young to understand?

Too many to count.

Mac had certainly left them well-provided for, beyond imagining. He had honored the commitment he'd made. But provision without presence was a poor substitute for love.

She took a deep breath. They would survive this, she and Noah. They had survived worse. And if, when, Mac returned, they would deal with that too, whatever it might mean.

Kelsey went to wake her son. The day was beginning, whether she was ready or not. The only way out was through.

Chapter 30

The late August sunlight beat its heat across the mansion's sprawling lawn. Noah and Tyler chased Amy's terrier, Ollie, their shouts and laughter drifting up to where Kelsey and Amy sat on the weathered stone steps. Kelsey swirled the last of her pinot noir and watched the boys rather than her sister's animated gesturing about the mansion looming behind them.

"The historical society practically had a collective heart attack when I mentioned updating the kitchen," Amy said, refilling her glass from the bottle nestled between them. "Apparently, the original cabinetry is 'irreplaceable period craftsmanship.' Never mind that it's falling apart and probably harboring colonies of mice behind the walls."

"Mmm," Kelsey murmured. Noah flopped dramatically onto the grass, allowing Ollie to scramble over his chest.

"And the wiring, my God, the wiring. The inspector said it's a miracle the place hasn't burned to the ground." Amy paused, studying her sister's profile. "You haven't heard a word I've said, have you?"

Kelsey blinked, then turned toward Amy with a guilty smile. "Sorry. Something about... wiring?"

"Never mind." Amy nudged Kelsey's shoulder gently. "Where were you just now?"

"Here. Just..." Kelsey gestured vaguely. "Thinking."

"About Mac," Amy stated flatly. Not a question.

Kelsey didn't bother denying it. "Noah talked to him Tuesday. Video call. They spoke for almost an hour."

"And?"

"And nothing. Noah said he's somewhere near the Azores. The connection wasn't great."

Amy's expression softened. "He didn't ask to speak with you?"

"Why would he?" Kelsey kept her tone deliberately light.

"Right. That's why you're sitting here looking like someone stole your puppy."

"I don't look like that."

"You absolutely do." Amy topped off Kelsey's glass without asking. "It's been what—seven weeks?"

"Six weeks, four days," Kelsey corrected, then winced at her own precision. "Give or take."

Amy's eyebrows rose. "Not that you're counting."

"Shut up." Kelsey took a larger sip of wine than she'd intended. Thankfully they had walked over on the footpath from their house through the cove beach, and then to the cottages. Tyler's mom was coming to get him after dinner.

They fell silent. The boys had invented some new game that seemed to involve Ollie, a stick, and elaborate running patterns across the lawn. It was a perfect late summer evening, the kind that hinted at autumn's approach while still clinging to summer's warmth.

"So the historical society is giving you grief," Kelsey said finally, steering the conversation back to safer territory.

Amy accepted the redirection. "Grief doesn't begin to cover it. Every modification requires forms in triplicate, photographic documentation, and probably a blood sacrifice." She sighed dramatically. "Truman's will specified maintaining 'historical integrity,' but what does that even mean? Do I preserve every crumbling baseboard? Every warped floor plank?"

"What does your heart say?" Kelsey asked, genuinely curious now.

A spark of real passion lighted Amy's eyes. "My heart says this place could be amazing. Not a museum, not frozen in time, but alive. A space where people create, connect, heal." She gestured expansively toward the mansion. "Music in that grand salon with the bay windows. Art workshops in the east wing where the light is incredible. Yoga out here on the lawn. Maybe even residential retreats."

"A healing arts center," Kelsey summarized, smiling at her sister's enthusiasm.

"Something like that." Amy hugged her knees to her chest. "But the logistics are overwhelming. The renovation costs alone..."

"You could start small. One room at a time."

"At that rate, I'll be ninety before it's functional." Amy frowned at her wine glass. "I almost wish Truman had left it to Mac instead. At least he has the resources to do something with it, unlike the limited fund Truman left and my invisible savings."

"Hmm. Not sure what Mac would have done with it. Maybe he'd have given it away." Kelsey pointed out. "He hates being tied to places."

The loaded observation hung between them.

"Have you considered what Mac suggested, about not working?" Amy asked after a moment. "About taking a position at the clinic board? Improving health care on the island?"

Kelsey shook her head. "I'm not quitting my job. The clinic needs nurse practitioners more than it needs board members."

"You wouldn't have to quit. Just... scale back. Consult. Direct resources where they're needed most."

"And live off Mac's money?" Kelsey's voice sharpened.

"It's not just Mac's money," Amy reminded her gently. "You're his wife. Legally, half of everything is yours."

"That's not why I married him."

"I know that. But the fact remains."

Kelsey watched Noah executing a cartwheel for Tyler's approval. "I need the structure of work. The normalcy. It's good for Noah to see nothing's really changed."

"Except for the giant, Mac-shaped hole in your lives," Amy observed dryly.

"We're fine," Kelsey insisted. "Noah's handling it well. He's made new friends over summer break. His grades are good."

"And his mom?"

Kelsey shot her sister a warning look. "His mom is fine too."

"If you say so." Amy didn't sound convinced.

"When did you become such an expert? Your last boyfriend had a man bun and played ukulele covers of death metal songs."

"First of all, Jasper was an experimental musician. And second, my disastrous dating history gives me a unique perspective on other people's problems."

Despite herself, Kelsey laughed. "Fair enough."

"My point is," Amy continued, more seriously, "you have options, Kels. The house, the money, it gives you freedom. You could quit the clinic and invest in this place with me." Her expression turned sly. "We could be independently wealthy arts patrons."

"Right. The York Foundation for Wayward Artists."

"I'm serious!" Amy's eyes lit up. "Well, half-serious. But think about it, what if we combined resources? You could finance some of the renovations, and I could manage the programming. We could create something amazing here."

The enthusiasm in her sister's voice was infectious. "You're actually considering this."

"I've been considering it since Truman dropped this massive responsibility in my lap," Amy admitted. "I just didn't think you'd be interested."

Kelsey glanced at the mansion, seeing it with new eyes. Seeing it as a possibility. A project they could build together. "I don't know the first thing about renovations and business planning."

"But you know healthcare. Community needs." Amy leaned forward. "What if part of the mansion became a teaching clinic? For preventative care, wellness programs? The island could use that, right?"

The seed of something interesting took root in Kelsey's mind. "There are a lot of underserved families here. Especially in the off-season when the summer clinics close."

"See? Perfect partnership." Amy clinked her glass against Kelsey's. "You save lives; I nurture souls."

"Quite the mission statement."

"We'll work on it." Amy's expression softened. "Seriously though, Kels. Think about it. This could be your project too."

Before Kelsey could respond, Noah came bounding up the steps, red-cheeked and breathless, Tyler and Ollie on his heels.

"Mom! Can we have pizza for dinner? Tyler's dad said he can stay over if it's okay with you."

Kelsey smoothed his wild hair, damp with exertion. "Did he? That's funny, because Tyler's mom said Tyler has a dentist appointment first thing tomorrow. She'll be by to pick him up after dinner."

Tyler's face fell. "I forgot about that."

"Next weekend," Kelsey promised. "But yes to pizza."

The boys cheered and raced inside with Ollie barking excitedly at their heels.

"You know he's going to expect pizza every night now," Amy remarked, gathering the wine glasses.

"Small price for that smile." Kelsey stood, brushing off her jeans. "It's been a while since I've seen him this happy."

"Kids are resilient." Amy followed Kelsey inside. "Unlike their mothers."

"I'm resilient," Kelsey protested. "I'm here, aren't I? Moving forward."

Amy paused as they walked back toward her cottage. "Moving forward isn't the same as living fully."

"Profound. Did you read that on a tea bag?"

"Mock all you want," Amy said, unperturbed. "But answer me this: when was the last time you did something just because it made you happy? Not for Noah, not for work, not for anyone else, just for you?"

The question caught Kelsey off guard. She opened her mouth to respond, then closed it again.

"That's what I thought," Amy said, not unkindly. "Look, I'm not saying quit your job tomorrow and become my business partner. I'm saying consider what would bring you joy, and then do more of that. Life's too short. You of all people should understand that."

From the path ahead of them, they could hear Noah and Tyler arguing good naturedly about pizza toppings, Ollie's occasional bark punctuating their debate.

"I'm not unhappy," Kelsey said finally. "Just... adjusting."

Amy's skeptical expression spoke volumes. "If you say so."

"I do." Kelsey nudged her sister.

They left Amy at her cottage and walked past their empty one. It seemed so small now. She tried to keep up behind the boys, following their voices through the dense pines as they argued. Apparently, Tyler wasn't happy with the idea of pineapple and ham on his pizza.

Amy was right. When was the last time she'd done something purely for her own happiness? She couldn't remember.

The realization was unsettling.

Mac couldn't stop looking at his watch. Eight hours and he'd be in port. Eight hours until he could step off the *Nereid* and get to the next harbor with a proper marine electrician. The satellite phone needed fixing, and quickly.

He adjusted the mainsail, catching the strengthening afternoon breeze. The horizon ahead remained clear, the weather report promising fair conditions all the way to Porto Santo. The small Portuguese island wasn't his first choice for making landfall, but it had the supplies and expertise he needed before continuing his journey.

Three weeks ago, he would have reveled in these perfect sailing conditions—steady wind, moderate seas, the vast Atlantic stretching endlessly around him. Even now, part of him appreciated the solitude and the rhythm of life at sea. This was what he'd wanted, wasn't it? Freedom, independence, the open horizon.

But his satellite phone lay useless in the navigation station drawer, waterlogged beyond repair. The electrical incident that had fried his communication systems had been concerning. One moment he'd been in contact with the world, the next, utterly alone—no way to call for help if needed.

From what he could tell, the damage was caused by some loose wiring that almost looked as though it had been tampered with. Regardless of the cause, the effect had been complete.

Standing in the cabin, staring at the dead equipment, Mac had felt a moment of unease. But he'd convinced himself this was just a temporary setback. He could make repairs in Porto Santo and be on his way.

Mac checked the wind indicator again, making a minor adjustment to catch the best angle. A sudden gust snapped the mainsail taut, and the boom creaked with tension. Mac adjusted the sheet automatically.

Lost in thought, Mac barely registered the darkening sky to the west. The approaching weather system wasn't on his charts, wasn't in the forecast he'd checked that morning. He frowned and double checked the instruments on his navigation station. The barometer was dropping rapidly—too rapidly.

"Damn it," he muttered, then returned to the deck to survey the horizon. The previously clear sky had developed an ominous band of clouds, moving faster than seemed possible.

He needed to reduce sail immediately. The *Nereid* could handle rough weather, but not with full canvas deployed. Mac moved quickly, securing loose items on deck before turning his attention to the rigging. The wind was picking up already, the gentle rocking motion of the boat transforming into a more pronounced pitch and roll.

Muscle memory took over. He shortened sail, checked lines, prepared for the squall's arrival. This was the danger of solo sailing—no one to take shifts, no one to help when conditions deteriorated rapidly. But Mac had decades of experience. He'd weathered worse.

The first lashing of rain struck as he finished securing the main. It came horizontally, driven by wind that had seemingly doubled in strength within minutes. Mac squinted against the stinging droplets, making his way carefully back toward the cockpit. The deck pitched beneath him, slick with rain.

He reached for the safety line he always trailed when sailing solo. Old habits, drilled into him by his father. Never move on deck in rough weather without being tethered. The ocean was unforgiving of mistakes.

But before he could reach the line, the boat lurched suddenly, caught between swells. Mac's foot slipped on the wet deck. He grabbed for the boom, but his fingers slid off the rain-slick surface. For a suspended moment, he felt himself falling, the boat tilting away from him, the dark water rising to meet him.

Then impact—cold that stole his breath, pressure against his ears, the sudden absence of sound replaced by a muffled roaring. Disorientation as he tumbled beneath the surface, the weight of his foul-weather gear dragging him down.

Mac fought the instinctive panic, forcing his body to still, to orient. Surface. He needed to find the surface. He kicked hard to propel himself upward against the sodden weight of his clothing. His lungs began to burn and demand oxygen.

His head broke through into air and chaos. Rain lashing down, waves towering around him, the *Nereid* already twenty yards away and moving fast under bare poles. The safety line—his only connection to the boat, to survival—trailed in the water behind it.

"No!" The word was torn away by the wind as Mac began swimming desperately toward the retreating vessel. The safety line dragged through the water like a lifeline just beyond reach. The distance between them grew with each passing second, each wave that lifted him and dropped him into the troughs between.

Cold penetrated his layers, his muscles already beginning to stiffen. How long before hypothermia set in? An hour? Less in these conditions? His mind calculated survival odds with detached precision even as he fought to close the distance.

The *Nereid* rose on a swell, momentarily further away, and in that instant, Mac confronted the distinct possibility of his own death. Not someday, not in the abstract, but here, now, in this expanse of indifferent ocean.

Images flashed through his mind—not the worn clichés of his youth or achievements, but a kitchen on a small island in Maine. Noah, laughing at the counter as he mixed pancake batter. Kelsey, sleep-rumpled and beautiful in the morning light, reaching for the coffee Mac had made.

The realization hit him with the force of the waves around him: he loved them. Not as convenient companions, not as a business arrangement, but deeply, completely. And he might die out here, alone, without ever having told them.

Mac redoubled his efforts, forcing his tired arms through the water. The safety line continued to trail behind the boat, tantalizingly close and impossibly far. His breathing grew labored, each gasping inhalation bringing spray with it.

Another wave lifted him, and this time, he caught a glimpse of the line's end—the trailing portion had formed a small loop where the knot had begun to slip. One chance. If the boat rose on a swell while he was in a trough, the line might—just might—come within reach.

Mac stopped swimming directly toward the boat and adjusted his angle to anticipate where the next wave would place him relative to that trailing line. The cold was numbing his extremities, his thoughts beginning to slow.

A particularly large swell lifted the *Nereid* high, the stern rising as the bow dipped into the preceding trough. The safety line went momentarily slack as the boat pivoted, and the loop at its end dipped lower in the water.

Mac lunged with the last of his strength. The rough texture of the line brushed his fingertips, started to slide past—and then he had it. His frozen fingers closed around the wet rope with desperate strength.

He clung to it, breath heaving in great gasps as the boat's movement pulled him through the water. Hand over hand, he began the agonizing process of drawing himself toward the *Nereid*, fighting the drag of the water, the weight of his waterlogged clothing, the increasingly clumsy movements of his cold-numbed limbs.

It might have taken minutes or hours—time lost meaning in the singular focus of survival. When his hand finally closed around the boat's stern ladder, Mac almost couldn't believe it. He hung there for long moments, gathering strength for the final effort.

With painful slowness, he dragged himself up the ladder, muscles trembling with exhaustion and cold. He rolled over the gunwale and collapsed onto the deck, chest heaving. Rain continued to lash down, but he barely felt it. The solid fiberglass beneath his body was the only reality that mattered.

Alive. He was alive.

When he could move again, Mac crawled to the cockpit, seeking shelter from the worst of the weather. The autopilot was holding course admirably despite the challenging conditions. He only needed to get below, to change into dry clothes, to warm his core temperature before hypothermia took a firmer hold.

But for the moment, he simply sat in the relative protection of the cockpit, shaking with cold and delayed shock.

Alone in the midst of a vast ocean, he had come within seconds of death—not from dramatic violence but from simple physics, from the implacable mathematics of distance and temperature and time.

And for what? To run from the one thing he'd been searching for his entire life?

"No more," he whispered, the words lost to the storm. "No more running."

He had nearly lost everything without ever having truly claimed it as his own. What was the point of protecting himself from potential future pain if it meant missing the life that waited for him back on that small Maine island?

Hours later, warmed and changed, Mac checked his course for Porto Santo. The storm had passed, leaving a clear night sky scattered with stars. Eight hours to landfall, perhaps twelve to the airport. A day, maybe two, of flights and connections.

He'd figure out the boat logistics along the way. Maybe arrange for it to be sent back to Maine. After this experience, he'd had enough of long-distance sailing.

In a few short days, he'd see them again. And this time he would never let them go.

Chapter 31

The sun was low in the sky as Kelsey, Noah, and Tyler made their way back from Amy's. Noah kicked a pinecone ahead of them, keeping score in some improvised game he and Tyler had concocted.

"Twenty-three points!" Noah crowed as the pinecone skittered across the path.

"No way," Tyler protested. "That was clearly out of bounds."

"Mom, wasn't that in bounds?" Noah appealed, walking backwards to face Kelsey.

"Hmm?" Kelsey pulled her thoughts back from their wandering. "Sorry, I wasn't watching. Want to try again?"

Noah rolled his eyes with the specific exasperation reserved for parents who failed to pay attention to crucial sporting moments. "Never mind. We're almost home anyway."

Home. The word still caught in Kelsey's mind. Mac's house, their house now, rose ahead, welcoming in the fading light. Despite nearly three months of living there, part of her still felt like a visitor, especially with Mac gone.

As they approached the driveway, Kelsey noticed an unfamiliar sedan parked near the front door. Dark blue, luxury model, tinted windows.

"Who's that?" Noah asked, abandoning the pinecone game.

"I'm not sure." Kelsey slowed her pace. A sense of unease prickled at the back of her neck.

"Should we go around back?" Tyler suggested, already picking up on her hesitation.

Before Kelsey could answer, the driver's door opened. A petite woman stepped out, expensively dressed in a pale blue cardigan and tailored pants. Her chestnut hair was pulled back in a perfect chignon, but something about her appearance seemed off, slightly disheveled, as if the polished exterior had begun to crack.

Jennifer Prescott.

A jolt of surprise shot through Kelsey as Jennifer stood looking at them with an unsettling rigidity, her smile too fixed as she spotted them.

"There you are!" Jennifer called, her voice pitched oddly high. "I've been waiting for ages."

"Jennifer," Kelsey acknowledged, instinctively placing herself slightly in front of the boys. "What are you doing here?"

"Oh, I wanted to surprise Noah." Jennifer's gaze fixed on the boy with an intensity that made Kelsey's skin crawl. "Hello, Noah."

Noah edged closer to Kelsey, his eyes wary. They had told him about the restraining order, so he was aware that it was wrong of her to be there.

Indeed, something was very wrong. Jennifer's eyes had a glassy, unfocused quality, and despite the cool evening air, beads of sweat dotted her forehead.

"Noah," Kelsey said quietly, "why don't you and Tyler go inside? I'll be right in."

Jennifer stepped forward abruptly. "No, no—stay, Noah. I've come to take you home. To your rightful home."

Kelsey felt Noah stiffen beside her.

Alarm bells clanged in Kelsey's mind. She needed to get the boys away, but Jennifer had positioned herself between them and the front door.

"Noah is exactly where he belongs," Kelsey said firmly. "You need to leave right now, Jennifer. You shouldn't be here. Does Jason know you're here?"

Jennifer's smile sharpened. "Jason doesn't understand what needs to be done. But I do. I've prepared everything, your room is all ready, Noah. Blue walls, just like you told me you liked. Sailing prints on the walls. A telescope by the window."

Noah pressed against Kelsey's side. "I never told you that."

"Of course you did, sweetheart. You just don't remember." Jennifer's tone remained honey sweet, but her eyes darted frantically. "We're going to be such a happy family."

Kelsey's nurse training kicked in, and she recognized the signs of someone in a delusional state. Calm, clear communication. No sudden movements. De-escalation.

"Jennifer," she said gently, "I think there's been a misunderstanding. I can call Jason for you."

"No!" The word exploded from Jennifer with unexpected force. "Jason doesn't know I'm here. He thinks I'm at my sister's in Portland. He doesn't understand what needs to be done. Especially after your husband ruined him."

Kelsey nodded slowly, buying time. "I see. And what needs to be done, Jennifer?"

"Noah needs to come home. He's the Prescott heir." Jennifer's hand slipped into her cardigan pocket. "Only we can take care of him the way he needs."

Behind her, Kelsey could feel the boys' fear like a physical presence.

"Boys," she said quietly, not taking her eyes off Jennifer, "I think dinner might be ready at Amy's. Here, take my phone. Then ask her to call Dr. Mitchell about that prescription I mentioned."

It was a code they'd developed for emergencies at the clinic. Dr. Mitchell was their signal for calling 911. She prayed Amy would remember. It would set Jennifer off if she asked Noah to call 911.

"But Mom..." Noah began.

"Now, please," Kelsey interrupted firmly. "Tyler, make sure he doesn't dawdle."

Jennifer's eyes narrowed. "They don't need to go anywhere. We're all going to the Prescott house together."

"The boys need to eat," Kelsey improvised. "And Noah needs to get his things. They can go collect them while we talk."

Jennifer seemed to consider this, her attention momentarily diverted. Taking advantage of her hesitation, Kelsey pressed her phone into Noah's hand, whispering, "Tell Amy. Go. Now."

Noah's eyes widened with understanding. He grabbed Tyler's arm, and both boys backed away slowly before turning to sprint down the driveway. To the path he knew by heart.

"Hey!" Jennifer called after them. Her hand emerged from her pocket—holding a small pistol. "Stop right there!"

The boys froze momentarily. "Run!" Kelsey shouted and stepped between the gun and them.

They bolted, disappearing into the trees.

Jennifer turned back to Kelsey, the gun now pointed at her chest. "That was stupid. Now I'll have to find them after I deal with you."

Kelsey raised her hands slowly, heart hammering. "Jennifer, please. Put the gun down. Whatever you're going through, we can get you help."

"Help?" Jennifer laughed, the sound sharp and jagged. "I don't need help. I'm fixing everything. Cleaning up the mess."

"What mess?" Kelsey was desperately trying to keep her talking, to give the boys time to reach Amy's.

"The Prescott legacy. It's been corrupted." Jennifer gestured with the gun. "Walk toward the car."

Kelsey obeyed slowly. "Jennifer this isn't going to fix anything."

They reached the car. "Open the door. Get in."

"Where are we going?" Kelsey asked. Her hand trembled as she reached for the door handle.

"Somewhere we can finish our conversation privately." Jennifer's smile returned, eerily calm again. "Before I bring Noah home where he belongs."

"Jennifer, Mac will be back soon," Kelsey tried, sliding into the driver's seat. "He'll look for us."

Jennifer's laugh was chilling. "Mac won't be coming back. There are always accidents on the open ocean. Pirates. Storms. A lone sailor doesn't stand a chance against the right arrangements."

Ice flooded Kelsey's veins. "What did you do?"

"Move over," Jennifer ordered, ignoring the question. "Passenger seat."

As Kelsey shifted across the console, Jennifer slid into the driver's seat, keeping the gun trained on her. "It's really better this way. Much cleaner than what Jason wanted, all those lawyers, custody battles. So messy. But now, with Mac gone and you... well, no one would question a bereaved widow taking her own life, would they? Especially one abandoned by her husband."

"You're talking about murder," Kelsey said, fighting to keep her voice steady. "People will know."

"They'll know what I tell them," Jennifer replied. She started the car with one hand, the gun steady in the other. "And I'll tell them how tragic it was, how I tried to help you."

The car began rolling down the driveway. Kelsey's mind raced. Her keys jingled in her pocket.

The emergency fob on her key chain! The one from the clinic. Without hesitating, she stealthily reached in her pocket and squeezed the device three times and prayed silently that it worked.

How long would it take for help to arrive? She needed to buy time.

"Where are we going?" she asked again.

"Somewhere appropriate." Jennifer's tone was almost conversational now.

As they turned onto the main road, heading away from town, Kelsey realized with growing horror exactly where Jennifer was taking her. Widow's Point overlook. The craggy cliff face that looked out over the ocean on the wild Atlantic side.

Twenty minutes later, the car crunched to a stop on the gravel parking area that was deserted. The sun had set, leaving a dusky light. Below, the ocean crashed against jagged rocks like distant thunder.

"Get out," Jennifer ordered, waving the gun.

Kelsey complied, still frantically searching for a way out. The wind whipped around them, carrying salt spray and the promise of an early autumn storm.

"Jennifer, please," Kelsey tried again. "Think about what you're doing. Noah will be devastated."

"Noah will be fine," Jennifer snapped. "Children are adaptable. He'll forget you eventually."

She fought against rising panic, forcing herself to breathe slowly. She had to survive this.

"Walk," Jennifer gestured toward the dark line of the cliff edge against the night sky. "Nice and steady."

"Jennifer," Kelsey tried one more time, "The boys are calling for help. People will be coming."

"Then we'd better hurry," Jennifer replied calmly, prodding her forward with the gun.

Kelsey stepped gingerly toward the cliff. The edge loomed ahead, a steep rocky incline formed from centuries of rockslides and then seventy-foot drop to the rocks and churning water below. No one could survive that fall.

"You don't want to do this," she pleaded, trying to slow their pace.

They were nearing the edge now. Kelsey could feel the ground beginning to slope downward, hear the waves crashing more clearly.

"Stop here," Jennifer instructed when they were perhaps ten feet from the cliff's edge.

Kelsey obeyed and turned slowly to face her captor. "Jennifer, please. Think about what you're doing."

"I've thought about nothing else for months," Jennifer replied, her voice eerily calm. "You out of the picture entirely."

"If you want me over that cliff, you'll have to push me yourself."

Jennifer's expression hardened. "I won't hesitate."

"I know," Kelsey acknowledged. "But Noah will know what happened. He'll never forgive you. Or Jason."

Something flickered in Jennifer's eyes—doubt, perhaps. But then her resolve visibly hardened. "He'll forget. Children do."

"Not this. Never this." Kelsey held Jennifer's gaze steadily. "He'll hate you forever."

"Walk," Jennifer repeated, raising the gun higher.

In the distance, Kelsey heard it—faint at first, then growing stronger. Sirens. Help was coming. All she needed was a few more minutes.

Jennifer heard it too. She whipped toward the sound. In that moment of distraction, Kelsey lunged.

Jennifer reacted instantly, grabbing for Kelsey's arm. They grappled, the gun caught between them. Kelsey's foot slipped on the loose gravel near the cliff edge. She fell on the steep incline, dragging Jennifer with her. Loose rock cut into her skin, and a sharp cutting pain on one arm made her cry out.

For one horrifying moment, they teetered at the brink, the dark void of the cliff yawning behind them. Then Kelsey found purchase, bracing herself against a small outcropping of rock. Jennifer wasn't so fortunate. As their bodies separated, she slid further, the gun flying from her hand.

"Help!" Jennifer screamed, fingers scrabbling at the loose soil of the cliff edge. "Please!"

Instinct took over. Kelsey lunged forward, catching Jennifer's wrist just as she began to slip over the edge. The sudden weight nearly pulled Kelsey down with her, but she dug her heels in, anchoring herself as best she could.

"Hold on," she gasped, muscles straining. "Don't struggle."

Jennifer dangled over the edge, eyes wide with terror, all trace of her earlier madness replaced by primal fear. "Don't let go. Please don't let go."

"I won't," Kelsey promised, even as her grip began to slip. "Help is coming. Just hold on."

The sirens were closer now, headlights visible on the winding road approaching Widow's Point. Just a little longer. She just needed to hold on a little longer, but her arms felt as though they would pop from their sockets.

For a suspended moment, they stayed like that—Kelsey braced precariously against the cliff, Jennifer's feet dangling seventy feet above certain death, connected only by their straining hands.

Then the night exploded with light and sound—headlights sweeping the cliff edge, car doors slamming, voices calling out.

"Kelsey!" A voice she knew better than her own heart. A voice that couldn't possibly be there.

"Mac?" she gasped, unable to turn, unable to look away from Jennifer's terrified face.

And then he was beside her, his strong hands closing over hers, helping her hold Jennifer's weight. "I've got her. I've got you both."

More hands appeared—uniformed officers, firefighters. They secured Jennifer and pulled her to safety. Only when Jennifer was fully on solid ground did Kelsey allow herself to collapse, trembling with exhaustion and delayed shock.

Strong arms caught her. Mac's arms. Impossible, miraculous arms that somehow held her when they should have been an ocean away.

"You're here," she whispered, and reached up to touch his face, needing to confirm he was real. "She said you were... that there had been an accident."

"I'm here." He held her tightly as emergency personnel swarmed around them with medical kits. "I came back. I should never have left."

On the periphery of her awareness, Kelsey registered Jennifer being handcuffed, heard her still babbling about bloodlines and legacies as officers led her to a patrol car. But all that mattered was the solid reality of Mac beside her, his heartbeat strong against her ear.

"Noah," she remembered suddenly, pulling back to look into Mac's face. "Is he..."

"He's fine," Mac assured her. "He's with Amy. They called 911. Smart kid."

Relief flooded through her, followed immediately by the adrenaline crash. Kelsey sagged against Mac.

"You need medical attention," Mac said, his voice tight with concern as he tenderly assessed her blood-matted arm.

"In a minute," she murmured. She was unwilling to let go of him yet. "How are you here? Your boat—"

"I was at the island airport when Davey, he's driving one of the taxis now and also volunteers with the fire department, got the call about an emergency at Widow's Point. When he heard your name..." His voice broke. "Kelsey, when I thought you might be—"

She silenced him with a finger to his lips. "I'm not. I'm here. We're both here."

As paramedics approached with a stretcher, Mac reluctantly loosened his hold on her. "I'm not leaving your side," he promised. "Not now, not ever again. If you'll have me."

Despite everything, Kelsey felt something like hope unfurling in her chest. "That sounds suspiciously like a real marriage proposal, MacCormack."

His smile, though strained with worry, was the most beautiful thing she'd ever seen. "Maybe it is. We can negotiate terms later."

Epilogue

The late September air carried a hint of wood smoke and the sweet decay of fallen leaves. Kelsey drew her cardigan closer around her shoulders as she settled deeper into the Adirondack chair, cradling a glass of pinot noir. The expansive lawn of the mansion stretched before her, its emerald green beginning to accumulate the first golden offerings of fallen oak leaves.

Mac sat beside her, his chair pulled close enough that their elbows occasionally brushed, each casual contact sending a pleasant warmth through her that had nothing to do with the wine. Across from them, Amy was gesticulating enthusiastically, a half-drawn sketch of the mansion's east wing renovations balanced on her knee.

"So, if we take down this non-load-bearing wall," Amy traced a line on her drawing, "we create one large, open studio space with southern exposure. Perfect for painting workshops, or yoga gatherings,"

Mac leaned forward, studying the plans with genuine interest. "Have you had the historical society weigh in yet? That section might be part of the original structure."

"That's where Kelsey's new best friend comes in," Amy said with a wink. "Mrs. Callahan from the historical society seems much more amenable to 'thoughtful updates' now that Kelsey's joined the preservation committee."

Kelsey smiled into her wine glass. "I wouldn't call us best friends. She just appreciates someone who does their homework before proposing changes."

"She appreciates the sizeable donation we made to the island's historical society," Mac corrected, his eyes crinkling with amusement.

"That too," Kelsey admitted.

Out on the lawn, Noah's delighted laughter rose above the rustle of leaves as he threw a tennis ball for the two dogs: Ollie, Amy's terrier, and Pilot, the golden retriever puppy Mac had brought home three weeks ago. Pilot bounded after the ball with more enthusiasm than coordination, tumbling in a heap of gangly limbs and golden fur.

"Careful with him, Noah!" Mac called. "He's still learning his legs."

Noah waved in acknowledgment, his cheeks flushed with the cool air and exertion. Kelsey felt a familiar swell of emotion watching him. He looked so carefree, so unburdened. The darkness that had lingered after Jennifer's attack had finally begun to recede.

"Any news from Jason?" Amy asked, her voice dropping slightly though Noah was well out of earshot.

Mac's expression tightened almost imperceptibly. "His lawyers called yesterday. They're still handling the legal fallout, but he wanted to check on Noah."

"And to apologize for the hundredth time," Kelsey added, reaching for Mac's hand and giving it a gentle squeeze.

The weeks following Jennifer's arrest had revealed a disturbing picture. Jason had been genuinely horrified by his wife's actions, completely unaware of her deteriorating mental state. Her fixation on Noah had apparently developed over months, fueled by delusions and paranoia that she'd carefully hidden from her husband.

"It's not exactly his fault," Kelsey continued, "but I still can't quite separate him from it all."

"The Prescott family has issues that go back generations," Mac said quietly. "Jason included. But I believe him when he says he never imagined Jennifer would…"

"The doctors say she may never be well enough to stand trial," Kelsey remarked, setting her sketch aside. "Severe delusional disorder, exacerbated by untreated psychosis."

"It's sad," Amy said, her tone sympathetic. "To be so lost in your own mind."

They fell silent for a moment. The only sounds were the distant barking of the dogs and the gentle rustling of leaves overhead. Kelsey looked up at the sprawling oak that shaded their sitting area. Its leaves were just beginning their transformation from deep green to burnished copper.

"On a much lighter note," Amy said, clearly eager to shift the conversation, "I've scheduled the first trial workshop for next month. Just a small watercolor class, eight students. If it goes well, we can start planning a real calendar for spring."

"With my new work schedule, I can actually help," Kelsey said, still marveling at how quickly things had fallen into place once she'd decided to cut back her hours. The new nurse practitioner had been eager to relocate to the island and had brought with her a wealth of experience and an enthusiasm for community health care that matched Kelsey's own.

"The MacCormack-York Center for Arts and Wellness," Mac mused, testing the name they'd been considering. "Has a certain ring to it."

"You're just pleased your name comes first alphabetically," Amy teased.

"Guilty as charged," Mac admitted with a grin.

Kelsey watched him, still sometimes caught off guard by the easy happiness that now seemed to radiate from the man who had once been so determined to keep the world at arm's length. Since his return and since that terrifying night at Widow's Point, Mac had embraced their life together with a wholehearted enthusiasm that still took her breath away.

He caught her watching him and winked, which sent a pleasant flutter through her chest. Later, after Noah was asleep, they would have the house to themselves. The thought alone warmed her more effectively than the cardigan or the wine.

"You two are disgustingly cute," Amy observed dryly. "I'd be nauseated if I weren't so happy for you."

"We try," Mac said, unabashed.

A sudden commotion from the far side of the lawn drew their attention. Noah was running toward them and yelling, Pilot and Ollie barking excitedly behind him.

"Mom! Mac!" he called, slightly out of breath as he reached them. "You have to come see what Ollie dug up!"

"Probably a squirrel's buried treasure," Mac suggested, setting his wine glass on the small table between the chairs.

"No, it's bones," Noah insisted, his expression serious. "Like, a lot of bones."

Kelsey exchanged a glance with Mac. "Probably a fox or raccoon that died over the winter," she said gently. "Remember when we found those bird bones at the beach? Nature recycles everything."

"This is different," Noah persisted, genuine distress evident in his voice. He grabbed Kelsey's hand and tugged insistently. "Please come look. It's... I think it's important."

His tone, the barely concealed note of alarm in it, made Kelsey set aside her wine and stand immediately. Mac followed suit, concern replacing the relaxed contentment of moments before.

"Where are they, buddy?" Mac asked, his hand coming to rest protectively on Noah's shoulder.

"By the stone wall, near those bushes with the red leaves," Noah pointed toward the far edge of the property, where a centuries-old stone wall marked the boundary between the mansion grounds and the thick woods beyond.

Amy rose as well, curiosity overcoming her initial reluctance. "Lead the way!"

They followed Noah across the lawn, while the boy glanced back repeatedly to ensure they were still coming. The dogs raced ahead, clearly excited by the renewed attention to their discovery.

As they approached the old stone wall, Kelsey noticed a freshly dug hollow at its base, partially obscured by a large burning bush whose leaves were just beginning to redden with autumn's touch. Ollie stood proudly beside the hole, tail wagging, while Pilot paced nervously behind him.

"See?" Noah pointed into the shallow pit. "I told Ollie to stop, but he kept digging."

Kelsey stepped closer and peered into the disturbed earth. At first, she saw only dirt and rocks, a few tangled roots. Then, as her eyes adjusted to the dappled lights beneath the trees, she saw it. Pale, unmistakable, partially embedded in the dark soil.

The bones of a human hand.

The delicate metacarpals curved slightly, as if reaching upward from the earth that had concealed them for who knew how long. A tarnished ring still encircled what had once been a finger, its stone dulled by time and soil.

Kelsey stepped back involuntarily, her shoulder bumping against Mac's solid chest. His arm came around her automatically to steady her.

"Is that...?" Amy's voice trailed off, though they all knew the answer.

"Noah, take the dogs back to the chairs," Mac said quietly. His tone left no room for argument.

For once, Noah didn't protest, perhaps relieved to be given a reason to retreat from the grim discovery. He whistled for the dogs, who followed him reluctantly, Ollie looking back at his find with canine disappointment.

When Noah was out of earshot, Mac crouched carefully beside the excavation.

"That's human," Kesley confirmed grimly. "And it's been there a very long time."

"We need to call Sheriff Winters," Mac said.

"Old houses, old secrets," Amy murmured, staring at the partially revealed remains with a complex mix of horror and fascination.

"This isn't just an old secret," Mac said, rising to stand beside Kelsey again. "This isn't a cemetery or a private family plot. It doesn't look like there was a coffin. It looks more like an old flower garden bed."

A cool breeze swept across the lawn. Kelsey shivered, unable to look away from the pale bones emerging from the dark earth. Bones that had once been a person with a name, a life, a story. The mansion loomed behind her, its many windows like watchful eyes, cold and unblinking. Centuries of history were etched into its weathered stone and carved wood. The air smelled of dirt and decaying leaves, carrying the whispers of long buried secrets.

"Why would someone be buried here?" Amy wondered aloud.

"I don't know," Kelsey said, already retrieving her phone from her cardigan pocket. "But I think we're about to find out."

From the Author

Dear Reader,

Thank you for joining me on this journey to Widow's Point Island. Writing *Last Wish Wedding* has been an incredible adventure, and I'm so grateful you chose to spend your time with Kelsey, Mac, Noah, and the rest of the island's characters.

Widow's Point Island isn't just a setting—it's a living, breathing place in my imagination, inspired by some of my favorite summer trips to Maine and the unforgettable beauty of Acadia National Park. The rugged coastline, the scent of salt in the air, the way the early morning light dances over the water—it all found its way into the pages of this book.

The image from the epilogue of hiking boots resting above Eagle Lake, with the ocean stretching beyond, is a moment from my own life. Those are *my* boots, and the serenity I felt in that moment became the foundation for Widow's Point—a place that feels both timeless and full of secrets waiting to be uncovered.

This book is only the beginning. As the trilogy unfolds, there's more to discover about the island's rich history, its hidden mysteries, and the love stories that intertwine with them. I hope you'll join me for the next chapter of this journey and continue to explore the world of Widow's Point Island.

To those who supported this special edition of *Last Wish Wedding*, thank you from the bottom of my heart. Your enthusiasm and belief in this story mean more to me than words can express.

Here's to second chances, the power of love, and the beauty of a windswept island that will always welcome you home.

With love and gratitude,

Jeulia Hesse

www.ingramcontent.com/pod-product-compliance
Lightning Source LLC
Chambersburg PA
CBHW021956130726
47903CB00014B/1484